Tales From The Sea

Eddie Gubbins

Cathy

Best Wishes

Eddie Gubbins

6/11/2023

Published 2013 Ceatespace

Tales From The Sea

Eddie Gubbins

Rombuli Saga fantasy novels:
Book 1 The Teacher of the Rombuli
Book 2 The Return Of The Exiles
Book 3 The Prisoner Of Parison

Other books by the author:
Running After Maria
Brotherly Love
A Ceremony of Innocence
An Ordinary Life

The Sailor's Mistress

When the cargo is loaded and all falls quiet
The sea itself is calling,
Beckoning the sailor out there beyond the dock.
His mistress is waiting
Where the river meets the sea.
He has no real knowledge of what her reaction will be
When he sails out to meet her.
She may greet him in a calm, balmy mood,
Like a gentle lover entwining him in her arms,
Leaving him refreshed and happy when they part.
It might be that she is angry
And will meet him with unmatched violence
A violence that beats upon the senses
And leaves the lovers drained and exhausted,
Ready to rush apart,
Ready to find a place of peace and quiet
Not the feeling of complete satisfaction.
Like all lovers, the sea and the sailor
Will never quite know what moods will greet them
when they meet
Or how the mood can change very quickly.
This is the excitement of the sea.
Every time a ship leaves port,
The sailor approaches that love
With a mixture of exhilaration and apprehension.
Will they together make beautiful love under a clear
blue sky
Or will they fight?
It is not for the sailor to subdue the sea
But to live with her moods
In the hope that he can survive.
The sea is calling, always calling
As a lover calls.

Chapter 1

I had been destined for a life at sea for as long as I could remember. In fact, I can recall vividly the first time my family started to take it for granted that I was going to sea when I left school.

It was at one o our family get togethers when I was about six years old. All of my aunties were there sitting in a line in the front room, pulling all their friends and acquaintances to pieces. It was a room which at that time was only used for special occasions or when some so called important visitor came. There was a fireplace with black cast iron surround and coloured tiles with pictures of flowers.

The uncles, my dad and granddad were in the sitting room drinking beer and talking of football and politics. The grandchildren in the conservatory playing with the toys they had brought with them.

We all came together for a buffet supper prepared by my grandmother, the aunties, uncles and eleven grand children. Somebody, I cannot recall who, started to speculate about what would become of all the grandchildren when they grew up and left school.

Suddenly Granddad put his large hand on my shoulder and announced in a voice which brooked no argument. " Edmund is going to sea when he grows up. He will be the first Captain of a foreign going ship in the family."

Everybody in the room nodded sagely and I did not protest. I suppose at six years old, I did not fully appreciate the true implication of what was being decided on my behalf. Oh, I had sat at the feet, so to speak, of my grandfather and listened to his stories of when he was at sea on White Star Liners. He had talked of the people, the ships and the sea. He made it sound so glamorous, mysterious and fascinating that I had been attracted to the sea from that time.

Even at such an early age, I had felt the excitement of being on a ship when my family took the ferry from the Town Quay to Hythe across the river to visit my aunty and uncle. To feel the vibration of the engine through the soles of my shoes and the slow roll of the boat when we passed another moving craft had made me feel as though we were at sea. At those times I could let my imagination run wild.

Then there had been that first summer when my family had taken a holiday on the Isle of White. Once on board the ferry, I had stood looking out over the bow with the wind ruffling my hair mesmerised by the bow wave and the movement. Passing through the docks and on down the Solent, I had watched the ships and imagined where they had come from or were going to and secretly sailed away with them to all those exotic places I had only read about in books or seen in the cinema. When we sailed passed the tankers moored at the Fawley Oil Refinery, they looked large and strange with their hulls so far out of the water. Fascinated, I had watched closely as the ship was manoeuvred alongside the quay and tied up when we arrived in Cowes.

As you can see, this goes to show that I was destined for a life at sea from an early age. It was accepted by my mother and father and the wider family. Others might discuss university or an apprenticeship in the shipyard but there was no doubt in the family's mind that I was going to sea.

This ambition spilled over into my school life. All the top pupils at the grammar school I attended were destined for university after taking A levels. When I informed the headmaster when discussing my future that

I was going to sea in the merchant navy, he was not impressed.

" You are among our top pupils," he had said looking at me over the top of his glasses. " There is no question but our top pupils go to university. The success of failure of the school is measured by the number of pupils who go to Oxbridge first and then other universities second. Nobody from our school goes for a career in the merchant navy."

Even when I assured him that I was planning to become a Captain, he was not reassured. I could not understand his attitude at the time but came to understand later when I became an academic.

One of the geography teachers at the school was in the Royal Naval Reserve and he set out to convince me that I ought go to Dartmouth and into the Royal Navy. An officer in the Royal Navy was, it sounded, more acceptable than an officer in the merchant navy. Even now I do not understand the thinking behind this assertion.

Periodically, Mr. Jenkins arranged visits to Portsmouth naval dockyard, including staying for a few days on HMS Vanguard. Whenever these trips were arranged, I was included. It was not long before I realised that my parents could not afford the expense of sending me to Dartmouth so I settled down to enjoy the trips but finding out all I could about the merchant navy.

Before sitting my O levels, I had sent an application to become a deck cadet with an oil tanker company and, after attending an interview, I had been offered a cadetship if I passed the required grades. In the September, I would go to pre sea college in Stepney, London and join my first ship in January. My grandfather was more excited than I was when I told him.

" I told you," he informed anybody who would listen." Edmund is going to become the first Captain in the family."

After finishing school at sixteen, much to the disgust of the headmaster who still harboured the hope that I would relent and go to university, my uncle found me a position as a deck boy on one of the Isle of White ferries for the summer. It was a glorious summer. The sun shone, the ferry sailed back and forth between Southampton and Cowes and I was doing something I enjoyed. It was not much of a ship. A modernised landing craft with some accommodation built on above the engine room and the ramp at the bow. I learnt a great deal about the various things that take place on board a ship. A few times when they were short of crew, I was transferred to the Calshott, a tug tender that met the ocean liners as they approached Cowes. It could carry five hundred passengers but the few times I was on board all we carried were the Dockers going to meet a liner and get the baggage ready for discharge. I did make a little extra money by making them mugs of tea and sandwiches during the trip down the river. Though I did not think about it at the time, it was good grounding in sea life without having to leave home before I actually started my sea career.

In September, I took myself off to pre-sea college. There I shared a room with Andy Brookes, who like me was a cadet for the same tanker company. Andy was about the same height as me but much broader and stronger. I was lucky. We got on well even though I was hard put to maintain my friendship when he played his accordion some nights. The Triumphal march from Aida I seem to remember. After hearing this many times, even now every time I hear that tune brings back memories of pre-sea training. We were thrown into the ring together during the boxing but maintained our friendship by agreeing not to hit each other too hard. Unfortunately Buster Brown the instructor, a true east end product noticed. Well I suppose we were naive to think that we could get away with it. Andy was put into the ring the next time with the most accomplished fighter and was soon overwhelmed. I was put into the ring with Douglas Moorhouse. I must admit I had taken a dislike to him from our first meeting. He was tall, handsome, always got his own way and always won. It was no match up even though I had spent time training with an amateur boxing club. With his long reach and height it was almost impossible to get to him. He knocked me down as soon as I tried to hit him. I got up and tried again. Ducking and diving, moving sideways and away from his right hand, I managed to hit him a couple of times in the chest. He knocked me down. Andy screamed for me to stay down. I got up. Buster stepped in grinning and stopped Douglas hitting me again.

" I admire your courage young man," Buster told me. " In life you have to learn when the odds are too great. Then you have to retreat and work out some other way of defeating your opponent."

Douglas grinned and held out his hand once the gloves were off. I shook it in return and grinned back. Deep down I vowed to make sure I beat him at something while we were in college. I was learning lessons that I hoped would help me when I was at sea.

The college had a small motor yacht that was used to sail down the Thames and back from Wapping Dock. It was painted white with a yellow funnel. There was a tall mast and a sail. It was provided to give the students experience of running an actual ship at sea.

There was a small professional crew but the idea was that most of the tasks were carried out by the students.

The students set off on their training voyage early one morning after we had been at the college for a few weeks. We had learnt the rudiments of seamanship and navigational chart work. Most of us were eager to put some of this theory into practice.

For me, the voyage did not start too well. Captain Duncan, the teacher in charge, was a tall imposing figure though with that hangdog look of somebody who wondered how they had got themselves into this situation. I suppose looking after twenty sixteen year olds on a yacht is no pleasure. When he came aboard, he demanded to know who it was leaning on the rail with his hands in his pockets. Of course that was me. All the teachers at the college called themselves Captain. The students had suspicions that not many of them had actually been the Captain of a ship before leaving the sea to become teachers. In the three months that we were in the college, not one of us had the courage to question whether this was true or not. Not that it made any difference to me at the time. On board the yacht, Captain Duncan was in charge.

In a stern voice, he said. " One of your jobs will be to clean out the latrines twice a day."

The other students laughed but they made sure they were presentable from then on. I suppose that was what Captain Duncan was trying to achieve. If it had not been me, he would have found somebody else. I did what I have always done when this happens to me. Sink into my shell, don't show any emotion and get on with the job. It was a horrible job but I stuck at it.

On the third day as we started to return to Wapping, Captain Duncan found me cleaning the latrines as ordered.

" Get cleaned up and report to the bridge," he commanded me.

When I came up the ladder onto the bridge, he smiled at me for the first time. " You have done well and accepted your punishment without histrionics. I want you to take over the wheel and we will start you on the path to your steering certificate."

The seaman stood by my side and offered advice but after a while let me continue on my own. It was wonderful. Concentrating on keeping the ship on a straight course whether by following the compass heading or points on land. I was in my element. The familiar landmarks on the banks of the river passed on either side and ships sailed by destined for places round the world.

Captain Duncan smiled again after watching me for a while. " You have done this before."

" Yes Sir," I answered with a grin. " I was a deck boy on the Isle of White ferries while waiting for my O level results. Because I was going to sea, they taught me how to steer when the ship was in Southampton Water. I even took a turn when, in an emergency, I was seconded to the tug called Calshott."

" I remember the Calshott," he said ordering a different heading as we passed Gravesend. " Steam driven tug tender. I used to see her when docking aboard the Southern Cross."

When we were approaching Tower Bridge, the sailor took over the wheel for the docking in Saint Katherine's dock. With an effort, I tried not to show my disappointment at not being allowed to take the yacht into the berth. Deep down I was pleased with my time on the wheel.

I passed out of the college as the second highest student. Andy congratulated me but I was disappointed not to be top, especially as Douglas Moorhouse had been the best student. He was one of those infuriating people who were good at everything and knew it. His arrogance got under the skin of most of the other students but I learnt a valuable lesson from that experience. It was more important when in a situation where one could not get away from those one worked with to find an accommodation and a way of so called rubbing along.

When we left college, Andy and I had to report to the head office of the tanker company. The Marine Superintendent went over our reports and assigned us to our first ships. Andy to the Fernando, me to the Fortunato. After three months sharing a room, we said goodbye on the steps of the office but hoped we would meet some time.

In the first week of January after a pleasant Christmas with my family, I found myself on a train bound for Heysham. It was the first time I had ever been north of London and the country and accents were strange to me. A taxi took me from the station to the berth and I got a good look at my first ship as we approached along the quay.

To me she was huge but later I came to understand that she was really of medium size for a tanker in the late nineteen fifties. The accommodation was amidships, three levels including the bridge. Running the whole length of the tanker was a catwalk raised about ten feet above the deck. The funnel was rather squat and above the aft accommodation. It was painted with two narrow yellow rings separated by a larger white ring. On this was the eagle, black with drooping wings. The smoke cowl was black. Two tall masts rose above the deck one aft of the accommodation the other forward. The hull was black with a yellow stripe and the structures in yellow. This was my first ship.

Once on board, the chief officer allocated a cabin to me, the middle one of four small cabins designed for the cadets and situated on the starboard side of the amidships structure. My porthole looked out on the walkway leading between the after deck and the fore deck. When I had stowed my gear in my lockers, John Reid, one of the other cadets introduced himself. He had been sent by the chief officer to showed me round the ship and explain what was going on. I was soon in a daze at all the technical language and unfamiliar sights. It was one thing to learn about life on board ship, cargo loading and ship routines in college but quite different when presented with these in practice. I found I was one of four cadets sailing on the ship and that we had a number of routine tasks to carry out. Over dinner in the saloon that evening, I was introduced to the other cadets at the table where we would take all our meals. As dinner was served by stewards, I was glad that at college they had taught us how to act when being served with a meal.

That night was even worse. I had to keep watch from midnight with the second mate as the cargo discharge continued. Not only had I to keep myself awake at times when I was usually asleep but I found the physical labour hard. It involved turning valves to switch discharge tanks, climbing up and down the almost vertical ladder into the pump room and going to the kitchen to make mugs of coffee for the second mate. And all the time, I was trying to learn this technical language and the jargon of sea life. When dawn was breaking, I had breakfast with the second mate and fell into my bunk, asleep before my head had hit the pillow as the saying goes.

The next afternoon I met many of the crew and soon realised that these were the people with whom I had to, not only work, but also live with for the next few months. It was soon obvious to me that it was very important for me to establish a way of dealing with these people which did not take away my own individuality but which would be flexible enough to avoid conflict. It is usually enough for somebody to rein in their feelings when working in an office during the day because at night they can walk away from the job and choose whether to meet their other office colleagues for recreation later in the evening or not. I know a great number of people work and play with the same set of people especially when the out of work hours life of an organisation revolves around the social club but it is the choice an individual in those circumstances is free to make. Nobody is going to force such a person to mix only with working colleagues, though colleagues and bosses may put pressure on somebody to take part in some of the activities of the company. It is, at the end of the day, up to the person what they do with their non-working time. At sea things are different. Not only must you find a way of keeping stable relationships during working time, you are shut up with the same people for the rest of the time as well. Tolerance of the different attitudes to life, tolerance of other peoples point of view and a quickness in forgetting past wrongs are called for aboard ship. The most successful seamen soon learn how to practice restraint.

Late on the second day on board the Fernando, I experienced that special feeling which comes to all seamen. It is amazing to the lands man but quite suddenly on board a ship in port there comes a time when all activity ceases. The cargo has been discharged or loaded. In our case the tanks battened down and the 'nes lifted ashore. The berth workers collect up gear and walk down the gangway talking about their next job or the weekend at home. All attention is on the office ashore where all the various pieces of paper are being assembled. For a short while the ship will lie quietly waiting, the diesel generator a muted noise in the background, waiting as though gathering strength in the same way as a sprinter waiting for the gun before the explosive action.

It does not matter for how long a time a sailor has been sailing the oceans of the world, how jaded the sailor's senses have become to the child like excitement of viewing the world as full of wonder, there is a certain expectant thrill running through a ship and it's crew just before the ship leaves port. It does not matter whether the crewmember is young or old, whether the ship is large or small, the expectancy, the thrill and excitement is felt by everybody on board. It even transmits itself to the shore people even though they experience the same thrill several times a week, it is still there. One can see it the faces of those connected with the ship and feel it in the vibration under the feet of those who walk the decks. At this time more than any other it is possible to believe that the ship itself is alive, waking from a long slumber in port and ready for the adventure and challenge of the sea. The pulsation grows as the engine is tested, sailors walk the deck in a purposeful fashion, ready to get this complex system of man and machine into motion. It feels as though the sea itself is calling, beckoning out there beyond the dock.

The mistress of the ship and the crew is waiting. She waits beyond the dock and there is no real knowledge of what her reaction will be when they go out to meet her. She may greet them in a calm, balmy mood and like a gentle lover entwine them in her arms, leaving them refreshed and happy when they part. It could be that she is angry with unmatched violence which beats upon the senses and leaves the lovers drained and exhausted, ready to rush apart, concentrating on finding peace and quiet rather than wallowing in the feeling of complete satisfaction. Like all lovers, the sea and the sailor never quite know what moods will greet them at the times of their meeting or how the mood can change very quickly as the time passes. This is the excitement of the sea and, every time a ship leaves port, the sailor approaches love with a mixture of exhilaration and apprehension. Will they together make beautiful love under a clear blue sky or will they fight? It is not for the sailor to subdue the sea but to live with her moods in the hope that he can survive.

The sea is calling always calling even when the sailor has long left voyaging behind. The sea calls over the noise of this sometimes dreadful life. To sail away but to where? That is what adds to the thrill. Let the voyage be long or short, let the love making be calm or fierce, in the urge to sail away lies man's eternal quest for something new. Why oh why does man always strive after the new when acccpting the present would save a lot of heartache? It has long been a mystery to me but, more than in any other profession, the sea seems to offer a greater chance to satisfy this need. The sailor never arrives because each new port is a stepping stone to the next and on to the next until the nomadic lifestyle grows too much. It maybe that the sailor observes other people settling into a pattern of life which brings rewards from such things as family and home, anchored to other aspects of living rather than constantly on the move. So the sailor leaves the sea and puts down roots or does he? The sound of a seagull screaming over an inland rubbish tip, the wind moaning around the roof of his house or the sound of waves lapping on the shore will awaken in the hidden recesses of his mind the longing to feel the excitement once more as the ship goes silent, ready to leave for the sea.

We sailed in the evening from Heysham out into the Irish Sea. As soon as we were clear of the coast the chief officer arranged for the tanks to be cleaned. The crew were split into gangs and I was assigned to the first gang. How I survived that first night I still can't believe. The work was dirty and hard, pulling pipes across the deck and lowering them into tanks. Timing the height for each wash and then lowering them further into the tank. All the time the ship rolled to me violently and water washed across the deck. By the time my watch ended, I was wet, cold and exhausted. John helped me undress and have a shower before I collapsed into bed.

" It will get easier," he assured me with grin as he dried his rather thin body with a towel. " At least you didn't throw up all over the deck. I did the first time I sailed and had to do tank cleaning."

He was right. It did get easier and I was soon involved in the routine of the ship. The bane of all cadets' existence, I found out, was Saturday morning. It was our job to clean the brass on the bridge under the watchful eye of the third mate. I was surprised at the amount of brass needing cleaning. Somehow, Captain Morris always managed to find his way onto the bridge just as we were finishing. For some reason, he always found a bit that we had missed. As senior cadet, Malcolm always went onto the focastle to clean the ships bell and the brass plates on the winches. I took note of this. By keeping out of the way, he always missed the ire of the Captain.

Captain Morris was a stickler for procedure. On Sundays, he did his rounds of inspection through the ship seriously. It was a ritual. Unless the ship was clean he would get the cleaning redone to his satisfaction. We cadets had to stand by our bunks until he had inspected our cabins. Afterwards, Mister Marsh, the chief officer invited us to his cabin for a beer with the other deck and engineering officers who were not on duty. In that way, he felt the cadets would be part of the officers' circle. It was important because most of the time we were neither officers nor crew but some undefined position in between.

We crossed the Bay of Biscay with an almost flat calm sea and the winter sun shining. Nothing like I had anticipated or dreaded. The stories I had heard while in college about the terrible weather and the gigantic waves, the warnings that it could be hell were unfounded. Most of the seamen ignored it but I was on the bridge when we passed the white bulk of Gibraltar and entered the Mediterranean Sea.

We hardly saw any land as we sailed east towards Port Said. Then there were ships converging from the west and we picked up the pilot just off the Suez Canal. The pilot took us to an anchorage in a line of tankers and we waited. Boats suddenly appeared and men were shouting their wares for the crew to purchase. Wafting on the breeze was the unfamiliar smell of Egypt a mixture of rotting vegetation, unclean drains and sweaty bodies.

The bosun organised the cadets to rig the spotlight on the bow. I was curious and Andy explained that this was used to light the bank of the canal as we transited during the night. One of the crew had to be stationed by the spotlight to position it on orders from the bridge.

We lay at anchor for most of the day, peaceful but hot and sweaty except for the persistent bum boats as they were called. Then suddenly there was a great deal of activity. The pilot arrived with his bags and everybody was looking towards the Canal entrance. Then they came in a line astern. First a couple of ocean liners, their passengers lining the rail to look at all the waiting anchored ships. Then cargo boats of every description and colour. Their funnel colours and badges told the informed which company and the flag at their stern the country. Then the oil tankers. One was another company ship and we dipped our flag in response as she passed.

" Captain Marshall," John informed me as we stood by the rail and watched. " I sailed with him on my last ship."

" What happens now?" I asked naively.

" When the north bound convoy is clear, the south bound convoy will form and enter the canal. I expect we will anchor in the lakes half way through the canal to let another north bound convoy pass."

The last ship of the north bound convoy cleared the canal and ships started to weigh anchor in a predetermined order. They sailed away from us into the canal as the sun was setting in the west. As one larger tanker passed our position, the order was given for the anchor to be weighed. Once under way, we followed the tanker ahead into the canal. It was getting dark as the sand banks and dunes beside the canal engulfed our ship. The spotlight was turned on and the banks lit up. That is all we could see. A round patch of moving sand with the stern lights of the ship ahead and steaming lights of the ship behind.

The next morning I awoke to find the Fortune anchored in what looked like a large lake. All the ships of the south bound convoy were there. It was not long before the north bound convoy passed. I stood by the rail and watched in wonder. A couple of Royal Navy ships leading, their weaponry covered in canvass. Some ocean liners with the passengers standing looking at all the ships anchored in the lake as they passed waving occasionally. Then came the cargo liners of some of the companies listed in my book of ships funnels and company flags. I had seen some of these in Southampton before leaving to go to sea but most were only studied in books. Then last came the oil tankers and I had to rush aft ready to dip our flag to any of the company's ships. Before long the last of the north bound convoy passed and we were weighing anchor and sailing south through sand banks leaving the green oasis of the lakes behind.

It was hot in the Red Sea. Hotter than I had ever felt. With no air conditioning, even in the shade of the cabin it was hot. It took a few days and then I started to get used to the heat.

We turned into the Persian Gulf through the Straits of Hormous joining the line of tankers sailing towards the loading ports. Coming the other way, another line of tankers lower in the water making for Europe or the Far East. The heat beat down and the decks were too hot to walk on bare feet. The Chief Officer made me keep my shirt and a hat on for most of the day fearing that I would get sun burnt. The Second Mate dished out sun tan cream for our faces and salt tablets to take with water, something I had never seen before. The sea was flat calm stretching ahead like the floor of a cathedral. The only breeze came from the forward movement of the ship.

In the middle of nowhere a pilot joined the ship and we sailed into Mina Al-Hamadi. There was nothing there like normal habitation. A jetty jutted out from the sandy shore to join the longest berth I had ever seen. Tankers were tied one astern of the other for as far as the eye could see. Some were high out of the water indicating they had just started to load, while others were almost down to their marks ready to leave. The pilot guided us parallel to the berth until we could see a vacant spot beside a gantry with rubber pipes hanging free. We tied up here between a Danish tanker and Japanese one. It was not long before the ballast was pumped out and we started loading. The oil poured into the tanks and we shut each tank down as it filled. Lastly we filled a central tank and ordered the shore to stop. Papers were exchanged, we blew the whistle and we were off. I had not set foot on foreign soil.

We reversed the trip and sailed for Eastham Docks on the Mersey at the entrance to the Manchester Ship Canal. In fact we sailed this trip for the next seven months and during that time I did not set foot in any overseas countries. Mina Al-Hamadi was the closest I got but, apart from walking along the jetty to the recreation club, there was no going ashore. It appeared to me that the authorities were quite willing to sell us their oil but they were not confident enough to let us mix with their people in case we contaminated them with western ideas. Maybe in my case it was a good thing. There is no question that I would have disputed the way they lived and their general philosophy. They did let us hold a Christian service in the clubroom by the jetty operational control building. It was inspiring actually to say the Lords Prayer accompanied by thirty other men talking in ten different languages.

On the forth trip I did get a glimpse of the dangers associated with sailing on oil tankers. Until then I had not thought too deeply about risks involved in floating on top of eighteen thousand tons of crude oil. To me it was a joy to be at sea. To see the stars in the sky at night far more clearly than on land. To stand on the bridge and watch the sun come up out of a calm sea. To feel the motion of the ship and the thrill of moving through the sea. These were the things that dominated my life. Well in my case going to foreign exotic places had not happened. I was stuck on the same worn track just like a train running along the same rails between the same stations. I could still sense the excitement in the crew and listened to the stories of the exotic places they had all travelled to. I assured myself that it would come in the future.

I happened to be on the bridge one day as we came out of the Red Sea into the Indian Ocean when there was a flurry of activity. The radio officer came out and talked to the second mate. The second mate called the Captain and he soon appeared on the bridge. I could not stop myself listening.

" The Radio officer has picked up a faint SOS. He thinks it is an automatic one like those from the lifeboats. He reckons by the DF it is on our course. Obviously he has no idea how far away it is,"

" Get him to inform the authorities. Set a course to intercept if we can."

The radio officer appeared again. " I have a communication from a British war ship. I gave her our position and they confirm that the source is about thirty miles from us. Could we go and investigate? They have given me the position of the ship in trouble and a bearing."

He placed a piece of paper on the chart table. The second mate was soon plotting positions and bearings on the chart when the Captain spotted me on the bridge wing.

He smiled. " Don't just stand there. Take those binoculars and keep a look out."

I stood staring at the horizon through the binoculars. The Captain watched the radar trace while the second mate navigated the ship.

Suddenly the captain exclaimed, " There is an echo two points on the port bow at about twenty miles."

We stood in a line looking in that direction. Then I saw it. A small smudge on the horizon and told the Captain. A sailor appeared and the steering was put on manual. The smudge got bigger and was now definitely a ship even to the naked eye. We sailed closer and closer and the ship now took on features. From this distance it looked intact, bow into the wind and swell. Then I realised something was missing.

Like most smaller tankers of that time, the bridge was over the officer accommodation amidships. As we approached it became apparent that this was missing. All I could do was stare. The crew were lining the ships rails but all were silent. In place of the accommodation structure was some twisted girders and a hole in the deck. All the structure was missing.

On the deck above the aft accommodation, some sailors waved as we approached. The captain ordered the motor lifeboat to be made ready. Turning the Fortunato into the wind and slowing parallel to the other tanker, the Captain got as close to the other ship as he dared. When this was done the chief officer and the third mate sailed our motorboat across to the tanker with some medical supplies and to find out what had happened.

It appears they were cleaning the tanks when there was an explosion which ripped away all of the accommodation. It had happened in the early hours of the morning and all the officers were asleep except the second mate on the bridge and the engineers aft. The second mate had been blown off the bridge and into the sea. They had rescued him in the lifeboat. He was injured but helping the bosun tend the ship. All the other officers had been killed.

The crew had rigged up a system so that they could steer the ship from the steering engine and had managed to turn the ship into the wind. The generator was going so they had power.

We stood by the disabled ship for the rest of the day. That evening as the sun was going down a British warship arrived and took charge. Captain Morris was not really amused by the way the warship officers appeared to arrogantly assume that we would hand over to them but we had commercial considerations to take into account. Unlike the Royal Navy whose sole purpose at that time was to spend taxpayers' money, our purpose was to carry cargoes for payment so that our company could survive. We dipped our flag in reply to their farewell and set course for the Persian Gulf and Mina Al-Hamadi once again.

I did get to stand on foreign soil before I left the Fortunato. The ship was sent to Rotterdam on the last voyage and I was sent on leave. I did not see much of this country because those crew returning to the UK were taken by taxi to the railway station and then to the ferry for Harwich. Still, I could truthfully say I had been abroad.

And so my first voyage ended without visiting any of the exotic places I had dreamed about all those years while I was waiting to join my first ship. I had listened in awe to the tales of my Grandfather of foreign shores, of storms and of sun kissed days when the sea was flat calm. I had been through storms, lent on the rail at night looking at the stars in a cloudless sky but not visited any exotic places. Kuwait was abroad but we had not been allowed ashore. The nearest I had come to the country of Kuwait was the clubhouse in the centre of the long jetty. I went home wondering what I was going to tell my Grandfather about the places I had visited and the sights I had seen. He had been anticipating tales of the sea when I came on leave.

Chapter 2

After my leave, I was ordered by the company to join a ship called the Wilfrido in, you guessed it, Eastham Dock. Not again I thought as I boarded the train at Euston Station after visiting head office. Was I destined to sail from Liverpool all my sea life? There was nothing I could do to influence any decision of the company so I settled back on the train for the journey to Liverpool.

When the taxi pulled up at the gate to Eastham dock, I looked down the slope at the next ship I was joining. Even from a distance I could see she was old. The funnel was more like a stovepipe than the funnel of more recently built ships. Her masts were like rugby posts attached to the deck until a single mast rose vertically from the crosspiece. The accommodation was held up with girders and on each deck there were walkways passing all around the structure. The wheelhouse was small and above this the ventilation was through horn shaped hoods rather than the grills of power driven air blowers. The funnel markings and badge were the same as the Fortunato. I found out later that she had been built during the war and her plates were riveted rather than welded. The engine was steam triple expansion with cylinders rather than the steam turbines of most ships in the fleet. Her top speed was ten knots flat out so we were not going to race across the oceans or overtake many other ships.

Once on board, I reported to the chief officer, a small neat man called Roger Frost. He informed me that Captain Venables was ashore so showed me to my cabin. This was on the Captain's deck at the rear of the accommodation block with one porthole looking aft. The significance of this was not apparent until we sailed. I was to be the sole cadet so had the cabin to myself. I was glad of this. It was small but had two bunk beds on either side. It meant that the cabin was designed to take four cadets. What it must have been like with four cadets sharing that tiny space is beyond me.

When the Captain returned, he signed me on and assigned me to the chief officer. I found this meant I had to keep the watch with the chief officer from four to eight while at sea and his cargo duties while in port.

The day after I joined the ship, I heard what our orders were to be. We were to sail that evening when the discharge was finished for the Caribbean Sea to load in a place called Curacao. We would find out what we were loading and were we were taking the cargo once we had arrived in Curacao. I was excited. This was it, I kept telling myself. I would be sailing across the Atlantic Ocean and into the Caribbean Sea. At last I would get the chance to sail to exotic places. Maybe I would be able to set foot on foreign soil and visit some foreign town.

When the ship sailed through the locks and out into the Mersey, I was on the focastle with the Roger Frost. It was hard to believe that we would sail west when we came out of the Saint George's Channel for the West Indies rather than South towards the Bay of Biscay. As the ship passed the Liver Birds I imaged that we were following in the wakes of all the ships that made Liverpool famous and prosperous, trading to the West Indies. Obviously, I could not ignore the fact that many of these ships had sailed south to West Africa to load slaves before crossing the Atlantic.

I had read though that as the volume of trade increased, there were a great number of ships sailing from Liverpool to the West Indies that never took part in the slave trade. Bulk sugar and other tropical produce exported to Britain went for the most part in West Indiamen. There is little doubt that it was regular West Indiamen which carried most of the traffic in a direct two way trade between the West Indies and Britain The difficulties of obtaining large cargoes without a long wait in the colonies meant that the ships were relatively small in the trade with the typical West Indiaman from London being in the range of 150-200 tons while provincial ships were often of less than 100 tons.

I remembered that agriculture in the colonies became the major form of enterprise when it was discovered that sugar and tobacco could be grown to commercial advantage in large plantations. Even today this was true and we were going to distribute the oil that drove those enterprises.

The major problem with the way plantations were organised was the labour intensive methods used in sowing and harvesting crops. After early attempts to recruit European and American labourers to man these plantations failed, planters turned more and more to the import of African slaves to solve their labour difficulties. The demand for labour on the plantations in the colonies provided the impetus for the rise of the slave trade from West Africa that was to be another factor in the development of Liverpool as a major seaport.

However, what is often overlooked but is important for the later development of the British merchant navy, it was not only the slave trade which provided Liverpool's only connection with West Africa. Throughout the period of the slave trade to the West Indies and America, there were merchants in Britain who traded to West Africa for the products of the area, sending these direct to British ports. These traders took no part in the slave trade. In the later decades of the 18th and the first decade of the 19th centuries, Britain was maintaining and extending its interests in the produce trade direct from West Africa. The proportion of ships leaving Liverpool for this direct trade may not have been too great but it came to about 5% of ships in the years between 1804 and 1807. This was a good base to launch a trade policy with the abolition of the slave trade and Liverpool merchants and ship owners were in a favourable position when the scramble for colonial expansion into Africa began.

It was gold which first attracted the Europeans to the Gold Coast of West Africa but despite the attraction of gold, there proved hardly enough gold available on the West African coast to make the voyages profitable. It was the direct sea export of slaves from West Africa to the new world that proved most profitable commodity. The slave trade increased to meet the demands for labour in the colonies being established in the Americas and as the plantations increased the amount of land under cultivation. It must be said that the slave trade was not unique to the English, although I will concentrate on the effect on the development of the British merchant service, but was practised by all the countries that had possessions in the West Indies and was part of the colonial expansion of all the European nations.

The physical and financial risks in the slave trade were high. There was the uncertainty over the time spent on the West African coast looking for enough slaves to fill the ship. The ever present chance of slaves dying on the voyage west across the Atlantic added to the risk. The market for slaves was not controllable and the ships could arrive in the West Indies to find the market flooded with slaves for sale, with the price of slaves being too low for the ship to make a profit. Although these factors made the slave trade speculative, large profits could be and were made by some operators making the trade attractive to both traders and ship owners.

In addition to the speculative nature of the trade, the operation required a high degree of organisation on the part of the trading companies or the shipmaster for it to be successful in the longer term. Ships had to be chartered or bought, fitted out for the trade and manned. Goods had to be purchased and carried to the African coast to be exchanged for slaves. The slaves then had to be carried to the West Indies arriving relatively fit to be sold for work on the plantations. All the costs of the voyages had to be incurred by the operators before the rewards were forth coming when the ship arrived back in Britain.

So we sailed across the Atlantic in the historic wake of those early West India men. The Wilfrido trundled along at her ten knots, not much faster than the sailing ships with a favourable wind. As I was to observe, we did not overtake many other ships. We had gales in mid ocean and the Wilfrido was tossed about like a cork. The riveted structure creaked and groaned in a different way than the Fortunato. I soon got used to the noises. The engine sound was different too. The whine of the turbine was missing, replaced by the swish of pistons in cylinders with the triple expansion engine.

After what seemed an age at sea without seeing land, we sighted some islands. On a gloriously sunny day, we passed between St. Lucia to the south and Martinique in the north. Both islands rose green and cone shaped in the distance. As they dropped astern, I realised we were in the Caribbean Sea.

We approached Curacao Island from the east. It rose out of the sea, barren for the most part with patches of what looked like scrub on the hills. The sea was deep blue and flat calm. Even though it was hot, it was not the oppressive heat of the Persian Gulf. On the breeze from the south could be smelt the jungle of British Guyana and Venezuela.

We broke out the Dutch flag and ran this up the foremast. For some reason after this it became my job to climb that bloody mast and unravel the flag every time it became entangled in the rigging.

" We can't have our Dutch friends insulted by a tangled flag can we?" Roger Frost stated with a slight grin.

It appeared to me that the courtesy flag got twisted round the mast and ladder five times a day though this might be an exaggeration. Of greater importance to me at the time, I was frightened of heights. Not freezing frightened where I have seen somebody unable to move but really nervous. The journey up the vertical ladder on one side of the goal post masts, walking along the cross piece and then up the single mast was agony. I clung to the ladder for dear life, my heart pumping and my palms sweaty. But I managed somehow to do what I was told. I have a suspicion even today that Roger Frost knew that I was nervous of going up that mast and made me do it to overcome my fear. It became easier and I found in the end I was running up the ladders. But I never did it one handed and I always had to pause to still my heart half way up. I can still remember the relief I felt whenever I reached the deck after climbing down. Of course there was one compensation if I could keep my eyes open for long enough. The view of the port in which we were berthed was phenomenal.

We anchored off Willemstad, the capital of Curacao. There was a line of tankers waiting for berths. For some reason we were not at anchor for long but soon had the pilot on board and were sailing towards the harbour.

Willemstad, and the bay beyond where the refinery was built, was entered through a narrow channel that effectively cut the town in two. There was a pontoon bridge opened by a tug towing it back against the entrance bank. The houses on each side of the entrance looked very Dutch with high gables and narrow windows. It was obvious to me that ships coming to the port through the entrance were such a common sight that nobody on shore looked in our direction. They carried on with their business as though a ship passing within yards was of no interest.

We berthed at the refinery and discharged the ballast. I took the first watch with the second mate, Joe Phillips. When we had finished, he asked me if I would like to go ashore with him. I jumped at the chance of setting foot on foreign soil and seeing the town during the daylight.

We took a taxi from the gates and went to Willemstad. First he took me to the floating market along the quay. Boats from Venezuela and some of the other islands came to Willemstad with cargoes of fruit and other produce that was not grown on the island. It was a vibrant, noisy and colourful place. We walked along the boats and there were fruits and vegetables I had never seen before. The stallholders held out samples to try. The whole population was black and their clothes were vibrant colours. At last, I thought, I am in a foreign place.

After the market, Joe Phillips took me to a cafe looking out over the entrance to the harbour. He ordered a bottle of Bacardi, a large bottle of coke, some ice and a bowl of lemon and limes. It was my first introduction to Bacardi and I was hooked. We sat outside in the shade letting the world go by, drinking our Bacardi until it was time to go back to the ship. At last I would be able to tell my grandfather about an exotic place abroad.

After loading a cargo of fuel oil, we set sail as ordered for Cartegena in Columbia. Most of the crew had been there before and talked excitedly about the cheapness of the booze and girls.

We sailed into Cartegena early one morning. It was my first time in South America. Since joining the Wilfrido my time was apportioned by the Roger Frost but as I was the only cadet on board, he gave me as much leisure as was possible. He also allowed me to mix with some of the sailors as long as I stayed within the boundaries of what he considered normal living.

The sailors invited me to join them on a trip ashore that evening after I had finished my discharge watch. I asked Roger Frost if that was all right and with a grin he gave his permission. As I showered and dressed I was excited at the prospect of drinking with some of the sailors. Back in England I was considered by law too young to enter bars.

The sailors ordered a number of taxis to take us into town. One of them who had been here before knew of a bar and recommended this. When we arrived, to me it was like a hacienda. Through an arch in a fence covered in bourganvilla was a garden surrounded by chalets. Flowers bloomed in beds and the lawn was carefully groomed. Opposite the entrance was the bar. It was how I imagined a colonial building would be, wooden with a corrugated iron roof. Along the front was a covered veranda with round tables and cane chairs.

Joe, one of the sailors who always appeared to be in the lead, paid off the taxi and did not ask me for a contribution. He found a large round table and we all sat around. A waitress wearing a skimpy top, no bra and short skirt appeared. Everybody ordered drinks and somebody paid.

Looking around curiously, I noticed that most of the tables were occupied by groups of men drinking and talking. There was loud music playing and inside the bar was a dance floor. Several couples were dancing very close. At the other tables sitting with the men were obviously local girls all dressed like the waitress.

It was not long before more girls appeared and after some banter with the sailors, sat down at the table. I have no idea how it was sorted whether by the men or the girls but soon each man had a girl sitting next to him. Joe ordered another round of drinks.

Dennis, one of the other sailors, lent over and pushed some money into my hand. " Buy a round of drinks," he whispered. " Don't say anything about who gave you the money. I know how little you earn. This is on me."

Next time the waitress appeared, I went to order a round. One of the other sailors pushed my hand away, told me to sit down and ordered a round. I tried to give the money back to Dennis but he told me to put it in my pocket until the opportunity came up again. This happened a few times during the evening with different sailors and by the end of the evening, I had accumulated a tidy sum of money.

The girl who had sat next to me was young, about my age I suppose. She was dark skinned, black hair with a round face and thick lips. Her body could be described as chunky though from the feel of her leg against mine, not fat. When she reached over me to get to her drink, her top fell away from her body revealing that she did not wear a bra. Her breasts glimpsed under her top were like two pointed cones. She sat holding my hand, singing softly to the music and stroking my thigh. Unlike some of the other girls who were all over their men, she made no attempt to get me to kiss her or fondle her body.

Bob the cook, a good looking man, went off with the best looking girl in the brothel. She had an almost perfect figure, round face with large dark eyes and well proportioned lips. Her hips swung provocatively as she walked. They disappeared into one of the chalets.

Fifteen minutes later the girl rushed out of the chalet without any clothes covering her body.

She was screaming causing her breasts to bob up and down. " I can't take it! It is too big! It will break me in two!"

Bob followed looking bemused also without any clothes. His member stood proudly to attention. I gasped as I realised it was as large as my forearm. The sailors sitting on our table all cheered. Some of the girls went to comfort their friend. One of the older women took Bob by the hand and led him back into the chalet. Her eyes were large and round. We did not see Bob again until it was time to go back to the ship.

One after the other after some bargaining, the sailors drifted away to the chalets. Angela, as my girl was called, took my hand and pulled me to my feet. She indicated that we should follow. I walked beside her to one of the chalets and she opened the door with a key. Inside was dark until she t switched on a bedside light. The room was sparsely furnished. A double bed dominated the space with a garish cover thrown across. A chest of drawers with a mirror above. Opposite the window a cupboard. A stand in one corner with an old fashioned, to me. wash basin and jug of warm water. I noticed that above the bed was a picture of the Virgin Mary.

Angela held out her hand and I paid the going price. She pushed the money into a bag hanging in the cupboard. Only then did she kiss me. She undressed me slowly, pushing my hand away every time I attempted to help.

Smiling she said. " Slowly, slowly. More pleasure."

Once I was naked, she pushed me onto the bed. Standing above me at the foot of the bed, she undressed slowly. Once naked, she knelt on the bed at my side and kissed every bit of my flesh. Every time I reached for her, she pushed my hand away. It went on like this for what to me seemed an age. Finally, she lay on top of me and made love. It was the most satisfying encounter I had ever experienced. After that she let me explore her body and we made love until Joe knocked on the door to say it was time to go back to the ship.

So ended my first encounter with a seaman's trip ashore after being locked in a ship for weeks.

The Wilfrido loaded diesel oil back at Curacao and sailed down the Brazilian coast to a place called grandly Rio Grande de Sul. It was a town whose main purpose was to serve the beef cattle industry that dominated that province of Brazil.

At the end of the voyage along the Brazilian coast, we sailed through the narrow entrance to the river and up stream to approach a rather rickety looking jetty with one rubber discharge hose. Ashore through the tree could be seen the rust streaked storage tanks with the paint peeling away.

As we approached the berth, the anchor was made ready. It was a good job it was. I was on the bridge operating the engine telegraph on instructions from the pilot. Captain Venables thought this would be good experience for me to accompany the third mate on the bridge and observe what duties he performed. Hence my standing by the telegraph and operating this on instructions from the pilot.

The pilot ordered stop and I pulled the handle to the stop position. The engine room answered by positioning their telegraph to stop. Then the pilot ordered slow astern. The telegraph rang and was answered. Nothing happened. The engine kept moving ahead. Frantically, as the berth came closer and closer at too fast a speed, the third mate rang the engine room.

He listened to the phone and then shouted. " The gear change lever has come adrift. They are having difficulty stopping the engine!"

The pilot panicked and started shouting in Portuguese and throwing his arms in the air. He rushed out onto the bridge wing.

The Captain reacted calmly and shouted through the intercom. " Let go the port anchor Mister mate."

Turning to the wheelman he ordered. " When the anchor hits the bottom steer the bow towards the jetty."

The pilot rushed in shouting in broken English. " What do you think you are doing? Hard to port."

The Captain shook his head slightly in the direction of the wheelman and turned to the pilot. " We have let go the port anchor. That will hold the bow away from the jetty. If we are not careful the stern will come round very quickly and smash the jetty. We have to steer the bow towards the jetty."

The pilot's eyes were almost popping out of his head but he shrugged and went out onto the starboard bridge wing to watch what was happening. It was obvious, though he did not say as much, that he was handing sole responsibility to the Captain.

The ship continued to churn on against the pull of the anchor. The jetty came closer and closer. The people watching started to run away down the pier towards the shore including the rope handlers. I suspected some of them from their size had never run as fast for a long time.

With a sickening thump, the ship hit the jetty. Because of the prompt action from the Captain and despite the lack of help from the pilot, the ship came against the jetty along its length. The fenders bounced the ship away from the quay and then the engine stopped. Steam screamed out of the pressure valves. Rust and dirt flew in a cloud from the ironwork and the rubber pipe swung violently from its place of suspension under the gantry. The piles under the jetty groaned but nothing was broken.

Two men ran back onto the quay and took a rope. Soon the ship was tied up securely and the steam had stopped releasing into the atmosphere. Silence reigned. The pilot wiped his forehead with a handkerchief. The Captain was on the phone to the Chief Engineer. I put the telegraph to stop engines and left the bridge to join the Roger to set up the pipes and tanks for discharge.

We lay at the berth for the rest of the day while a team from the oil company inspected the jetty and the oil pipes connecting the ship to the shore. The company was worried about leaks in the system when we started to discharge. As the sun was setting, they gave the all clear and we could start to discharge.

In the morning the Captain sent me to the engine room to find out how long they were going to be. When I climbed down the ladder, I found pieces of machinery

its laid out near the engine with the engineers
ing at them.

The second engineer saw me and grinned. " Spying on us are you?"

I blushed. " No. The captain sent me to ask when you thought you would be ready for us to sail."

He looked and indicated a piece of equipment that looked to me as though it was gear wheels. " The pin for the lever broke. We don't carry a spare but the third engineer is a turner and he is making one. We should be ready by dinner time tonight tell Captain Venables."

True to his word, over dinner he informed the Captain that the engine was fully operational and we could leave any time.

On the way back to Curacao the ship called into the mouth of the Amazon River to load fresh water. As we sailed up the river, I stood on the gangway platform and took hygrometer readings of the water density until it passed a certain number. Then we loaded six cleaned tanks of fresh water to deliver to Curacao.

When we arrived back in Curacao, we received orders to load for Hamble and then go to Glasgow to dry dock. It was surprising but the Captain called all the officers together in the saloon while we were waiting for the loading to start. We all sat talking quietly about many things but nobody was prepared to come out with what most of us felt. Why had the captain called us all together? was the question on most of our minds.

He came in with a folder under his arm. Placing this open on the table, he looked up and smiled. " I know it is strange but the Company wanted me to request something from all of you. They have decided that the Wilfrido has out lived here natural life span. It is costing too much to keep running. The latest incident where we almost demolished the jetty at Rio Grande de

Sul was the last straw. Therefore after dry dock, the ship is to go to Hong Kong for scrap. It is due there in December. You might think it strange that we are going to dry dock in Glasgow when the ship is due to be scrapped. The only way we can sail the Wilfrido to Hong Kong is to get the seaworthiness certificate renewed, hence the dry dock. On the way to Hong Kong we will carry cargoes to other ports. What I would like is for most of you to sail with me and take this venerable lady to the scrap yard. I know many of you are over due for leave because the company have difficulty in recruiting steam reciprocating engineers. I can assure you that the company will not refuse leave if that is what you want. Those who agree to this proposition can come and se me after wards. Unfortunately, Eddie you have no choice."

Almost all of the officers agreed to sail the ship to Hong Kong for scrap. In many ways it was a sad day. To think that the Wilfrido would cease to be a ship in a few months.

We sailed for Hamble on Southampton Water with a cargo of fuel oil the day after the Captain announced the plan to scrap our ship. Most of the officers were ambivalent about taking the ship to scrap. On the one hand they were sad at the end of a ships life. Moreover the end of a ship on which they had faithfully served through the good times and the bad. On the other hand they remembered the frequency of the occasions when things had gone wrong due to age and they had struggled to keep the ship operating. Roger told me of the trip before the one I had joined when they had had to put over one hundred fish bolt in the side to replace sprung rivets. This came about because it was observed as they left port that one of the tanks was leaking.

Seeing my look of incomprehension, Roger explained. " Some times rivets come loose and pop out. A few does not matter but if a number come loose they have to be replaced. What this entails is some of the crew going into the hold and identifying the rivets. These are then knocked out by cutting off the head inside the tank. We had to rig ladders to do this. Then another of the crew has to be lowered over the side in a bosun's chair to push the fish bolt through the rivet hole. Those inside then tighten the nut against a washer until the plates are tight."

It sounded so easy when he explained but I could imagine what it must have been like in the hold. The beams and floors must have been slippery and oily. Even with the lights it must have been dark in the shadows. On top of all that it must have been hot. The man on the outside had to sit just above the rushing water because the Captain would not have stopped the ship. To get to the holes low down in the ship, the Wilfrido would have been heeled as far as possible making clinging to a jury ladder in the tank scary. I was glad that this job had been undertaken before I had joined. Those thoughts came back to haunt me latter in the voyage.

It is a strange feeling coming back to ones home port by ship. It reminded me of the times I had sailed along these waters on the Norris Castle and the Calshott. I stood watching as we sailed passed Ryde on the port side, Southsea on the starboard with the forts guarding Portsmouth at the edge of the channel, Cowes and then round the bends at Calshott with the power station near the beach. Then passed the Fawley oil refinery and so across the river to Hamble terminal. It was so familiar unlike most other places I had visited many of which I had been seeing for the first time. I was back home.

Twenty four hours later we set sail down the Solent for John Browns shipyard on the Clyde. This was the place where the Queens had been built. Those graceful liners with which I had been brought up. Funny really. When I was younger, like many people who lived in Southampton, I had been passed the docks on numerous occasions and not even glanced at these queens of the sea. Only when my parents had visitors did they take them down to the docks to look at these ships. I did see a great deal of them when I was on the Isle of White ferry and the Calshott before going to sea.

We were in drydock for two weeks during which time the drydock managers and surveyors walked round the ship shaking their heads. Mysterious men in boiler suits banged the hull with hammers standing listening to the note. Others scraped of the layers of paint and drilled the palates to test their thickness. It became one of my jobs to show them around. At last they approved of the ship and gave it a seaworthiness certificate. I still believe that they only awarded the certificate on the understanding that the ship would sail to Hong Kong for scrap. As a mere cadet I was not privy to the inner discussions of the company, the captain and the surveyors. It was an old ship lets face it and unlike humans, when a ship gets old and tired, it is scrapped.

One thing that did happen was that in Glasgow the agent had difficulty in engaging a crew. They took one look at the ship or had heard stories of the accommodation and the conditions on board, and they refused to sign on. We sailed down the Clyde and anchored off Greenock. The crew were engaged without seeing the ship. The first sight they ha of the Wilfrido was when they sailed out to the ship on a tender. As I was to learn during that trip, they were what can only be described as the dregs of the pool. Many had bad discharge reports, many were social misfits but a few were normal sailors.

" This lot mean trouble," Barry Mason, the bosun had remarked as we stood by the rail watching the tender approach. " You mark my words. There will be fighting, drunkenness and difficulty in getting them to work. Still it is only for a few months and then we can get back on a civilised ship once more."

Barry Mason's words came back to me a week or so later. The Wilfrido was rolling gently through a low swell in the Mediterranean Sea with the sun shining and hardly a cloud in the sky. Since leaving Glasgow, Barry Mason had struggled manfully to keep the crew working normally and fulfilling the tasks set each day by Roger Frost. With a few exceptions, most of the sailors were lazy and ill disciplined. They were late turning out for work or going to relieve the watch. Indeed it was not long before the bosun identified the most reliable and assigned these to the watches. The others he organised for maintenance. The whole episode showed me once again that a ship is an enclosed, twenty four hour society. The system of work on board ship relied to a great extent on trust. The crew members had to find ways of getting along with each other. On most ships the tolerance sometimes broke down and the disciplinary code had to be enforced by the officers. If one or more of the crew were trouble makers and set out to disrupt the smooth running of the ship, they had to be dealt with internally on the ship. There were no circumstances where the captain could sack any crewmember and send them home. All in discipline had to be handled on board. Some Captains were better at handling this situation than others.

On that trip on the Wilfrido from Glasgow to Hong Kong for scrap, the worst crewmember of a very tough crew was called McCluskey. Once upon a time he must have had some pride in his ships and his work. Not on that trip he didn't. What had happened to him in the past I have no idea, I never heard his life's story from him or anybody else. This was strange because with most of the ships complement sailing together for long periods, everybody found out some background to the other crewmembers. With McCluskey, whether it was something that had happened while at sea or in his home life I was never told.

He was of medium build with a wiry body. For some reason he was one of those men who look as though they needed a shave all the time but never end up with a beard. His face could only be described as battered. His nose had been broken at least twice and there were scars all over his cheeks. One ear looked as though somebody had taken a bite out of the top. His clothes were ragged and unpressed even when he went ashore for a night out. When he did report for work, he smelt as though he had not had a shower for a week.

It might have been prejudice on my part but his accent was so east Glasgow I could not understand what he was saying even when he was looking directly in my direction. I tried but it was impossible. To my ears it was as though he was uneducated and unintelligent. With most of the rest of the crew, even though they also came from Glasgow, I found I could make out a sense of what they were saying.

In addition to all of this, McCluskey drank. Well all seamen drink, some more than others. I have had a far bit of drink in my time. McCluskey drank and was permanently semi-sober and many times blind drunk. I suspect he did not need much drink to tip him over the edge of drunkenness like many alcoholics I know. Where he got the drink from was uncertain. The sailors were only allowed so much beer a week. They denied it if ever confronted with an accusation but it was suspected that some of the crew sold their allowance to McCluskey at inflated prices. It was rumoured though never confirmed, that his drinking over the years and his disposition had resulted in his wife kicking him out of their home. All I know was that when he was not at sea, he stayed in the seaman's mission hostel near the docks in Glasgow.

Late one afternoon just as the sailors were knocking off for the night, I was clearing away the equipment and wires in the store under the amidships accommodation. Bill, the bosun had been instructing me in wire splicing that afternoon. I was amazed at the complications in splicing a wire as compared to a rope but the bosun had praised me for getting fairly competent. There were hurried footsteps along the deck and Tom Alcock the carpenter burst into the store.

" You had better come quickly Bill," he said trying to catch his breath. " There is a fight in the seaman's mess. If we don't stop it soon, somebody is going to get killed."

The bosun dropped his bronze hammer by the table and rushed towards the door. " Eddie. Leave that for now. Get up onto the bridge and tell the Mate. I will meet him outside the seaman's mess as soon as he can get there."

He was gone. I dropped the wires and the tools onto the deck and raced out of the store. Not looking aft, I did not hesitate. I climbed the ladder two steps at a time, raced across the boat deck and up the second ladder to the bridge.

When I burst through the door into the wheelhouse, Roger Frost looked up from the chart table where he was preparing for his star sights that evening to fix the position of the ship. I was due to join him at dusk for my navigation instructions. He raised an eyebrow at my hurried entrance.

" The bosun sent me," I reported gasping for breath. " There is a fight going on in the seaman's mess. I don't know the details but he wants you to meet him outside the mess as soon as you can get there."

Roger shook his head and sighed. " I knew this crew were trouble. You look after the ship for a moment. There is nothing about. I will tell the Captain as I go aft. He will most likely relieve you in a couple of minutes."

With those passing words Roger left via the stairs to the Captains accommodation. For the first time in my sea career I was on the bridge on my own. I nonchalantly lent on the rail looking forward and scanning the horizon. The sea rolled away to the horizon sparkling in the low sun. There was not a ship or any land in sight. That did not matter. To me, I was in charge of the ship. I could alter the autopilot and the ship would turn onto another course. What power! It felt good being in charge of the ship.

The captain hurried onto the bridge before I could get too carried away with my feeling of control. He took a quick look around the sea.

" What happened?" he demanded.

" I was clearing away the wires I use to practice my splicing when the carpenter came and told the bosun that there was a fight in the seaman's mess. The bosun instructed me to tell the chief officer. I came up her and told him. Mr Frost left me here and went aft to sort things out. That is all I know Sir." There was nothing else I could tell him.

He scanned the horizon again. " You keep a lookout. I am going down onto the boat deck to see if I can find any more about what is happening. Call me or fetch me if you see anything or are worried about anything at all."

With that passing comment, he climbed down the ladder and disappeared aft on the boat deck. I heard him calling for his steward but turned back to keep watch on the sea in front of the ship before I could hear any more.

A smudge appeared on the horizon almost dead ahead of the ship. I watched as it slowly took shape and after a while could clearly see that it was a ship. It was soon apparent, as seen through the binoculars, from the derricks that it was a cargo liner. From this distance I could not work out which company owned the ship.

I called the captain as instructed and he returned to the bridge. " Take regular bearings as it approaches. You have had lessons in seamanship and know that if the bearing changes, the ship will pass safely. I will be looking aft."

I did as I had been ordered. As the ship approached, the bearing changed constantly. Other ships appeared heading in our direction. I took bearings and watched closely. They all looked as though they would pass safely down our port side. I then realised that these must be the first part of a convoy that had passed through the Suez Canal.

Just as I was enjoying myself acting out my boyhood dreams of being in charge of a ship, Roger Frost came back to the bridge. The Captain appeared and joined him in the wheelhouse.

" What happened," Captain Venables demanded in a harsh voice. " Is everything under control?"

Roger Frost smiled slightly. " Everything is under control. There was a fight in the seaman's mess. When the bosun, the carpenter and I walked into the mess, McCluskey and two other sailors were backed into a corner confronted by some of the other sailor. McCluskey had a large spanner in his hand and was threatening anybody who came near with a beating. It had not worked too well because one of his eyes was closed and he had a cut on his cheek. We managed to separate the two groups and herd them into different parts of the accommodation. It sounds as though when the sailors packed up this afternoon, they went back to the mess for a drink before getting ready for dinner. There they found McCluskey already sitting drinking a beer. He was throwing darts into a picture of the Queen. Roper told McCluskey to stop but he laughed and threw one of the darts at Roper. Millar then thumped McCluskey and McCluskey hit him back with the spanner. McGregor joined in on McCluskey's side and all hell was let loose. All the sailors took sides and a general fight took place. With the help of the carpenter and the bosun I was able to sort things out. The chief steward is there now tending to their wounds. I hope you didn't mind but I told them all that they would have to answer to you in the morning."

Captain Venables looked grim. " Oh, they will have to answer to me all right. In the morning have them all outside the cargo office. I will see them one at a time from nine o'clock. Make sure McCluskey is there. Make him wait outside until I have seen and heard all the others involved. I will then throw the bloody book at him. After dinner, I will go and study the Merchant Shipping Act and the Company disciplinary code. I will charge the bastard with every offence I can find. How dare he put my ship in danger? If I have my way he will not recover from this for a long time."

Turning to me, he grinned. " How are those ships progressing, young man?"

" Two have passed safely down the port side. There are four more approaching but they are all going to pass safely," I answered very seriously.

Roger Frost laughed and looked out on the port side at the approaching ships. " I will take over now, young Eddie. Go on down and put the gear away you were using. Then get ready for dinner. Don't be too anxious to take over up here. Always remember you have to qualify first. With that in mind, make sure you are back here at dusk so that we can continue teaching you how to navigate using the stars."

I walked off the bridge wondering what the Captain could do to the crew the next morning. Visions of prison cells, handcuffs and walking the plank were the most fanciful. At the same time I was thrilled at having been allowed to look after the ship if even for a brief time. I had to accept that in reality the Captain had been only a few yards away but I could wallow in my belief that I had been in control of the ship. The episode had convinced me by the time I was back in my cabin that I was more determined to pass my certificates and become a fully fledged officer.

The next day I found out what the Captain had meant by his orders to the chief officer. I was helping the carpenter retag a steam pipe which ran between the engine room and the amidships accommodation under the catwalk. From where we were working, I had a good view of the door to the cargo office. The sailors who had been involved in the fight lined up outside and then were admitted one at a time. Most were in the office for only a short time. Finally McCluskey went in, there was the sound of angry voices but we were too far away to make out what was being said. When he emerged, he kicked the rail and stormed off down the catwalk.

He stopped above where I was working.

" What are yoose staring at, you English bastard," he shouted in his unintelligible Glasgow accent. His hands gripped the rail so hard the knuckles were white.

Tom Alcock straightened by my side, balancing a bronze hammer in his hand. For the first time I realised what a big man he was.

He smiled slightly. " You mind what you are saying, McCluskey. Leave this young man alone or you will have to answer to me. You might be able to bully some of the other crew but you do not scare me. Now get your ass aft and report to the bosun. He will tell you what you are expected to do today."

McCluskey scowled at Tom, held my stare for a moment and then, muttering to himself, staggered aft.

" Thank you, Tom," I said to the carpenter.

" Watch him young Eddie. He is trouble that man. He will not come up against me though and as I have told him to leave you in peace, he will. Now lets finish the job."

" Before we finish the job, what happened in the office this morning?" I asked nodding towards the office.

" Oh, I expect McCluskey was fined a couple of weeks wages and warned as to his future conduct by Captain Venables. He could have been put on a charge and had him taken before a magistrate when we get back to England. Most Captains try to sort out their disciplinary problems on board without recourse to outside people. Knowing Captain Venables reputation, it will have been two weeks wages. It won't make any difference though. Give McCluskey a couple of days and he will be just as bad. His type never learn lessons because their brains are scrambled. It is the result of too much booze and too many fights. He will die young will our McCluskey. Either in a ships hospital bed from a heart attack or in a gutter in some port after a brawl. He is no good to anybody either as a person or a seaman. We must have been desperate to sign on a crew that included him. That is enough of my social observations. We have a job to finish today."

Tom was to prove accurate in his forecast. McCluskey knuckled down for a few days, was on time when reporting for duty and, apart from the twitches, appeared sober. He still glowered at me every time we met but the rest of the crew made it clear that he was to leave me alone. I have no idea why he picked on me as an example of the establishment but he did. Then he reverted to type. He was found dead drunk in his bunk mid morning and the cycle started all over again.

We sailed through the Suez Canal and into the Persian Gulf. Our orders were then to go to Abadan up the Shat Al Arab to load fuel oil for Colombo in Ceylon at the oil refinery there. Even in Abadan McCluskey managed to get drunk and upset the authorities. They delivered him back to the ship in a police van and set a guard on the gangway to make sure he did not go ashore again.

The river flowed sluggishly passed the Wilfrido as we lay loading. On the other bank was sand and to the north the large town of Abadan. I was disappointed in not being able to go ashore. It was hot and sticky and I was rather relieved when we sailed.

Once we had entered the Persian Gulf before arriving at Abadan, I came the closest I had ever come to having an argument with Roger Frost. It was hot both by day and night. The Wifrido had no air conditioning though most ships at that time did not have air-conditioning. The cadet's cabin as I have observed before had one porthole facing aft. When the ship was underway not a breath of air entered my cabin. Even in the Mediterranean it had been hot. In the Persian Gulf it was intolerable. Many of the crew took their bedding and slept out on the aft boat deck in an attempt to stay cool. Of course the crew had an almost insurmountable difficulty with staying cool. Their accommodation was above the three Scots boilers and did they give off some heat. That was great in the winter around Europe but in the Persian Gulf it was hell. The crew sweated and grew even more irritable with lack of sleep. Those with portholes at the side of the ship put out wind chutes. I asked the Chief Officer whether I could sleep on deck but he informed me that the Captain did not allow his officers to sleep outside of their cabins. For weeks I lay on top of my bunk without clothes and suffered. Sweat poured from me and I had to drink pints of water and take salt tablets to survive.

In Colombo the problem of McCluskey came to a head. We had completed the discharge and loaded the ballast. The bosun took a count of the sailors, the chief greaser of the engineering staff. McCluskey was missing. I was ordered to search the ship in case he had fallen down into a store or some other lightly used place. After scouring all the places I thought he could be there was still no sign of McCluskey. I reported this to the Chief Officer.

We waited for the final papers and the pilot. Still no McCluskey. The pilot came on board and ordered us to get ready to sail. The ship's personnel breathed a sigh of relief as it looked as though we were about to leave McCluskey behind. The rope men were in place, the crew at stations fore and aft. Still no McCluskey. The pilot ordered the ropes to be let go one at a time.

Blue flashing lights appeared along the jetty and two police cars escorting a police van appeared racing towards the ship sirens blaring. Much to the noticeable displeasure of the Captain, the pilot ordered the last lines to be held in place. We all watched as the police cars skidded to a halt turning sideways to block the jetty. The van stopped and three burly policemen got out. This was strange because most of the policemen in Ceylon were shorter than the average British man. The back doors of the van wee flung open and McCluskey was hauled out by his legs. He was out to the world. Blood smudged his face and one eye was swollen shut. The policemen picked him up and threw him unceremoniously onto the deck. The Chief Steward rushed to his aid but the pilot ignored the body and ordered the ropes to be let go. We sailed away from Colombo as McCluskey's limp body was carried back to his cabin. We never did find out what had happened to him. The last he could remember was engaging a girl and falling asleep in her bed. How he came by the cut on his head or his swollen eye he could not recall. Belligerently, he blamed the police. I suspected he had fallen foul of the girl's pimp. Knowing McCluskey I suspect he had refused to pay.

The captain shook his head and remarked to the Chief Officer. " I thought we had got rid of him there. Bad pennies and all that."

We sailed for Singapore to load a cargo for Japan. It was a peaceful voyage across the Indian Ocean and down the Malaga Straits. The sea was calm, the sun shone every day, the stars twinkled in a dark sky at night and the temperature was balmy. Even McCluskey caused no trouble.

In Japan I learnt more about life. The ship was going for scrap. The company sent an inventory of what was included in the sale. The crew with, I must admit, the connivance of the officers, scoured the inventory and worked out what was included and what was not. Armed with this knowledge, they proceeded to sell everything that was not on the list and split the money between them. How agreement was reached about the proportions of the money or the split I have no idea. I was not included in the arrangement. Later I was to learn that this was at the expressed instructions from Captain Venables. Something to do with my cadetship agreement. The problem for everybody was that I kept watch over the ship those nights in Japan while the ship was discharging the cargo and could not help observe the way in which items of equipment were disappearing over the side of the ship into waiting boats. For me to keep quiet, the bosun offered what amounted to cash bribes. I pocketed the money and said nothing. Actually the crew were over cautious. Even though I knew what was going on, I would not have said anything to anybody out of loyalty to the bosun and the carpenter. When we did get to Hong Kong I had a tidy sum of cash to spend. Thinking about the episode now, it might have been the bosun and the carpenter's way of getting me included in the rewards without going against the Captain's instructions. I did mange to detach the eagle emblem from the bow one night and took this home in my case.

We sailed from Japan destined for Hong Kong. Before arriving in Hong Kong, the crew had to clean the tanks. It would take us the best part of a week so we proceeded at half speed. This time the tank cleaning was different. The tanks had to be cleaned by hand held hose to make sure that all the oil was washed away. Then as each tank was cleaned, the rest of the crew had to climb down and dig out all the rust and gunge from the bottom. We were to work twenty four hours in two shifts.

I was assigned to the carpenter. Dressed in oilskins including hoods and goggles, rubber boots and thick gloves, we climbed down into the tank with a hose and blasted the oil off the tank sides. Two sailors paid out the hose as we progressed and attended to the safety harnesses. It was horrible, back breaking and messy work in the arc lights. I soon worked out that the best way to retain my footing on the slippery beams was to lean against the pressure in the hose. After the first beam we progressed down the tank until every part had been cleaned. It was crazy but I quite enjoyed the intense concentration we had to employ. Before long our oilskins were covered in oil from head to toe.

This went on for a week and it became a nightmare. Get up in the morning, have breakfast early. Don the washed down oilskins. Waddle out on deck. Don the goggles. Take over from the bosun. Twelve hours later, strip off the oilskins, wash and shower, have a meal and off to bed. Our other meals were brought to us by the tanks and we ate sitting in our oilskins by the side of the tank combing. At the same time, the rest of the crew were shovelling rust and gunge, placing this in buckets, heaving these up to the deck and emptying them into a chute over the side. Actually, the carpenter and our gang were kind of lucky. At least we did our stint mainly in daylight. The other group under the bosun had to work all night.

Late one afternoon, the carpenter and I emerged from the last tank and flopped onto the deck. We were exhausted.

Roger Frost came up to us and grinned. " Thank you. That was a job that had to be done. You have done great work there. The mucking out gang will go down and clear away the last of the rubbish now. When they have finished, I will put some beer and rum in the mess for them to drink. Lets hope when we get to Hong Kong they accept the tanks."

The carpenter grunted. " Knowing what happens in these circumstances, that will depend on whether they are ready to take over the ship. It is the same as when we were loading chilled meat on one ship I sailed on. If the meat was ready they would accept that the hold was clean. If the meat was not ready they would claim that we had to do some more cleaning. That way, the ship would have to pay for the delay no matter who was at fault."

We approached the pilot station for Hong Kong as the sun was setting a big red ball behind the islands. Lights were starting to show along the shore and on the boats sailing between the islands. The leading lights flashed ahead of the ship one above the other. The ship slowed, stopped and the red painted pilot boat came alongside.

After the pilot was safely aboard, the chief officer and the anchor party were ordered onto the focastle. I stood beside Roger Frost and watched the islands pass close on either side. The trees were hardly visible, lighter patches against the dark of the hills. The waves lapped on the shore, a line of white phosphorescence in the wake of the ship. Except for the sound of the throttled back engine, all appeared quiet.

After a while, the islands parted and a bay opened up in front of the ship. It was to me as though we were entering a magical kingdom. Multicoloured lights climbed away from the water towards the stars. They twinkled and winked like diamonds in Aladdin's cave. On all sides of the ship the lights were reflected in the water and moved gently as boats and ferries disturbed the water and altered the patterns.

It was like looking into a fairy grotto. I stood captivated and was pleased that it was dark on the focastle because I suspected that my mouth was open. I will remember that first sight of Hong Kong harbour all my life.

The ship traversed the harbour between the crossing ferries, the sampans and the speedboats. John pointed out all the landmarks that were etched in lights. Sticking out into the harbour was the airport runway. Further on from the runway I could see the flash of cutters like lightening against the sky. The ship headed in this direction and anchored opposite the place where the broken down hulks of ships lay on the beach.

Once the ship was securely at anchor, those members of the crew who were not wanted the next day were taken off by boat and bussed to the hotel. The skeleton crew left on board settled for the night. Their belongings, except for a small over night bag had been sent on ahead to the hotel. It was strange walking round the ship that night to find there were so few people on board. The Captain, Chief Officer, Chief Engineer, Second Engineer, Bosun, Carpenter, two sailors, greasers and me. Everywhere footsteps seemed to echo into empty space.

Early the next morning as the sun was climbing above the hills, the pilot came aboard. The tall buildings I noticed as I led the pilot to the bridge were now visible all around the harbour. The green ferries ploughed their way across the water from Kowloon to Hong Kong Island. Once the pilot was safely on the bridge, I took my place on the focastle with the Chief Officer, bosun and carpenter.

At the order, we weighed the anchor, the chain clanking as it came aboard. A boat was by the bow and we lowered the anchor all dripping wet as soon as it was above the water onto its deck. Another boat took the other anchor. At a whistle signal, the two boats headed for the shore with the Wilfrido closely following. When the stem touched the mud, the pilot ordered the ship to stop. The boats continued towards the shore.

The anchors were lifted by a heavylift crane ashore and attached to large diameter wires. At a signal from the shore we slowly paid out the cable as it was pulled further ashore by the wires. We could not see how but the cables were fixed ashore. At another signal we started to heave in the anchor cable. Slowly unnaturally with a sound like a sigh, the Wilfrido slid up the beach. More and more of the black, rust streaked hull became visible. On either side were the shells of half demolished ships.

With just the stern in the water, we were ordered to stop. The engineers opened the safety valves and vented the steam into the air with a long drawn out scream. We secured the anchor chain and left the focastle.

Even as we walked towards the amidships accommodation, men were swarming all over the ship, pulling pipes and equipment after them. The crane was landing heavier machinery on the deck.

We collected our overnight bags from our cabins and assembled near the steep gangway that had been placed against the ship's side. The Captain joined us soon after having signed away the ship to the scrap yard manager. He shook hands with manager of the demolition gang and led us down the gangway and along the walkway beside the ship. He did not look back but resolutely led us to the waiting bus. It was as though his emotions were under strict control but would break loose if he looked back at his ex-command.

Three days later after a fascinating time in Hong Kong, my first taste of the east, I sat by one of the windows of the plane that was taking us home. It taxied down the runway, out into the harbour. I caught sight of the Wifrido or what was left of her. The tall funnel with the smoke hood was gone, half the accommodation blocks were now missing. No longer were the masts shaped like rugby posts at the bottom and a tall mast at the top standing proud. Those masts which the chief officer had made me climb to unravel the flag of the country we were visiting or the company house flag. As I have told you, I had been scared the first few times clinging to the ladder for dear life though determined to reach the top so that the crew would not bate me about being a coward. What remained reminded me of pictures I had seen of stranded whales.

The plane turned and rushed along the runway between the flats leaving what was left of the Wilfrido bereft of life and on its own. It had been made of steel and now was a pile of scrap waiting for the trader to find a buyer. A ship is more than a pile of steel, I thought. It had been a home for countless seamen. When they were on board it had been alive. It had battled storms, rolling and heaving through heavy spray. At times it had smiled serenely into the mirror like sea of the Persian Gulf. How many ports had it visited with how much cargo? As I said, above all of this it had been a home. Through the voyages it had been a platform for friendships, feuds and arguments and some indifference. It made me sad to think that the Wilfrido had ended up as a pile of scrap metal on the banks of the harbour in Hong Kong.

Chapter 3

After having Christmas at home, something that many of the seamen I had sailed with longed for, I was sent to join the Edmundo in dry-dock at South Bank in Middlesbrough. All my family made fun of the fact that I was joining a ship with my name.

When I arrived at the drydock, I saw that the Edmundo was a much more modern tanker than those I had sailed on before. The stem was more raked and flared, the accommodation was rounded and smooth while the funnel was a little more streamlined. Apart from that it was designed and laid out in much the same fashion as the majority of smaller tankers. I say smaller because while sailing on the Wilfrido we had passed the first one hundred thousand ton tanker as it sailed towards Mina Al-Hamadi on its maiden voyage. So at eighteen thousand tons, the Edmundo was small.

After picking our way through the equipment seemingly scattered around the drydock, the taxi stopped at the bottom of the gangway. When I had paid off the taxi and collected my bags I noticed a grinning face looking over the rail at the top of the gangway. It was Andy Brookes. We hadn't seen each other for almost two years. He ran down the gangway to help me with my bags. Andy appeared to have lost weight. He looked thinner and even fitter.

" Eddie! Is it good to see you," he exclaimed shaking my hand. " I arrived yesterday. The chief officer Ron Fisher was here along with the old man, Jenkins."

We reached the deck and he led the way towards the amidships accommodation. " We have cabins on the starboard side which seems standard for this class of tanker in the fleet. Three cadet cabins on the starboard side near the second mates. This ship is fairly new. Built in nineteen fifty eight two years ago."

We reached my cabin and I left my bags while we went off to see the chief officer. Ron Fisher was what can only be described as a bruiser. Big and square built with a nose that looked as though it had been broken quite a few times. His voice sounded as though the words were being dragged over gravel. His fists would enclose mine without squeezing my fingers. In reality, he was a gentle person who never raised his voice or appeared to take offence. I came to see that the crew respected him and there was never trouble. This after the Wilfrido was heaven.

After introductions, he ushered me up to see the captain. " Never keep Captain Jenkins waiting," he advised. " He is very strict and acts by the book. He would be most upset and you would start with a question mark against your name if he thought you had been aboard this ship for a long time without reporting to him. He is also strict about the training of his cadets. Have you brought your books and correspondence course material with you?"

" Of course," I answered. The company paid for a cadet's correspondence course and we had to send the assignments to the company training officer rather than straight to the college. At times it was hard to keep up to date and cadet's then would receive an admonishment from the training department.

" Good," Ron Fisher grinned. " He will ask to see your work schedule. I don't suppose this has happened on any other ship but he will lay down a schedule of work for you and build in time for you to undertake this. I sailed with him before and he had all the cadets in his day room once a week to do their assignments or exercises. If you are still on board for the end year exams, he will make you sit down in examination conditions and take the paper."

He knocked on the Captains door and an obvious Welsh voice ordered us to come in.

Ron Fisher introduced me. Captain Jenkins was a shorter than me with a round face, curly grey hair cut short and a round body. His small piggy eyes stared hard into mine and his lip seemed to curl at the edges in contempt. As you can see I took an instant dislike to Captain Jenkins.

" What ships have you been on?" he demanded.

" The Fortunato and the Wilfrido, sir," I replied.

" You were on it when it went for scrap with Captain Venables,?"

" Yes sir."

" You will be assigned to the second mate when he arrives later this afternoon. The chief officer will tell you your duties. Once we sail we will arrange a time for you to study in my office next to my cabin. Make sure your correspondence course notes are to hand. I will send off the completed scripts. They will be returned to me when they have been marked and I will inform you how well you did. One of my cadets always either wins the annual exam prize or comes close. You make sure you work hard. I see from your records that you came second at college. We will make that a first this time won't we?"

" I will try," I answered truthfully.

" Trying is not good enough," he barked back. " You will study hard and win me that prize young man. I will watch yours and Andy Brookes' progress closely while you are on my ship. If I see you shirking, I will come down on you like a ton of bricks. Just you keep that in mind. Now off you go and settle in before reporting back to Mister Fisher for your work schedule."

I came to hate Captain Jenkins. He hounded me ever time he caught sight of me through out those fourteen months I sailed on the Edmundo. He would look down from the bridge wing and on seeing me shout in that infuriating Welsh voice of his, " Gubbins, I'll make a man of you or kill you on this voyage." Andy for some reason escaped the major part of the Captain's tongue lashing.

As we approached a port, I started to dread the return of my correspondence course papers. They were returned to Captain Jenkins not to me. He would look at them before calling me to his office. With obvious relish, he would then proceed to point out all the mistakes I had made, all what he called the sloppy work and the miserable marks. Even though I did better in all my papers than Andy, he appeared to pick on me. He would then make me do extra work in the evenings while Andy was drinking with the junior engineers. It was hell. I hated that man. Many was the time when I imagined getting him near the rail and pushing him into the sea. Andy and I used to sit over a few beers and make more and more outrageous ways of getting rid of the tyrant.

But it wasn't only me who thought he was a tyrant. His nickname among the crew was D.R. Jenkins. Why D.R.? That came back to his reputation. In some ways the company was like one big family. Those serving on the company ships heard about other seamen from what can only be described as the grapevine. Over cans of beer or ashore, the crews would talk about the other ships they had sailed on and the people they had sailed with. With the various captains and other officers the discussion was mostly about how they ran the ship or treated the crew. Obviously there were the stories of incidents some funny, some scary, some routine which had occurred on the various ships that the seamen had sailed on. Captain Jenkins had a reputation for being hard. Every seaman had what was known as a discharge book. It contained a photo and all the details of certificates and the competencies. The main pages of the book were reserved for details of the ships signed on in chronological order and the position held on the ship. At the end of the voyage the Captain signed the seaman off the ship and recorded a report on the seamen's conduct and competence. The Captain had a choice of Very Good (VG) if satisfied with the seaman, Good (G) if not up to the highest standard and Declined to Report (DR) if bad. Thus, the DR in the Captain's nickname. He dished out more DR's than any other Captain in the fleet. Many officers secretly called him a vindictive bastard. He justified his conduct with throw away remarks about most seamen not being worth their wages. That was another thing he did. Fine them at the first opportunity during the voyage.

He said to me one day when we were on the bridge together, " You will learn young man. Stamp on the crew as soon as possible or they will take advantage of you."

The other thing that annoyed most of the crew was when he held lifeboat drill in the middle of the ocean. Admittedly it was a calm day with hardly any swell. Now usually with lifeboat drill the crew would muster at boat stations, except those on watch, lower the boats down to the boat deck, embark, disembark and put the lifeboats back in their cradles. This exercise was undertaken every other week. The other week a fire drill was held.

Captain Jenkins on this afternoon decided that not only were we going to muster at lifeboat stations but we were going to lower the boats and row them round the ship before putting them back in place. There was almost a riot by the crew my lifeboat but the second mate calmed everybody down. He pointed out that there were provisions in the act for the boats to be manhandled like this. Yes, the crew replied, but usually in port with volunteers. It was hard work. They are not the most manoeuvrable boats in the world and they are heavy. The crew, a mixture of sailors, greasers and stewards did their best. With a lot of splashing at first, a great deal of swearing and some laughter we managed to row in unison in the end. It did not help that the chief officer had the boat with the engine and circled us all with the engine going. In our boat we were all praying that the engine would break down. It didn't happen. The chief officer and his crew were spared the physical effort to propel their boat and were back on board before we had attached ourselves to the davit cable again. When the boats were all stowed safely, I resumed my stint with the second mate on the bridge.

The second mate, Vincent Burke, was entirely different. He was one of these perpetually charming people with impeccable manners. I never asked him out right but the story was that his family owned half of Yorkshire. He did admit to me one night, while I was sharing the midnight to four watch with him, that his two brothers had entered the family business. He had resisted all attempts by his family to get him involved. For as long as he could remember he had wanted to go to sea. It was with a blush that he admitted to reading all those sea stories in his youth and on holiday while he sat watching ships pass along the coast near Canne where his relations kept a villa. It was obvious from early on during that voyage that he did not need the money. Indeed he confessed to me that most of his wages from sailing with the company went in tax rather than into his bank. Why he had not gone into the Royal Navy like many upper class second or third sons I was not too sure. Suffice to say that he had been influenced by a director of the company finding him a cadetship on one of the company's newest ships.

The consequences of his wealth were two fold. Captain Jenkins held no fears for him. Vincent Burke was very good at his job. There could be no questions about his competency and his dedication. Captain Jenkins could not fault Vince. Though with other members of the crew, he could always find something to criticise, with Vince it was futile. Very early in the voyage Vince made it plain to the Captain that if there was something wrong with his work, he would take responsibility. If on the other hand, the Captain could not justify his criticism, Vince would sign off at the next port and fly home. I did not come to sea to have some bitter and twisted Captain trying to make my life miserable, he told me.

The other consequence manifest itself in every port. It appeared to Andy and I that no matter what outlandish place we ended up, there was always somebody who knew Vince or his family and would turn up in an expensive car to take him ashore. Not that Vince let this interfere with his duties. He did his watches like all the other officers before he went ashore. Then showered and dressed in his beautifully tailored clothes, he would wave to me and disappear with his friends. I got the distinct impression that the Captain was not amused but Andy and I were consumed by jealousy.

The ship berthed in one of those South American ports bordering the Caribbean Sea to load crude oil. As seemed often the case it was the middle of the night. After securing the ship, Vince and I had watched from the catwalk as guards were posted, one on deck the other at the foot of the gangway. I asked him why in this tin pot dictatorship they needed to post guards. He shrugged.

" What are they looking for?" I asked as our bags were searched as we went ashore to deliver papers to the agent.

" Subversive material," he muttered while smiling at the guard.

When we took over the loading of the cargo from the Chief Officer, it was mid morning. The water ballast had been pumped ashore and the crude oil was now flowing into the ships tanks.

As we opened and closed valves to start loading into one of the tanks, the sun was beating down on the black painted deck. Heat haze rose causing the structures to shimmer and waver. The only shade was under the catwalk which joined the amidships and aft accommodation. This was high above the deck to give safe passage when the deck was battered by waves. Joining the heat haze was the cloud of gas from the open vent through which we measured the oil depth in the tank.

By the amidships accommodation, a guard in his green uniform, gun slung over his shoulder, lounged against the rail watching our efforts. Ashore, another guard sat on a bench by the foot of the gangway chatting loudly to a refinery worker.

I measured the oil depth and reported this to the second mate.

He grinned. " Another forty minutes until we have to change tanks. I'm off to the cargo office to enter the figures in the book."

" And get a mug of coffee," I muttered.

" I heard that," he laughed. " Privileges of yer officer class my boy. I'll bring one back......"

He never finished what he was saying. Like a statue he was fixed to the spot, his eyes bulging from his head. I turned in the direction in which he was looking and froze.

The guard had straightened and was pulling out of his pocket what looked like a large cigar. Calmly, he unpacked it from its silver case throwing the case into the sea.

We stood our boots rooted to the deck, unable to move. Both of us were silently willing him to put it back into his pocket but, after rolling it between his fingers, he raised it to his lips.

After that it was as though everything happened in slow motion. The lifting of the arm to place the cigar in his mouth. The reaching into a pocket and extracting a lighter. The hand going round the lighter thumb on the striker. The cupping of the hands against the breeze.

His thumb moved and the lighter sparked. Flame leapt from the wick. His head lowered until the end of the cigar disappeared into his cupped hands. He straightened and the end of the cigar glowed red.

The second mate had ducked under the catwalk and I quickly joined him, hunching down behind one of the pillars.

Nothing happened.

I took a quick look.

The guard was standing looking straight down the deck through the gas cloud pulling contentedly on his cigar. All I could see was the glowing red end. It appeared to get bigger and bigger.

" You'll have to order him to put it out," I told the second mate trying to sound calm.

" Not me after what happened to Joe the last time we were here." The second mate sank further into the shadows under the catwalk. " All he did was let the national flag touch the deck when he was lowering it one night. The guard shot at him and arrested him. He spent two weeks in jail before the company could get him out."

I stepped out of the shadows and took a measurement of the oil. About half filling the tank, I noticed.

A sound made me turn sharply and I once more froze to the spot. In measured steps, his gun slung jauntily across his back, the guard was walking along the catwalk towards the stern contentedly puffing on his cigar. Screaming at me from behind his back in big letters on the accommodation bulkhead NO SMOKING in three languages.

I stood rigid and glued to the spot. The measuring tape dangled unnoticed in my hand. Clouds of gas drifted upwards over the catwalk from the tank opening. The smell of oil filled my nostrils. My stomach was filled with ice.

Clank, clank. Measured footsteps along the metal grating over my head. The red tip of the cigar big and round, bright even in the sunlight. As though out for a Sunday stroll round the village square, the guard passed overhead, leaving a trail of smoke in his wake. My eyes followed his progress but my feet were fixed to the spot.

I wondered how much I would feel when the ship exploded.

The guard walked out of the gas cloud and continued until he reached the end of the catwalk. Turning towards the port side, he strolled under the NO SMOKING signs, took one last puff on his cigar and threw the butt over the side of the ship.

Looking in my direction, he grinned. " Very good cigar. Come from Cuba."

When I looked round, Vince was slumped back against a pipe, his face white and hands shaking. His eyes were closed and perspiration dripped from his chin. I sank to the deck still clutching the measuring tape and lent back against one of the catwalk pillars. My hands were wet with sweat more than accounted for by the heat. There was a thumping in my ears and I realised this was my heart beating far too fast. I had difficulty breathing. For a moment I could not see, my mind filled with visions of the ship exploding. Then my heartbeat returned to normal, my breathing became more measured and I thought about the oil pouring into the tank.

I got to my feet rather unsteadily and took a measurement. Vince joined me his face still white.

" Christ," he exclaimed. " I need a drink. We will have a few when our watch ends."

The rest of the loading passed off without incident. Even now I can still, as I write this, feel the fear deep inside and shudder at what might have happened.

We laughed later, the second mate and I. After coming off watch, Vince invited me into his cabin and we sat drinking Bacardi trying not to think too much about how close to disaster we had come that morning. That evening for the first time Vince took me ashore dressed in my white dinner jacket to meet some of his friends. A car arrived at the berth and took us to a country club to mix with well dressed and wealthy people. Vince spoke fluent Spanish but most of the people I spoke to used English. By the time we returned to the ship, we were both rather merry and the danger that afternoon had been forgotten.

We sailed from Curacao to various ports in South America without incident. Even the weather was clement with hardly any storms. Captain Jenkins still hounded me but most of the time I was able to ignore his attention. One voyage, we loaded a cargo of diesel oil for Trinidad.

After helping Vince with our watch during the discharge, it was late so I went to bed early.

It was pitched black in my cabin when I was awoken by a banging on the door. The generator hummed but there were no other sounds. All appeared perfectly normal. Locating the clock, I noted it was three o'clock in the morning.

A voice was urgently shouting through the closed door. " Eddie! Eddie! Wake up. The Old Man and the second mate want to see you in the cargo office as soon as possible. The Old Man is steaming, so I would be quick if I was you."

" The door is not locked so you could have come in," I replied, starting to awake. " Tell the Captain I will be with him as soon as I have dressed."

Not long after being called, dressed in an old pair of shorts, tee shirt and flip flops, I shuffled down the corridor trying to shake the sleep from my mind. At the same time, I was wondering why the Captain would want to see me so early in the morning. Not only me but also the second mate. One's mind plays tricks in anticipation of something and, as I approached the cargo office, I imagined all sorts of things. These ranged from trouble at home to neglecting part of my job.

When I stepped out of the accommodation into the night, I looked around with all my senses alert. The silver stars shone from a cloudless sky. A gentle breeze tousled my hair. The generator hummed from the engine room. The sound of a pump whined from the pump room. There was not a heavy list, just a small angle that was associated with discharging cargo. In fact all looked and felt normal.

The Captain was waiting dressed in his striped pyjamas and a silk dressing gown. His baldhead shone in the overhead light and his shoulders were slumped as though he was weary. His eyes were bleary with sleep and, it must be said, the effect of too much drink. On his feet he had what could only be described as granddad slippers. The telephone receiver of the line that connected the ship to the shore was clamped to his ear. He was red faced and angry from what he was hearing. The second mate stood nearby listening to what Captain Jenkins was shouting down the phone. I wondered whether whoever was on the other end could understand what he was saying.

" Ah Gubbins," he greeted me with a scowl. " As I have been telling the second mate, I have the ship's agent on the phone."

Into the telephone, he said, " I have the second mate here. Tell him what has happened and what you think needs doing. The second mate can then handle it for me."

Vince took the telephone receiver and listened holding it away from his ear so that I could hear what was being said. The ships agent, Mr. Johnson, who I had met that morning, greeted Vince

In a mournful voice, heavy with a West Indian accent, he said loudly as though wishing to emphasise his words, " Morning second mate. How are you this morning?"

" I'd be better if you had left me to sleep," Vince replied unable to keep the coldness out of his voice.

" Wouldn't we all, wouldn't we all," he growled back equally cold and weary. " As I have just told Captain Jenkins, I have had a phone call from the central police station. It seems they have most of your crew locked up in their jailhouse. They want somebody from the ship to come and collect them. They will have to be bailed and escorted back to the ship. Man, the Captain suggested you were just the person to undertake this chore."

" If it was up to me I would leave them to rot in their cells until the ship was ready to leave," Vince growled back.

" That is not possible. The police chief wants them out of his cells and back on the ship as soon as possible. I will meet you at the central police station as soon as you can get there."

Vince handed the telephone back to the Captain with a heart rendering sigh. Experience told me this was the end of any thoughts of a good nights sleep or of any time ashore in the morning before the ship sailed that the evening. I knew the sun would be climbing into the sky before I got back to the ship from the police station. In frustration, I could have shouted to the night sky that it was not fair but understood shouting would do no good.

A short time later dressed in my best whites with gold braid on the epaulets and my cap on my head, I joined Vince in a taxi at the foot of the gangway. The admonition from the Captain still rang in our ears such was the force of his voice.

" Do what is necessary to get my bloody crew back! We cannot sail without them even if we wished!" With a twisted smile, he had assured us in a harsh tone, " No matter what happens to them now, they will have to deal with me in the morning when they are back and sober. You just tell them that!"

The journey from the ship to the police station was rough. The main road from the terminal to the town was at least tarmaced though crumbling and pot holed. As though impatient to get off duty, the driver took the short cut along a dirt track passed the sugar cane fields bordering the oil terminal. He appeared to take great delight in finding every gully, crater and ridge in the road. I gripped the seat in an attempt to protect my life because there were no seat belts. At times I was suspended in the air above the seat, coming down with a bang each time the car landed testing the shock absorbers. Dust hung like a mist behind the car, blowing in clouds over the scattered groups of corrugated iron roofed dilapidated wooden houses near the road. I gasped with relief when the car stopped bouncing and arrived on relatively smooth roads. With difficulty, I managed to smooth down my uniform, adjust my cap and emerge from the taxi with something approaching dignity. Vince shook the dust from his cap and rammed it onto his head.

The taxi had stopped in front of a single storey building looking like a large blockhouse in the gloom. The plaster walls were painted white though showing signs of wear and tear. The paint was peeling off in places to revel the grey plaster underneath. Indeed in patches the plaster had crumbled to reveal the dirty concrete beneath. The street running past the building was almost dark with a few isolated lamps at sparse intervals providing isolated spots of dim light. Most of the other buildings lining the street were dark and lifeless.

After the driver had made Vince sign a receipt, we climbed the few steps to the black painted door. I noticed that all the windows had bars, whether to keep people in or out, I had no idea. Before pushing open the door, I paused to wipe my brow. More and more I wishing I was back in my bunk on the ship.

When I pushed open the door, heat and the smells of sweat, dirt and unmentionables assaulted my nose. Inside the room opposite the entrance there was a counter behind which was a brown painted door leading to the rear of the building. Along the wall to the right of the door were some broken plastic chairs. A single unshaded bulb hung on a threadbare flex from the ceiling illuminating somewhat the dirty concrete floor but keeping the walls in shadow. There was nobody in sight.

On the counter was one of those brass bells with a mushroom shaped plunger. Vince banged this with the palm of his hand and was startled at the loudness of the sound as it echoed round the building.

There were some shuffling noises from beyond the brown door, which opened to reveal a policeman hastily tucking his shirt into his trousers. With the opening of the door, the smell of sweat and other unmentionables welled out even stronger. I tried rather unsuccessfully not to gag.

" Yes?" the policeman barked when he had gained the counter.

" I am the second officer of Edmundo," Vince informed him very politely. " I have come to oversee the release of our crew who are being detained by you."

" Take a seat," he ordered with a look of what could only be considered as contempt. " Mr. Johnson, the ship's agent will be here shortly. We will deal with the matter then."

He turned away and started to deal with some paperwork, before disappearing through the brown door. Sticking rigidly to the rules, I thought. Gingerly I studied the chairs until I found one that had a semblance of cleanliness and sat down to wait. Vince took a handkerchief from his pocket and wiped his chair before sitting next to me.

Thankfully, we did not have long sitting in that smelly not too clean room. The door to the street opened and a round faced, overweight man in a white suit heaved himself into the room. He wiped his face in a white handkerchief. Behind him came a dapper man in a dark suit, thin faced with a pencil moustache. A gold watch prominently circled his thin wrist and gold teeth punctuated his smile.

" Second mate?" the plump man inquired raising his eyebrow at me in question. " We met yesterday morning. This is Abraham Croft, our lawyer."

Vince got to his feet and shook his hand. " Mr. Nubbins my cadet."

Mr. Croft smiled and nodded. I noticed that neither of them took a seat.

" What happened?" Mr. Johnson asked Vince.

Vince shrugged. " The policeman insisted that I waited for you to arrive before telling me anything."

Mr. Johnson banged the bell vigorously.

When the policeman emerged, Mr. Johnson asked. " What have you done with his crew?"

The policeman grinned for the first time. " Abe Johnson. Another mess to dig these foreign seamen out of. When will they learn? Why do they have to drink so much and then want to take on the rest of the world? May the Good Lord forgive them."

Mr. Johnson shook his head. " Joshua, I have not come to this police station at this time of the morning to hear your worldly grumblings. Why have you locked up the crew of the Edmundo?"

" We were called out by some villagers about a lot of shouting on the track passed their village leading to the oil terminal," Joshua replied evenly not disturbed in the least by Mr Johnson's attitude. " When we arrived at the scene, we found this group of men fighting. We arrested them and brought them back here. They will be charged with disturbing the peace."

Mr. Johnson sighed deeply. " Can the second officer, his cadet and I see the men? Mr. Croft will stay with you and sort out the bail conditions. I have ordered a bus to take them back to the ship and this will arrive in a few minutes."

Joshua shrugged. " We will be glad to get rid of them. I will get my colleague to take you to the prisoners. "

He opened the door behind the counter and shouted. Even more so than before, the smell of sweaty bodies, effluent and dirty drains swept over me. Try as I did, I could not stop my eyes watering or the cough that caught in my throat making me gag again.

Another policeman appeared and waved for us to follow him into the building. With my stomach churning, I stepped through the door. A narrow corridor of bare concrete, ceiling, walls and floor opened up ahead blocked by a door of rusty iron bars. The policeman opened the door and the iron bars clanged back against the wall. Five yards ahead, the corridor ended in a cross passage. The smell was just bearable.

When we reached the cross passage, the policeman turned left. Two other policemen sat on chairs, dozing. On the left was a wall of iron bars revealing a room filled with men.

I recognised my crew. They were sitting on the few benches round the walls or on the floor with their backs to the iron bars. It was hot. Well, more than twenty people crowded into a small space with hardly any ventilation can generate a great deal of heat. All the eyes were looking out into the corridor.

When they spotted us, several started talking at the same time. Vince held up his hand for silence. The policeman opened the barred door and motioned us into the room.

" What happened?" Vince demanded in a harsh voice. They all started talking at the same time. Once more he held up his hand for silence.

Spotting Joe, a seaman who I had always found could talk sensibly, Vince said to him," Joe. You tell me what happened."

" Well Mr. Mate," he began hesitatingly and looking round the room seeking reassurance. " All the off duty crew went ashore at the same time. We found a great bar in the town where there were girls and cheapish booze. When it was time to return to the ship, Prodo thought we should walk back. On a night like this, why get taxis? he said. We all agreed. He led us through the streets of the town and then down this dirt track. A short cut to the terminal, he said. It was rutted and full of potholes."

" I know where you mean," Vince muttered. " The bloody taxi driver nearly killed us coming here to get you. He drove at ninety miles an hour. I must have hit my head on the roof a hundred times. "

They all laughed nervously.

" When we left the town there were no lights and once on the track, it was really dark," Joe continued. " Prodo was leading with Will. Then Dick fell down a crater and hurt his ankle. Brian, the greaser has some first aid training but it was dark. Somebody found some paper and made a torch. Dick looked bad but that might have been the amount he had drunk or the thought of the girl he went with. She was ugly, God was she ugly. He must really have been desperate to go with her. Lets face it Mr Mate, we were all quite drunk. Brian reckoned it was only a sprain and we ought to carry him back to the ship. That was when the trouble started."

Brian, a big man with oil stained hands and an almost totally baldhead, butted in then. His words were a bit slurred. " Dick is a sailor. As a gesture of goodwill, the engine room men offered to carry him back to the ship. Prodo objected, saying it was for the deck staff to carry him not oily greasers. We objected to what he called us but went to pick Dick up anyway. Prodo hit me. I hit him back."

Joe shrugged. " Then we all joined in. Well we couldn't let a greaser hit a sailor, could we? Some of the people from the nearby village came out with sticks and tried to stop us. So we turned on them. Somebody must have called the police. They arrived ready for a fight. It took a while for them to subdue us. Those truncheons like base ball bats don't half hurt."

Prodo laughed and said proudly. " It was a great fight. We would have won if they hadn't cheated by pulling their guns."

Vince shook his head and raised his eyebrows. " Do you mean to tell me that all this started over a dispute about who was going to carry Dick back to the ship?"

Prodo laughed again. " Yup. We had to uphold the honour of our deck department. Then when the villagers and the police attacked us, we all had to up hold the honour of the ship."

Brian grinned and I saw that one of his eyes was closed. " We couldn't let their insults to the engine room staff pass could we? But then we were all mates when the villagers and the police attacked us."

Vince raised his eyebrow to me. " What will we do with them, Young Eddie? No don't answer that until you have had some sleep."

I looked around the room and noticed for the first time that every member of the crew had a bandage or sticking plaster on some part of their bodies. Dick sat in pride of place with his heavily strapped ankle resting on a bench and a pair of crutches by his side.

" Can you walk?" I demanded bluntly.

" On crutches yes," he replied grinning. " I feel humble that they all cared so much for me that they fought over who was going to carry me back to the ship."

" Oh shut up Dick," I snapped. " You know you will all have to answer to the Captain later this morning. He was pretty angry at being woken up in the middle of the night."

They all looked nervously at each other. Such was the reputation of Captain Jenkins when it came too disciplinary matters.

Mr. Croft joined us and stood smiling broadly. " Mr Mate will you tell me please. How is it that British sailors can cause such mayhem on the way back to their ship? Why do they have to fight with each other?"

" It was a matter of honour," Vince snapped not in the mood for casual banter. " What now?"

" No need to take it out on me young man," Mr Croft laughed even louder. " We have all been taken cruelly from our warm beds and our women, to come to this stinking hole. But don't blame me. Blame them. Now I have paid the fine and smoothed things out with the police. It was not hard. All they wanted was to get rid of this lot so that they could go back to bed. Which is where I am off to right now. It was nice meeting you."

He shook our hands and hurriedly left.

Mr. Johnson mopped his brow once more. " A bus will be here in a few minutes. This will take them all back to your ship. A couple of police cars will escort the bus. Part of the agreement was that they will not come ashore again. A guard will be placed on the gangway to check who goes ashore."

Once the bus arrived, they all filed out like a line of foreign troops being taken to prisoner of war camp. Some had bandages on their heads, many were limping and most looked as though they could do with a change of clothes. Bringing up the rear escorted by Prodo was Dick. He wobbled on his crutches that made a clicking noise on the concrete floor. As he passed me he grinned and it took all my control to stop myself from punching him on the nose.

Back at the ship, I waited at the foot of the gangway as they all filed aboard behind Vince, shook Mr. Johnson's hand and went back to my cabin. The sky to the east was getting light and I realised I could either go to sleep or get breakfast. After a shower, breakfast won.

Chapter 4

After fourteen months on the Edmundo I had a long leave over a summer. One thing that sailors look forward to is a long leave with their family and friends when they can live a normal life. By that I mean staying in one place and meeting people in different places rather than within the confines of the ship. One problem they all have when home on leave after an extended time away is the belief that everything has stayed the same as it was before they went away. They soon realise that everything does not stay the same. In fourteen months that I had been away most things had changed. Couples who were together when I left had now split and were now with other people. Others had even got married some to somebody else other than the person I had understood that they were devoted to the last time I had seen them.

As an example of this take what happened with my best friend. Before I had left to join the Edmundo, we had boozed and hunted women together. Neither of us had been attached to one woman. To me it was natural that when I was at home I would accompany Percy on his nights out.

As was the custom, I had walked into the local pub that first night after leaving the Edmundo and returning home on leave. Sitting at the bar nursing a pint of beer, I found Percy as expected. He had blinked at me through his glasses in that earnest way he had whenever I greeted him and ordered a pint for me without asking if

I wanted one, an automatic gesture between friends. His rather chubby face was glistening like I had never noticed before and he seemed nervous and excited at the same time. A girl came into the room through a door at the side of the bar and took his arm.

" June," he had said, a grin spreading all over his face." Meet Eddie."

The girl, round faced, dark brown hair, brown eyes and a great figure stood looking at me with that open smile which seemed to offer an invitation. I found later, she always presented such a smile to the world. She told me how much she had been looking forward to meeting me. I had thought then, as I grinned back to match her welcoming smile, that I could really get to like her and we have been friends ever since. To the clack of dominoes, the sound of a jute box and the clink of glasses, they told me, while holding tightly to each other's hand, that they were going to get married. June then showed me the engagement ring, sparkling in the overhead light. Then Percy asked me if I would be his best man. I remember smiling like an idiot and flinging my arms round their shoulders in pure pleasure. Deep down, though, I accepted that our friendship had changed. It was sad but we would not be able to chase women, booze as much or even spend so much time in each other's company. While at sea things stayed the same, at home the move on.

A is often the case for the seaman; sadly, it wasn't to be that I should be the best man at their wedding. Circumstances made it impossible for me to arrange to be home on leave at time their wedding took place. Oh, they sent me some cake and some of the photos but this was scant consolation for not being with them on the day. Since their wedding, we had made a point of meeting whenever I was on leave and had sat long into the night swapping stories of what had happened to us since we last met. It had become one of the rituals of our lives and had provided me with an anchor when I returned home after months away.

It is a fact that time at sea can be uneventful. Such was the case with the next few voyages I sailed from the Persian Gulf to various places in Europe.

Then I joined a ship called the Heldia for my last assignment as a cadet. Once more I found myself in Curacao. We loaded a cargo for Buenos Aries. The voyage down the South American coast was unexceptional.

What I remember about the first time I visited Buenos Aries was that we tied up to the next berth to the Armour corned beef factory. We were supplying a cargo of diesel and fuel oil. The pipeline from the shore to the quay was of a small diameter that meant for the first time we would take a few days to discharge.

On the land side behind the factory were the stockyards. They stretched to me as far as the eye could see. Through the stockyards were marshalled cows. Thousands of cows. All day they mooed and sometimes bellowed. They walked up a ramp into the building in a constant stream. As the stockyards emptied more trains arrived with more cows.

On the river side were the berths. Tied up along the quay Blue Star Line ships. Conveyor belts rumbled down from the upper shores of the factory into the holds of the ships. These carried cases of tins of corned. Bundles of hides and other products were craned aboard. Seeing this put me off eating corned beef for years. Cranes loaded bundles of hides and other products into the hold. In many ways it was boring with only one pump and the oil taking an age to pump out of each tank.

The slow discharge did give me a chance to get ashore with the other cadets. We fund a city of contrasts. Down the centre ran a broad avenue flanked by large buildings and trees. There were eloquent squares and fountains. A few streets away from the main road the buildings were dilapidated and poorly maintained. The people looked as though they were also poor.

We dined in an elegant restaurant with white table clothes, polished wooden floor and white shirted waiters. The people sitting at the other tables were well dressed and well fed. I must admit it was a very well cooked and presented meal.

After the meal a band played dance music. To my surprise some of the young women indicated that we should dance. They laughed at our attempts to tango but it was a pleasant evening.

I did notice that during the dancing, a man in a uniform cam and talked to some people sitting at one of the tables. It was strange that they all immediately left.

On the way back to the docks I made the connection. It was strange but the streets appeared very empty. There was an oppressive silence the only sound being a few barking dogs. It was as though the citizens were waiting, as though many were frightened of what was going to happen.

Then there was the sound of aircraft and paratroops started to land in the parks all around. We had not gone far when a soldier thrust a gun in our direction. He shouted something but I did not understand. The end of the barrel of his gun looked like a tunnel. He was waving it around in a very undisciplined way. We all froze. Dave could speak a little Spanish and pulled his papers out of his pocket. We all did likewise. The soldier had been joined by an officer who looked at our papers.

In English, he said. " Get back to your ship as soon as you can. Go straight to the docks and do not wander away from the main road. It might get hot before the night is over. If anybody asks to see your papers, just show them and do not say anything. We had to get this corrupt government out."

We were stopped at least three times before we arrived at the docks. The dock gate was guarded by soldiers and they were patrolling the quays. We were relieved to get back on board. The next morning we sailed down the river Plate passed the place where the Bismarck had sunk and on out into the South Atlantic. Rolling in the swell from the northeast, we were all glad to be back at sea and away from Buenos Aries.

After an uneventful voyage back to Curacao, we were ordered to sail up the Amazon River to a place called Manaus. The main problem was the ship. She was the largest ship to navigate the river.

The pilot came on board in the river mouth far from land. Indeed there was no sight of land on either side. All that showed that we were in the stream from a river was the brown of the water. We had been given a position to reach and the only way we could find the way was by using the radar.

Once on board the pilot laid a folio of charts on the plotting table. He then consulted the captain and chief officer. I was on the bridge and managed to hear what was being said.

The pilot pointed to the chart he had smoothed out on the table. " We can get to here by night fall. We will then anchor to wait for daylight. Is your motor lifeboat serviceable?"

The chief officer bristled. " Of course. The engine was serviced and tested last week."

The pilot smiled. " We will need it at various places as we navigate the river. In the rainy season the channel markers are washed away. Then the deep channel changes. What we have to do is anchor and launch the lifeboat. I will then go ahead of the ship and test the channel. We will need sailor to measure the depth and one to note this down. I will draw a on the chart the channel depths and directions. That way we will manage to get up the river without putting your ship aground."

The Captain looked worried. " Eddie you will go in the boat with the chief officer, the bosun and one of the seamen. Do exactly as the pilot orders. I do not want my ship sitting on a mud bank."

We sailed towards the land until the river mouth was plainly visible. Low down on either side were the banks of the river. The water flowed swift and muddy brown with large pieces of vegetation floating on the surface. That night we anchored until dawn.

The next day we followed the river path the pilot using to us unseen landmarks by which to navigate. There was no satellite navigation system and the river channel was always changing. The strength of the current tended to wash away the channel markers.

The river narrowed and the pilot ordered the Captain to anchor the ship. I was told to join the Chief Officer on the boat deck and the motorboat was lowered into the water. The Pilot, the Chief officer, the bosun and a sailor. For the next hour we traversed the river from one side to the other making progress up stream. The pilot took soundings of the depth of water, noting these on his chart. He also took bearings of the bank presumably to fix navigational landmarks for us e later. When we were back on board, the pilot ordered the ship to proceed.

We did this four times. In some ways it was exciting doing something unusual but I could see the Chief Officer was nervous every time the boat set out from the ship. I think he was desperately hoping the boat's engine would not break down in the middle of the Amazon River. From my subsequent experience, I can now see what he was worried about. Lifeboats even the motorboat were not designed or expected to sail for any length of time.

As the river got more narrow, it was fascinating to see the rain forest passing quite close to the ship and the villages close to the shore. The one thing I do remember quite distinctly was the size of the bugs that kept flying into the wheelhouse windows.

We arrived in Manaus as far up the Amazon River that a ship of our size could travel. The history of Manaus situated so far up the River Amazon is fascinating. Of all the places I went while serving at sea, Manaus was the most strange. It is in fact the story of a provinces rise to prosperity and glamour and then the slow decline in fortunes. When I visited in the early nineteen sixties the town was rundown and had the air of neglect. From my reading, the history of Manaus begins in 1669. That is when Manaus began as little more than a small fort, created by Portuguese settlers to defend themselves against incursions by the Spanish. Indeed it was not until the nineteenth century that it began being called Manaus that came from an indigenous tribe (the Manaos) who had once inhabited the same area.

Its prosperity came from the Brazilian rubber boom in the late nineteenth and early twentieth centuries. It led to a rising tide of prosperity. Unfortunately, this prosperity was short lived. The allure of riches and comfort attracted floods of immigrants who found the conditions of poverty and drought in northeastern Brazil to be intolerable. This was combined with the advent of synthetic rubber and the rise of cheaper plantations in Asia to deliver a decisive knockout punch to the rubber boom. Rubber prices plummeted to unprecedented lows and Manaus descended into poverty.

I went ashore riding through the jungle on the edge of town on the road from the oil terminal to the town. I found a rather neglected and rundown town. Since I was there attempts have been made to regenerate the area and it looks as though Manaus might once more see prosperity.

In its pomp, the citizens had built an opera house and this became the crowning glory of all the luxury and extravagance of the city. It was called the Teatro Amazonas. It became famous throughout the world and in some ways infamous. Governor Ribeiro commissioned a Portuguese architect to build an Italianate opera house that would have cobbled streets with elegant houses, plazas and gardens surrounding it. What started as a modest project wound up costing two million dollars, which was an enormous sum at that time.

Architects, painters, sculptors, and builders arrived from Europe to work on the new opera house. Built almost exclusively from materials imported from Europe, the iron framework was from Glasgow, Scotland; the 60,000 tiles in its cupola were from Alsace Lorraine; and the crystal chandeliers from Italy. The main material used in the construction was stone but the entrances and supporting pillars were finished in Italian Marble. In keeping with the" spare no expense" attitude, some locals thought the cupola should be of gold rather than tiles. The governor wasn't worried. He said before the theatre was even open "When the growth of our city demands it, we'll pull down this opera house and build another".

The interior of the theatre was brilliant with gold leaf and lush red velvet. The decorations, painting and sculpture had as their theme the classical Greek and Roman mythological figures together with the Indian legends of the Amazon. Indian heads were on the balustrade of the staircases, and there were murals of the gods and goddesses playing in the Amazon.

On opening night, January 6, 1897, the Grand Italian Opera company played Ponchielli's La Gioconda. The elaborate opera house in the middle of the Amazon forest became a symbol of the incredible extravagance of the elite during the rubber boom and became a legend in itself. Through the years stories were told of the famous performers who came to Manaus. It was alleged that the tenor Enrico Caruso, the Russian ballerina Anna Pavlova, and the actress Sarah Bernhardt had performed at the Teatro Amazonas. When I visited this it was so rundown there were only tattered posters to show its purpose.

I was rather sad when I returned to the ship ready to sail. Like the Wilfredo left stranded on a mud bank in Hong Kong bereft of its purpose, the Teatro Amazonas sat with the plaster peeling from the walls and the seats rotting. It is sad to see something neglected and left without the purpose for what it was designed.

We went back to Venezuela and sailed for Rotterdam. When we arrived in port, I was informed that I had only a few months left on my cadetship. When these months had passed I would be sent to college to study for my second mates certificate of competency. As the ship had a Chinese crew, it was being sent back to Hong Kong via the Persian Gulf to change the crew. We were to proceed first to Nigeria to load for Durban. In Bonny I would transfer to another tanker. This was to be used as what they called the topping up tanker. The approach to Bonny loading port along the channel is too shallow for a tanker to load a full cargo. The idea from the company was to position a ship in Bonny that would then sail along the coast topping up the other tanker. It was a technique used by naval ships over the years but this was the first experiment between two tankers. I was fascinated to see how this would go.

Bonny was a rather ramshackle town at the entrance to the Bonny River that flows through the oil fields of the Delta area of Nigeria. There was not a berth big enough to take our tanker or any other tanker of our size. To load the oil we had to moor at some buoys in the river. The pipeline was raised from the riverbed. It was attached to a bow and men in a boat attached our derrick hook to the line. We then pulled this on board. It was wet and muddy work to take the blank flange off the end and then attach the line to our manifold. The loading supervisor came on board to agree the amount. He then used a radio to keep in touch with the shore. In order to read the draft numbers at the bow and the stern, I had to go down into a boat.

Before leaving we loaded two enormous fenders from a barge that came alongside. The ship had only one set of derricks amidships so both had to be placed on the after deck It was decided by the Captain and chief officer that we would tie up to the other ship with our port side to their starboard. The fenders were place on the portside.

We sailed once the correct draft was reached and anchored in the river mouth to wait for our first ship. The Captain used the time in having the crew manoeuvre the fenders into position. They were lowered over the side and winched into position fore and aft.

The attempt to make a moving transfer was what could only be termed a disaster. We put the fenders in position and weighed anchor. The tanker needing to be topped up, loaded to her full draft, sailed out of Bonny to join us. Side by side we sailed out to sea.

The connection worked as planned. Using a compressed air gun we managed to get a thin line to the other ship. This was attached in the normal way to the large mooring rope. The sailors on the Henis pulled this across and attached to their bollard. At the same time the second mates crew aft had accomplished the same result. Slowly we pulled the ships together. The Captains had great difficulty in maintaining the same speed but after a few scares as one ship and then the other moved ahead, this was accomplished.

Then we made ready to lift the rubber hose between the ships. There was a loud bang and the ropes holding the bows level parted. We managed to get another rope on board but the rope aft parted. As the ships hit the swell in the Atlantic Ocean they started to roll not too violently but enough the make the mooring ropes slacken and tighten. There was no way we could maintain our positions. The Captains were reluctant to connect the hose and we abandoned the attempt.

After collecting our thoughts and setting parallel courses the two ships made another attempt. The outcome was exactly the same.

There were frantic messages back and forth to he head office while the officers from the two ships suggested alternatives. What was needed we were told were what they called self tensioning winches These so I was informed would maintain the required tension on the ropes while letting the ships roll. We did not have these. In the end it was decided to anchor in the lee of an island called Fernando Po. Then the transfer could take place in calm waters with our ship at anchor and the other ship tied up along side.

We sailed for Fernando Po knowing we would have to pick up a pilot because we were to anchor inside territorial waters. In practice here was no need for this but that was the rule. In the end we anchored in sight of the main port but were not permitted ashore because we had not been through customs or immigration. Thus we had to sit at anchor in sight of the shore.

The ship we had tried to top up running along the coast arrived and tied up successfully. The hose was attached and we pumped oil into their tanks. It went smoothly. After this the operation became routine. We sat at anchor and ships arrived, tied up, the cargo was transferred and the ship left.

I became aware of the differing approaches of the Captains of these ships. Some swept alongside with a flourish and left with the same flourish. Others crept alongside leaving it for our ships company to pull their ship alongside. One miss judged the approach and smashed into our unused anchor with their bow. I split appeared in their bow and some stores fell into the sea. After loading, they anchored nearby and used a concrete patch to get them back to Europe.

After three months we were replaced by another tanker and loaded to sail for Rotterdam. My cadetship was almost over. Four years of sailing the globe meant I could go to college and take my second mates certificate of competency. If I passed I would then have the chance to become a ships officer. So in Rotterdam I said goodbye to my friends and colleagues and took the train and ferry for home.

I found it a strange experience to return to college as a student after a long time working on a ship at sea. The rhythm of college life is entirely different to life on board ship. Shipboard life is dominated by watches even when working day shifts. Three watches namely twelve till four, four till eight and eight till twelve. These were repeated twice a day. Then there is the arriving and leaving port with the handling of the cargo. I found I missed the call of the sea. For the six months I was at the college and the two months leave the sea was no longer beckoning me out there beyond the dock. I no longer had to think about what the weather would be like when the ship sailed out of port to meet the sea. We always hoped the mood of the sea would be calm and balmy. Sailing out onto the oceans can be like meeting a lover. Sometimes she is like a gentle lover entwining the sailor in her arms, leaving him refreshed and happy when they part. At other times she is angry and will meet the sailor with unmatched violence, a violence that beats upon the senses. It is a violence that fills the whole world and needs all the sailors' concentration. The sailor never knows what moods will greet him when leaving port or how the mood can change very quickly. This is the excitement of the sea that mixture of exhilaration and apprehension. Every sailor knows that there is no way they can subdue the sea. I had learnt that we had to live with her moods. Thus for months I left the sea behind but could not forget.

Life in college involves subjecting oneself to a laid down timetable which is designed and implemented by somebody else and cannot be violated. Although many may argue that this is the same as being at sea with a strict watch system, in college one is not in control and has no direct input.

In case of students at a nautical college, the end result was vital. On passing the exam most of the students would immediately gain extra money and wider promotion prospects. Failure would mean having to try again at our own expense and in our own time. All efforts of both the staff and the students was focused on the passing of the examinations at the end of the course, not on gaining all round knowledge, which should be the purpose of education. Any extra information presented by the lecturers, no matter how interesting but which was not purely helpful in passing the exams, was greeted with cries of 'get on with the teaching'.

It was not an atmosphere that made use of or developed fine educational principals but in many ways, it was a hot house forcing reluctant students through the process of gaining the qualifications that they needed to pursue their career

After a few days at home collecting my thoughts and watched over by my mother, I went to the college and signed on for the master's certificate course. I was determined to slip into the role of a student and to concentrate on the task I had set for myself. Roy had convinced me of the soundness of the idea of gaining my master's certificate.

There were a few other students in the class whom I had met before, either while at sea or when I had been in college studying for other exams. Some of these greeted me like a long lost friend. It was a relief to see some familiar faces but at first I resisted all attempts to get me to go to out with them either at lunchtime or in the evenings. I was acting the part of an intense and hard working student and actually liking the role. My mother raised her eyebrows every night when I settled down to work or sat talking to her over a drink.

My time at the college went smoothly. Then time came for the exams. This was the main reason for coming to college. This what we had all been preparing for all those months. Well even before. There were all those periods when Captain Jenkins had made me study. I hated that man but now as I prepared to sit he exam, I began to realise how important his insistence on my studies while at sea had been. I know I had not been the best student while sailing with him, I had come second once again but it had helped when I was at the college.

We all assembled in the exam centre some nervous and trying to revise at the last minute, others appearing calm and ready. The exam room was

Everything went well until the oral part of the exam. For every exam candidate there was an oral exam lasting anything up to an hour. There were usually two examiners taking a candidate each and as there were twenty candidates, it took two and a half days.

I was collected from the bare waiting room with the instructions on the notice board and the iron tube with stretched canvas chairs by the examiner. He had a pipe in his mouth and blew smoke over me through out the oral. I sat the other side of the desk spread with books and paper. He shuffled the papers in what appeared random fashion and asked me questions. I managed to answer most questions adequately. Then near the hour mark just as I was anticipating the finish, he asked me a question I did not know the answer. It was a new M notice and what it ruled. M notices were at this time put out by the Government giving advice. In many cases they became part of the maritime law when agreement could be reached through the international maritime organisation. In reality any breach of the M notice would be taken into account. Because I could not answer, I failed.

The examiners arranged a specially reset oral for the following week. I found out there were nine of us who had to reset. For the rest of the week I read and reread M445 and M 653 and all the accompanying commentary. You see it was such a traumatic experience I can still remember the numbers.

The following week, I turned up in the afternoon to reset my oral exam. I was the only candidate to be seen in the afternoon because I lived locally while the others lived away. When I arrived in the exam waiting room I found a large poster on the notice board. It said " Good Luck Eddie. We all passed. Signed by all the others. I was looking at this when somebody spoke from behind me.

" And you will need it."

Turning I found the examiner with his pipe in his mouth. I tried not to blush. Once in the exam room, he said bluntly. " Tell me all about M445 and 463."

I told him all I knew. In fact I could have repeated these by heart.

Reaching into hid drawer, he pulled out a piece of paper" Take this to the shipping office and they will prepare your certificate. That will teach you to ignore things that are important to the seaman. Good luck young man. See you when you come for your First mates."

Chapter 5

It was freezing cold that January day when armed with my pristine certificate, I went to the head office to get my air tickets. The proud words of my father were engraved on my mind as I went to Heathrow and caught the plane bound for Singapore. It was a Comet 4 and only my second flight. On instructions from the marine superintendent, I was to join the San Felipe a tanker permanently based in the east. The heat hit me when the plane arrived in Singapore but I was used to the heat when I joined the ship after a wonderful three days in a hotel waiting for it to arrive.

We sailed from Singapore with fuel oil for Shanghai and were the first British flag tanker to dock in Shanghai since the communists took over the country. To my surprise before we left Singapore the Captain had to supply the Chinese authorities with the names of all the crew. On the way, the company sent us a list of five members of the crew who were not allowed into China. We had to put into Hong Kong to put these people ashore. They were to be put up at the seaman's mission until we picked them up on the way back to Singapore. We were also served notice by the United States consul in Hong Kong that the ship would be barred from United States ports for two years along with all the crew. As we did not go to the United States very often, this did not seem to matter.

We arrived in Shanghai to find the berth lined with people. There was a band under a canopy decked out with bunting and some dancing to greet us. Then we were not allowed ashore except on a supervised tour were the coach picked the crew up at the ship, toured the main sights and returned. No contact with the Chinese. I did not go ashore because I was needed to unload the cargo. It was many years before I went back to Shanghai.

We sailed back from Shanghai after picking up the crew members we had left in Hong Kong to load a cargo at Balak Papan in Borneo. We were then to proceed to Geelong in Australia. It was in Balak Papan that I got a taste of what it must be like to be an officer on passenger ships.

The ship arrived in Balak Papan late one evening as the big red ball of the sun was setting into the dark green of the jungle. As soon as the ship docked, the agent boarded and informed the Chief Officer that the cargo would not be ready to load for two days. In normal circumstances, the ship would arrive in a port, load the cargo in twenty four hours and depart. The delay in getting the cargo ready had some compensation for the crew. It meant that they had the opportunity to relax and a chance for some time ashore. Not the usual pound down the gangway for a short break but at least two nights.

The weather was glorious the next morning after breakfast when I took over the managing of the ship from the Chief Officer. First, I had a quick stroll round the decks to make sure all was in order before returning to my cabin to enter information in the safety log. The phone rang in the middle of noting the dates and times fire drills, lifeboat inspections and exercises, fire fighting equipment maintenance and lifejacket audits.

" Good morning Third Mate," It was the Captain sounding amused and cheerful. " Mr. Bolton, the Managing Director of Eastern Operations, is visiting the ship for lunch. He will be accompanied by his aide and his daughter. She has requested to be shown round the ship. As you are the youngest officer, I feel you will be the ideal man for that job."

" Do I have to?" I asked, imagining a morning spent in the company of such a girl. " She will be impossible. Educated at some private boarding school. We will have nothing in common. Why not ask the second mate? He mixes with people like her all the time."

The Captain laughed. " This is an order, Third Mate, not a request. I have asked the chief officer to look after the ship while you are entertaining Mr. Bolton's daughter. Try not to upset her with too much of your social comment! Remember she is a guest on board and he can influence your future career with any comments to head office."

As I put the phone down, I had a mental picture of the Captain chuckling to himself about how I would be uncomfortable showing this teenager round the ship. I sighed, anticipating the morning was not going to be much fun for me.

Later that morning, a sailor opened my cabin door after knocking loudly. " Third Mate. There are couple of official looking cars approaching the ship along the jetty. I think it would be a good idea if you were on deck to greet whoever is in those cars when they arrive."

I sighed, packed away my logs and followed him out onto the deck.

Standing at the top of the gangway a few minutes later, I watched curiously as two Mercedes cars approached along the jetty. They stopped at the bottom of the gangway. Three white shirted, dark trousered Indonesian men got out of the second car and adjusted their sun glasses. They spread out along the jetty facing away from the ship and the cars. Like the bosun who was standing by my side, I laughed out loud. It was straight out of one of those B gangster movies I showed to the crew while the ship was at sea.

Once the bodyguards were in place, the doors of the lead black car opened and a man got out. He was tall with slicked back grey hair and glasses, dressed in an immaculately cut tropical suit and shiny shoes. As soon as he alighted out of the car, he placed a panama hat on his head. Trailing him, a younger man carrying a brief case and dressed in a short sleeved white shirt and white trousers emerged. Finally, a girl followed. From where I stood she looked about fourteen and my heart sank. Her brown hair glistened in the sunlight and like her father, she donned a hat as soon as she was out of the car. She wore a short white dress and white sandals. This was the girl I was going to have to show round the ship. The duty seaman stood politely at the foot of the gangway ready to help if needed. I noticed that like all the seamen who had stopped their work to watch, he ogled the girl.

Mr. Bolton ignored the duty seaman and climbed onto the gangway unaided. The girl and the man with the briefcase followed. When they reached the deck where I was standing, Mr. Bolton nodded to me.

" Show me the way to the Captain's cabin, Third Mate," he ordered without so much as a good day. His accent was clipped and what I regarded as upper class.

The girl looked at me with large brown eyes. Close up, she was pretty with a good figure and was older than the fourteen I had first estimated. Her expression was that adopted by the local Lady of the Manor for one of the local peasants she happened to meet. The next few hours were not going to be pleasant, I concluded

" This way, Sir," I answered indicating the ladder leading to the accommodation deck. As he followed me, he was looking round the ship as though checking that all was in order. The girl looked right ahead. The man with the briefcase trailed in their wake mopping his forehead with a white handkerchief.

After showing them to the Captain's cabin, I returned to the deck and walked round the ship. As everything was in order, I returned to my cabin and the safety log. I had not been there for long when the phone rang.

" Come to my cabin and collect Mr. Bolton's daughter, third mate." It was the Captain and he still sounded amused.

I grunted into the phone but dutifully climb the ladder to his cabin. Deep within myself I was cursing the Captain. How was I going to show this apparently bored, spoiled girl around the ship without saying something out of place or upsetting her? I imagined the rest of the crew laughing behind my back at their egalitarian Third Mate looking after a girl from a very privileged background.

Mr. Bolton smiled when I entered the Captain's cabin. " Lydia is ready to be shown round the ship. I will leave her in your capable hands."

Lydia climbed to her feet, smoothed down her white, short dress and placed her sunglasses on her small nose. She was almost as tall as me.

I led the way out onto the boat deck and waited for her. The sun was high in the sky and the jungle looked particularly green across the river from the berth. Heat haze distorted the trees and the boats drifting with the current further down the river.

" Well Miss Bolton," I said smiling," What would you like to see?"

She looked at me, though I could not read her expression with her eyes hidden by dark glasses.

" If we are to spend the next hour in each others company, you had better call me Lydia," she said without a flicker of emotion.

" Eddie," I replied.

She shrugged. " Daddy said you would show me all over the ship. Lead on McDuff."

Taking her instructions literally, I led on. Viciously ignoring her white dress and sandals, I started with the engine room. Well not exactly ignored the white dress but took a certain pleasure in the thought that she might learn what dirt was all about. I know now this was being petty and she most likely knew what dirt was like from mucking out her horses. She listened politely as the engineer told her about the boilers and the turbines. Followed me down to the propeller shaft and the steering engine room. Going back up on deck I climbed the ladder behind her. The dress was so short I had a good view of her sturdy legs and floral panties. Stop these lewd thoughts, I seemed to hear my mother saying.

Then to the galley to glimpse lunch being prepared and the dining room. Down the corridor to the games room. I followed this by walking along the deck to the focastle, the anchors and the chain locker. What amazed me was that despite my best efforts, when we emerged back on deck again, she appeared as clean as when we started.

Finally I led her onto the bridge. We lent over the chart table looking at the charts of the area. Rapidly I showed her the wheel and the magnetic compass on the top deck. Lastly we went to the radio office and the sparks explained the wireless system. I had reluctantly to admit that though I might have been prejudiced against her at first, by now the atmosphere between us was much friendlier.

We stood on the bridge wing looking over the deck when we had finished. " Would you like to come to my cabin for a drink before you go back to your father?" I asked tentatively.

For the first time that morning, she smiled. " That would be nice. What can you offer?"

" I have beer, fruit juice, coke or gin."

" A beer would be fine."

She looked curiously round my small cabin when I showed her inside and sat her down in the chair. After I had served the beer, we talked about ourselves. I found out that she had lived a sheltered, rarefied life compared to mine. It sounded great but there were drawbacks. Her father and mother had moved around the world on company orders. Lydia had been deposited in various boarding schools for most of her life. Then in the holidays, if she could not join her parents, she would stay with relations. I started to feel sorry for her.

" I take my A levels next year," she remarked which told me she must be seventeen. " If I get good grades I will be off to Oxford. I already have the promise of a college place."

" What will you study?" I asked being polite.

" Ancient history." She smiled. " There is no need to pretend interest. Daddy cannot order you to listen to me or take an interest I what I am doing."

" I was enjoying hearing about your life," I remarked truthfully.

" I did enjoy you telling me about what it is like going away to sea. I have only known one other seaman and he never said much about his life away, besides he was older than me and treated me like a little girl. He works for the company. Vincent Burke."

I laughed. " We have a mutual acquaintance then. I was his cadet on the Halvid a couple of years ago."

" You know him then? I met him a few times at my Uncle's house for parties and weekends. What do you mean you were his cadet?"

" On that ship each cadet was assigned to one of the officers and we had to follow them around and learn about their job. We ran errands for them and did the bits they found either boring or dirty. Actually that is not fair as far as Vince Burke was concerned. He is a gentleman and treated me like a friend. He is the only officer I have sailed with who appeared to know rich and aristocratic people in every port we went to. Sometimes he would take me ashore to exclusive clubs and I would mingle nervously with the influential men and women from that place. He taught me a great deal."

" I met him at weekends and balls at my Uncles House in Yorkshire. His family appear to own half the county."

" We have to get you back to the Captain's cabin so that you can go to lunch."

" Thank you for showing me round," she said kissing me on the cheek as we entered the Captain's accommodation.

Over lunch, Mr. Bolton invited me to spend the afternoon with his daughter at the club in the compound. The Captain concurred.

That afternoon, I rode to the company accommodation compound through the oil refinery in the car sent for me. Lay out like a village were bungalows of differing sizes surrounded by manicured lawns and flowerbeds. At the centre was the clubhouse with bar, shops and a gym. Across the road from this was a nine hole golf course. A bit apart from the other buildings was the large, sprawling bungalow of the Boltons.

The car dropped me outside and the driver told me to phone the car pool when I needed a lift back to the ship. I stood at the edge of the lawn for a while looking round and then walked along the path to the bungalow. A maid met me at the door and took me around the back where Lydia was waiting. She smiled in welcome. Pulled round her body was a wrap.

" Come on," she said taking my hand. " We must get to the pool."

The pool was large surrounded by tiled terraces with sun loungers. Lydia chose a spot and waved to the other people sitting or lying on other sun beds. She pointed to a changing room back from the sun terrace and I quickly changed into my swimming trunks. When I rejoined Lydia, there were towels on the sun bed. A white coated waiter stood waiting, a tray in his hand.

" I have ordered my drink. What do you drink?'

" Bacardi and coke." I said quickly reaching for my wallet.

Lydia laughed. " You don't have to pay. Everything goes on my father's account. In fact every member of the club pays for their guests because there is no cash used on the compound."

It turned out to be a wonderful afternoon. Though Lydia had at first appeared superior and stuck up, by the pool we were like any young people enjoying each other's company. As we talked and swam, I came to realise that Lydia must be lonely unless other expatriates brought out their teenagers to stay. Also, when coming aboard the ship, she must have been nervous. Why she could have been apprehensive, I could not imagine. Her up bringing must have taught her to handle such situations. That afternoon, I suppose she grasped the opportunity to talk and be with somebody close to her own age.

I was invited to stay for dinner at the bungalow of the Bolton's that evening after our swim. The car took me back to the ship to dress properly. The Captain was there and some of the other higher managers and their wives. I sat close to Lydia and mostly talked to her.

After dinner, Lydia and I went for a walk around the garden. It was very pleasant with the insects chirping in the shrubs, a soft breeze and stars twinkling in the sky. To my surprise Lydia took me to a summerhouse at the bottom of the garden and we made love on a bench illuminated by the moon. A perfect way to end our day, Lydia remarked, as we walked back to the house.

As the ship sailed, I was surprised to see Lydia waving good-bye from the river bank. There had been no promises of long lasting friendship or undying love. Just a pleasant day spent in each other's company.

After discharging the crude oil in Geelong the San Felipe loaded fuel oil for Sydney. On a par with Hong Kong, Sydney harbour is one of the most beautiful in the world. Turning round the headland at the entrance and seeing the harbour bridge ahead and the green clad slopes reflected in the sun kissed blue water is wonderful. Then to sail under the bridge is magic.

We did many trips around the Australian and New Zealand coasts. It was a wonderfully peaceful time. The Captain did highlight on the chart of the Great Barrier Reef an island called Gubbins Island. He has pencilled in a note telling me to avoid going too close out of curiosity! On one notable trip we went to Fiji. There we docked close to a ship I had long known but never seen. The John Williams, the missionary ship. I had tea (no booze) with the Captain talking about the collection box shaped like a ship we had displayed at home trying to get everybody to put some of their change in the box. Here was the ship we had supported from Sunday school. Sadly it was not long before the service was discontinued. Independence and air travel combined to supersede the service.

It was while we were there that I noticed the second mate get very nervous whenever he heard or saw a low flying plane. There were a few of these because Suva had a number of flying boats stationed there.

Sitting over a beer that night I asked the second mate why he was so nervous of low flying planes. When he told me I realised that I had herd of what had happened.

" The sun, low down to the east, was shining from a clear blue sky that day," he said in a quiet voice. " Hardly a ripple disturbed the water of the bay. To the starboard of the San Fernando, lying at anchor off the small oil terminal on the island, were the golden sands of a beach. In Britain, on a day like this, such a beach would be crowded. That morning it was almost empty. Arcing around the bay, green jungle and forest climbed steeply from the sand towards the ridge of a line of hills."

" Directly shoreward from the ship, a jetty pushed incongruously out of the jungle into the clear blue water, the piles holding up the decking, grey and weather beaten. Forming a tee at the end of the jetty was a berth occupied by some brightly coloured but rust streaked fishing boats and three navy patrol vessels. Hanging from a metal structure on the jetty were a couple of black rubber pipes connected to two silver pipelines marching shore wards and disappearing into the jungle. In the distance, half shrouded by trees, the tops of several silver tanks shone dully in the sunshine."

All this I took in at a glance as I came out of the accommodation dressed in a pair of shorts and flip flops," he went on. " In my hand, I carried a mug of coffee. Standing by the rail, I breathed deeply of the warm, fragrant air. The almost empty golden beach invited me to spend a lazy day lying in the sun and doing nothing. Away towards one end of the beach, a few fishermen were tending their nets by their fishing canoes.

" This is, I thought, a perfect morning."

" It was early and, as I stood looking out over the bay and the island, the ship's crew were just stirring around me. The bosun, his shorts and tee shirt emphasising his wiry frame and tanned skin, waved as he hurried by on his way to the bridge to get his daily orders from the Chief Officer. The overweight chief steward staggered, with an armful of towels and boxes of soap, towards the mid ships accommodation where I stood. He stopped to wipe his sweaty face with a large white handkerchief, before disappearing through a door. The lookout sailor remarked what a beautiful day as he walked jauntily aft from the focastle to get his breakfast. Just a normal morning with the ship at anchor waiting for the berth to clear before docking and discharging its cargo."

" While I slowly drank my coffee, I was gazing out to sea through the mouth of the bay watching the small waves break on the rocks near the headland. Abstrusely, I noticed two black dots approaching low over the water. Then, born on the slight breeze, I heard the faint sound of aircraft engines. Before long, it possible to make out the outlines of two single engined planes. Curiously, I watched as the planes rushed towards the bay wondering what they were looking for. As far as I knew there wasn't any oil under the sea near this island. Therefore I reasoned, they could not be surveying the seabed. Then they banked steeply left and climbed over the jungle clad hills ahead of the ship. Very soon, they disappeared from my view."

" Having finished my coffee, I was just about to return to my cabin to dress properly for breakfast, when I heard the planes approaching from the landward side of the ship. Inquisitively, I strolled across the deck to the other side of the ship to take a look at what the planes were doing."

He paused and took a long drink of his beer. " One behind the other, the two planes were diving down the slope just above the trees and heading straight for the tanker. It was just as I had seen in a dozen war movies as the Japanese planes attacked the American fleet. I wondered idly if they were filming a scene from a movie."

" When it was above the beach, the lead plane levelled out and headed straight for the ship across the blue water of the bay. I watched transfixed as a black object detached itself from the underside of the plane. It fell slowly in the direction of the after deck. Suddenly I realised it was going to hit the ship. In a panic, I dived for cover behind the bulwark."

" There was an almighty bang and the ship shuddered as though it had run full speed into a very big wave. The stays on the mast and the wireless arial twanged. Diesel oil spattered the accommodation from the geyser which exploded from the damaged deck. Pieces of metal splashed into the sea. Over everything was the sound of hissing as steam escaped from fractured pipes. All over the tanker, alarm bells were ringing and hooters wailing."

I noticed he was sweating profusely and his hands were shaking such that he gripped his glass tightly " Nervously, I lifted my head above the bulwark and risked a look. I was in time to see the first plane wheel away, rushing out to sea and climbing into the cloudless sky with its engine screaming. "

" Turning back, I saw a black object fall from the second plane. Once more I flung myself for cover behind the oil streaked bulwark There was another ear splitting bang. The shuddering and shaking of the ship was followed by the screaming of fractured steel. The second plane headed out to sea, rushing after the first."

" Except for the ringing in my ears, all sound had gone. Then there was the grating of steel plates twisting apart, steam whistling from holes in the pipes and the splash of oil landing back onto the deck. What had happened was so fantastic, it was unbelievable. A tanker innocently anchored in a sun brushed bay being bombed in broad daylight in peacetime. It could not be true but I only had to look around the deck to understood that it had taken place."

" Cautiously, I climbed to my feet and looked over the bulwark. Oil was bubbling out of the holes in the deck but no longer shooting skyward. At first, I thought my eyes were playing tricks for it appeared the ship was bending in the middle. Yes, I told myself on closer inspection, the aft end is higher than the centre. The funnel looked as though it was slowly falling towards the main deck such was its angle to the vertical. At the same time, the ship was settling deeper into the water."

" Shaking my head to clear the ringing in my ears, I did not have time to think too much about that had happened. Looking up, I spotted Captain Ruddock on the boat deck above my head staring aft at the buckled deck and the funnel bending towards him. His face was white which matched the knuckles of his hands gripping the rail so tightly I thought he was going to snap it away from its anchor points. As though he could not believe what he was seeing, his eyes were staring in horror at the after deck and his mouth was hanging open. Incongruously, I noticed white shaving foam still clinging to his chin."

" Spotting me on the deck below, he demanded in a hoarse voice. ' What happened?'"

" 'Two planes came over and dropped bombs on us,' I answered bluntly still too much in shock to be diplomatic."

" 'Whatever for?' he muttered more to himself than me. ' Those bloody rebels, I suppose.' "

" Then pulling his shoulders straight, closing his mouth and wiping the shaving foam on the towel he held in his hand, he was the Captain of the San Fernando again."

" ' Run up to the bridge and get the Chief Officer to sound boat stations. Remind him to get the radio officer to send out an SOS. After you have done that, meet me in my cabin.' His order was crisp and firm."

" Other crew members were pouring out of the accommodation both amidships and aft calling out in alarm. They were dressed in a variety of clothing, many having that minute risen from their bunks. Alarm bells started sounding the long pulses that told the crew to assemble near the lifeboats. Looking rather confused and scared, the crew started to make their way to the boat decks."

" As I raced up to the bridge, Captain Ruddock was already issuing orders to organise the crew. When I arrived breathless in the wheelhouse, I found the Chief Officer and the bosun staring aft and issuing orders over the emergency phone."

" ' The Old Man orders everybody to muster by the lifeboats,' I shouted as I rushed through the bridge to the stairs leading to the Captain's cabin. ' He says to make sure that the radio officer sends out a mayday or SOS.' "

" ' Where are you off to?' the Chief Officer demanded harshly. ' I need you here with me.' "

" ' I have to help the Captain.' I replied."

" ' Make sure the radio officer has sent out an SOS as you pass his office,' he shouted after me."

" Stopping by the radio office, the radio officer assured me that he had sent out an SOS in answer to my question."

" Leaving the radio officer waiting for a reply to his SOS, I raced down the stairs to the Captain's accommodation. Loudly above the sound of the alarms and the noise of creaking metal plates, I knocked on the door of the Captain's cabin. When bidden to enter, I found Captain Ruddock on his knees, dressed in his uniform and stuffing papers from the ship's safe into two brief cases."

" ' Everybody is mustering and getting into the lifeboats, sir,' I said rather breathlessly. ' The radio officer has sent out an SOS and is waiting to see if there are any replies before going to his boat station. He has the emergency radio ready for use in the lifeboat.' "

" Captain Ruddock smiled slightly. ' Good work. You are to take one of these brief cases up to the bridge. I will bring the other. Try to make sure it stays with you no matter what happens. It contains copies of all the ships papers and records. I have the originals. Between us we should be able to make sure that these are taken ashore and saved.' "

" Taking the brief case from the Captain, I ran down the stairs to my cabin. On the way my shoulders banged painfully into a bulkhead as the ship took a lurch but I ignored the pain. When I got to my cabin, I quickly dressed in my uniform ignoring the shuddering and bucking of the ship and the groaning of the plates. I shoved my personal effects, my discharge book, identity book, photos, letters and money into a bag I kept for this purpose. Some of the other cadets during my time at sea had scoffed at my caution but it was vindicated now. Slinging this over my shoulder, I raced back up the stairs to the bridge still clutching the briefcase with copies of the ship's papers."

" On reaching the wheelhouse, panting from running on a heaving and vibrating deck, I saw Captain Ruddock standing on the bridge wing looking aft. By the time I joined him, the water was lapping over the main deck and when I looked forward all I could see was the focastle. Looking back aft, it was as though the engine room and the accommodation in the stern were completely cut off from the amidships. The decks were at crazy angles and the funnel looked as though it might fall into the water. The four lifeboats were now being filled with crew under the supervision of the other officers. Air and oil were bubbling up from the holes in the tanks spreading a black sheen over the waters surrounding the ship."

" Out of the corner of my eyes, I looked at the captain not wanting him to feel I was staring. His face was lined and drawn. To me, he had that broken look of somebody who had come to accept defeat. Where they gripped the rail, his hands were shaking. His shoulders slumped as though he had aged considerably in a short time."

" Seeing me for the first time since I arrived on the bridge as ordered, he nodded. ' You had better get down to your lifeboat.' "

" ' What about you?' I asked even though I knew the answer."

" ' There is a life raft at the end of the bridge. I intend to stay here until just before the bridge goes under.' He laughed sadly. ' Actually, unless the ship capsizes, I think she will ground before the water reaches the bridge. There was only twenty feet below the keel when we anchored, so when it settles on the bottom, the top of the accommodation should remain above the water. Go on. Go for your lifeboat. I can see the third mate is waiting for you.' "

" ' If it is all right with you, I would like to stay.' I never understood what made me say that but it appeared to help the Captain."

" Captain Ruddock put his arm round my shoulder and squeezed. ' Thank you. You have to have some sympathy with the ones who ordered this. Up in those hills some men are fighting the central government for some measure of autonomy.' "

" ' Why bomb us?' I was curious."

" ' They see this ship as a part of the government machine. Again I suppose they are partly right. Some of the oil we are delivering will be used in the army's trucks and equipment. Therefore, to them, we are helping the government suppress the rebels. In these situations, young man, there are no grey areas. To the rebels, those not helping them are their enemies and fair game for assault. I am afraid we have been caught in the middle. I must say that was some precision bombing from a small plane. The pilots must have been skilled. As far as all the reports to me have indicated, nobody on the ship was really hurt.' "

" He waved the last lifeboat away commanded by the Third Mate. I have to admit as the lifeboat moved away from the ship and deck under our feet bucked and shuddered, I was more frightened than I would ever admit to anybody. Despite my fear, there was no way in which I could have left this vulnerable man on his own."

" The Captain and I stood and watched as the lifeboats pulled away from the sinking ship. Two patrol boats had left the jetty and were racing in our direction. Once again my heart stopped as we felt the grinding of broken plates beneath our feet. At one time, we had to cling to the bridge rail as the ship lurched and heeled over to starboard."

" The water was steadily climbing up the structure, level now with the main accommodation deck. There was a groan and a long hiss as though an old lady had lowered herself painfully into a chair. The bridge rocked and swayed. The Captain and I saw the stern twist and then settle. The tanker heeled over to port. With a whoosh, the remaining air bubbled from the superstructure in a rush. Then there was silence. Even the hiss of escaping steam had ceased. With a lurch, the ship was still."

" The water was now level with the boat deck and the oil sheen spreading out from the ship into the clear waters of the bay look thick and ugly."

Captain Ruddock turned to me and said, ' Thank you for staying with me.' "

" We walked down the twisted stairs together to the boat deck below the bridge carrying the ships papers, my personal belongings and the Captain's bag. By the time we arrived, a patrol boat was alongside the boat deck waiting. I stepped aboard, helped by the crew. The Captain took one last look round his command and stepped aboard after me, leaving his ship to the mercy of the elements."

" So you see Eddie every time a plane flies over a ship I am on it brings back memories of that day when the Fernando was bombed.' The second mate smiled ruefully.

We loaded fuel oil and diesel oil in Geelong for the Queensland coast. There was cargo for three ports.

Townsville was different. It reminded me of a wild west town with wooden pavements and canopies over the shops. In many ways it was not typically Australian.

In Gladstone we had an experience, which was somewhat different from the usual. The tanker arrived on a Saturday morning and was to take three days to discharge the cargo. It was the largest ship to visit the port and oil was delivered twice a year. The population from miles around turned up to see the ship and organised a party for the crew in the local hotel. It was a boozy evening and many of us had great difficulty in reporting for work the next day.

On then to Cairns and a berth in the middle of the jungle. Don't fall into the river or the crocodiles will have you the pilot warned. This really was a town of eccentric people.

We took on the pilot and sailed by the inner passage of the Great Barrier Reef on passage for Indonesia It was sublime. The sea was flat calm and a deep blue. The shore was green and the island like paradise. The pilot was dropped in the Torres Strait.

Out into the Coral Sea. It was dead calm, the sky blue and the dolphins played games in the wake of the ship. The routine of the ship took over. Breakfast at seven thirty, bridge at eight to relieve the chief officer. Off watch and lunch at twelve thirty, afternoon looking after lifeboat maintenance and dinner at six. Then onto the bridge at eight until midnight. Included was the sun sight early morning, and at noon to plot the position of the ship. Everybody on board was relaxed. The swimming pool was filled and well used. Not a problem to disturb the work or leisure on the ship. Rolling gently and the dolphins playing in the waves of the ships wake.

One day against the clear blue sky the Island of Bali rose over the horizon. It was green and cone shaped. To me to looked like the paradise island I imagined. Then on the other bow Lombock. We sailed through the Lombock Strait dodging the fishing boats and their nets.

A few days later after one of the most pleasant voyages I had sailed since coming to sea, we picked up a pilot and sailed up a jungle shrouded river. Turning a bend, the berths suddenly appeared as though sticking out of the forest. The tanks could just be seen through the trees but I was assured that the town was just beyond the gates. Three berths lined the river bank. Two were already occupied, one by a sister ship the other by one of the company's small coastal tankers that plied their trade around the Indonesian and Malayan coasts. Small so that they could deliver fuel to smaller ports.

When the agent came on board, the Captain informed me that I was to leave the ship in Singapore and fly back to the U K to attend college to sit for my first mates certificate. My eastern adventure was coming to an end. In a few days I would be in Singapore and boparding a plane for home.

Chapter 6

It did not work out how I imagined. We had arrived in Indonesia at the time when there was tension between the British government and the Indonesian government. As we sailed around Australia and New Zealand, we had been aware that trouble was brewing but as we were far away, it appeared it would not affect us. Even as we sailed for Tanjong Priok, we had convinced ourselves that all would be well or the company would not send us there. The second mate shook his head and looked more and more nervous as we approached the oil terminal. He was still thinking about what had befallen him in the past. We all tried to reassure him that all would be well.

When we sailed up the river and approached the terminal everything appeared calm. The night after arriving those crew members who were not on duty went ashore without any objection from the military guards or the officials. The local bars and the girls welcomed us with open arms. On the way back to the ship, the roadside food sellers served us without question. All seemed peaceful.

It all changed the next morning. I have no idea what the British government had said or not said but the atmosphere by the river changed. Suddenly the dock was swarming with soldiers. They lined the shore facing the ship with their guns in their hands. An officer and his escort climbed the gangway and marched to the captain's cabin. At the same time, the oil stopped filling the tank I was monitoring. Looking up I saw the shore people shutting the valves controlling the flow of oil along the rubber hose connecting the ship to the shore. The sailor with me looked puzzled. Suddenly the captain appeared on the boat deck beside the army officer and flanked by the escort also with guns out.

" They have ordered us to stop loading and blown the oil out of the pipeline before shutting everything down on the shore. The chief officer is on his way. Start shutting all the valves on the ship.'

The sailor and I were well under way with the shutting down when the chief officer arrived. " What has happened?" I asked him.

He shrugged and started to help. " We have been told to stop and leave the berth. From what I gather on the radio there is a dispute between the British government and the Indonesians. Once we are ready and the engine is operational, we are to leave the berth and anchor in the river to await instructions. The same goes for the other two ships."

Once the pipelines were secured and the engine made ready, we let go the ropes and the ship was anchored in the river. Soldiers remained on board stationed on the bridge wing, the focastle and on top of the stern accommodation near the funnel. A gunboat moored by the gangway and a naval officer climbed on board. I went to meet him but he ignored me and marched without looking left or right up to the bridge. The tension between the officer and the Captain was like electric sparks as I followed the officer into the wheelhouse.

" Why have you detained my ship?" the captain demanded.

" You and your countrymen are no longer welcome in my country, captain." The naval officer's english was very laboured. Then he smiled and shrugged his shoulders " Look. I am a naval officer and carry out my orders. I have no argument with you. Your ship is to remain anchored here until the authorities decide what is to happen. The patrol boats will make sure there is no attempt to sail."

For four tension filled days we sat in the river with guards on the ship and two gunboats blocking our escape. We could see the shore and the berths but even the agent was not allowed to board the ship and contact the captain. We had no idea of what was happening and at the least sign of crew making moves to move the ship the guards started to point their guns.

The small coastal tanker suddenly one night raised the anchor on the incoming tide and made off down the river. It was dark and they did not show any lights. Slow to react, one of the gunboats gave chase as the tanker disappeared round a bend in the river. All the officers who were awake lined the bridge wing and willed the tanker to make the open sea. We all looked shocked when we heard gunshots but had no way of finding out what had happened. Nobody came on board to ask. The gunboat returned the next morning and resumed its guard behind the remaining tankers.

Then we were ordered to leave. The soldiers disembarked as the pilot came aboard accompanied by a naval officer.

" You will sail down the river and then for Bango Island off the west coast of Sumatra. There we will wait for instructions. I and my men will stay on board until decisions have been made."

The Captain raised an eyebrow but did not reply. Turning to the chief officer, he gave the order for the ship to sail.

We raised the anchor, turned in the river and, followed by the other tanker sailed down the river. The gunboats took up station ahead and astern as escorts.

When we came to the mouth of the river there was the kinder anchored. There was silence on the Felipe as everybody lined the rail. There were bullet holes in the funnel and the wheelhouse. We found out later that the chief officer was injured and taken to hospital. The captain had been arrested and taken into custody. Later we heard that the chief officer had died.

We joined several other British flag tankers anchored off the nearest Indonesian island to Singapore. The gunboats positioned themselves out to sea from our anchorage. On the horizon just outside Indonesian territorial waters several Royal Navy ships were patrolling. They signalled us by lamp to hold fast until this was sorted out. If there is any danger, they said, we will come for you. They must have thought we were a bit thick because it took us ages to get the whole message. It was OK for them they had signallers and could send out morse code really fast. We had me and my morse code reading was slow. I have no idea what was more frightening, the Indonesian gunboats or the thought of the navy coming to our rescue all guns blazing.

One morning after we had been anchored for three days, the naval officer took a call on his portable radio.

Smiling to the Captain, he held out his hand. " It has been resolved and you can proceed to Singapore."

The Captain shook his hand. " I cannot say that I will be sorry to see you go. Third mate see the officer off my ship."

As soon as the gunboat left, we weighed anchor and sailed towards the Royal navy Frigates. With flags flying they formed up line astern and escorted us to Singapore.

Saying goodbye to the chinese crew, I left the ship ready to go home. It was not so easy. A great many British expats from Indonesia were trying to get planes home. In the end the company had to put me up in a hotel for five days while trying to find a flight. It was great because I was on a daily expenses rate. In the end they found me a flight leaving from Kuala Lumpur. To get there I had a lift on an exploration plane being moved to a northern airport.

It was the most hair raising flight I had ever undertaken. Sitting writing this now it reminds me of the time years later when I flew from Port Harcourt to Lagos while working a consultancy in Nigeria. The plane flew at a few thousand feet and appeared to skim the trees. I tried shutting my eyes but had to look. The plane was small and buffeted by every wind current, bouncing up and then plunging down. I clung to the seat in front all the way. On the Nigerian flight we took off in a thunderstorm the pilot manoeuvring round the stacked up thunder clouds. The man sitting next to me remarked that this was is first flight from Port Harcourt for a year. He explained that on his last flight the plane had hit a cross wind on landing in Lagos and ended up in the hanger. He had been in hospital for six months. All I could do was swallow and pray.

The plane did arrive safely in Kuala Lumpur and I boarded a Lufthansa flight for Frankfurt. It was a flight filled with German peace corpse youngsters and they sang German drinking songs all the way home. Luckily in Frankfurt I was put on a positioning flight as the only passenger among a great many flight crew. I was well serviced for that flight.

Back at college, I found the First Mates Certificate straight forward. It was in one way like entering a familiar territory. Many of the students who had been there when I took my second mates were again at college. It helped me sink once more into the world of study. Even though the studying went well it was still with relief that I went along to the exam centre to find out I had passed. Like all the students, I imagined that when I had gained my first mates certificate, I would get promotion from third mate to second mate. You cannot believe my shock when the company appointed me to my next ship as third mate. I was to join the ship in Spezia in Italy along with two other officers. When I asked the company why I was still third mate they went into a long explanation about the accelerated promotion during the war. This resulted in many young captains who still had not retired thus the log jamb in the promotion schedule. If I waited a few years promotion would take off and I would soon find myself as chief officer.

For the entire journey by train across France and Italy I wrestled with this conundrum. Should I have the patience to wait in the hope of promotion or should I find another company. While studying at the college many of my friends came from dry cargo companies or passenger ships. Speaking to them had opened up the possibility in my mind of joining a dry cargo company. I had for sometime deep down wanted to see what sailing on a dry cargo ship would be like. Even more I wondered what it was like on a passenger ship. Before the train arrived in Spezia, I came to the conclusion that I should see out the remaining six months on my contract and then leave the company. I could use the time to get in touch with companies to see what was available.

The Calisto was had not reached the port when the train arrived at the station. A woman from the agents met us and took us to a hotel for the night. The next morning I sat on the balcony of my hotel room and watched the Calisto sail through the breakwater and tie up at the oil terminal. Shortly after this the agent phoned to say a car was waiting to take us to the ship.

I climbed the gangway with my bags and found the third mates cabin. He as usual greeted me with open arms, his bags already packed. He advised me to go and sign on with the captain straight away. He will be waiting for you and does not take kindly to being ignored he added.

My suspicions should have been aroused then. I had found it strange that the company had not told me who the captain was. In my indignation at not being promoted, I had really noticed this oversight. At the top of the stairs, I knocked on the captain's door.

That familiar welsh voice ordered me to enter. My heart sank. Captain Jenkins.

He sat behind his desk, his expression bleak. " Well Gubbins I see they have sent you to me again. I hope you are better now than before. I will be keeping my eye on you."

Without a comment, I signed the papers and left. On the way down the stairs to my cabin, I vowed to myself that I would not let him get me down.

In the main it worked. I did my job and Captain Jenkins left me alone most of the time. He did complain about the maintenance of the lifeboats on one inspection but I knew the maintenance had been carried out competently.

The ship sailed from Mina Alhemadi to European ports through the Suez Canal. It was like running a regular service and most of the time it was routine. The officers kept watch and did their extras in their off time. The ship ploughed on day after day without much drama.

There was one thing. It stemmed from the food. Like an army is said to march on its stomach, the morale of a ship is affected by the food served. With hard physical work many times in hot sweetie conditions, sailors look forward to their meals.

This all came to a head with a sailor called Murdo McCloud.

Murdo was one of my aft crew when arriving or leaving port. Tall, broad shouldered and powerful, he came from Barra in the Outer Hebrides. Like many large men, he was surprisingly softly spoken and talked very slowly, as though thinking deeply about the effect his words would have on those around him. I remember a time in Genoa, Murdo asked me whether I would come up the road as soon as we were off duty for a pint. Having endured weeks at sea, I agreed. In the bar, Murdo spotted a couple of other sailors and walked across to their table with me trailing in his wake. They greeted each other like long lost friends. Well, it took them so long to say hello, it was like the Ents in conclave.

In addition to being soft spoken, Murdo was immensely strong. Over six feet tall with blond curly hair and a square jawed face, his neck to me was twice the size of mine and his arms seemed like tree trunks. Usually he had a dour expression on his face but his look could suddenly brighten when something amused him. I recall a day when we were tying up in Mina Alhemadi. One of the eight inch ropes broke as the ship was caught by the wind and current. The stern started to swing away from the berth and I warned the bridge. To my astonishment, Murdo hauled in the rope hand over hand, tied a bowline in the end and heaved it back ashore before the others could get the next rope ready. We tied up the ship without any other incident.

Murdo was slow to take offence. Once he did have a falling out with two other sailors over what I have no idea. He challenged them to a fight. It did not work out how I imagined. The next time the ship was in port. I watched the three disappear behind a shed after we docked. A few minutes later Murdo appeared carrying the two unconscious sailors on his shoulders.

Late one night as the ship ploughed through the Mediterranean I was awoken by angry voices outside my cabin. Opening the door slightly, I saw Murdo and the Chief Steward in the alleyway.

Murdo was angry. You could see that from the redness of his face, the tension in his body and the way he spoke much faster than normal. With his left hand he had the Chief Steward by the throat. What was astonishing was he had the one hundred kilo Chief Steward off the ground so that his feet dangled banging the heels against my cabin bulkhead. In the other hand, he held a two gallon fire extinguisher. Now I would not have been able to lift the Chief Steward even with two hands let alone at the same time as a two gallon fire extinguisher. I knew intimately how much the fire extinguishers weighed because it was my job to fill them when they had been discharged during a test. Then I had to lift them back into position on the bulkhead.

Between clenched teeth, he was saying. " You are in charge of the food, you and that fat, lazy cook. What you serve up is uneatable rubbish. My mother would be ashamed to put that on our table. It is not fit for the animals on my Uncles farm. Either the food improves or I will be back again."

With that he dropped the quivering Chief Steward and stalked out of the accommodation, placing the fire extinguisher back on its bracket.

I stepped out of my cabin and helped the Chief Steward to his feet. He was visibly shaking, his fat stomach vibrating like a jelly and his chins moving like waves breaking o n the shore.

" Are you all right?" I asked smoothing down his clothes.

He glowered at me. " Why did you not rush out and help me?"

I lied easily. " I had only been in bed a short while after coming off watch. Lets face it. I must have fallen into a deep sleep. By the time I was fully awake and realised something was happening outside my cabin, he had dropped you and was going back to his cabin."

" I will go and report this to the Captain!" he almost shouted.

" Don't you think it can be left until the morning?"

" No!" he snapped and waddled off in the direction of the Captain's cabin.

In the morning Captain Jenkins came to the bridge during my watch to have a mug of coffee. It was a morning ritual and done in such a way that he was making sure I realised he was keeping his eye on me. He asked me what had happened the night before. I described what Murdo had done, adding what I took to be the reason for his outburst. When I mentioned the state of the food and that everybody on board had a great deal of sympathy with Murdo, I caught the hint of a smile. Captain Jenkins ordered me to report to the ship's office at two that afternoon.

Unlike many Captains I have sailed under, Captain Jenkins was a man of principle as I had seen when I was a cadet. Disciplinary rules were all covered in statute and agreements. This was in a document called the disciplinary code. Under these laws, Captain Jenkins had the power to fine members of his crew. He would never do this without first holding a properly constituted hearing.

When I arrived at the ship's office wearing my best uniform whites and my cap, the office was set up very precisely. A table opposite the door was laid out with the official logbook to record the proceedings, a copy of the disciplinary code, a copy of the Merchant Shipping Acts and the Captain's hat with the gold laurel edging. To the right at an angle was a table for the accused and a supporter, to the left at an angle a table for the witnesses.

Captain Jenkins sat behind his table. He smiled at me and indicated that I should sit beside the Chief Officer to his right. The Chief Steward came in and sat next to me.

Murdo arrived accompanied by Dick Hearn, the union representative on the ship.

Captain Jenkins called the court to order. The Chief Steward described what had happened to him. I then told the Captain what I had seen and heard. Then Murdo was asked to give his side of the story.

In his soft spoken way, Murdo explained. " What they have reported is all true. I do not deny any of it. After being on watch for the eight to twelve, I went back to the sailor's mess for my supper. It was almost uneatable. I was hungry. Then it all caught up with me. All those uneatable meals. The Chief Steward gets an allowance for food the same as every other Steward in the fleet. Why I asked myself is the food on this ship so much worse than every other ship I have sailed on? Either the Chief Steward is on the fiddle or the cook is hopeless. I decided it must be a bit of both though the cook says he can only cook the food he is given. Then I thought I'd go and have it out with the Chief Steward. You have heard what happened after that. I would not have hurt him. All I wanted to do was scare him into providing us with better food."

Captain Jenkins looked around the room. " Fined two days wages."

He entered this in the Official Logbook and got the Chief Officer, me and the Chief Steward to sign the entry. " You can all get back to your duties now."

When the ship docked in Rotterdam, the Chief Steward and the cook were sent on leave and replaced. The food took a turn for the better.

The other incident happened when I was on my last voyage with the company. I had decided finally to leave and written to the personal department to inform them that I would not be renewing my contract. The ship had loaded crude oil at Mina for Rotterdam.

I was in watch as we sailed through the Western Approaches nearing the English Channel when the fog descended. I immediately slowed the ship and called the Captain. He arrived on the bridge and placed himself by the radar ordering me onto the bridge wing and the sailor on the wheel. I stared into the fog but could not see anything. Indeed at times it was so thick the focastle almost disappeared. The lookout had been posted and he was bundled up in his oilskins.

The Captain called. " Ship approaching on the starboard side. Shout if you see anything."

The fog cleared a trifle and I made out the red port light of a ship shinning through the whiteness. There was only a vague outline of the structure. I went into the wheelhouse and told the Captain.

For some reason and this was not like Captain Jenkins, he ordered in a shaky voice. " Hard a port!"

The sailor on the wheel was very experienced and he stared at me with a white face.

I looked out of the wheelhouse window and acted on instinct. " Hard to starboard."

The wheelman looked relieved as he obeyed. The red light swung across our bow and disappeared down the port side. I sighed and looked at the Captain.

His face was white and at first I thought it was anger but then I noticed the twitch at the corner of his mouth. Still looking at me, he wiped his face in a large handkerchief. Looking back in the radar he ordered the ship back on course. I went into the chartroom to plot the position of the ship from the Decca electronic position system that was relatively new.

Captain Jenkins looked in at the door. I braced myself for a tirade but he half smiled. " Thank you young Eddie. I do not know what came over me. You will make a fine officer in time."

I was so astonished, I did not reply.

I found out later how much he was sincere. As I said I informed the company that I was not going to renew my contract. For the only time in my life, I was called up to the head office for what the described in the letter as an exit interview. It turned out to be more of a chance to try to make me change my mind. There was the marine superintendent, the personnel manager and the pay and pensions manager. They used all the arguments they could. First that the block in promotion would soon end and I would be a second mate. I made plain I was sceptical. Then the advantages of pension, schooling for any children, wife's accompanying officers and the eventual chance of a job ashore with the company. When it was obvious that I had made up my mind, they took out my report file and pushed the reports from Captain Jenkins under my nose. I read these and became almost angry again. All that brow beating and harassment. Now I find that the reports were glowing.

" You are one of the few cadets and officers who has had such glowing reports from Captain Jenkins. If he thinks you are that good, we do not want to lose you." At least the marine superintendent was being honest.

" I have had a great time with the company but I would like a new challenge," I stated equally bluntly.

" When you require a reference, just give them my phone number. I will tell them how reluctant we are to let you go." He got up and shook my hand.

I was in London a few weeks later just before Christmas for an interview with a small dry cargo company whose ships sailed to Finland Russia and Poland. I was informed that I had the job after a very brief interview. It appeared that the marine superintendent of this company had been at see with the o one from my previous company and he was prepared to take his word and appoint me.

Chapter 7

After Christmas I packed my bag, said goodbye to my mother and took the train to London. I was to go to Surrey Docks to join a ship called the Vanguard. It was cold and the rain was pouring down from a grey sky.

All I could make out through the grey dimness outside was streets and buildings I did not recognise any of the places we passed. We were travelling south of the river round the Elephant and Castle roundabout and down the Great East Road towards Bermondsey.

The taxi turned into a road with the blackened outline of a brick wall that I supposed had once been red. Not another living soul was visible through the rain, only that plain, unbroken brick wall. The only movement came from a few passing cars throwing up clouds of spray for all the world like ships rushing through a choppy sea.

Turning a corner, but still following the line of the wall, the cab came to a stop half through a gateway. Double gates, green paint clinging in patches to the almost bare wood, were flung back against the wall on either side of the opening, stuck in place as though they had not been shut for a long time.

As the car came to a halt, the driver sounded the horn, strident and echoing across the docks. A policeman, his coat collar pulled high around his helmet, hurried out of the nice dry interior of his box to investigate the source of the sound. The need for protection against the downpour was obvious as the wet wind blowing from the direction of the river sent the rain like stair rods horizontally through the gate, drenching everything with which it made contact.

" Nice day for a drive, even better for a swim," I remember the taxi driver greeting the policemen cheerfully. Without any sign that he had heard, he stuck his head through the open window of the cab.

" Second Mate for the Vanguard," the taxi driver informed him, continuing to grin.

The policeman growled sourly at me, whether in greeting or as a warning I could not judge, and then withdrew his head. " Too wet to remain here too long," he muttered to nobody in particular. " Berth 43 is what you want. The gangway is at this end of the quay so I would go round this end of the shed. Not that it really matters at the moment. All the dockers are sheltering from the rain. Bloody weather. The damp gets right into my bones it does. See you on the way out."

The taxi driver shook his head, muttered something about miserable sods, wound up the window, put the taxi into gear and drove onto the quays.

Feeling much like a provincial coming to the capital city for the first time, I stared out of the taxi window. Unconsciously, I was contrasting the sight of lorries drawn up in rows, their drivers huddled under the shelter of the overhanging roofs of the unloading bays or sleeping at the wheel of their vehicle, with the more familiar sight of lines of pipes leading from the berth to tanks on the shore of a typical tanker terminal.

The taxi turned the corner at the end of the shed, shutting out the sight of the lorries, and drove parallel to the edge of the quay. Through the grey of the pouring rain, I could make out a line of dock cranes, their skeletal fingers pointing into the grey sky, the hooks hanging forlornly in the rain like so many bodies on a row of gibbets. Groups of dockers gathered by the doorways of the shed, gazing forlornly out into the rain, whether wishing it would stop so that they could resume work or whether it was so heavy the foreman would send them home for the rest of the day, I could not tell. Even to my untutored eye, there was no cargo being worked in the rain. On tankers the discharge never stopped no matter what the weather.

The driver deftly manoeuvred the taxi between the crane rails and the piles of cargo handling equipment littering the quay, coming to a stop by the foot of a gangway leading up the rust streaked sides of a ship. After paying off the taxi driver and watching it drive away round the corner of the shed, I had a chance to look around. The black painted side of the ship rose over me, zebra like running rust streaks giving it a blotched and cancerous appearance but what really hit me was how small it appeared. My mind turned to the oil tankers on which I had sailed, small in comparison to some but gigantic in relation to this ship I was about to board.

My feeling of apprehension rose once more, filling my mind with panic and making me want to turn and run away but the sight of the curious expressions on the faces of the waiting dockers got me moving. I ran up the gangway holding tightly to my bags, through the door into the dry of the accommodation, more scared of appearing foolish to a lot of anonymous dockers than to allowing my sense of foreboding to overcome my confidence.

Once inside the cover of the accommodation, I was able to take stock. The familiar sound of a diesel generator greeted me and helped to steady my nerves. Through a window I was able to see the length of the ship and a part of the docks. God, I thought, the docks are a sorry sight in the pouring rain. A ship lay like a stranded whale, tied to the quay but bereft of any purpose. Water ran off the closed hatch covers, forming small rivers across the deck and into the scuppers to cascade over the side in miniature waterfalls adding to the zebra streaks of rust down the plating. The cranes and derricks stand as children abandoned by their parents outside a pub with nothing to do but wait mournfully for their parents to come out and take them home. Men, usually so active pushing, pulling, signalling, shouting, laughing, arguing and sometimes fighting, stand around in groups, in any shelter they can find, drinking endless cups of tea while they wait for the rain to clear. What a waste of men's time to stand idle when there is so much to do but the weather is such a fickle mistress as all who sail the sea know, I thought. In a twinkling of an eye, all would change, the sun would come out and the men would be back to their proper role.

Turning from the window overlooking the deck, I was confronted with a long corridor stretching the whole width of the ship, lined by a series of doors to cabins and another corridor leading away to the left into the bowls of the ship. The passage was full of men, some leaning against the walls, some sitting propped up but all gently steaming as their clothes dried in the comparative warmth. The atmosphere was closer to a fetid jungle in the tropical heat than a cool, wet autumn day in London. The smell of drying clothes, sweating bodies and cigarette smoke was overwhelming and with difficulty I pushed my way through the crowd until I found some stairs. With relief, not only from the increasing sense that I was in a dragons den, hot fetid and rumbling, a feeling that helped me to understand how Jonah felt inside the whale, but also to escape the stares of enquiry which had greeted my entrance. Nobody had moved since I came through the door but several pairs of eyes had stared unmoving in my direction. Nobody asked who I was or why I was there but several of the men were obviously curious. With a sigh of relief I reached the top of the stairs and dropped my bags to the deck.

It was quieter on this level, the sound of the diesel engine louder in my ears. Looking around, all I could see was a corridor lined by walls made of a light green coloured material which shone faintly in the bright overhead fluorescent light. Like the deck below, doors punctuated the wall on one side, again I assumed leading to cabins. The other side was smooth and unbroken but for one door made of steel. The corridor turned sharply to the right and disappeared some way in the distance. With an effort, I worked out that in that direction lay the forward part of the accommodation.

Just as I was starting to wonder where I should go, a man dressed in a well worn boiler suit, which had been white at one time, the sleeves of which were cut off at the elbow, came out of one of the cabins. On seeing me standing indecisively at the head of the stairs, he smiled broadly and came to where I was standing. The grey streaks in his hair and beard made him seem far older at a distance but this close I could see he was in his early thirties.

" You must be the new second mate? " he said in a cheerful voice and I nodded in reply. " I'm Bill Douglas the second engineer."

" Eddie Gubbins," I said by way of introduction.

Bill's handshake was firm and warm. " The Chief Officer's cabin is down the corridor and around the comer to the other side of the ship. Captain Harris is ashore at the moment so I would go and see Dick if I was you. I can't stop because I am wanted in the engine room. You should be able to find your way from here. See you later." Bill turned and went into the engine room through the steel door, leaving me to pick up my bags and find the Chief Officer's cabin.

All the doors to the cabins lining the corridor along which I walked had the name and the rank an officer on a brass plate screwed to the surface. It was soon obvious that the engineers lived on the port side of the accommodation and the deck officers on the starboard. I passed the second mates cabin and came to an open door but the plate saying ' R. Mortimer - Chief Officer' was plainly visible. Putting down my bags, I paused to steady my nerves and then knocked, entering when a voice told me to come on in.

The room I entered was fairly large, square with the same green walls as those lining the corridor outside. Behind the door was a large double bunk, a desk covered with papers beside the bunk under a window and a settee running along the wall and round the comer. A wardrobe and washbasin took up the space on the forth wall with a door which I took, correctly as it turned out, to lead to the bathroom. A coffee table and two armchairs faced into the comer towards the settee.

Hesitating just inside the door on seeing five men sitting drinking beer or coffee, I stood blinking as I looked around the room. " I'm Eddie Gubbins, the new second mate," I announced rather dramatically.

All five men stopped talking and turned to look at me as though I had interrupted some serious conversation. Feeling rather foolish, I felt a blush coming to my cheeks and wished that I were somewhere else. Swinging his feet to the floor from off a partly opened drawer, a large grey haired man sitting in a chair by the desk got to his feet and waved me further into the cabin.

" Hello. I'm Dick Mortimer the Chief Officer," he said extending his hand. "Come on in and find a seat. Would you like some coffee? "

At my nod, he lifted his phone and spoke rapidly into the receiver. I sat down on the end of the settee, nodding politely as Dick introduced each of the men in the room in turn. Johnie Cousins, the stevedore's foreman dressed in a greasy mackintosh and a flat cap, nicotine stains on his fingers. Brian Burtex, the company's port man, dressed in a rather well cut suit and shiny black shoes. Harry, the shed foreman sitting in one of the arm chairs, a small man constantly on the move whether it was shifting in his chair or taking off and replacing his cap from his head. Rex Berisford, the third mate, dressed in a uniform with a pair of working gloves by his feet.

My coffee arrived and the rest soon lost interest in me, much to my relief, picking up the bones of to the conversation that my arrival had stopped. I tried to listen and understand their conversation but it was about cargo stowage, hold space and the way the weather would hold up the loading, all this interspersed with jargon that I found hard to follow. My mind slipped away and once more I found myself wondering whether I had made the right decision when I had decided to leave oil tankers and join a cargo ship, to step from the understandable and the familiar into the unknown or at best only vaguely known. My attention was returned to the cabin when the third mate addressed me directly.

" You an oil tanker man, then? " the third mate asked. He was a small, rather stocky young man with a round weather beaten face, close cropped curly hair and rough hands with short thick fingers. To me he looked exactly like a farmer, bleached by the weather and strengthened by the passing of the seasons. " You'll find working on the Vanguard rather different, then. Have you sailed on a cargo ship before? "

" No, " I replied truthfully, not knowing where the conversation was leading us. " I have sailed on tankers ever since I first went to sea as a deck cadet."

" Oh, there will be none of this turning valves and standing back to wait for the cargo to load itself like it is on a tanker, " the third mate said with a knowing grin. " The officers on this ship have to climb up and down the hatches to check the cargo all the time it is being handled and thrown around by his men. " The third mate waved his hand at Johnie Cousins sitting on the settee by the desk. " All the dockers swear at you if you point out how bad they are treating the cargo and take no notice unless you swear back."

Johnie cut in before the third mate could say anything else about the dockers and turned to grin at me. " My men don't do all the damage, you know. If I was you, second mate, I wouldn't believe everything the third mate tells you."

I looked from one to the other, expecting a big argument but caught the shake of Dick's head out of the corner of my eye. From the way everybody were looking at me and smiling, it was apparent that everybody else realised that the third mate was going to enjoy, for as long as he could, his position of having somebody on the ship with less knowledge about handling general cargo than he did. It must have been the chance he had been waiting for, something he had dreamed about ever since he joined the Vanguard, to be able to give advise to one of those above him in the hierarchy.

" How long did you sail on tankers? " asked Brain Burtex from the corner of the settee where he lounged back for all the world as though he owned the ship. His dark eyes appraised me from out of a rather podgy face, a face that had seen too many good meals and bottles of duty free whisky, topped by tight curly black hair. Whether it was the natural colour or dyed was hard to tell because it was difficult to judge his age. Without the podge he could have been in his early thirties but with the effects of the whisky, he looked fifty.

" It was six years," I answered defensively, looking round the cabin in an effort to gauge the reaction of the men. I felt as though I was in a laboratory, a specimen to be watched closely, tested and analysed, and this put me on the defensive. Much later when I had come to know these people better, I realised they were only making conversation, trying to include me in their circle and put me at ease. " I joined Shell when I was sixteen, served my four year apprenticeship and then a two year contract."

" What made you leave? " Dick asked. " Surely, you must be taking a cut in pay to join Baltic Steamers? "

" I suppose I wanted to find out what it was like sailing on a general cargo ship," I answered rather vaguely." Besides the sight of sand from a jetty sticking out into the sea and only a few days in port at the end of each voyage can become extremely wearing even to the most hardened tanker man."

" You'll find things different on the Vanguard then. " Rex remarked with as close to superiority he could muster.

" I expect you can show me the main aspects of the job, " I said, knowing that Rex would get a boost from answering any questions I may have about the working of the ship. " Where is the second mate I am relieving? "

" Up on the bridge making sure that the navigation equipment is in order before handing over to you, I expect, " Rex said. " I'll show Eddie the way if you can spare me for a few minutes," he added to Dick as he got to his feet.

Dick laughed loudly. " Don't be so sarcastic, young Rex. Until the rain stops there is not much you can do. Go on. You show James to the bridge but come straight back because it looks as though the rain is easing off. Eddie, leave your bags here for a while until the Captain returns from the office. I have to find out where you are sleeping tonight and where he wants you to sign on. Leave that to me. I'll tell you what he has in mind when we have lunch together."

I found the navigation bridge of the Otter a lot smaller than the bridges of the ships I had sailed on previously. It was as though I had entered a world in miniature but that was only natural because the whole ship was smaller. Besides the size, everything was familiar, equipment seemingly spread around in a random fashion when looked at by the untrained eye. A radar set just inside the starboard door at the front of the bridge, next to this a plotting table, in the centre an autopilot with what I took to be an engine control by the side. The forward facing windows were sloped outward with clear view screens at each end to give some kind of visibility even in bad weather when spray was breaking over the bridge. The steering wheel stood back near the front edge of a chart table that divided the floor space of the bridge in two. In one corner by some electrical switch boxes was a gyrocompass and behind the chart table a hatch through which could be seen the radio office.

A man looked up from the chart table when Rex and I entered the bridge and wiped his blond hair out of his eyes with an ink stained hand, showing the two gold stripes on the sleeve of his uniform jacket.

" Hello," I said. " I'm Eddie Gubbins, your relief second mate come to let you go on leave. "

" Thank goodness you have arrived at last, " the man said putting down the pen with which he was drawing on a chart, wiping his hand on a tissue and moving into the space by the auto pilot to greet me. " I'll look after him now thanks, Rex."

" Come on, " he said taking my arm. " I'll show you round the ship and then we can look at the navigation equipment that is your responsibility. With a bit of luck the rain will stop and we will be able to look at the cargo being loaded. You must be wondering what it is like to load general cargo after all those years in tankers. I know you have your mate's certificate but there is a difference between theory and practice."

The Baltic Steamer Company must have had a good grapevine because everybody I met that day seemed to know about my background, about what I had been doing before I joined the Vanguard. Looking back now, I suppose I should not have been so surprised. To all the people I met, it must have been a little strange for a somebody trained and then spending most of their seafaring life on oil tankers to suddenly leave all that behind and join a small cargo ship. Again, I was to find out later that it was nothing to do with my being a tanker man but the openness of a small company that allowed everybody to know what was happening. I was used to the closed nature of the large company where every new ship represented new people who one had never met before and in the main who had never even heard of each other before joining the ship. The Baltic Steamship Company was different. With only a handful of ships, about fourteen while I was serving the company, sailing to a restricted number of ports, it did not take long for a ship's officer to get at least a passing acquaintance with most of the officers sailing with the company. Whenever two or more of the company's ships were in port together, the officers visited the other ships to see their colleagues and talked about their mutual friends. In many ways sailing with the Baltic Steamer Company was like belonging to a large family with all the gossip, argument and fun that that entailed. .

Thus my first day on the Otter passed, working with the second mate, learning about the ship and climbing in and out of the holds to look at the cargo as it was loaded. Laying back in my bunk that night, in the spare cabin behind the Captain's accommodation, I tried to sort out the jumble of impressions which floated on the surface of my thoughts, aided by the amount of the gin which I had consumed. For all my anxiety about joining a different type of ship like the Otter, the system of duties once the ship was at sea would be exactly the same as for those with which I was familiar. The second mate taking charge of the twelve o'clock to four o'clock watch morning and afternoon. The only difference was in port where the dockers knocked off at night and other than the duty officer and sailor, the rest of the crew could go ashore. During the day I had been conscious that the steady hum of the pumps so familiar on an oil tanker when the cargo was being discharged was replaced by the noise and sudden vibration caused by the ship's cranes or the roar of a fork lift truck. All the people I had met, some introduced formally, some only nodding on passing, blurred into a vast sea of faces, names and voices which did not connect one to the other as I fought to bring some semblance of order out of the chaos of my first day. The expressions people had used when explaining things to me had at first made me wonder whether I was on a different planet or at least in a different country. However, like the student in the language class, by evening I was starting to understand enough to follow the pattern of their speech.

The next two days passed in confusion, for me, of new sounds and sights. Cargo arrived alongside the ship on fork lift trucks from the sheds lining the inner edge of the quay or on lorries, was lifted aboard the ship by either the ships cranes or the shore cranes and stowed in the hold by the dockers accompanied by much grunting and swearing. Tally clerks kept a record of every box, bag, bundle or whatever that was put into the holds. These recordings were taken by a runner to the port office of the stevedoring company to be translated into what was called a manifest and a plan of the cargo aboard the ship. All the time I concentrated on making sense out of the process because the drawing of the cargo plan was to be one of my duties while the ship was being loaded in Finland. Moving around the decks of the Vanguard, I asked questions of everybody who would listen and answer. In addition I paid frequent visits to the cargo office on shore and generally discovered what was going on. Rex lorded it over me just as I had suspected, revelling in a newfound sense of superiority but for some reason I did not resent what he was doing. It had become plain to me that although I had only a theoretical knowledge of how to load a cargo ship gained during my studies for my certificate of competence, it did not take long before the theoretical started to match the practical. With a few days experience I would not need Rex to instruct me, so while it gave him a feeling of confidence, I let his attitude ride. I had become completely absorbed in the work and no longer questioned whether I had made the right decision in leaving tankers to join the Otter.

Of course, like anybody sizing up a new job, I learnt a great deal from my fellow officers besides Rex. It was soon obvious that Dick Mortimer ran the deck department very efficiently and had the respect of the sailors because he could, at a moment's notice, actually successfully complete any task that he ordered the sailors to undertake. I stored this knowledge away for future reference though, on reflection, I did not realise at the time that Dick had an easy task when compared to the task of a chief officer on a tanker. The crew of the Otter all lived in London, wanted a regular sailing and to get home to their families as much as possible. Indeed, by mutual agreement with Captain Harris, they had signed on an extra man so that at the end of each voyage one of the deck crew had the opportunity for a voyage off. This led to a very stable crew and moreover a crew who valued their jobs and did not want to stir up unnecessary trouble. Captain Harris stayed in the background sticking to his cabin and some said drinking a lot though over the two days I had been on board I could not tell, but everybody was agreed that he was the best shipmaster in the company. Watch him, Dick told me, and you will learn a lot about the way to command a ship.

Of the others, Bill Douglas who I had met as soon as I came aboard was short of money but had a reputation, which unknown to me at the time, was to be tested in Finland, of being able to chat up anything wearing a skirt. Lock up your wives, daughters and girlfriends when he is around because he cares nothing for reputations or for status. He it was who arranged parties on board every so often and it is rumoured that at one of these he had three girls in different beds on board at the same time though I could never satisfactorily prove this. I believe it was one of those stories that get out of hand and expand at every telling. I must admit, when I first met Bill, I did not think he had enough energy to match his reputation but sailing with him, I was to come to know better.

Like at most places of work there is always one person who can get you anything. On the Otter that person was Brian Robinson, the electrician. He had contacts all over the place and in every port, having sailed on Baltic Steamship Company's ships for a long time, and was willing to deal in any merchandise as long as no questions were asked. Whether he did anything really illegal, I have never found out, though some people would say that was because he became a lifelong friend. I did not want to investigate his activities too closely for fear that I would have to make a choice between my friendship and my sense of right or wrong.

Rex, when not telling me how to do the job, was looked on as the mascot of the ship by both the officers and the crew. He had taken three attempts to get his second mates certificate, was slow at grasping details but, in contrast to the way they treated most other people, everybody on board made allowance for Rex and he got away with murder. Rex was saving up to get married and like all the officers of the Baltic Steamship Company was always claiming poverty because of the low wages paid by the company. He has been saving up to get married for so long, Brian whispered to me one night, it is a standing joke in the company and causes a certain tension between Rex and Pat, his girl friend.

These were the people that I had to, not only work with, but also live with over the next few months. Nobody is going to force such a person to mix only with working colleagues, though colleagues and bosses may put pressure on somebody to take part in some of the activities of the company. It is, at the end of the day, up to the person what they do with their non-working time. At sea things are different. Not only must you find a way of keeping stable relationships during working time, you are shut up with the same people for the rest of the time as well. Tolerance of the different attitudes to life, tolerance of other peoples point of view and a quickness in forgetting past wrongs are called for aboard ship and the most successful seamen soon learn how to practice restraint.

It is amazing to the landsman but quite suddenly on board a ship in port there comes a time when all activity ceases. This is especially true for a cargo ship. The cargo has been loaded and the hatches closed. The sounds of the cranes and the forklift trucks cease. The dockers collect up their gear and walk down the gangway talking about their next job or the weekend at home. All attention is on the office ashore where the various pieces of paper are being assembled. For a short while the ship will lie quietly waiting, the diesel generator a muted noise in the background, waiting as though gathering strength in the same way as a sprinter waiting for the gun before the explosive action.

Once the ship was ready to sail and all the paper work on board, I stood on the poop at the stern of the Otter waiting for the order to let go the ropes and set the ship free from the land. The three sailors stood with me leaning on the rail talking loudly with the people on the shore. Jokes and insults flowed back and forth but even among these men, hard bitten by experience, I could detect an undercurrent of excitement. The loudspeaker on the bulkhead behind my head crackled into life telling us to let go the ropes and for a few minutes chaos reigned as the heavy lines were hauled aboard and stowed on deck. I told the Captain the ropes were clear of the propeller and the ship was suddenly alive, vibrating with the expectation of getting away from the dock. The quay moved away as the ship started to move, slowly at first and then gathering speed. The men standing on the shore waved goodbye and turned to return to their homes.

" Helsinki here we come, second mate," one of the sailors observed as we tidied up the deck. " I expect you will like it there, after all those years on tankers."

" I am looking forward to it," I said gazing back at the fast receding quay and wondering what lay ahead. All thought of having done the right thing or not had now vanished in the realisation that, for good or ill, I was now committed to the Vanguard and to Finland.

The Vanguard sailed for Finland, a land I was to discover of vivid contrasts. Unlike all the time I was sailing on oil tankers, I found I had the time to explore. There were the blazing summers with clear blue skies and temperatures into the eighties. These rapidly turned, through the wet mush of a very short autumn, to the clear winter days with the temperature so low that the ground and the sea turned to ice.

Leaving the front of the wheelhouse, I went to the chart table and plotted the position of the ship. As I bent over the chart, the radio officer came and gave me a message from the icebreaker. He looked out through the windows at the driving snow and shivered.

Battered by gales in the North Sea, I found the motion of the ship more pronounced that the tankers I had been used to on tankers. Sea water did wash across the decks of a loaded tanker but spray very rarely smashed against the bridge windows. For a while the ship had to be slowed to stop the pounding of the bow. It was with relief that I watched the sea state drop as we entered the Elbe River and picked up the pilot for the Kiel Canal.

It was cold when we came out of the canal and sailed into the Baltic Sea. I had been warned that the radio officer would make sure we found out where the ice started. It was not long after I came on watch at midnight that the snow started coming down. Over the next day it did not give up and the temperature dropped further and further. Luckily the sea was relatively calm and no ice formed on the rigging or the hatches. Again I was told that if this happened, the crew would have to get out on deck and knock the ice off the structure with hammers.

The radio officer passed me a piece of paper and I called the Captain as instructed. He soon bustled onto the bridge taking the paper from my hand.

" This is the last reported position of the ice edge and the meeting point of the convoy," he said shaking his head. " By the look of things, this weather is going to hold us up even more. What a trip! Force ten in the North Sea and now driving snow in the Baltic. I hope the icebreaker can get us through to Helsinki quickly. We are going to be a couple of days late as things are without any more hold ups. My wife will be wondering what has happened to us."

I took the paper into the chartroom and concentrated on plotting the positions on the chart. After calculating the course we should steer and the distances to go, I went into the wheelhouse to inform Captain Harris. He listened to my instructions and adjusted the course accordingly.

" On a night like this I hope we pick up the ice edge on the radar because we are going to have a hard job seeing it through the snow before we hit it," Captain Harris remarked, his face illuminated by the glow from the radar screen. " Tell the engine room we will get to the ice edge in about one and half hours."

Having telephoned the engineer on watch about the time to the ice edge, I took my place by the wheelhouse window. Peering out into the snow laden air, I thought of my warm cabin and sighed. The snow started to clear and though it was hard to tell in the dark, I began to believe that I could now see about a mile passed the bow of the ship. Indeed the lookout was now much more plainly visible.

" Radar echo!! Twenty miles on the starboard bow! " Captain Harris's voice broke into my thoughts and for the next thirty minutes I had no time to think of anything other than the ship and what was happening. The Captain called out bearings he had taken from the radar and I plotted these on a chart. The echo on the screen came closer and closer and for all my staring out into the snow between plots, I could not see any lights. I went out onto the bridge wing, letting a blast of cold air enter the bridge to listen for any sound of a whistle from the approaching ship. The whistle of the Vanguard blared out above my head like a love sick cow but there was no answering sound from out of the fog. I was startled when the loudspeaker by my side burst into life.

" I think I can see a light three points on the port bow! " the excited voice of the lookout echoed round the bridge.

" Thank you! " I answered into the microphone, hearing the metallic echo of my words in the distance. Picking up a pair of binoculars from inside the bridge, I went back outside and peered into the snow. At last I detected the faint glow of a light but soon the white steaming lights and the red port light of the other ship were plainly visible.

" Two miles," Captain Harris said, leaning on the door and looking out into the murk at the other ship. " The snow seems to be clearing. There is nothing about so take over for a while. I have to send a message to the agent about the delay. " He went into the radio room leaving me alone on the bridge. I could see the other ship clearly now and a quick glance in the radar showed me that there was nothing else about.

As I stood looking in the radar, my eyes became more focused on the screen as some in built instinct brought my full attention back to the task in hand. There was something different about the picture I was looking at. About five miles ahead of the ship the clutter on the screen formed by the echoes of the waves was not so pronounced.

" The ice edge about five miles ahead! " I called to Captain Harris reasoning that this must be what we were looking for even though I had never seen the echo of ice on the radar before

He strode purposely into the wheelhouse and took up his station by the radar. Once again, I pulled the hood of my coat over my head and went outside into the cold. The flakes of snow were falling lazily now and visibility was rapidly improving. There was a glow ahead of the ship as though we were approaching a large city on a dark night. This must be the reflection of light from the ice, I reasoned. It was an indication that the ice edge was not very far ahead.

" Crushed ice about three miles ahead! " the voice burst out of the loud speaker.

" Thanks! " I answered.

At that moment the snow stopped falling and, as though a curtain had been pulled aside, the ice was plainly visible. I could now see that the water immediately in front of the ship was covered in crushed and broken ice pieces. Then a couple of miles further on was the hard edge of the sheet ice, looking solid and unbreakable. Beyond the edge, the flat plain of the ice stretched away into the dark. I moved back inside to stand by the engine control watching Captain Harris who had moved away from the radar and was standing pipe in mouth staring ahead through the window.

" Half ahead! " Captain Harris called as the ice approached. The engine sound altered slightly as I eased back the control. The ship's forward rush slowed. I have found that at these times every sound takes on significance and sharpness as the level of concentration increases. Soon the Vanguard entered the patch of crushed ice accompanied by a low hissing sound as the ice rubbed against the hull. Close ahead, the hard edge was plainly visible against the sea.

" Stop!" Captain Harris ordered and I pulled the engine control to stop.

" Keep her head at right angles to the edge of the ice!" he called to the seaman at the wheel, who had taken over from the automatic pilot when this had been turned off.

The engine noise dropped further as the ship slowed quickly in the crushed ice. I braced myself against the front of the bridge waiting for the impact as the stem of the ship hit the edge of the ice. The bow rose into the air, hung for a moment and then fell as the ice cracked beneath the weight of the vessel.

" Full Ahead! " Captain Harris called. The structure of the ship shuddered as I pushed the control lever forward and the propeller bit into the open water at the stern. I noted the position at which we had entered the ice, plotted this on the chart and went to the radio room so that it could be sent to the icebreaker.

" Fifteen miles to the convoy assembly point, Eddie." Captain Harris smiled and stretched. " The light is getting much better now. We should be able to see the other ships' lights soon. I'll go and have a shower before the chief officer comes on watch. Call me if you need any help."

Captain Harris knocked the ash from his pipe and left the bridge.

Looking in the radar, I could see a group of targets at about fifteen miles away which I took to be the convoy assembling ready to get through the ice, bound for Helsinki. Altering the course slightly to put these echoes straight ahead, I lodged myself between the radar and the engine control. For a while I concentrated on keeping the ship as far as possible away from any hard looking ridges in the ice while keeping the course as closely as possible towards the cluster of ships. As the last of the snow cleared away and the stars started to twinkle in the sky, a group of lights became clearly visible low down ahead. There was now no need to look in the radar. The ship began to slow as I tried to negotiate an ice ridge that stretched away in either direction and was impossible to avoid. The ship got slower and slower as the ice got thicker and squeezed against the sides. I stood listening and feeling the vibration with the engine control in my hand. My excitement mounted as I started to judge the right moment to change course.

" Hard to Starboard!" I called to the wheelman. The bow of the Vanguard turned agonisingly slowly to starboard. " Mid ships, Hard to Port! "

I waved my hand to port in a gesture to go with my commands but the wheelman did not need my wave. The bow stopped its progress to starboard, for a moment hesitated and then started swinging to port. In this way I was hoping the ship would push the ice away and open up a crack ahead of the bow. After a little progress through the ice, the Vanguard stopped going forwards. We lay stationary, caught by the pressure of the ice. The engine power and the turning of the propeller had no effect except to vibrate the ships structure.

" Mid ships! " I ordered the wheelman and stood watching the rudder indicator return to the centre. Once I was certain the rudder was back amidships, I pulled the engine control to stop and then full astern. The ship bounced and vibrated madly as the propeller bit into the water at the stem but nothing happened. Then slowly at first, but with gathering speed, the ship started to move astern. Pieces of ice were thrown against the hull clanging and banging. I eased the engine control to stop and waited for the ship to slow.

" Keep her steady, " I said standing by the control and easing the handle to the ahead position. Once more the ship vibrated and bounced as the power built up. The wheelman clung to the wheel and I braced myself against the effect of the expected impact. The bow of the Vanguard rose above the ridge of ice and all forward motion stopped. Suddenly the ship began to turn to port and a crack in the ice appeared leading away in that direction. For an instant the Vanguard appeared to hesitate and then she sprang forward like a greyhound out of a trap. She gathered speed and the wheelman had to fight the steering wheel to maintain control. I slowed the engine once we were clear of the ice ridge, turned the bow onto a course that would intercept the convoy and grinned at the wheelman. Only then was I aware of Captain Harris standing at the back of the wheelhouse watching what I was doing.

" You enjoyed that, didn't you?" he said, the lips around his pipe smiling slightly. " You did that as well as I could and with out much practice."

After coming off watch, I was absorbed in making myself familiar with the plan for the start of cargo work to give to the chief officer before we arrived. Indeed, as the day wore on and the icebreaker kept the convoy waiting, everybody on board resigned themselves to having to wait a little longer before we arrived in Helsinki. It was frustrating. The weather had cleared and the wind dropped. The ice sparkled in the weak winter sun, the glare hurting the eyes unless wearing sunglasses. Five ships lay waiting for the convoy to start but the icebreaker wanted to wait for another two that were approaching through the ice from the south.

At midday I climbed the ladder to the bridge to begin my watch. As I walked into the wheelhouse, a voice over the radio was giving instructions to Captain Harris. I had arrived just in time to hear what was said.

" Captain Harris, welcome back to Finland. Would you please take up station at the rear of the convoy? I would like you to help the Burbeck, if that is necessary. Call me if you require any assistance. Try to keep both ships moving because I have to tow one of the other ships. If I have to let go the tow to come to your aid, we will be even later arriving in Helsinki."

" I understand," Captain Harris answered. " I've done that job before. See you in Helsinki in about five hours if the wind does not get up."

" Hi!" the third mates voice broke into my thoughts and the feeling of relief that we were finally to be on our way. " As you must have gathered, we are about to sail. All systems have been checked and are operating. All you have to do is sit back and follow the track left by the ice breaker."

There was soon a great deal of activity in the vicinity of the Vanguard as the icebreaker circled the ships breaking up the ice. When this was finished, the icebreaker took one of the smaller ships in tow by pulling its bow into a V shaped notch at the icebreakers stern. Like a family of ducks on a pond, the icebreaker as mother, the ships making up the convoy moved off one behind the other. For the rest of my watch nothing happened. The group of ships moved steadily through the ice in the direction of Helsinki. All I had to do was keep the Vanguard behind the Burbeck and in the ice channel. It was not exactly a major feat of navigation.

By the end of my watch at four o'clock, the glow of the lights of Helsinki was clearly visible and the lighthouses easy to see in the gathering gloom. After handing over to the chief officer, I went below. I tried to rest before dinner.

When I was called again, the ship was approaching a group of lights low down on the ice. As we got closer, I made out some men standing waiting. One after the other the ships stopped against the side of the ice channel, a ladder was lowered and s pilot climbed aboard. He handed the third mate his bag and a stout pole. Then we were off along the channel to Helsinki.

I did not sample the night life of Helsinki that trip. Because I was the newest officer, I agreed to look after the ship at night while the others went ashore. I did explore a little of Helsinki while having time off during the day.

The schedule of the Vanguard was to discharge in Helsinki for two days and then sail round the coast to a port called Kotka near the Russian border. To get there we followed a channel cut through the ice between the islands dotting the coast. The third mate told me that in the summer, the ship sailed outside the islands.

In Kotka, the return cargo of timber products was loaded. Once more I agreed to stay on board for the nights the ship was in port. That was from Friday to the following Wednesday. This was bliss for me used as I was to only having at the most two days and nights in port. When we got back to London we would have from Sunday to Friday in port.

Chapter 8

During my second voyage on the Vanguard, Dick Mortimer the Chief Officer, grandly announced to anybody who would listen, and as though he was making a great sacrifice, that he would stay on board on the Friday evening in Kotka so that I could go ashore and partake of the delights of the town. It was not a charitable gesture really because it was the turn of either the chief officer or the third mate to look after the ship.

To my surprise, before leaving the Vanguard, Bill and Rex came into my cabin, each took a beer out of my cupboard and instructed me on how I was to conduct myself when we had arrived at the restaurant. They were treating me as a first voyage cadet.

" You must follow the conventions and unwritten rules of the place," they instructed me. They were so serious, I had to suppress an instant urge to laugh. " All you have to do is follow what we do and you will be all right. Remember this is Finland not Hamburg."

After my instruction period and a couple more of my beers, we left the Vanguard and climbed the snow covered road from the docks to the town The central square proved to be an unpresupposing snow covered cobbled area with a bus stand in one corner. The grey statue of some long forgotten hero covered in the white splashes left by disrespectful sea gulls in the centre. My first immediate impression of the town was of a drab uniform greyness, of rows of dull wooden houses lining the road up from the docks and of equally grey two storey buildings lining each side of the central square.

The only colour in the whole scene was from the neon signs over the shops and the displays of goods in the windows, the lights from which were just casting a glow over the surrounding area.

Directly across the square from the road leading from the docks was a building somewhat taller than the rest of the structures fronting onto the square. As though in a hurry to get out of the cold and into the bright lights, Rex hurried ahead of Bill and I towards this building, neither looking to left or right. Whenever I paused to look around, Bill pulled me after Rex, telling me I could act like a tourist some other time. Closer inspection revealed a cafe on the ground floor, shrouded now in darkness. Next to the entrance to the cafe, double doors opened into the street and over these doors a flashing sign in red neon saying 'HOTEL' and something in Finish that I could not translate. Through the open doors I could make out a red carpet covering a flight of stairs but not much besides. Without any hesitation, Bill led us through the doors and up the stairs.

After climbing the red carpeted stairs, we left our coats, hats and gloves at the reception desk before pushing our way through double glass doors into a large, square room. Tables, covered in white table cloths were arranged randomly round the room but leaving a space for a highly polished piece of floor in front of a raised stage on which musical instruments were propped against some chairs. To one side of the room was a small bar decorated as though fronting a beach in the south seas and some doors that I took to lead to the kitchens. A number of people sitting at the tables looked up when we entered. On seeing that we were another group of men, the men already in the room soon resumed their drinking and conversation but the glances from a few of the women lingered a bit longer. One thing I noticed was the way most of the men sat together in twos or threes separated from similar groups of women sitting at other tables.

A waitress, dressed in a black dress and white apron, came to the door and led us to a table beside the dance floor. She smiled at Bill as she took our order.

" Hello, Bill," she said seeming to push her breasts, which were straining the fabric of her dress, very close to his eyes. " I heard the Vanguard had docked and thought you would be in here tonight. Who is your new friend? I haven't seen him before."

" This is Eddie, our new Second Mate." Bill waved a hand negligently in my direction. " Eddie this is Anna. She usually tries to bring us our drinks when we are in here."

I smiled and said hello.

Anna gave me a huge smile, though it tended to emphasise her broken and stained teeth, and went to fetch our order. While we waited for our drinks to arrive, Bill and Rex sat back in their chairs and openly surveyed the room paying special attention to the tables at which the unaccompanied women sat.

" Aren't we supposed to have a meal?" I asked innocently, having read that in Finland alcoholic drink was only available with a meal.

Bill looked at me as though he was trying to figure out if I was being sarcastic and then laughed when he realised my question was genuine. " You are right, as far as it goes. The law is quite explicit and we are supposed to have a meal while we are here if we want to drink. The management of most restaurants near ports in Finland let visiting sailors off the need to buy a meal. As far as I can make out, the regulation states that the inspectors will assess whether bar takings are in line with food takings, or something like that. It appears that most nights the relationship is true without us having to eat and so we get away with only having drinks." He grinned and turned to Rex. " Not many people in yet."

" No," Rex answered but his eyes never left the occupants of a table across the room. " See that girl over there, the one with the long hair and blue dress? She is the one I have been trying to chat up for the last few visits." Bill followed the direction in which Rex's eyes were looking and nodded.

" I hope the band is reasonable. Last time we were here the music was impossible to dance to." Bill thanked the waitress as she placed the drinks in front of us.

At this point, five young men dressed in black trousers, black waistcoats and green frilly shirts strolled into the room through the door I had assumed led to the kitchen. The band, I thought and as though to confirm my thoughts, they proceeded, as all bands do, to fiddle with their instruments, blow experimental notes and scales, get into a huddle and ignore the audience. With a quick introduction as though they were loath to speak but wished to let their music speak for itself, they were off, playing for all they were worth. Mid Atlantic Latin American with a sprinkling of pop was what the sound they made immediately suggested.

I was taken completely by surprise by what happened as soon as they started to play. During all my years at sea and in all the ports I had visited, I had never experienced anything like this. In an instant the atmosphere in the room was transformed. One moment there were groups of people sitting at tables talking and drinking quietly, the next the room was full of movement. Chair legs scraped across the floor, men rushed across the spaces between the tables and with a great deal of bowing and heel tapping, if not to mention a little pushing and shoving, asked the lady sitting at the table they had approached for a dance. Suddenly the dance floor was alive with couples dancing. It was astonishing, like a throw back to the golden age of Hollywood film and the great dancing era. I had this thought that I had been transported back to the nineteen twenties instead of nineteen sixty five. The whole process was so formal, so traditional and in many ways old fashioned, I had difficulty believing my eyes.

Lifting my drink, I sat back to watch. I was only aware when I turned to say something to my companions that they were no longer there. Rex and Bill had left the table unnoticed by me in the bedlam that had accompanied the start of the music. After a brief search, I discovered them both on the dance floor, chatting away as fast as they could speak to their partners. After two dances, like all the men, they shepherded their partners back to their tables and came to rejoin me.

" I reckon I have a good chance to take that girl back to her place tonight," Rex said, panting with the effort to recover from his exertions on the dance floor. His face was red and he mopped his brow with a large white handkerchief just like a farmer on a hot summers day. " She tells me her husband is away at the moment and she was quite chatty, which is a good sign. I'll have to be quick next time I want to dance with her so that I get to her table before any other bloke. What do you think Bill?"

" I think you are right about being on with her tonight," Bill remarked looking over to the table where Rex's girl was sitting with a friend. " As far as I could see, she seemed to wait for you to get to her table as you elbowed that Finn out of the way. I must say that was a nifty piece of work, young Rex. If I was in your shoes, I would chat her up as soon as you can and then get away early. Anna, the waitress told me Judy will be in later tonight and you know my feelings for Judy. The trouble is, I never know if she is going to want me to go home with her until it is too late to get anybody else. I will take things a bit easy until she arrives. I always like to find out how I stand with Judy before I try chatting up any other woman. It wouldn't do me any good if Judy arrived wanting me to be her date and I had to say I was already occupied for the night."

Bill looked at me and raised his eyebrows. " Eddie, why are you just sitting here? You have to be quick if you want to dance with a woman. All you have to do is pick out the one with whom you wish to dance, get ready when the band looks like they are going to start playing and, on the first note, make a straight line for her table. If you get there in time to get her on her feet, chat away like anything while you are dancing, even if she doesn't understand a word of English. What you are doing is making sure she grasps the fact that you are interested and wish to dance with her all night. Always remember, you have only two dances to get the message across but if you are successful, sometime during the evening, she will give you a nod even before the band starts playing and then wait until you get to her table, refusing the offers of any other man. When that happens you know you are in and it saves a whole lot of rushing around."

Bill's wide set, brown eyes sparkled as he spoke, excited by his theory of how to chat up women in a Finnish bar. He was obviously in love with the whole concept, alive to what he would call the chase and sunk into solving the problems of what to say and how to say it. I had the distinct impression that Bill did not mind if nothing came of his exploits as long as he had played, what to him, was a glorious game. The art and the excitement, for him, were in the subtle eye contact, the out manoeuvring of a rival, the getting through to a partner in broken Finnish, in other words the chase. What followed afterwards was a bonus but not too important to the success of the evening. What was maddening to many of his friends was that despite his seeming indifference to success or failure, it was in all the time I knew him the exception when Bill had to go back to the ship rather than to some girls flat.

" I think I will sit here for a while and watch what goes on, drink in the atmosphere so to speak," I said rather tentatively in the face of his obvious excitement.

" Don't wait too long! " Rex cut in, never taking his eyes off the woman he was trying to talk into letting him take back to her home. " Get up and dance with somebody, anybody, it does not matter who. You have to show all the women in the place that you are interested in them and you are available. "

" It's all a game to you two, isn't it? " I asked innocently smiling indulgently at their enthusiasm.

Bill rounded on me as though I had touched a raw nerve, his eyes for the first time rather hard and more black than sparkling brown. Now he really did look like a pirate. " If you want to enjoy sailing to Finland and to end up in one of these woman's beds of a night, you have to play the field their way," Bill said fiercely thrusting his face across the table towards me. " The Finns like a formal approach or the game as you call it. In many cases it will take a few trips to actually get invited back to the woman's flat but it is well worth the effort. On a good night, if you are lucky, a woman will consent to come back to your table for a drink at the end of the evening. If that happens you know you are in with a chance of going to bed with her that night,"

Bill looked round the room as the band finished another set. " In this country you have to work at relationships, talking to the woman you want to get to know at every available opportunity and making sure that even if you don't get any opportunity to talk, the woman is aware of your interest. When the band starts, even if you are too slow across the floor and somebody else gets to dance with her, by getting up and trying to get there you are showing your interest. If she wants to dance with you later on, she will give you a chance to ask her for a dance."

The band started to play, interrupting the passionate flow of words. Bill and Rex were off across the floor, each intent on their intended victim. I ordered another round of drinks, sat back in my chair and watched them guide their victims onto the floor. It wasn't long before the atmosphere overcame my cynicism, or maybe it was the drink, and I found myself being drawn into the game that all the other men in the room were playing.

A small, dark haired woman looked across at me during a pause in the music while the band members were discussing what to play next, smiling slightly when our eyes met before she looked away. Without being conscious of moving, I found myself standing by her table asking her to dance when the band next started to play. She smiled hugely and followed me onto the floor. Dancing close together, I talked about anything that came into my mind while she answered in broken, fractured English. At the end of the set, I led her back to her table and returned to my place.

Rex grinned broadly and nodded approvingly as I sat down. " That was a good start. You'll soon get the hang of it. Are you going to try to get her to dance again? "

What he said passed completely over my head because I wasn't listening to a word he was saying. Over Rex's shoulder, I was watching a tall blonde woman who had just walked into the restaurant. Out of the corner of my eye, I caught a flash as Bill waved to her. The face was round, almost fat with a very full mouth and wide set deep blue eyes. Silver blonde hair fell in cascades down over her shoulders and contrasted with the low cut black dress showing her clear tanned skin. The full breasts pushed hard against the fabric of her top, rounding out the material above a slimmish waist. Her skirt was that bit shorter than the other women in the room, not a lot but just noticeable, showing off her shapely legs. Almost all the men in the room, even those with female companions, had stopped talking and were looking at her. Judy I thought, from the way she smiled in answer to Bill's wave.

There were three other girls with Judy and they followed dutifully behind like obedient attendants or ladies in waiting, as she swept through the room to her table obviously aware of, but paying little attention to, the reaction of both men and women to her entrance. All eyes in the room seemed to watch her progress. As though on cue, the band had stopped playing the moment she entered the room leaving her the centre of attention but started to play again once she was seated and normal conversation resumed. Two of the girls accompanying Judy, sat back in their seats and surveyed the room as though assessing their prospects for the evening making remarks to each other as their eyes took in the clientele of the restaurant.

The third sat sipping her drink, talking quietly to Judy and hardly glancing at the other people in the room. She was rather short with wavy brown hair and wearing a tailored dark grey suit with the collar of her navy blue blouse over the top of her jacket. I was gazing in her direction when she looked up and her eyes met mine with a steady gaze. Her face was rather plain with only a trace of makeup but her eyes had endless depths. Those eyes appeared sad, drawing me into their depths much as a lake draws the eyes of a watcher on a moonlit night. I felt myself being drawn into those depths even across the floor of the room, drawn deeper towards the mystery that lay beneath the surface, drawn steadily down beneath the calm exterior. The spell was broken when the eyes looked away towards a man who was asking her to dance and she dutifully rose from her seat to follow him onto the dance floor.

I cannot now remember why the idea occurred to me then but as she started to dance I was certain before the evening was through I was going to charge across the floor and try to get her to dance with me. It was a conviction that grew as I watched her dancing with her partner but I lost sight of her when I saw Bill dancing with Judy. They were oblivious to all the other couples, completely tied up in each other as though they had been waiting for this moment and were excited at it's arrival.

After two dances, the band stopped playing and left the room for their break. All the customers sat down to wait out the pause in the dancing and to continue drinking. I lent back in my chair, trying to catch the eye of the girl who had come into the room with Judy and only half listening to Rex and Bill discussing what the were going to do for the rest of the evening. Once more the woman sitting with Judy looked in my direction and once more I was drawn into the depths of her eyes. When she looked away there was a slight smile on her lips as though she had scored some sort of point. I was trying to fathom this out when Bill pulled my arm.

" Judy has told me she is on her own this weekend. I will be going back to her place after the restaurant closes," Bill said matter of fact. " She found out from the ships agent that we were in port today and has been preparing the ground for us to be together while the Vanguard is here. How are things going with you two? "

" I'm not sure what is happening," Rex remarked looking across the room to the girl he had been dancing with. " Anna lives out in the country and it would mean a taxi ride there and back if I want to take her home. I am not sure I want to go that far. Besides, I can't really afford to pay for a taxi. You must know I am due back in Helsinki tomorrow afternoon to see Hilda and I don't want to put my relationship with her in any danger by spending all my money on a taxi trip just for a night with Anna."

" Oh don't be so silly!" Bill exclaimed grimacing in mock horror at Rex. " You don't often get the chance to line up somebody here because you look after the ship so that you can have the time off to go to Helsinki. Take Anna home tonight with what money you have now and then get some more off the Old Man when you get back to the ship in the morning. That way you can enjoy a night with Anna and get to see Hilda in Helsinki over the weekend."

" It's all right for you to talk that way. You earn a lot more than me. In addition, I have to consider how much I send home every month towards the cost of buying a house after I get married." Rex said indignantly.

" That's no excuse! " Bill answered. " I have a wife, two kids and a mortgage to finance from my earnings. As you are aware, I have to be very careful with the money I earn, which is one of the reasons I never get too hitched to one girl and have to do a lot of travelling. Do you think he should draw some more money tomorrow so that he can take Anna home tonight and still see Hilda in Helsinki over the weekend? " Bill turned to me for help.

I didn't know what to say, deciding to stay as neutral as possible so as not to upset one or the other. " How am I supposed to give advice when I haven't got all the facts? Everybody I sailed with on tankers took every opportunity to go to bed with a woman whenever it arose. What you have to realise however, we had no idea when the next chance of meeting, let alone sleeping with, a woman would come. I don't know how much you need to go with this Anna tonight or whether you should wait until you get to see Hilda on Saturday. If you are as broke as you are making out, surely you can hold your sexual drive in for a day? "

" You aren't much help are you with that holier than thou attitude," Rex growled looking sourly at me.

" Hey, don't take your frustration out on me! " I shot back feeling trapped between the certainty of Bill and Rex's lack of funds. " You're the one who has a fiancee at home, goes to see a girl in Helsinki and now wants to have the same here as well. On top of that, you want to do all these things without spending any money. I haven't a girl in England, have not been out at night in Finland until now and am not too short of money, so how am I supposed to advise you? I know it sounds silly to both of you but if I was married or planned to get married, I would not be chatting up women here. I would be saving all my money. "

" That's all very well for you to talk but it doesn't help me, " Rex snapped back angrily.

" For Christ sake Rex, go and ask her if you can take her home and then decide what you are going to do,

" Bill said losing interest in Rex's problem. This was not surprising because, as I was to find out later, Bill did things and then thought his way out of the consequences afterwards.

" I'll lend you the money for tonight, " I told Rex on a sudden impulse. It was well known fact on the Vanguard that Rex was short of money and for some reason despite his grumbling, I was feeling sorry for him. " You can pay me back when you get your finances sorted out."

Rex looked at me for a long time as though weighing up my motive, working out what I thought I would gain from lending him the money.

" OK, " he said suddenly making up his mind. " I'll see you when I get back to the ship in the morning. You can lend me the money to get me to Helsinki. If Anna wants me to take her home, I expect I will have to leave early. She was telling me earlier that she has to leave before the band finishes so that she is not too late home."

Bill and Rex continued to dissect the 'talent' as they called the women sitting round the room and to speculate on who would end up with whom. Looking across the room to the table at which Judy and her party sat, I did not join in because my mind was on other things. After a while the band wandered back from their rest, had a consultation and then began to play.

Without a conscious effort, not realising what I was doing, I found myself beside Judy's table looking into those deep, sad eyes. The woman looked up at me with one eyebrow raised but she smiled the same slightly secretive smile I had seen earlier and she got up from her chair to accompany me onto the dance floor.

" Do you speak English?" I asked as we started to dance and the relief flooded through my body when she nodded.

" My name is Eddie, " I went on remembering Bill's advice to keep talking.

" Kirsti." she said, her Finnish accent very strong. " I studied English at school and now work for a company which does a lot of business with England. Translating the documents gives me a lot of practice in using English. The company sent some people to London to meet our clients a few years ago and I went with them. It gave me a chance to practice my English among English people. "

" Did you like London? " I asked. At least, I thought, we have found something to talk about straight away and I am not desperately trying to find things to say.

" It was so big and busy compared even to Helsinki not to mention Kotka, that I was confused all the time I was staying there. Everybody in the streets or on the tube are rushing along as though they did not have time to stop and think. It gave London a sense of being exciting but rather breathless. " She screwed up her nose before going on. " One thing I did notice was that we seemed to get wet every time we left our hotel!"

" It doesn't rain in London all the time," I said defensively.

The rest of the dance and what we talked about has faded from my memory, lost in the mists of time and mixed up with similar occasions in other places and at other times. With an effort, I can still recall the closeness of her body, the smell of her perfume but mainly the memory is of those eyes pulling me down into their depths. Big brown orbs, pulling me down, making me want to disappear, to explore the mystery that lay under the surface. It was with a feeling of being cheated that I escort her back to her chair at the end of the dance. I could have stayed on the dance floor looking into those eyes for the rest of the evening, not concerned about what happened afterwards. Floating in those depths, exploring the half hidden mystery sinking without trace, that is what I remember about my first encounter with the night life of Finland.

" You will let me dance with you again? " I asked tentatively as I helped her with her chair.

" You will have to take your turn with all the other men," she said but smiled at the flash of my disappointment that I could not keep from my face. " I was only making fun of you, Eddie. I will have to dance with whoever gets to my table first for a while, it is what is expected of me. If you have trouble getting to me before other men, then later in the evening I will refuse all offers and wait for you to come to my table. " She squeezed my hand as I turned to go. A feeling of elation swept over me as I walked back to, our table.

True to her word, Kirsti looked across to my table later in the evening and brushing all other offers aside waited patiently for me to come and take her onto the dance floor. We dance close together, hardly talking but very conscious of the warmth of our bodies through our clothes. Towards the end of the dance I asked her where she lived.

" Just round the corner in a block of flats," she answered. " I have Rachel staying with me. " She nodded at one of the women sitting at the table with Judy.

" Can I walk you home when the band stops? " I asked a bid formally but I could think of no other way of broaching the subject.

Kirsti laughed, the first time I heard her laugh, and pushed herself closer to me. " Of course you can take me home. Anyway, there is no need to ask too many questions now because it looks like we are going to have a drink all together for the last part of the evening."

I looked across at the table where Bill and I had been sitting. A waiter was putting some more chairs round the table and Bill was already seated with Judy. At the end of the dance, Kirsti and I joined them. Rex was saying good night to his friends and getting the doorman to phone for a taxi, obviously ready to take Anna home.

Later, when the band finished playing and had put away their instruments, we collected our coats and drifted down into the street. Judy with Bill, Rachel with another man I did not know though by the way they talked, Bill had met him before, Kirsti holding tight to my arm and a tall heavily built man on his own. Before we had left the restaurant, Kirsti had asked us all back to her flat for coffee.

Kirsti's flat was on the first floor of a block overlooking the harbour, a typically large window providing a view of the ships and the port approaches dotted with rocky islands. Off the entrance hall on one side was the bathroom and on the other a kitchen. The lounge or living area was large with a kind of raised stage at one end reached by three steps. On the raised platform was a dining table and chairs cut off from the rest of the room by a rail. A door led off the dining area to what I took to be a bedroom while another door opened into another room at the end of the flat. Kirsti took all the coats, put them on hangers in the hall and went into the kitchen to make some coffee. Coffee served, Kirsti sat beside me on the settee ignoring the man who had come on his own and who now sat on my other side. This Finn sat glowering at us, his bulk and size looking even more pronounced in the close confines of the flat. Kirsti made her intentions for the rest of the evening plain by the way her hand strayed over my thigh but I began to wonder what the big Finn's intentions were if Kirsti continued to show affection for me.

Bill and Judy left after a while but still the Finn sat on the settee showing no signs of leaving but ominously flexing his muscles. He and Kirsti argued in Finnish at one point, an argument that I could not understand but from the Finn's gestures it concerned me. By the thunderous glances he cast in my direction, my presence in Kirsti's flat after he left to go home was not desired. The situation was getting out of hand and I did not know what to do. It was obvious even to me that the Finn was not going to budge until I left. Rachel said something to Kirsti, got up and went to her bedroom holding her boyfriends hand. Still the Finn sat massive and immovable on the settee.

" I'll help you with the cups," I said, collecting them onto a tray and carrying them into the kitchen. Kirsti followed me, her lips drawn into a thin line and her eyes no longer deep mysterious pools but blazing with anger.

" My husband's friend," she said with a shrug. " As soon as he saw me at the restaurant on my own, he wanted to come home with me. He has been trying to get into bed with me for years but I won't let him. When he saw that I was coming home with you, he set himself up to protect me. Not that he is worried about me being with you, just jealous that it is you rather than him." She slammed the coffee pot onto the top by the sink with such force I thought she had broken it.

" Look," I said, being very gallant though not feeling that way in the slightest. " I don't want to cause any trouble for you and, besides, he could pick me up with one hand and throw me out of the window if he wanted. What do you suggest we do?"

She considered her reply for a moment and then grinned. " Say good night to me and then leave to walk back to the docks. He will leave with you to make sure you have gone back to the ship. You will have to go on board if you think he is still following you when you reach the ship. When you think he has finally gone home, come back here and I will be waiting for you."

" What happens if he doesn't leave with me?" I asked in a strangled voice.

" Oh, he will if he wants to think he has any chance with me in the future! " Kirsti was emphatic.

I had difficulty in suppressing a giggle of fear but went to fetch my coat anyway. As soon as he saw me enter the lounge with my coat, the Finn heaved his bulk out of the chair and made ready to leave. He towered above me, looking even larger than he did before, the hands that fastened his coat so large, the fingers had trouble getting hold of the buttons. For a brief moment, I had second thoughts about leaving the flat at the same time as him, visions of him picking me up and throwing me into the harbour flashing through my head but I grinned bravely and led the way from the flat.

We walked down the road towards the harbour together, the tall and the short, not saying anything, each wrapped in his own thoughts. At first I was scared especially when the road became particularly dark but it was soon obvious that he was only going to make sure I went back to my ship. I would have found the situation funny if he had not looked so serious and capable of tearing me apart with his bare hands. Actually, later I did laugh and embellished the tale to my friends to make it sound amusing. I know people say that really big people are often gentle at heart but I can tell you, I was not about to test the theory with him.

When we approached the docks, I cheerily said good-bye and ducked between a pile of timber and a shed as though taking a short cut back to the ship. In reality, all I wanted to do was get out of the light and out of the sight of my companion. Looking over my shoulder, I saw the Finn, enormous in outline against the street lights, gazing after me. Involuntarily, my steps quickened to put as much distance between us as possible in case he thought of coming after me. I was too aware of the damage he could inflict with one blow from his massive fist. All right, he might have been as gentle as a mouse but through my head was running the refrain from Jack and the Beanstalk : I smell the blood of an Englishman! I wasn't about to take the chance of finding out if he was as tough as he looked.

Finding a hiding place close to the quay, I watched him as the minutes ticked away, agonisingly slowly until I thought I had been rooted to this spot for hours. Finally, he strode off into the night. When he was out of sight, I lent against a stack of timber, the sweat pouring down my face and my legs so weak, I almost fell. I began to wonder whether the prospect of a night with Kirsti was worth such a release of nerves and fear. Leaning back against the timber, I felt drained and tired, all I could think of was my bunk aboard the Vanguard only a few inviting steps away. Kirsti's flat seemed a long way away through enemy territory, the terrors of the journey back unimagined. With a sigh, deciding that after all this effort I had to get some reward, I stepped out of my hiding place to begin retracing my steps.

The road stretched empty before me but, like a thief in the night, I hugged the shadows expecting at any moment a tall figure to materialise and confront me. My heart was in my mouth at the least noise or sight of another person but nothing happened. All was quiet as Kotka slept, not a car passed, hardly a light showed in the windows of the houses. It was as though I was on my own, the only person silly enough to be out at this late hour.

After negotiating the streets from the docks to the building containing Kirsti's flat, I waited in the shadows across the road in case the Finn had returned here to wait for me. Nothing stirred. In a rush, I crossed the street flattening myself against the wall beside the entrance to her flat. With one last anxious look round, I rang the bell of Kirsti's flat. My heart was beating as waited anxiously for her to open the door.

A noise made me turn but it was only a cat or some other animal rustling through some discarded papers. The door lock clicked and I pushed it open to get inside as quickly as possible. Closing the door behind me, my breathing was shallow and coming in short gasps.

The corridor and the stairs were dimly lit but I found my way back to the door of her apartment by feel as much as sight. Kirsti was standing just inside the open door waiting for me and she smiled broadly when I came into her hall. A white dressing gown covered her from head to foot but from the way her nipples showed through the cloth, she did not have much on underneath. As soon as I was inside her flat, her arms came round my neck and she pushed the door shut with her foot. We stayed locked together like that for some time and then taking my hand, she helped me through the dimly lighted lounge and into her bedroom. We made love hungrily, exploring each other's bodies as if this was a new experience. After a time, we slept the sleep of the deeply satisfied.

The next night, after a day looking after the ship, I sat alone at a table in a different restaurant in another part of Kotka from the one at which I had met Kirsti. After lunch, Rex had come to claim his money and left for Helsinki. Brian had left on the same bus to be with his girlfriend Sylvie and it was Bill's turn to keep watch over the ship. Being Bill he had persuaded Captain Harris to give him a pass so that Judy could spend the night with him. It had been my turn to keep ship but Dick had told me to go ashore because he wanted to stay on board. Feeling rather alone, I sipped my drink and watched the other people drifting into the room ready for the entertainment

Kirsti arrived as we had arranged, dressed in a tight fitting dress which clung to the curves of her body and made her look even smaller than she really was. Spotting me sitting waiting, her face broke out into a big smile and she swept over to my table not waiting for the waitress to show her the way.

" Hello, Eddie," she said as the waiter helped her into a chair, her eyes deep pools behind her smile. " Have you been waiting long? "

" No," I answered. " I always arrive early when I am looking forward to something. Do you want to eat straight away or have a drink and a dance first?"

" I'll have a drink now and eat later, " she replied, those deep brown eyes of hers gazing into mine. " Did you get back to the Vanguard in time to start work this morning? It was a rush in the end even though we woke up early. Making love in the mornings certainly slows down my reactions during the day."

" I was back in plenty of time. In fact, the dockers did so little loading, there was nothing for all three of us officers to do. We sat round talking all morning. I suppose you lounged around in your dressing gown until it was time to come and see me."

" I went shopping and wrote some letters. Then I prepared myself to come and meet you, " she countered with a smile.

We sat at the table and talked about ourselves, what our lives were like, danced a little and had a typical Finnish meal. The time passed unnoticed and suddenly the band was playing the last dance and it was time to return to her flat.

It was snowing when we walked through the town. Our bodies built up by contact and promise an anticipation of our coming lovemaking. We did not hurry knowing that it was Sunday the next day and there would not be any need for me to return to the ship. There would be time to awake and lie in bed, to relax in each other's company.

Back in the flat, I sat on the settee listening to some music, at ease with the world and waiting for Kirsti to bring some coffee. The lights were low and the evenings drinking had blurred my perception of the passing time. This, I told myself is what life should be like. I was floating on a sea of goodwill, all my senses coloured by a rosy glow that told me that the world was whole and perfect. A good meal with a woman who I found interesting and the anticipation of love making to come, had relaxed me. I had no worries about the future, no worries about actions and reactions, only today and now was what mattered. At that time, that was how I wanted life to be. All I wanted was to sail in my ships, drifting with the trend of events in my small circle without the need to take on commitments. To me this was true happiness, divorced from the humdrum problems of so many relationships. Tomorrow would be another day but for the moment I could live as though there were no tomorrow. Such attitudes are selfish but that is the price society has to pay for letting people be free.

Kirsti poured out the coffee and sat down on the settee by my side, running her finger through my hair as she did so. She kissed me and wrapped he arms round my neck, holding me tight.

" We must make the most of tonight and tomorrow, " she whispered in my ear, a sad smile lighting her eyes. " My husband returns early next week and I have no idea when he will be going away again. We must make love as though we are trying to satisfy each other for ever."

I sat back, pushing her slightly away and looked into her eyes, wondering what to say. There was not a lot of conversation in a statement like that. She was telling me that very soon I must make way for her husband but before that, I had to make sure I satisfied her with my love making. I wondered whether she really was attracted to me or if I was the person who happened to arrive at the right place at the right time to fulfil her needs. From the first meeting the night before, she had appeared to have a huge need for a man. Pushing the thought of her motives out of my mind, I grinned and held her tight.

" My husband and I don't go out together very often when he is at home, so there is very little chance of you seeing me in town. If you do see me while I am with him, don't try to say anything to me though you can nod if you like. I can always say you are a friend of Judy and Bill. It is funny really. When we are together, he tends to be very possessive though I know he is no saint when he is away."

She laughed at my expression and stroked my brow. " Don't look so defensive and partly shocked. I wanted you to make love to me from the first time we danced. This will have been the best weekend I have had for a long time. I feel I am truly happy. When I am lonely in the future, I will look back and hug this feeling to myself. I will dream about you, about what we did together and try to recreate those feelings in my daydreams. My girlfriends will not say anything to anybody because they will not want to limit their own opportunities to spend the night with a man other than their husbands. They all carry on in the same way. I expect all the husbands know what goes on when they are away but ignore it as long as there is not a scandal. Lets face it, all our husbands want the opportunities this gives them. What we have to hope is that when he next goes away, you are still running to this port on the Vanguard. "

" I hadn't thought about what happens to us after this weekend, " I told her truthfully, smiling slightly. " When you came to the restaurant last night, I knew that of all the women in the room, you were the one I most wanted to dance with. After we sat at the same table, talking and laughing, it seemed only natural that we would come back here and make love. Come on. Drink your coffee and let the future look after itself."

She drank her coffee while never taking her eyes off my face. It was as though she wanted to etch the picture firmly in her memory to be recalled when she needed reminding of what it had been like spending the night with me. Putting down her cup, she stated to unbutton my shirt, softly running the tips of her fingers over my chest as she did so. Feeling a bit like a

Hollywood movie star, I lifted her off the settee and carried her into the bedroom. We abandoned ourselves to our passion that night and the next day, not knowing if we would ever meet again. It was as though we both felt we had to fit a lifetime of lovemaking into those few hours. Again and again we roused each other and finally we slept as darkness started to creep over the harbour the following evening.

Almost two months passed, the pattern of sea voyages broken by periods ashore in Helsinki, Kotka and London. True to her word, Kirsti did not come to the restaurant in Kotka again though I went there quite frequently in the hope that she would have the chance to come and see me again. On a few occasions, I did bump into her in the street or in a shop but we merely nodded greetings as we had agreed and passed on our different ways. The large Finn seemed to turn up all over the place but he only glared at me whenever I waved a cheery greeting. Life was peaceful and uneventful when measured against the dramatic happenings out in the world or the troubles and tribulations suffered by other people. By accompanying Rex and especially Bill ashore, my circle of friends expanded and there was always some woman to dance with and occasionally sleep with when I wanted to have companionship. Nothing came up to stir the calm serenity of my life and I do believe I was as happy as I have ever been. It may have been happiness at the expense of commitment to the world, it may have been extremely selfish in using women for my own satisfaction and giving nothing in return but at the time this did not trouble me. All I knew was that I was happy and did not want the times to end.

Chapter 9

One morning, as Vanguard sailed through the Baltic Sea bound for Helsinki, my friends Bill and Brian were lounging in my cabin drinking coffee and passing comments about the laziness of all Second Mates. I was propped up in my bunk sipping the sweet strong coffee they had brought me when giving me a call. This had become, for us, a ritual while the ship was at sea and I was working the twelve until four watch morning and afternoon. Bill would arrive straight from his rounds of the engine room and the two of them would sit talking at me, through me or ignoring me while I struggled awake, took a shower and drank more coffee.

That morning as I recall, the Vanguard was rolling gently, the rays of the sun casting moving shadows across the cabin bulkhead. Once more, the sound of the water washing along the side of the ship was background to their talk and I lay back only vaguely aware of what they were saying.

" It's about time we had one of our famous parties, " Bill was saying when I became fully aware of direction the conversation was taking. " Let us set the date and start organising."

" Why so formal and official? " I asked curiously, sitting up in my bunk and grinning. " Surely, all we have to do is get hold of some women and off we go."

" It is not as simple as that, " Bill replied looking so serious I had to suppress a laugh. " Captain Harris is very strict, as you must have noticed, about who comes on board his ship while it is in port. That is especially so if it involves a lot of people at the same time. He has only ever allowed us to have a party aboard the Vanguard if everything is done properly, in other words how he judges ship's officers should act. What he wants is for us to send out formal invitations, obtain passes for those people we invite to get into the docks, have proper food laid on and the saloon decorated with a place for a bar. You don't have to worry about the Captain, I will get his permission."

" I'll get the Steward to order any special food we need. I have a list of what we ordered last time, " Brian put in just as seriously. " The Steward is usually very good at getting what we want. Rex, the Third Mate, can look after the decoration of the saloon and the music. He maybe a bit slow but he seems to be able to manage."

" I'll get Dick, the Chief Officer, to organise some coloured lights for the deck and a sailor for the gangway watch to help everybody on board. " Bill was ticking everything off a mental list. " That is the music, decorations and food. How about the booze? "

They both looked innocently at me and then grinned.

" All right, I will try my hand at looking after the booze, " I said, realising that, from what had been hinted at, all the officers coming to the party contributed something to help the arrangements. " What sort of drink do we usually serve at these parties? "

Bill considered for a moment and then replied with a shrug of his shoulders. " Once we have designated the jobs, we usually leave the fine details to the person in charge of that part of the arrangements. If you want to be fancy, you could try your hand at a punch. If not, get together some different bottles of spirits, some mixers and cases of beer. You don't have to worry too much what we put out to drink because Finns drink anything filling the glass in their hands. You must have noticed what the Finns are like when it comes to boozing. All you have to do is tell any of the officers who are coming what you want them to contribute and collect their contribution before the party. "

" I make an excellent punch even if I do say so myself. All I need is the right ingredients and a large glass bowl, " I said trying to think of what I had put in the last punch I had made and when, " What about women? "

Bill laughed at my now serious expression. " Some of the other officers have girlfriends in Helsinki and they invite those if they want to. Brian and I, through our contacts, make up the numbers. Sylvie, Brian's girl, can be relied upon to get a few friends along. I have a number of contacts ashore who are more than willing to help at the mention of free booze. Thus, everybody leaves the women to us."

Turning to Brian, he said. " I think that is all the domestic arrangements. All we have to do next is make a list of who we are going to invite. There are eleven officers on board who will want to be there. If my calculations are correct, we need to invite twelve women to make sure there are plenty of partners plus any couples who might come. If we get the invites to them when we arrive in Helsinki this trip, we should be able to hold the party next time we are there."

Smiling in my direction, he remarked. " As the keeper of the booze, it will be your job to keep a record of what is spent. We demand a cash payment for the food, because that is brought for us by the steward, and for any other out of pocket expenses. The total at the end is divided by the number who come and you have to collect the money. As for the drinks. Each person will give you what ever you ask so you had better draw up a list and start getting people to supply their share."

" I suppose we will impose the usual rules? " Brian asked ticking these off with the finger of one hand against his palm of his other. " No monopolising one woman all night, even if she was invited by you. That way everybody circulates and gets to talk to all the other people. Part of the costs which Eddie will have to take into account is the cost of the taxis home after the party has finished."

I climbed out of my bunk and went to have a shower, leaving the two of them heads together, furiously writing on a piece of paper. When I came back to my cabin, they were good naturedly arguing about the merits of who to invite and whether the Captain would have any guests along.

The preparations for the party progressed slowly as the ship sailed towards Helsinki and more people became involved. Captain Harris gave his blessing and offered the spare cabin on the Captains deck as the ladies cloak room. Brian somehow produced some official looking cards with the company crest and the name of the ship emblazoned on the front. All those who wanted to invite their own guests busily filled in these cards all ready for delivery on arrival in Helsinki. Rex spent many an hour while off watch testing his 'sound system' in different places in the saloon until he was certain he had the right sound distribution. He asked me to come and help but it all sounded the same to me no matter where he placed the speakers, making Rex usher me out of the room in despair. A box of decorations, mainly intended for use if the ship was at sea for Christmas, was produced by Dick and after some debate everybody agreed they were adequate for our needs. Dick tested the coloured lights over the boat deck and made sure they could be attached at the top of the gangway. After the initial rush of enthusiasm, all went quiet as the ship returned to London and Helsinki seemed to get further away.

On the next trip, as the Vanguard sailed northwards through the Baltic Sea, the wind force rose and the ship started moving vigourously through a rough sea. The excitement on board mounted steadily as the ship got closer to Helsinki but everybody was looking anxiously at the weather. Would bad weather slow the ship and make it arrive late in Helsinki? everybody was asking. It was the fervent hope of the party organisers that the Vanguard would arrive in Helsinki the day before the party was due to take place so that there would be time to make any last minute arrangements and to prepare the ship properly. As the gale increased in strength and water started to wash across the decks as the waves increased in height, all hearts fell and the ship had to be slowed to avoid any damage to its structure.

Luckily, the bad weather did not delay the arrival too much and at dusk the night before the party, the leading lights of Helsinki came into view. The pilot was soon on board and in a short time, the ship was tied up alongside the berth. Impatiently, all the officers went through their duties for the arrival of the ship in port but at last the party planners assembled in Dick's cabin for a last minute briefing.

Sipping beer from a can, Bill referred to his list. " Rex are all the decorations ready to put up? "

" Yes," Rex replied. " I will need half an hour to get them into place after we finish cargo working tomorrow night but that should be plenty of time. The tapes are sorted in order ready to be played once we have the sound system set up and there are a few pieces of furniture to arrange. That will not be too much trouble after we have knocked off because I have all ready planned how to do it. Don't worry, Bill, I will have the saloon in working order long before the guests arrive."

" That's what I like to hear," Bill said. " Eddie? "

" My cabin resembles the out store of an off licence at the moment, " I replied having spent the time since leaving London trying to avoid tripping over cases of beer and bottles of spirits which the other officers had kept depositing on my cabin floor. As more kept appearing every time I came off watch, I began to wonder whether it was a party for alcoholics rather than guests. " I managed to get the cook to lend me a large stainless steel bowl for making the punch and I will prepare that a few hours before hand. I need all the glasses that people said they would lend me but they can wait until tomorrow. If there are not enough to go round, the steward has a few spare hidden away and he will break those out for us. I think it would be a good idea if we served the first drink to everybody as they arrive and then leave it to individuals to get their own drinks after that."

" Dick? " Brian looked at Dick over the list he was inspecting.

" The lights are all ready in place or they only need a small adjustment tomorrow night when we finish. I have arranged for one of the sailors to be on gangway duty tomorrow night while the party is taking place, paying him some fiddled overtime, but we should give him a few beers to ward off the cold! "

" Right," I said making a note on my list.

" I gave out the invitations the last time we were here so all I can do now is make a few phone calls to make sure that everybody can still come." Bill opened another can of beer and looked more closely at his list. " I will arrange to meet the guests at the dock gate. Is Captain Harris coming? "

" Yes," Dick replied. " He reckons he wouldn't miss one of your parties unless there was something really important he had to attend to. He says he has invited four people, the agent and his wife and dock manager and his wife."

The preparations all complete, the ship settled down for the night, peaceful and quiet in port.

In the gathering gloom of the following evening, with the sun sinking below the level of the trees west of the port, I stood impatiently on deck of the Vanguard watching one of the sailors drive a crane to pull hatch covers across the top of the holds. While Bill and the others were having their evening meal and then getting ready for the party, it was my job to make sure the ship was secured for the night. With the noise of the hatch wheels in their guides, the screech of steel on steel, drowning out all other sounds, the last cover closed with a bang against the stops and then silence descended over the ship. Seagulls could be heard again, screaming and fighting near the stern of the Vanguard as they tried to grab their share of the scraps discarded from the evening meal. Looking around the deck to make sure everything was secure, I noticed how the lights reflected brightly in the water as they beamed down from the now still and silent cranes on the shore. It was almost dark and all the ships tied up along the quay fore and aft of the Vanguard were settling down for the night.

" That's all the covers closed and secured, Second Mate," the seaman remarked as he climbed down to the deck from one of the ship's cranes. " If that is all for tonight, I am off to grab a bite to eat and then up the road for the night. See you in the morning."

I nodded briefly and wished him a pleasant evening with his girlfriend but he was away so fast I doubt he heard what I said. Wishing I was in my cabin getting ready for the party, I had to walk round the ship checking everything was secured and in order. In the seaman's rest room, I briefed the sailor who was to take the watch that night about where to find me and not to hesitate to fetch me if anything was wrong. He grinned wickedly, made some comment about even if I had gone to bed with one of the girls from the party, he'd fetch me and then assured me seriously he would look after the ship. With one final look around the decks of the now silent ship, I turned gratefully into the accommodation and went to my cabin.

When I had showered and dressed, I piled the ingredients for the punch into the bowl and went to the saloon. The others had already gathered, dressed and prepared for the party. Putting the bowl in the kitchen, I greeted them cheerfully. Fetching ice and lemons from the refrigerator, I measured the right proportions of ingredients into the bowl. With a flourish, I gave it a stir and stepped back. Dramatically holding the ladle like Fanny Craddock on television and making sure that there was at least one of the other people watching, I dipped the ladle into the bowl and then took an exaggerated sip of the liquid.

" What does it taste like? " Bill asked, looking over my shoulder to see what I was up to with the punch.

" Try some, " I said, dipping the ladle into the punch once more and holding it to his lips to help him sip. " The taste is not so bad and it is very drinkable, even if I say so myself. "

" Christ! " Bill exclaimed holding his throat. " This will knock their heads off if they have too much. Actually, joking apart, it is quite smooth and very drinkable. A few of these and all the inhibitions will drop away. What did you put into it? "

" That is my secret, " I answered, laughing at the look Bill gave me as though to say I had no right to keep secrets from him. To hide my amusement, I went back to my cabin to get all the other bottles and drinks. With a show of hard work, I arranged the rest of the bottles, the glasses and the ice bucket on a table covered in a white clothe at one end of the saloon. Once the punch bowl was in pride of place on the table, all was ready.

Brian arrived rather breathlessly with some small dishes full of crisps and peanuts and placed these at strategic locations around the room. On the way back to the pantry for some more, he took a sip from the offered ladle and nodded his approval as he disappeared through the door. Rex came down from a pair of steps, took a sip and surveyed the decorations he had been adjusting, making some remark about preferring beer. Satisfied with the decorations, he adjusted the switch on his tape deck and music blared out across the room, shattering the peace and vibrating the eardrums until they cried out in protest.

" Not so loud, " somebody shouted above the noise of the music, their voice strained and hollow as it fought to be heard above the beating drum and the bass guitar. " We are not all deaf! A few of us wish to remain that way! "

Having finished arranging the bottles, cans and glasses, I poured drinks for those in the room and took a seat in the corner to await the arrival of the guests. Looking round the saloon with the main lights still fully on, I noted it was not the Savoy, indeed it was rather shabby and in need of a coat of paint. Still, I thought with the lights turned down low and a lot of people filling the space, cigarette smoke and noise, it would pass for one of the seedier nightclubs in Hull.

Soon after I had sitting down, Brian and Bill left to go to the dock gate with the passes for the guests. As if this was a signal, all the other officers were suddenly in the saloon demanding drinks while they waited for the visitors to arrive and the party to start. As I dished out the drinks, I had to bite back a retort about helping to set up the party but I let it ride with a smile and a glass of my punch.

We didn't have very long to wait, indeed I had hardly served all the officers with drinks when I heard excited voices drifting up the stairs from the deck below. Suddenly the room was full of women, each taking off their coat and being introduced. I found it impossible to remember all the names and faces as I rushed around making sure that everybody had a drink in their hand. One of the girls I did remember, Sylvie's friend Maria, her eyes big behind a large pair of spectacles. For some reason I cannot fathom even now, when our eyes met on being introduced, I felt there was a spark between us as though there was an attraction like the opposite poles of a magnet. Before I had time to think about it, we were swept apart and some more people were calling for drinks.

Soon, Maria and that look were forgotten as other women, other faces and names bubbled in confusion around me. Voices filled my ears and colours swirled in a kaleidoscopic display that beat against my mind in a confusing picture, changing and reforming until it flashed like a dress on an African woman. Somebody grabbed my arm and I was dancing with a woman I could not remember seeing before but, remembering Bill's advice, talked as fast as I could. Time passed in a whirl of dancing, drinking and talking with people who I began to find hard to place or to put names to faces. Some food arrived and there was a temporary lull in the noise and the laughter but then the whole process started again.

By this time the world around me had taken on a rosy, misty glow where everything seemed to add to my happiness, where the people and the world looked wonderful, where all thought of strife and hardship had vanished. One of the women suggested she be shown round the bridge and, by general consent, it was agreed that I would be the best person to act as a guide. For a while I was solely concerned with conducted tours of the bridge for those who wanted a tour. Through my alcoholic haze, I found it very difficult to concentrate on what I was showing the visitors and my explanations must have been quite weird to the expert but the people gasped in the right places, appeared to be impressed by what I said and came away from the bridge talking and laughing as though they had enjoyed the experience.

After the last group had returned to the saloon, I poured myself a drink. All the people in the room seemed to be talking at once, making the noise of their chatter and the music vibrate inside my head as though a part of my brain had become a gigantic sounding board. Cigarette smoke hung in the air in sheets and layers, stirred languidly by a fan in one comer but not dispersing and the room had become hot and stuffy. Even in my heightened state of semi drunkenness, I could see that this was having some effect on a few of the women who appeared to be shedding clothes as though what they had on had gone out of fashion. The sweat was pouring down my back and the walls of the room had started to move in and out.

The music and the level of noise was now bashing away at my brain, mixing with the affect of the drink to make me feel I was floating a few feet off the deck, free and above the mere mortals attached to the earth.

Leaving my latest drink on the side, I poured myself an orange juice and fought my way out of the saloon into the comparative quiet of the corridor outside. There was a roaring in my head and I sank gratefully to the deck with my shoulders against the bulkhead. People who passed had become vague shapes of differing colours, observed from a long way off, swaying and moving against the glare of the lights. I knew I was grinning stupidly and tried to stop myself but to no avail. The attempt made my grin worse and I wanted to laugh out loud. Taking small sips of my orange juice, I slowly brought the corridor back into focus. People passing became people again instead of vague ghost like shapes, able to say hello, the noise from the saloon stopped vibrating my head and the walls had stopped moving. I was once more back in the land of the normal.

" It is rather hot and stuffy in there, isn't it? " A voice very close to my ear made me jump, breaking my concentration which had become focused on getting back to sanity. With a supreme effort of will and without the wall falling on me, I managed to half turn in the direction of the voice and, at the same time became conscious of a warm thigh pressing against mine. A pair of dark brown eyes were gazing seriously at me through large round spectacles. Concentrating all my remaining powers, screwing up my eyes, I focused on her face. It was round with a small nose on which the spectacles perched and a rather large mouth filled with very white regular teeth that smiled at me from very close. The face was framed in brown hair, neatly cut and not quite reaching her shoulders. It must have been the drink but the hair shone in the light above our heads and I had to stop myself from reaching out and stroking it. Those red lips looked so inviting, parted in a smile that I sat back a little to stop myself stealing a kiss. As usual I didn't steal a kiss. The eyes behind those spectacles blinked as though they understood what was going through my mind but then continued to hold mine in a steady stare.

" Sorry, " I said breaking the spell she was casting over me by looking away and focussing my eyes on the wall opposite to where we were sitting. " I was trying to bring everything back into focus from the alcoholic haze into which I had fallen. Events were just starting to pass me by, to become detached from reality and I came out here to recover. My name is Eddie Gubbins by the way."

" Oh I know that," she replied, her speech slow and stilted as though she was searching for the right word, as though her English had been learnt at school and she had to work at it in order to speak properly. " You were the one who showed the guests round the bridge and I was one of those. Actually though, I was introduced to you by Brian and Sylvie when I arrived. This is the first time I have been on a big ship. Are the parties on the Vanguard always like this?"

I realised that my first assumption about her English was not correct because her use of English though slow was better than most of the other women on board that night. " This is the first party I have been to since joining the Vanguard a few months ago. I think it is about normal judging from the comments about other parties I have heard Bill and Brian make. Have you been to a party on board a ship before?"

Above the noise of some special dance, I had to lean close to hear her reply. The dancers spilled out of the saloon door and along the corridor, all stamping their feet and shouting loudly at the tops of their voices.

" No, I have never been on a ship before," she waited for the dancers to pass. " I came with Sylvie and Brian because he asked me last time the Vanguard was in Helsinki whether I would like to come to a party on his ship. I was reluctant to come at first because of the stories I hear about what goes on at these parties on English ships. Brian is very persuasive. He convinced me that this would not be one of those parties but very official and formal. Sylvie told me, I would meet some nice people when she backed him up. She has known Brian for a long time and been to many parties with him. Oh, I suppose you know that. I have heard a lot from her about evenings on Brian's ships because she is always telling me all about them the next time we meet after the ship has sailed. She sometimes has friends round to her flat for drinks when Brian is stopping with her in Helsinki. I get the impression that Brian smuggles the drink ashore for her. I suppose you couldn't really call them parties when comparing them to this, more a get together of a few friends but I have been to one or two of those when I have been invited. A few of Brian's friends like Bill are always there so I get a chance to practice my English. I learnt English at school and now work as a secretary in a company that imports machinery from England. Sylvie works in the same company. That is why my English is a bit formal with none of what Sylvie calls slang."

" Do you live in Helsinki? " I asked my mind now starting to clear.

" Yes but I originally come from a little village in the east of Finland. My father owns and runs a timber products business." Her eyes were large, clear brown and pulling me into their depths. " Do you come from London?"

" No." I had to laugh at the assumption by all Finns that every Englishman comes from London. " I live in Southampton when I am on leave. It is a port on the south coast. Have you ever been to England?"

" Last year a group from our office went to London for a Finnish week and to meet some of our suppliers, the people who we write to or telephone but never meet. There were a lot of Finns there, a bit like being in Helsinki really. It was summer but it rained every day we were there. Does it always rain in England?"

I had to laugh as I recalled the conversation I had had on my first visit to Finland. Kirsti from Kotka had insisted that it always rained in England and I wondered whether they had been in London at the same time. " Do all Finnish people think that it rains in England all the time? The weather can be really warm when the sun comes out. The scent of flowers can fill the air and the very atmosphere makes one feel as though the world is a perfect place in which to live. When I leave the sea, I am going to make sure I can have time to see England in the summer and have a garden where I can grow all the flowers with the nicest scent and the brightest colours."

I grinned at the surprised expression on Maria's face and suggested we go and dance. After sitting and talking to her in the corridor away from the direct effect of the music and drinking fruit juice, I was feeling better. Once on my feet, I found I could now stand without the walls moving in on me, without the floor rocking under my feet as though the Vanguard was still at sea and without my body swaying too much.

We pushed our way back into the crowd in the saloon and started to dance. Maria put her head against my shoulder and we danced slowly to the music, not talking, content to let the feel of each other express our thoughts.

Brian and Sylvie pushed their way up against us. " Come on Eddie stop hogging one girl all night. You know the rules, " Brian shouted above the music. " I'll dance with Maria, you dance with Sylvie."

With that bold statement, he took Maria by the hand and dance off into the throng, his rather flabby body vibrating and rippling to the music. I wanted to stamp my foot like a child deprived of it's favourite toy but remembered, just before I cried out, the rules of the party which I had laughed about when Brian and Bill had outlined them to me. Left with Sylvie, I had no other choice but to take her by the hand and set off into the scrum.

A succession of partners followed but, whether by design or chance I have no idea now, my eyes seemed to meet those of Maria each time I looked around. She smiled every time our eyes locked, her eyes blinking behind those large round glasses giving her at times the wet eyed look of a barn owl. I felt drawn towards her, found myself hoping we would be able to have one more dance together before the night was through with the chance for me to ask her out next time the ship came to Helsinki. The lights sank lower and the music got softer, the party was coming to an end and still there was no Maria. She was dancing with other men and there was no chance of me getting anywhere near her.

Suddenly I found her by my side, an empty glass in her hand that gave me a chance to get her a last drink. We stood close together for a little while as she drank, hardly talking but swaying in time to the music. I put my arm round her shoulder and she moved even closer to put her arms round my waist. Somehow as the mood of slow romantic music took hold, as the party came to an obvious end, I found great difficulty in asking her for her telephone number and whether I would meet her again. Putting down her drink, she placed her hands behind my neck and rested her head on my chest. I could feel desire rising as her breasts pressed against me, the smell of her scent drifted subtly into my nose, her warm breath on my neck and her heart beating.

" It will be time for me to go home soon," she said looking up at me but not letting go. Her eyes were sad but her lips smiled as though she was sad and happy at the same time. " It has been a nice party. Will I see you again, do you think?"

" I expect you will if that is what you want," I replied, smiling broadly with a sense of relief that she had broached the subject. " Where can I find you? "

Before she had time to answer, the music died and Bill was calling out to everybody in a loud voice. " The taxis will be here in a few minutes. Follow me and we will get your coats."

He led the women out of the saloon up to the spare cabin and they all appeared soon after wrapped in heavy clothing ready to face the chill of the night air. The cabs were lined up at the foot of the gangway and I was soon standing at the top making sure the guests negotiated the first steps correctly. Maria kissed me as she came to the top of the gangway much to the amusement of Brian and Sylvie who were waiting for her.

Handing me a piece of paper, she said. " My telephone number. Call me when the Vanguard gets back to Helsinki in three weeks time. We can spend the evening together without him looking on. "

She ducked under Brian's pretend push and ran down the gangway into the waiting car with Brian in hot pursuit behind. Sylvie stood looking into my eyes for a long time as though trying to gauge my motives towards her friend. Her eyes seemed to be issuing a warning but, without saying anything, she kissed me and followed the other two into the taxi. I lent against the rail, watching the red lights of the cars disappear along the quay, waving one last time as they went out of sight behind a shed. Before returning to the saloon to help tidy the mess, I put the piece of paper into my wallet with the thought that three weeks was not too long to wait for a chance to meet Maria again.

I never did get to see Maria the next trip because when the ship arrived in London, I was sent on leave. Actually, it must have been strange for the shore people in both Finland and London because Captain Harris, Dick Mortimer, Bill, Brian and Rex all left the ship.

Chapter 10

It was like coming home. For the first time in my maritime life I was rejoining a ship I had sailed on previously. As is the nature of tanker life, the chances of rejoining the same ship were pretty slim. There w ere just too many ships in the fleet. Not only was it like coming home by going back to the same ship but the policeman on the dock gate recognised me with a greeting as though I was a long lost friend. Once the taxi dropped me at the foot of the gangway, many of the dockers looking over the rail or on the quay waved cheerfully. I had hardly reached the second mates cabin when Brian was there shaking my hand.

" Welcome back Eddie," he greeted me with a wide grin. " I arrived earlier and Bill was already on board. Captain Harris is due later this afternoon. As far as I know but the Captain will tell you officially, Dick has been promoted and is taking out the Swift from Whitby next week."

" That is great for him," I replied. " How was your leave?"

" Great," was all he said as he hurried off into the engine room. " See you in Bill's cabin for a beer later."

The second mate who had relieved me three voyages ago was in his cabin waiting his bags already packed. He insisted on showing me around the ship and the bridge as a way of handing over. With a grin he did acknowledge that I most likely knew far more about he Vanguard than he did. He was off to Hull to join Dick on the Swift. As soon as he thought it was prudent, he left and I had my old cabin back.

Captain Harris arrived and took command of his ship, as he liked to call it. He sent word for me to sign on when I was free.

After I had signed on and we had talked about our leave, he grew serious. " I have been asked by the head office to take on anew chief officer. You might know that the Royal Navy has had to make a few officers redundant. One thing they did do was to set up training courses so that the officers could be qualified to serve in the Merchant Fleet. Our company has agreed to employ one of these officers. He is called Commander Pierce. He is a very experienced officer and can most likely teach us a thing or two about navigation and ship handling. I have no worries on that score. What will be new is in handling the cargo."

He paused and looked out of his window. " Remember Eddie nine months ago you were like that. I told Superintendent Smith that I had a very competent second mate in you and between us we would be able to help Commander pierce come to terms with any problems he might have. Will you agree to this?"

I grinned. " I suppose we have no choice. I think we can manage as long as he is not too arrogant."

" What do you mean?'

" I have met a great many naval officers. They tend to loom on us as beneath them. I suppose I do not help by telling them hat they swan around spending tax payers money while we actually have to earn our wages."

Captain Harris looked at the ceiling. " Young Eddie try to be nice to him."

Adrian Pierce joined the next day. He came to my cabin after signing on. I was having a mug of coffee in between checking the loading. The third mate, Charlie Shaw, was now on deck.

" I am Adrian Pierce, the new chief officer," he introduced himself. I noticed his uniform was pristine clean and the gold braid shining in the sun beaming through the porthole. I thought he looked rather nervous.

" Eddie Gubbins, the second mate. Mug of tea? There is some left in the pot in the pantry.' I shook his hand.

He looked rather startled at my question but nodded. " That would be splendid."

When I returned with the tea he was sitting looking at the loading papers on the desk. " You have been on this ship before or so Captain Harris tells me."

" Adrian believe me when I tell you I was like you only nine months ago. I had never been on a dry cargo ship before. You will soon pick things up. When you have finished your tea, I will show you around and introduce you to all the important dockers. Then we can go up to the office and meet the clerks. They do the cargo plan here but we have to do it in Kotka. Don't ask me why. Tradition I think. On the other hand it could be about the language."

" One thing. There are no uniforms among the crew. How do you tell who is who?"

I bit back a sarcastic comment about so many on naval ships that they had to wear uniforms but replied. " There are not many so you soon get to know them all. I will introduce you to the bosun while we are looking round the ship. It is a shame that Merve, the last chief officer, was taken ill and was not here to help you. I will do my best. One piece of advice. The bosun is the man you need to get to know. He has been on this ship for the last two years and knows the maintenance routine. He will tell you what needs looking at each morning."

" Isn't it my job to decide how to allocate the crew?"

I grinned. " You are in charge, Adrian. You can change anything you like but it will be a great deal easier if you let the bosun help."

I collected the mugs. " Come on. After rinsing these I will show you around."

I noticed his raised eyebrows. " When you are in your office you can order the steward to fetch you coffee or tea. I do it myself because it is quicker."

I took Adrian to the shore office and introduced him to the clerks and especially Norman Winter who drew up the cargo plan. Adrian watched as the cargo plan took shape. Next into the office of the supervisor, Derek Boman. They discussed the loading schedule and what would be coming the next day.

On the way back to the ship, Adrian asked. " How do we load the cars and tractors?"

" We have a watertight door in the side of number three hatch. There is a ramp that we lower onto the quay. They are driven into the hold. If there are more cars than can be accommodated on the upper deck we have ramps which are fixed between the decks,"

Pointing I showed him the cars arriving on lorries to the compound behind the shed. "The dockers drive them from there straight into the hold. It gets a trifle like Brands Hatch on a bank holiday but surprisingly there is little damage. The dockers get paid per car so the quicker they do it the quicker they get home."

" Who rigs the ramps?"

" The bosun organises that with one of the crew driving the crane. They will put the ramps in place after the dockers knock off tonight. I will supervise. I think it would be a good idea if you came and watched. After that you will be familiar with the procedure."

" I will do that."

" One other thing. When the cars are being put into place, both the third mate and me should be in the hold with a couple of sailors noting any damages. At the same time we check that the cars are secure." I grinned at his look.

" Who secures the cars?"

" The company hires a rigging company. They have special securing gear and we have to make sure it is returned on the next voyage."

We were now back on the deck of the Vanguard watching boxes being loaded the holds. " You did not mention the tractors."

" Usually they are loaded by crane because they can get more in that way. The foreman will tell you in the morning."

Adrian smiled for the first time. " Thank you Eddie. Everything is much clearer now."

The next morning after breakfast, Captain Harris asked me to see him in his cabin.

" How is Adrian Pierce doing?" he asked bluntly when I entered his cabin.

I explained what I had shown him the day before. " I think he will make a good officer, sir."

Captain Harris grunted. " Keep an eye on him."

Adrian stood and watched the sailors manoeuvre the ramps into position. It was not an easy job. The ramps weighed a few tonnes and were too long to fit from one end of the hatch to the other. They had to be lowered with the ends in the corners of the hatch. Then landed in the hold so that they could be lifted into position using a different sling. I could see that this was something Adrian understood. It must have been something he was familiar with during his time with the Navy.

The next morning the cars came one after the other. Adrian stood on deck to watch. Charlie and me along with two sailors rushed around the holds checking that there was no damage visible on the cars. At the same time we checked that the restraints were properly secured. The atmosphere in the holds despite the fans sucking the air became thick with car exhaust fumes. Even when we took turns to climb back on deck to catch our breath, the taste clung to the back of the throat.

On one rip to the deck I saw that Adrian was watching the loading of the tractor on the forward hold. I did not have time to speak before I plunged down once more into the foggy, smelly atmosphere of the hold.

At last the final car was in place. I signed a paper to say that the securing was satisfactory. The tractors were all loaded and the ship made ready to leave for Finland. The clerk from the office came aboard with the final manifest and cargo plan. The hatches were secured.

I went to the poop to let go the ship and see her through the lock and into the river. Once we were in the river I left the poop and went back to my cabin. I met the bosun in the corridor and he stopped me.

" Second mate, I do not know how this new chief officer is going to make out." He looked seriously worried.

I grinned. " It is all a bit new to him but he will learn with our help."

" But Eddie you wee not there on the focastle," the bosun shook his head. " He turned up ion his best uniform and leather gloves. He looked around and asked where everybody was. When I told him that four sailors, him and me was all we had he looked shocked. I told him you had to do the job with three because there was one on the wheel. Then when I asked him to hold the securing rope as we unwound the rope from the bollard, he said it was not his job. I hope I will not get into trouble but I told him if he did not hold the bloody rope the ship would not leave. He held it like you would a rat by the tail. I hope he doers learn."

" I will have a word in his ear." The bosun went away shaking his head and muttering to himself.

I learnt first hand what Adrian was thinking. We sailed from London in the evening as daylight was fading. Adrian was on the bridge for the trip down the river and then the third mate took over at eight o'clock. When I came on watch at midnight we were well out into the North Sea rolling gently in a southerly swell. When the chief officer came on watch at four in the morning, he looked around the bridge with surprise.

" Where is everybody?" he asked anxiously.

" This is it," I answered trying not to sound patronising. " There is a watch sailor who can be contacted by phone if required. He will do rounds of the ship every hour and report to you here. There is coffee in the chart room with water and milk. At six the steward will bring you coffee and toast but you can tell him what you would like if toast is not your thing. I am off to bed. See you at four tomorrow."

The Vanguard arrived in Helsinki and Adrian was presented with more problems. We tied up at the Ford berth which was a purely roll on roll off berth. Once the cars and tractors were discharged, the ship would move across the harbour to the main discharge berth. There were no cranes or other cargo handling equipment. The ramp to the quay was in place and the watertight doors opened, the cars were driven off onto the quay. When the watertight door to the forward hold was opened, it became apparent that there was no possibility of driving the tractors off the ship. The dockers had done a good job in London in making sure as many tractors could be fitted into the hold. The trouble was that they were jammed in so that there was no room for manoeuvring them round so that they could be driven off.

We stood at the hatch top trying to decide what could be done. There was only one solution. One of the tractors would have to lift out of the hatch top making space to turn the other tractors to face the door. That way the rest could be driven off. It proved more difficult than appeared at first. For a start there were no cranes on the quay because this berth had been designed as a roll on roll off berth. In addition there were no cargo handling dockers available or the cargo handling gear. After much discussion it was decided to send for the appropriate gear and use one of the ship's cranes.

I was called into the chief officers cabin while waiting for the gear to arrive. Captain Harris and Adrian Pierce were drinking coffee.

" Ah Eddie come in," Captain Harris smiled. That smile made me nervous.

He poured me a mug of coffee. " Adrian has informed me of the problem with the tractors. I have been onto the agents and the importers. They all agree that our solution is the best one. There is a problem. They insist that they will only accept a crane driver who has a safety certificate. The only person I will trust is you. Will you drive the crane?"

Now I understood the reason for the smile. " If I am required to help I will."

Adrian smiled now." Thank you. The cargo handling gear should be here any time soon."

In the end we had to lift three tractors out before the rest could be manoeuvred enough to enable the rest to be driven off the ship. I was relieved when it was all over.

When we arrived back in London, Adrian Pierce told me over a beer that he had handed in a trips notice. He was adamant that it was all too much for him without enough crew. I tried to get him to change his mind but he had already decided. The company had found him a post with P and O passenger ships that I understood would be more in his sphere than small cargo ships. With this in mind he left the loading virtually to me.

At midnight as we sailed through Baltic Sea on the way back to Helsinki, I climbed the ladder to the bridge of the ship to take my watch. Half asleep from being woken a few minutes before. As always on reaching the bridge, I looked around. It was a typical autumn night, overcast with a calm sea.

Even though I was not mentally sharp, something alerted me to danger. It is as though some sixth sense was working even though there was nothing overt to indicate that anything was wrong. Looking all round, I tried to make out what was out of place, my eyes checking all the instruments I could see and my ears straining to sense any difference in the peculiar sounds which emanate from a ship. Everything appeared in order. Then my eyes rested Charlie Shaw in the gloom of the bridge. He was standing rigid at the front of the wheelhouse, staring out at the sea ahead of the ship. Some lights were visible close to the starboard bow, and my brain suddenly registered that they were the accommodation and stern lights from another ship.

I reacted instantly and automatically, my years of training and experience taking over. Suddenly I was wide awake, the adrenaline rush causing any lingering sleep to vanish. Rushing to the front of the bridge, I grabbed a lever and changed the steering gear from automatic into manual. I yelled at the second mate to take over the wheel. He came out of his trance at the sound of my voice and rushed to the stand by the wheel. I could see in the reflected light of the compass that his face was white and his eyes wide with fear.

" Hard a port!" I yelled even louder as I came to terms with the true situation. The Vanguard was only a few yards from another ship and in a few minutes we were going to smash into it's stern.

" Are we overtaking or not? " I yelled never taking my eyes of the rusty grey hull as it was getting ever closer and closer.

" Overtaking, " Charlie Shaw replied in a voice that quivered with fear. The knuckles of his hands on the wheel were white he gripped it so tight.

As the bow of the Vanguard swung away from the other ship, I yelled for the wheel to be put amidships and raced out onto the bridge wing to watch our stern come round. The aft ends of the two ships were now closing each other very fast and I yelled for the wheel to be put hard to starboard, towards the other vessel. The two ships were now running parallel and water was being thrown into the air as it was squeezed between us. Looking over to the other ship, I caught a glimpse of a white face looking out of their wheelhouse but had no time to wave. Once the two ships were running exactly parallel, I yelled for Charlie Shaw to steer a steady course hoping all the time, the two sterns would not be pulled together. As the bow of the Vanguard edged passed the other ship, I waited holding my breath.

There was nothing I could do other than pray the two ships would stay apart long enough for me to take the next action. Charlie Shaw was fighting the wheel, trying to hold the Vanguard steady while casting fearful glances out of the wheelhouse at the other ship.

When I judged the time was right, I yelled for Charlie Shaw to steer to starboard, ignoring his look of horror, across the bows of the other ship. I did not look and concentrated on what I was trying to do. As the Vanguard's bow turned towards the other ship, I wondered whether I had judged things right. My heart was beating too fast and I felt as though I had a lead weight in my stomach. I had to remind myself to breath.

Actually, thinking back now there was nothing else I could have done because the sterns were starting to close. Our stern started to move away from the stern of the other ship and our speed was carrying us round his bow. It seemed to go on for ever and I must have stood holding my breath for what was an impossible time, watching the bow of the other ship slowly pass down our side and then slip away very close astern.

" Put her back on course," I ordered my voiced drained of all feeling.

I sank down against the front of the bridge wing, my hand gripping the rail tightly in an effort to stop the shaking of my arms. My legs were like jelly and I honestly thought I was going to collapse onto the deck. Never in my whole life had I been so scared, never had I used up so much nervous energy in so short a time. I felt as though I had stood and faced death, only to be reprieved. That is not so strange because there was every chance I would have lost my ticket if we had hit the other ship. Still shaking almost uncontrollably, I managed to pull myself upright and somehow walked into the wheelhouse.

The sight of Charlie Shaw standing there, his face chalky white and his hand pushing nervously back a lock of his hair from his eyes snapped my control. For the first time in quite a while I lost my temper.

" You bloody idiot! " I shouted even though he was right next to me. I was so beside myself with rage, I could not stop myself. " What the hell were you trying to do? You could have lost us both our certificates not to mention our lives. Standing there like that staring out to sea and waiting for something to happen is the worst thing you could have done. Do you call yourself qualified? I would make sure you never set foot on a ship again if I had the power. What the hell were the examiners thinking of when they gave you a ticket? If I was you, I'd get out of my sight now and make sure you keep out of my way for the rest of the trip."

I turned suddenly at the sound of a quiet voice behind me. " There is no need for you to manhandle my second mate. "

Captain Harris was standing in the entrance to the bridge frowning. It was then I realised I was holding Charlie Shaw by the coat collar and shaking him from side to side. Sheepishly I let go and pushed him away.

" Go down to your cabin now and I will be down shortly, " Captain Harris said to Charlie Shaw who left the bridge as fast as his legs could carry him.

" You will have to learn to keep your temper under control if you are to be a good captain one day." He looked round the bridge. " You did a good job there. Well done. I could not have done it better."

For some reason that praise of Captain Harris filled me with pride.

When we arrived back in London, Adrian Pierce packed his bags and left the Vanguard before the next chief officer arrived. Once more I was left in charge of the discharge while Captain Harris went to the office to find out who was to be the next Chief Officer. I must admit I enjoyed myself. I enjoyed the way people deferred to my opinions and carried out my instructions.

The Captain came back that afternoon accompanied by the new Chief Officer. He found me by one of the hatches talking to the dockers foreman.

" Hello second mate. I am the new chief officer. Bobby Render."

" Hello. Eddie Gubbins. This is the dockers foreman Graham Jones."

I hurried ashore to speak to the office leaving them talking.

Norman Winter showed me the cargo expected for that trip. " The shed is configured to sort the cargo into loading order. The compound for the cays is ready and the cars are arriving. There are no tractors this time. There are two vans that have been converted as television studios for what they call down here outside broadcasts. They are filled with equipment and must be securely secured. They will be loaded through the hatch last."

" You had better inform the new chief officer and he will plan their loading."

The cars were loaded and the chief officer left a space for the television vans. I came on deck from the cargo office and looked down the hold. The television vans were parked on the quay waiting for the crane driver to arrive. What I saw appalled me and I hurried to confront the chief officer.

He was leaning on the rail talking to the foreman.

He turned as I approached and smiled. " The cargo is all stowed. We are just waiting for the vans."

I looked at him wondering how to broach the subject but decided to be blunt. " The space you have left is wrong."

He looked angry. " What do you mean?"

" Looking into the hold, you can only stow the vans facing across the ship. That is dangerous."

" Are you questioning my competence and plan? I am the chief officer and it is my decision that counts."

" If you load the vans like that and we get bad weather there will be nothing to stop them shifting. Think of the damage that will do."

He laughed. " You are being to cautious. They stay like that. Go ahead foreman and load them."

I shrugged. " You are the one who makes the decisions but may the consequences be on your head."

As I turned away the chief officer said. " I will remember this boy."

We sailed that evening with the weather forecast echoing in my head. Gales in German Bight.

When I came on watch that night, the ship was rolling heavily in a northeast sea. Spray was washing across the decks and the structure creaking. Visibility was marginal with heavy rain.

I heard it faintly at first and then louder even against the sound of the sea. There was a crash in the hold followed by the sound of breaking glass. With growing apprehension, I listened closely. After a few more rolls of the ship, I was certain. The vans must have shifted.

I wondered whether to wait for the chief officer to come on watch but decided to call Captain Harris.

The phone rang for a while until the sleepy voice of Captain Harris answered. " Yes?"

" Sir I do not know if this is important but I can hear the noise of glass breaking coming from the hold."

" I'll be straight up on the bridge."

It was quicker than I thought but Captain Harris was soon on the bridge. He led the way out onto the bridge wing. We stood bracing our bodies against the rolling of the ship listening to the sound of crashes and breaking glass coming from the hold.

" Bugger!" the Captain exploded. " It sounds as though something has broken loose. Call the sailor on duty and go and have a look. When you report back, I can decide whether to rouse the Chief officer. You be careful down there. All I need is for you or the sailor to get injured."

Both Jim my watch sailor and I donned waterproofs and climbed down on the deck dodging the spray. I banged back the clips on the door to the hold and lit my torch. The ship lurched and rolled heavily as we climbed sown the ladder and we both paused to cling on tightly. The sound of metal hitting metal was now loud in our ears as was the creaking of the structure.

When I reached the bottom of the ladder I shone the torch along the hold. Above the roofs of the tethered cars I could plainly see the vans moving backward and forwards across the ship. There was another smash but we could not see enough to decide what was happening.

I indicated for Jim to follow me between the secured cars. It was hard to maintain our feet against the erratic movement of the ship. We bumped into the cars but finally made it to the space where the vans were stowed.

One of the vans had broken away from some of the securing restraints. It was not only moving from one side of the ship to the other but was slewing from side to side. This carried it into the other van. The cars in front and behind were crumpled and dented. Another wave caught the ship and the van bashed first against its twin and then pushed the cars with a crash further across the deck. There was more sound of glass breaking and equipment crashing from inside the vans.

Jim shrugged is shoulders. " We will have to try to attach a wires to the vans and secure them."

I shook my head. " Come on. We have to go and tell the Captain what has happened. Be careful making your way back. Think about what is required and we can tell the chief officer."

When we got back to the bridge, Bobby Render was there with the Captain. It was obvious to me that they had been having what in novels is described as words. The sailor described what he had seen and I filled in the details.

" Come on," he ordered the sailor. " The bosun and another sailor will be along soon. We will collect the wires and go and secure the vans."

As he left the bridge he cast a withering look in my direction.

" Right," Captain Harris barked. " Lets see if we can get the ship to stop rolling too much while they are down in the hold."

After he was satisfied that he was steering the best course, he turned his attention to me. " How the hell did you let the vans be loaded facing across the ship?"

I held my temper and tried to stay calm. " It is he chief officers job to plan the loading of the cargo."

" Did you not warn him about he danger of loading in that way?"

" He did not discuss it with me," I replied looking directly at Captain Harris. " I introduced him to the people in the office and the foreman of the dockers. He discussed things with them."

Captain Harris smiled crookedly. " All right young Eddie. We will leave it there. I hope the chief officer realises what this will mean to both him and the company. When the damage is assessed, he will have to put in a report to the company claims department so that they can alert the insurance people. There maybe a case for negligence that means the company will have to pay some of the costs. They will not be happy."

His words came to echo in my mind. When we arrived in Helsinki, the vans were lifted ashore first. The Finnish television people swarmed over them having been informed in advance that they had shifted in a storm and there might be damage. I was looking after the discharge and invited to look inside when they were on the quay. The chief officer was also there.

Much of the equipment was damaged beyond repair at first sight. The chief officer offered my services to help the owners make a list of damages. I could have killed him. It was not the making of a list of damages. I had compiled those in the past. Indeed I had had to justify the reasons for the damages to our claims department on numerous occasions. There was always some damage to the cargo either caused by the dockers during loading, the dockers during discharge or bad weather. With bad weather it was usually caused by poor stowage. I have to admit, bad stowage did not happen too often. The dockers in Surrey Docks for all their faults were very professional when it came to stowing cargo safely. I can recall getting to Helsinki after bad weather to find no damage to our cargo but finding other ships where the cargo had shifted in the hold. What upset me was having to work with representatives of the owners or the insurers and having to put up with comments about the competence of who had planned the stowage. There would be questions about why we allowed this to happen. It was not a pleasant morning.

The chief officer managed to glower at me again when he was summoned to the office after the damage assessment was finished. He ordered me in a voice dripping with malice to look after the discharge while he was away. He made it plain that he resented the inclusion of the Captain in the discussion of the damage.

The damaged cars were towed pout of the hold and the rest driven off. Then the discharge of the rest of the cargo started.

It was a very awkward voyage back from Finland to London. Bobby Render did not speak to me. Well we spoke to pass information when we handed over the watch from one to the other. It was that we did not indulge in what could be termed social chat. It was as though he blamed me for what had happened. I had the impression that he was holding his feelings tight all the way back. Bill and I still had a drink in the morning before I went on watch but Bobby never came near my cabin. It was one of the facts that I had understood soon after joining my first ship. Unlike most other jobs, being at sea meant not only working with but socialising with all your colleagues. There was no way you could decide at the end of your shift to go home and meet other people. Even when I did not really like somebody, I still made the social occasions that came about on board.

I was leaning on the rail by one of the holds talking to the bosun when Bobby Render climbed into a taxi to go to the office to sign off. He had told me that he was leaving at the end of the voyage, giving the impression that he had had enough. Observing his time with the Captain, I had come to the conclusion that he had been asked to resign.

" I wonder who we will get next?" the bosun asked. " We seem to be running through chief officers since Dick Mortimer left. I hope it is somebody with company experience."

" I think that is the problem, bosun. There are no spare mates left in the company without promoting the senior second mate. From what I gather the two who are next in line are in college studying for their Masters at the moment. I have about six months to go before I go to college."

Captain Harris returned to the Vanguard later. He sent his steward to find me and ask me to come to his cabin. Making sure the third mate was on deck and available to the dockers, I left my working gloves outside the cargo office and climbed he ladder to the Captain's cabin. I considered that he wanted to tell me who was the new chief officer.

As it happened I was right. After knocking on the door and being asked to enter, I found the Captain sitting at his desk the articles open in front of him. He smiled and pushed a letter across the desk.

" The company sent this for you." He smiled slightly.

Trying to stop any shaking in my fingers and keeping my face as expressionless as possible, I used a pen to open the letter.

" On the advice of Captain Harris the company would like to appoint you as the chief officer of the Vanguard as of now." It was signed by the marine superintendent Trevor Smith.

Captain Harris held out his hand and shook mine. " I have great faith in you, my boy. Now get ashore to Taylor's and get them to replace the second mate's rings with chief officers. The third mate can look after the ship while you are gone. Oh. Captain Smith is retiring in a few months and I have been asked to take over as Marine Superintendent. I have accepted."

When I came back to the ship a couple of hours later I dinned my uniform jacket with the three gold rings. With the help of the deck officer's steward, I moved my stuff into the chief officers cabin. Once settled, I called for the bosun and the third mate.

When he came into the chief officers cabin, the bosun grinned. " Congratulations, Mr. Gubbins. I am glad to see the company came to their senses."

So I became a chief officer of the Vanguard and was lucky that the next few voyages were relatively straight forward and problem free. I could not have asked for better introduction to life as the senior deck officer. There was only one incident to mar the calm.

I have a memento of that occurrence. It sits on the shelf above my computer and when seeking inspiration I often look at it and remember. It is really just a few pieces of wood glued together but it has a story.

Arriving in Helsinki one day, we were ordered to moor the Vanguard at the Ford berth to discharge our cargo of cars and tractors. It was the one berth in Helsinki where there as a flat quay on which we could easily lower our ramps. There were no crane rails to make it awkward to drive the cars off the ship. We had been through this before and there was no nervousness on board. I had made sure that the cars and tractors could be easily driven off the ship when they were loaded in London. I had burnt into my memory the time we had come here and could not discharge the tractors without a great deal of delay. Now I was confident that there was no problem.

It has to be admitted that it is a difficult approach to the berth along a narrow dredged channel with mud banks on either side. However, it was a manoeuvre we had undertaken many times without mishap. The method used was to approach the berth and drop the port anchor. This slowed the ship while ropes were passed to the quay. Then the ship could be moved sideways to come to rest gently against the fenders guarding the berth. The weight of the anchor also prevented the bow overshooting the berth area and grounding on a mud bank.

The day in question, we approached the berth in exactly the way we had planned. The sky was overcast and there was snow falling. It was very cold and wet on the focastle were I stood supervising the anchor party and the forward mooring. The shallow water near the shore was showing the signs of ice forming. As we approached the berth, the cargo manager waved cheerfully indicating that all was ready. Leaning against the small office building trying to find some shelter from the elements, bundled in heavy weather gear, were the drivers and rigging gang ready to rush on board to drive off the cars and tractors.

After we had negotiated the channel and approached the berth, the Captain ordered the anchor dropped. I waved for the bosun to release the brake of the windlass. With a metallic clang that vibrated the ship's structure, the anchor fell into the water with a splash. Unfortunately, the end of chain, which should have been attached to the anchor, flew up into the air and landed with a crash on the deck before sliding off into the water. Luckily the chain did not hit anybody on the focastle.

For a moment there was silence and then confusion. The bosun applied the brake and the chain screeched to a stop. Acting quickly, I ordered the starboard anchor to be dropped. Luckily the bosun reacted swiftly and this anchor stopped the ship before we hit the mud bank. I winced as the anchor chain wrapped itself around the bow of the ship, scrapping away great areas of paint. Another overtime job for the crew I thought. It worked however and we safely berthed the ship.

I shook my head at the bosun. " I do not know why that happened. Thank you for helping. Later we will pull in the chain and look at what happened. Lets go and get the side door open and the shore ramp in place."

Later that day, the dock authority did dredge up our anchor and we were able to lift it back in place with one of our cranes.

That evening over pre-dinner drinks, the engineers on the ship presented me with this trophy. They were all grinning. That is the story to the drift wood trophy that sits on the shelf above my computer. It is shaped like an anchor mounted on a wooden plinth. Attached to the plinth is a brass plate with the words " Lost anchor 1967."

A trip later I left the Vanguard to attend college to study for my Master's Certificate. I accompanied Captain Harris to the company offices. He told me how torn he was. On the one hand he was pleased to become the Marine Superintendent while on the other he was sad at leaving the sea.

Chapter 11

My father was so proud when I went to his work place o tell him that I had passed my Master's Certificate. He was not outwardly demonstrative. That was not like my Dad. But I could see in his eyes that he thought it was a great thing.

" Well done, Edmund," he said smiling crookedly. " It is a pity your Grandfather is not here to see this day. He would have been so proud. He would have gone out and told all the neighbours."

The company appointed me to join the Swift. This was the smallest ship in the fleet and did not have a regular voyage schedule. It filled in when there was cargo to take especially to some of the smaller Finnish ports. She did not sail from London but mainly from Hull but she had been known to sail from Whitby or Leith. I was pleased to hear that Dick Mortimer was her Captain.

I took the train to Hull that was different from what I had been used to in the past. When the ship turned into the dock I had my first sight of the Swift. She was smaller. From her configuration there were three holds. What was different was that the officers' accommodation was amidships under the bridge. The number one hatch was small and forward of the accommodation. The chief officers cabin was in one corner of the accommodation.

I had met the chief officer John Kelly I was relieving many times before in port. It did not take long to hand over the ship. Dick Mortimer greeted me like a long lost friend and I was soon settled in my cabin drinking a gin with John and the cargo foreman. The one thing I learnt from them was that the number one hold could be refrigerated if required.

The cargo loading was straightforward except for two containers that we were asked to carry on deck. It was a time when the container revolution was just taking off. There were a few specially designed container ships but most containers at this time were distributed from main terminals by ordinary ships. If possible they were loaded into the hold but this one would not fit into the hold. It was destined for Kemi right in the north of Finland and that is where we were bound. It was autumn so there should not be any ice.

We sailed from the Humber into the teeth of a southeasterly gale. The ship was rolling and pitching as soon as we left the shelter of the river and headed for the River Elbe.

The structure of the Swift creaked and groaned as the ship rose and then plunged through heavy waves in the North Sea. At regular intervals vibrations travelled along the length of the ship as the bow climbed up a rushing wall of water, left the water and plunged with a loud bang into the next wave. Over lying the protesting steel and the vibrating panels, was the scream of the wind in the rigging. All prudent sailors would have put into shelter long ago but the company had a reputation for getting to the destination even in the worst weather.

Braced against the uneven movements of the ship, I sat at the desk in my cabin on an armchair firmly fixed to the floor. Spread out before me were the cargo papers and the crews overtime sheets, all held down with paperweights. My gin and tonic was in a glass holder attached to the desktop, designed specifically to stop any drinks moving across the desk during a storm.

With half my mind I was listening, trying to put the sounds of the ship in storm to the background so that I could recognise any out of place noises. To many people confronted with the noises and movement of a ship riding a gale for the first time, the idea of the creaks, groans, vibrations and bangings being ignored is very strange. How can anybody put these things to the back of their mind? To me the sounds of a ship in a storm are familiar and to be lived with during a voyage. Like the conductor of an orchestra, the seaman notices the out of key sounds. While I listened there were no out of the ordinary sounds. Satisfied, I continued with my paper work.

Suddenly, the ship took a larger heel. Spray smashed against the portholes of my cabin and the ship shuddered violently before rolling back upright the steel protesting loudly. It felt like a wrestler throwing a great weight from his shoulders. There was a loud bang. The screaming of severed steel and the whole ship's hull vibrated. The ship rolled again and there was another bang as it came upright.

Without thinking, I was racing out of the cabin door when the phone rang. I turned back and lifted the receiver.

" What!" I growled.

" This is the Third mate from the bridge." The voice sounded scared and worried. " The captain is on his way. One of the containers we stowed on the hatch cover on the after deck has come loose. The Captain asked me to tell you to get down on deck and assess what has happened. Can you report to him on the bridge regarding what will be needed?"

" Tell the captain I am on my way. " I threw down the phone and rushed out of the accommodation.

The bosun was standing by the rail just outside of the door to the amidships accommodation. He was staring wide eyed along the after deck. Even in his heavy weather gear he was wet through. When I joined him all he could do was point. The container we had stowed on top of number three hatch had broken some of its lashings. As we watched, the box was caught by another enormous sea as the ship rolled to port and the deck edge submerged. Water boiled over the deck, smashing against the hatch combing, sending a cloud of stinging spray against the aft accommodation block. The remaining lashings twanged with the strain. Half the container was over the side of the ship and was threatening to smash into the aft accommodation if it came completely adrift. As it was the wave lifted the end, pushing it on board and as the ship returned to the upright shedding water over the side in a waterfall, it landed with a loud crash bending the rail and threatening to stave in the hatch cover.

The bosun remark as though rehearsing his lines to a committee of enquiry, " I checked the lashings with you before we sailed. They looked strong enough to me. What are we going to do?"

I did not hesitate. " Get all the deck crew to have a look and then assemble in the mess. We have to work out what can be done and I will not ask anybody to take any risks until we have all agreed what we can do. Some of them may have seen something similar in the past and they can tell us what they did then. I am going to the bridge to see if the captain can bring the ship round so that it stops rolling green water across the deck Then I will put on my heavy weather gear and join you in the mess."

The bosun looked startled and ducked as another bout of spray lashed across the deck. I did not see him dodging behind the hatch combing as he made his way aft along the slippery deck. After climbing the ladder to the bridge and arriving breathless, I found the captain on the bridge wing staring aft.

On spying me Dick asked bluntly, " Well?"

I shrugged. " As you can see, the container we loaded onto number three hatch has come adrift. It has broken the forward lashings but the aft ones are holding. It is now at an angle to the hatch with at least half its length over the side. The remaining lashings are not going to hold much longer with the pounding they are taking."

" What happens if they snap?" the Captain was trying to gauge the likely path of the container if it broke free. " Will the box float away?"

" As far as I can see not at that angle to the deck. The likely out come of the aft lashings breaking is for the box to lift clear of the hatch cover and smash into the aft accommodation. We can't be sure how much damage it will inflict or if even then it will be washed clear. Besides which it will most likely damage the hatch cover and flood the hold. I have no idea whether the bilge pumps will cope with that much water. That is in addition to the ruined cargo."

" What do you want me to do to help?"

" Can you try to turn the ship so that we are running down wind? That way the sea will tend to push the container back on deck."

" I can try though the ship will roll like a model boat in the bath while we are turning. See what you can do about that container."

I thanked the captain and raced back to my cabin. As I donned my heavy weather gear the ship bucked and rolled alarmingly. I had to steady myself against the desk to pull on my waterproof trousers but I managed somehow to dress. When I came back on the deck, the ship was pitching violently with the waves picking up the stern and planning the ship along on the crest before falling into the trough. As I battled along the deck towards the aft accommodation, I did notice that there was less water coming across the deck. Every so often there was a violent lurch and I had to hold onto the rail as the waves rushed over me.

Arriving dripping wet, the bosun and five sailors were in the mess waiting. The bosun explained that the other sailor was on the bridge steering the ship.

" Well," I said looking around at their tense faces. " As you have all seen the box is half over the side. Have you any suggestions?"

There was a shuffling of feet but none of them spoke.

The bosun intervened. " Look men, I have sailed with the Chief Officer before on a number of voyages. He is genuinely asking for your opinions."

" I know you might not be used to an officer asking your opinion but there must be somebody with some experience of similar situations. I have never been in this position before. Some of us are going to have to go out there in the teeth of the gale and do something about that box. I want to make sure that we come up with a feasible solution before I ask somebody to help me."

Like nervous school children, they stuttered at first but soon a discussion was taking place. They started to relate incidents that had happened of previous ships or that they had heard about I was surprised at the depth of experience they could call on.

After a while I held up my hand. " That was fascinating. Distilling the essence of what you have discussed, I see there are two alternatives. One is to cut the wires and cast the box away. The other is to somehow get a rope attached and heave the box back aboard. As you have all pointed out there are dangers in both suggestions."

One of the sailors interrupted. " Have you ever experienced what happens when a wire breaks?"

Quietly I replied. " Yes."

The bosun butted in before I could go on. " The chief officer was the second mate on the Vanguard when the wire broke leaving Hull and the third mate lost his leg. So he knows the dangers. He went and told the third mates family and girl friend and took them to the hospital."

The sailor said equally quietly. " Sorry Mister mate."

I shrugged. " OK. Taking things from there. We have no control over what happens when the wires are cut. They are going to be stretched like piano strings. The main danger is to the one who cuts through the wire. I would not like for any of you to get hurt so I would have to do that. But I would need somebody with me to make sure I am not swept away if a wave breaks over the deck and to pull me clear of the box as it is swept up by waves. There is no knowing where the box will go It could smash into the aft accommodation and do limitless damage."

I paused. " I must admit from what you have all said and from my experience, I favour the second option, trying to get a rope attached. If we can get a rope attached there is a fair chance we can heave it back on board. I know there are dangers in this option. One of the sailors will have to come down on deck with me and climb onto the hatch by the moving container. It will be slippery and we might have waves coming aboard. At the same time we will have to dodge the end of the container if it is lifted by a wave. Bosun, have you got a line with a hook spliced to the end?"

The bosun frowned. " I have a large strong hook that will do the job. I will have to go and splice it to a rope. If you manage to get it hooked into the eye of the box I hope it will be strong enough."

" Who is going to come down on the deck with me?" I asked looking round at the concerned faces. I knew it was asking a great deal, maybe outside the normal duties of a sailor but I needed somebody with me when I stepped out on the deck.

" I will," the bosun interjected before anybody else could answer. ' I think you should stay by the accommodation directing operations from there."

" I am sorry bosun but I think this is a job I will have to do. I will go onto the deck with one of the sailors. We will take the rope with the hook and make this fast to a tackle attached to the eyebolt near the central winch platform. The rope will then be led back to the aft winch. You will direct operations from there. Now who is going to come down on the deck with me?"

Jock Winters volunteered. He was a stocky, small sailor with tattoos on his arms and a face that looked as though it had run into the back of a bus. He was not the most reliable of characters and in port always got drunk. However, he was the best rope thrower on the ship and he did volunteer. I never asked him why.

We all waited impatiently while the bosun spliced the rope to the hook and arranged the tackle. When he rejoined us in the mess, we all went out on deck. Jock and I descended onto the deck. Jock carried the rope with the hook. I had the tackle over my shoulder, the rope trailing away to the winch. It was difficult to carry these and get our balance against the heaving and rolling of the ship. As we left the shelter of the aft structure, the ship lurched violently and a wall of water washed over the deck almost knocking us off our feet. Jock grinned but my heart was beating too fast for me to grin back. Almost overhead the container moved, banging into the hatch and making the remaining lashings twang. Another wave broke over the deck and I had to grab Jock as he lost his footing. He grinned again. I did not have the courage to look at the bosun standing by the winch anxiously following our every move.

Gingerly we climbed onto the hatch cover, the container towering above our heads. The ship rolled and another waved washed over the deck catching the corner of the box. It lifted from the hatch and moved in our direction. I held my breath but it dropped with a bang before it caught us. Jock's face was now white and he had stopped grinning. I was glad I could not see mine.

We cautiously made our way to the forward part of the hatch and made the tackle fast on the eye bolt. The bosun tightened the rope. Jock walked towards the corner of the container the hook in his hand, while I held the rest of the rope. As the ship rolled I braced myself and held onto Jock by his coat. He swung the hook back and forth. At the right trajectory, he let go. The hook sailed up into the air but it hit the side of the container with a loud clang and fell back onto the hatch at our feet. As spray lashed us once more, Jock calmly recoiled the rope, set himself and threw. This time the hook landed on the top of the container. Slowly, to me agonisingly slowly, Jock eased the rope through his hands. Even above the sound of the wind, the sea and the waves, we could hear the hook scraping against the roof of the container. It fell with a loud clunk into the twist lock holder. Almost holding our breath, we pulled on the rope. The hook held fast. I let my breath go in a long whoosh realising I had been holding it for quite a while. As we signalled to the bosun to start tightening the rope, a wave caught the container and it rose in the air to smash back as the wave passed. The hatch covers creaked and groaned as though on the brink of breaking.

We watched as another wave caught the container lifting it clear of the hatch. I signalled for the bosun to heave away on the winch. In this way each time the container lifted on a wave, we heaved in on the rope. After what seemed to Jock and me an age during which we were battered by spray and slipping on the metal hatch cover as the ship lurched and rolled, the container was back in position.

The rest of the sailors swarmed onto the deck, some climbing onto the container the others on deck. Soon wires were attached to all the lashing points and the container was secured in position.

I phoned the Captain on the bridge to tell him that we had secured the container back in position. He started to turn the ship back on course. It rolled violently but the container remained lashed to the hatch top. I ordered the sailors and the bosun back to the mess. Before going to join them I grabbed a bottled of rum from my cabin and ordered the chief steward to deliver some cases of beer to the mess.

We sat and drank to our success. In a way it was a triumphant party. We were all proud of what we had accomplished. We had saved the ship from major damage and rescued a container of cargo. Like true seamen we thought we had acted for the benefit of the ship ignoring the danger to ourselves. The drink and companionship allowed us to release the tension and fear. It moulded a group of seamen into a close knit team.

As I walked back along the deck sheltering from the spray and water, I examined the damage. The bulwark was twisted and bent but not beyond repair. While stripping off my heavy weather gear, I was quietly pleased that we had managed to succeed without any outside help.

My phone rang and it was Dick Mortimer. " Come on up for a drink. I know it is early but I expect you need it."

After that we had an uneventful voyage through the Kiel Canal and the Baltic.

When we left Kemi there was a strong wind in the Gulf of Sweden. We were sheltered from this as we sailed down the coast. We were bound for Kotka to load a cargo for Hull. It was also snowing. When we cleared the coast, we hit the full force of the gale.

The wind howled out of the northeast sending the snow horizontally across the decks. Curtains of spray and tons of solid water crashed over the ship as it ran before the wind, forming ice on the rigging and coating everything in a white translucent sheen. Like a toy boat tossed about in a toddlers bath tub, the Swift pitched and rolled, rushing forward on the crest of each huge wave only to crash with a shudder which vibrated along the length of the ship as the wave passed and the bow slammed into the sea. Wires once the size of a finger now started to look the size of an arm and the frozen spray formed tattered banners of some mediaeval army from the lifeboat tackles over the boat deck. The snow did not settle on anything, blown away into the dimness beyond the ship by the strength of the wind.

Standing on the bridge wing with the snow coating the backs of our fur lined coats and stiffening the leather of our hats, Captain Mortimer and I looked anxiously out into the murk but could see nothing more than a few yards ahead of the bow, The ship shuddered as another wave washed across the deck, adding more ice to the equipment, the rigging and the hatch covers. The wave raced foaming white away into the gloom and the almost horizontal snow. Even the lookout on the other bridge wing was hard to distinguish from his surroundings covered in snow as he was.

" We have to turn into the Gulf of Finland," the Captain remarked calmly looking back at the waves coming out of the snow from the direction.

" Do you think she will come round?" I asked trying to keep my voice as calm as that of Captain Mortimer.

" Your guess is as good as mine, Mate but we have to try." Captain Mortimer grimaced. " Go and tell everybody to hang on to something fixed. This is going to be rough."

Captain Mortimer walked purposefully into the wheelhouse and positioned himself by the engine telegraph. I followed and noted in passing that the wheelman was fighting to keep the ship on course, the wheel spinning back and forth in his hand. Picking up the microphone, I advised all the crew to hold onto something immovable, hearing the metallic tones of my voice echoing through the corridors of the ship

Clamping his pipe firmly between his teeth, Captain Mortimer gave the order to the wheelman. " Port ninety degrees!"

The wheelman turned the wheel, holding tightly to the spokes until his knuckles were white. The bow started to turn to port. As the ship swung to the left, the wind screamed even loader through the open door of the wheelhouse. Those on the bridge hardly noticed the sound. At the same time, the ship rolled violently. The movement of the Swift was like a corkscrew causing the structure to grunt and groan. Soon the ship was heeling more and more to starboard as each wave swept over the decks. When almost side on to the howling wind, the bow stopped turning. The ship heeled over even further until those on the bridge were clinging onto the handrails. Then the bow fell away from its heading and the waves were battering the ship in such a way that I thought it was not going to come back upright.

With obvious reluctance, Captain Mortimer gave the order and the ship turned away from the wind and continued her ahead long rush before the raging sea with the waves lifting the stern and almost flinging the ship forward. All of the time, the snow continued to rush horizontally passed across the wheelhouse door and the bridge wing. As though with a mind of its own, the Swift sailed through that howling wind, with spray and snow restricting visibility to a few metres. The noise of the groaning structure, the violent vibrations felt through the feet and the sickening lurches where at times the ship felt as though it was not going to come upright beat at our senses.

The wheelman stood stiff legged and fought the ship through the wheel trying to keep a steady course. My face was highlighted by the glow of the radar as I fought down the building panic as I watched the echo of the approaching land. Staring one moment out into the gloom and the next at the echo sounder, the third mate tried to keep his voice untroubled as he related the lessening depth of water under the keel. Like a statue carved out of wood, Captain Mortimer, gripping the rail with his fur lined mittens, stood on the bridge wing pipe clamped to his teeth staring at the ice accumulating on the structure and rigging.

Suddenly the snow was no longer hurtling passed the wheelhouse door horizontally but was falling much closer to vertically than before. At the same time, the wind appeared to have dropped and the sea had moderated a trifle. The third mate announced that he thought he saw the beam of a lighthouse on the port bow but could not be certain. On hearing this, Captain Mortimer strode into the wheelhouse and consulted the chart.

" How far do you make it to the shore?" he asked me frowning.

" Five miles." I replied looking up from the radar.

" Depth?" he barked at the third mate.

" Fifteen fathoms and shallowing." There was a hint of hysteria in the third mate's voice.

" Now is the time to alter course. We do not have much leeway. Third Mate, get everybody to hold on. I will turn to starboard this time, hopefully away from the shore." I had to admire the way the Captain still managed to sound calm, as though he was in complete control.

The third mate picked up the microphone, announced that they were about to turn the ship and told everybody to hold on, like mine had before his metallic sound echoed through the ship.

With a last look back at the raging sea, Captain Mortimer gave the order to turn the ship to starboard. The wheelman turned the wheel and in silence we all held tight to the rail and watched. The bow turned slowly to the right, hit a wave and came back to port. With a roar that wave passed and the bow was turning at a giddying pace to starboard only to slam into another wave and stop dead in its tracks. The bow came back a little to port but I noted that the Swift had turned a lot more to starboard than it was being pushed back to port.

As though to emphasise the precarious nature of their plight, the ship rolled violently as she came beam onto the wind making the watchers cling ever harder to the rails. There was the sound of breaking crockery and

Captain Mortimer muttered something about bang goes my afternoon tea. For one horrible, breathtaking moment at which the thought that this might be the end, the Swift hung side on to the wind and waves heeled over at an impossible angle. Then with what sounded like a relieved whoosh, the bow turned, the ship came back upright with a rush and heeled over the other way.

Now the Swift was heading into the wind and was riding the waves in a way for which she was designed. Captain Mortimer unclasped his pipe from his jaw and looked around as though awaking from a nightmare. Almost gently, he gave the order to steer a northeasterly course, ordered the engine to be slowed so that the ship did not pound into the waves too much and looked out over the decks.

Turning to me, he said with a relieved grin, " You had better get some of the crew turned out to chip the ice off the deck, Chief Officer. While you and the crew are on deck, I will try to avoid too much water coming aboard. When things calm down a little, join me for a drink in my cabin."

The ship still bounced and shuddered through the waves but there was a feeling that they were once more in control.

Chapter 12

After six months on the Swift, I joined the Star in dry-dock in Sunderland. She is an older version of the Vanguard with derricks instead of cranes. Unlike the Vanguard, the Star's hatch covers had to be pulled over using a winch and wires instead of a hydraulic motor. She had two derricks per hatch and a twenty ton heavy lift derrick amidships. All the accommodation was aft.

When I came on board from the hotel where the officers were lodged, the equipment was in pieces on the quay. Men in boiler suits were clambering over the ship. The electrical manager showed me the winches and explained what had been done to make them serviceable. All the gear on the derricks had been renewed and tested. Painters were clambering up and down scaffolding and coating the hull. All seemed in order aboard a ship in drydock.

Surprisingly, in a week all was back in place, the painting completed and the ship ready to sail. The dry dock was filled with water, the engine started and tested and we sailed for Hull to load cargo for Turku in Finland.

We left Hull to find the passage across the North Sea was fine with the wind from the southwest and the sun shining from a blue sky. The banks of the Elbe River were low and almost lost in the mist when we picked up the pilot. Soon we joined the line of ships waiting to enter the locks leading to the Kiel Canal. I was on the bridge towards the end of my evening watch when the order came to enter the locks. The wind had stiffened and the ensign on the gaff was blowing straight towards the bow of the Star.

Captain Ross looked nervous. " I always worry about this ship going into these locks with the wind astern."

I raised my eyebrows. The locks for the Kiel Canal were wide and long especially in relation to the Star. Indeed at times the locks could accommodate four ships of her size at a time with room to spare. In all my experience of sailing the Vanguard through these locks every ten days we had never had any trouble. The whole process had gone smoothly.

Captain Ross sighed. " You haven't been on the Jet or the Star before have you? Well when the wind in strong astern these two ships lose steerageway if the speed falls below eight knots. It has something to do with the way the accommodation is designed. Going into the locks at eight knots or more can be hairy. We are ready. You had better go to the focastle."

I stood on the focastle watching the lock entrance approach. The wind appeared to be stronger now than it was when we arrived off the canal entrance. The lock entrance approached far quicker than I was used to. Then we were rushing through the gates. I made sure the bosun and the sailors were ready with the wire for the spring. In other words their job was to get the wire from the ship to the shore leading aft. Then they would run this round the bitts and let it out slowly rubbing against the bitts, letting friction slow the ship. The big problem was to let the wire pay out rather than jamb it solid. The result of jamming the wire most likely would be it breaking.

The sides of the lock were rushing passed too fast. I stood by the loudspeaker waiting for the order to send out the wire spring. The sailor stood by with the heaving line ready to throw this ashore. The order came and I waved my hand to the bosun. The heaving line sailed out over the ships rail and the shore man grabbed this before hauling the wire ashore. He attached this to the bollard and hastily stepped away as the wire twanged as it took the weight of the moving ship. The sailors turned the wire on the bits and started paying out the wire between their hands waiting for the order to hold.

I left this to the bosun to supervise and turned my attention to the forward rush of the Star. The side of the lock appeared to be rushing by. Then the ship started to vibrate as the Captain ordered the engine astern. The bow started to swing to starboard. I looked onto the quay. A customs man was standing leaning against a wooden hut near the end of the lock. He was watching us approach smoking a cigar. Suddenly his eyes opened wide as he realised that the bow was swinging towards him. In panic he dropped his cigar and started to run away from the Star. The bow swung back but the anchor caught the hut with a sickening crash. Bits of wood flew up into the air and the hut was flung down the quay into the canal.

The bosun gave the order to start holding the spring. The wire twanged but slowly started to hold. I looked over the bow and started to shout into the intercom the distance to the lock gate. It got closer and closer. I thought we were not going to stop but the ship came to a halt two metres from the gate. Quickly we sent another rope ashore and the ship was secured. It had been a scary experience.

I went ashore with the Captain to assess the damage. Except for some scratches on the paint of the bow, there appeared to be little damage to the ship. All that was left of the hut was the concrete base and some pieces of timber. The Captain was informed that a canal official would come aboard at the other end of the canal with the paperwork. Once back on board the captain informed the head office.

The approaches to Turku compare favourably with most ports I had visited round the world. From the gulf of Sweden the approach winds its way through wood clad green islands and bare rocky outcrops. The sea was blue and clear. Dotting the sea between the islands were yachts of all sizes and colours. Their sails were stiff in the breeze and they were all colours as well. I had to steer the ship between the yachts under the watchful eye of the wheelman. The yachtsmen and it must be said women, waved as we passed close. It was summer and hot with all the officers in shirtsleeves with epaulets.

The cargo was being discharged the next day and I was sitting in my cabin content to let the second and third officers supervise. It was a straightforward discharge and from the papers I was working on a straightforward loading. It was warm in my cabin the ship not having air conditioning. Indeed the main emphasis on the Star was heating for the very cold winters. There was a knock on my door. I called come in and the third mate entered.

" There is an officer from that American ship asking if he could come aboard and see you," he said frowning.

I got up from the desk and looked out of the window at a much larger ship moored along the quay from where the Star was berthed. She was obviously waiting for cargo but the shore cranes were still and silent with their jibs pointing upwards. The large stars and stripes were prominent at her stern.

" Tell him he is more than welcome and show him up here," I smiled.

The third mate was back shortly accompanied by a large man dressed in a blue shirt and jeans. " Mr Briggs from the Reynald J."

" Come in and take a seat." I waved at the settee. " Thanks Joe."

Turning to the man Joe had shown into my cabin, I smiled broadly and said." Welcome aboard the Star. Eddie Gubbins the chief officer."

" Melvin Jones, first officer from the Reynold J." He shook my offered hand.

" Beer?"

" That would be great." His southern american accent very pronounced.

While I collected the beer from the fridge I left him looking round my cabin. He was standing looking down the deck watching the cargo being loaded.

" Well," I said. " It is good to meet you but you must have some other motive. After you have told me what is on your mind we can sit and drink beer while talking."

He laughed. " Straight to the point I see. Yup I do need your help. On American flag ships it costs a fortune to turn the crew to outside their usual duties. My derricks are in the wrong positions. The crew pulled them away from the holds as requested when we arrived. That is my crews duty under the agreement. Now the dock people have decided that we cannot have cranes and we need to re-rig the derricks."

He paused and scratched his head. " What I was wondering was if you could order your crew to position my derricks for me. I will pay them a cash bonus."

I laughed which made him frown. " I cannot order my crew to take on extra work like that. Lets face it, I have no idea where work like that appears in their agreement. What I can do is get the bosun up here and he will tell you whether his sailors will be willing to help you."

" You can't order them? I thought the Brits had authority over their crews."

" Not in that way. If it was to do with our ship, yes I could tell them what to do." I shrugged.

We sat talking about the sea and the differences between the American Merchant Marine and the British. Eventually the bosun walked into my cabin.

" You wanted to see me Chief?"

" Yes. This is the chief officer from the Reynold J. He wants to ask you something."

Melvin Jones put is proposition to the bosun. They haggled about the price but in the end agreed.

" You OK with this?" he asked me.

" Yes bosun. You go ahead. The money ought to be shared by all the deck crew because I will have to insist that two sailors stay behind to look after the Star. You choose the men and I will agree."

" Mr Jones, I will collect my sailors and meet you by the gangway in a few minutes."

" You coming to see what they are up to?"

Melvin Jones looked at me.

" Not particularly though I will come to see your ship."

" No booze I am afraid. All I can offer is coca cola or coffee."

It did not take the sailors long to rig all the hatches with derricks in the union purchase formation. That is where one derrick is positioned over the hold, the other over the quay. The runners are joined. The cargo is attached to the runners on the quay. Using the derrick over the quay runner, the cargo is lifted higher than the hatch combing. It is swung aboard by heaving on the hold derrick and paying out the quay derrick runner. Then using the hold derrick runner, the load is lowered into the hold. That way neither derrick needs to be moved. If the winch men are skilled it can be almost as quick as using a crane. The one drawback is that the cargo load has to be placed in the same place in the hold each time. With a crane the load can be placed more specifically.

Having spent a pleasant morning on the Reynold J looking over the ship, I returned to the Star to make sure the cargo was being stowed properly.

When we arrived back in Hull once more after an uneventful voyage, I was informed that we were to load for Poland. It appeared that there was a heavy lift to be carried on deck and the Arrow was not suited to carry this load. The hatch covers, like those of the Swift, were boards and tarpaulins with a ridge down the centre. I remembered back to the container that had come adrift on the Swift and was glad this was the Star.

Big Bertha the floating heavy lift crane was manoeuvred alongside when all the hatches were closed after the loading of the rest of the cargo. Steam and smoke billowed from the funnel as it was made ready for the heavy load to arrive on the back of a low loader.

When it came, it proved to be a large stainless steel cylinder with pipes and valves attached. I have no idea even now what it was to be used for or attached to. I suppose another ship had taken out additional pieces of the equipment to be assembled on site. I watched closely as the cylinder was lowered into position and noted the way in which the rigging gang made it secure. When the dockers' foreman and the rigger boss came and reported that it was in position and secure, I took the bosun and third mate to make sure it was stowed to our satisfaction. It looked secure and I signed the papers accepting the load was safely stowed.

The voyage from Hull to Gydnia was trouble free. Indeed there was hardly any wind and we managed to get into the locks of the Keil Canal like a normal ship. To me this is what going to sea was all about. Being able to see for miles while at sea with plenty of time to avoid all other ships. By day the sun shining from a cloudless sky and sun bathing on the boat deck while off watch. At night being able to clearly see all the stars though with an electronic Decca Navigator there was no need to take star sights to fix the position of the ship. As with many things the weather affected the mood of the ship. On that trip all was peace and good will.

The problem came when we arrived in Gydnia. It was arranged for the Star to moor at the heavy lift berth to discharge the deck cargo. After the Once the heavy load was ashore, we would then move to the cargo berth. Unfortunately the heavy lift berth was occupied. We were informed that there was no chance of the ship moored there leaving the berth that day. Indeed the dock supervisor told us in confidence that it would most likely be another two days. With a deck cargo of this size there was no way in which we could start the discharge of the rest of the cargo until the deck cargo was put ashore.

" Unfortunately Chief Officer," he said in his heavily accented English as he drank a beer in my cabin, "the floating heavy lift crane is out of commission. You will have to use your heavy lift derrick if you are to get that machinery ashore today."

" I will have to consult my Captain and crew about using our derrick. Finish your beer and then I will be in touch as soon as possible."

He drank his beer and went ashore to consult the dockers' foreman.

Captain Ross was sitting drinking coffee with the ship's agent when I entered his cabin. He frowned when I relayed the information from the supervisor.

" What do you feel about using the heavy lift derrick?" he asked.

" I have used the one on the Swift before so I know what to do. The bosun and some of the crew are familiar with the workings and rigging. I will go and consult them. It might not be possible because of the height of the machinery and the reach of the derrick."

" It is imperative that we get that piece of machinery ashore today," the agent stated bluntly. " We can get compensation from the dock people if we are delayed but that takes a great deal of time and administration to get the money."

I bowed ironically. " I will see what I can do."

He grunted but did not reply.

I called for the bosun and asked him to meet me on deck by the heavy lift derrick.

" We have to rig the heavy lift derrick," I told him bluntly when he joined me. " The agent tells me that the shore heavy lift crane will not be available for two days. He wants us to lift the machine ashore."

The bosun looked hard at the heavy lift derrick and shook his head. " It has not been used for a long time, if at all from what I gather."

" It has been maintained properly or has since I have been in charge," I answered. " We have no choice. Take all the sailors off their other duties and get the derrick rigged."

The bosun shrugged. " I'll get right onto it, chief."

When the derrick was rigged, the bosun called me to join him on deck.

" It is already, chief."

I looked over the rigging and noted that every thing appeared in order. The guys lead aft with the tackle wires led to winches. The runner hook from the lifting tackle was over the centre of the machine.

The bosun pointed. " The lifting cradle was left in place so all the dockers have to do is attach the hook."

I nodded. " Thank you bosun. I will go and inform the agent that all is ready for the lift."

I found the agent in the captain's cabin. " All is ready with our heavy lift derrick. You can inform the stevedores foreman that the dockers can start now."

The agent collected his briefcase. " Come with me and we can see the foreman together."

We walked off the ship together. He led me across the railway lines running along the quay and into the transit shed. To one side of the large double doors were some offices. Dockers were sitting in groups at the back of the shed drinking coffee, reading papers and some playing cards. It was the same scene as would greet any ships officer anywhere in the world where dockers were waiting for cargo work to start.

The foreman bid us enter or I suppose he did because I did not understand Polish. The agent pushed open the door.

Three men were sitting talking around a table covered in papers. Pushed up against the corrugated iron wall of the shed was a desk with a red telephone. The top was also covered in piles of papers. A swivel chair was near the desk.

The agent indicated me and said something to the foreman. He replied shaking his head.

The agent turned to me and said in english. " The foreman is not very happy about his men using your heavy lift derrick to discharge the machine. He says your sailors should man the winches while his men will tend the guide ropes."

I looked at the foreman who was rubbing his stubbly chin. It was obvious from his demeanour that he was not going to give way on this point.

I was not going to give up easily. " I thought their job was to discharge the cargo whether using a shore crane or the ship's gear."

The agent sighed. " That maybe your understanding but in reality he is in control. If he says they will not do it, they will not do it. The authorities will back them up. Besides the dock manager is the brother of his wife. You will not win any argument with him. Those with influence always win in this country."

I glared at the foreman. " Tell him I am disappointed but we will discharge the machine."

With that parting comment I turned on my heel. The agent hurried after me. He caught up as I was climbing the gangway.

" This is not England, mister mate. This is Poland. You have no choice."

" Thank you," I grunted.

Seeing the bosun, I shouted. " Get all the sailors on deck straight away. I am off to see the captain. I will be back in a few minutes."

Captain Ross was still sitting in his cabin looking through some papers from the company. " Yes?"

I shook my head. " The dockers refuse to use our heavy lift derrick. We have a choice. Either we wait two days or more for the heavy lift crane to be available or I get our crew to lift the machine ashore."

Captain Ross smiled. " Eddie welcome to Poland. As you can see this is not Finland. If they will not do the job we will have to ourselves. I leave it up to you to organise things."

" Thanks," I said leaving the cabin.

The bosun and the sailors were waiting for me by the heavy lift derrick when I climbed down onto the deck.

" We have to discharge the machine," I told them. " Organise the sailors, bosun, while I go and ask the engineers to put ballast into one of the low tanks."

The bosun looked puzzled. " Why are the dockers not doing the discharge?"

I shrugged. " Don't ask me. Something about them not trusting our gear. There is politics as well. I suspect though I have no proof of this that they want extra money for using our gear and the company will not pay. Whatever the reason we will have to discharge the machine. Are you and the sailors willing to do this?"

The bosun grinned. " Don't take it out on me, mate. Yes we are more than capable of doing this. We will be ready when they give the order."

I went to the office and phoned the engineer. Though he was startled, after I explained that we had to get the centre of gravity of the ship lower, he said he would do it straight away. The need to get the centre of gravity of the ship lower stemmed from the fact that when the load was lifted, the effective point of the load would be at the head of the derrick. This could make the ship unstable if the centre of gravity was too high to start with. As it was I anticipated that the ship would heel to a great angle as we manoeuvred the load. There was nothing else I could do about that except to warn everybody.

A low loader drew up alongside the ship. I measured by eye the place the lorry was stopped and went ashore to make sure the lorry was in the correct position. Looking at the load and the reach of the derrick, I waved the lorry into the position that I deemed where the load would land. As I was doing this, the foreman and his dockers appeared. I pointed out what was needed and the walked aboard the Star. They attached ropes they carried to the corners of the load and stood waiting. Everything being ready, I went ashore to stand near the lorry and signalled to the bosun to start.

Gingerly, with the gear creaking and groaning, the winch started to move. The runner tackle tightened and the hook gripped the ring in the lifting cradle. I waited with baited breath as the slings tightened until the shackles were taking the load. I signalled for the bosun to stop. He ran down from the winch platform and examined each wire and shackle. He signalled that all was in order and ran back to the winch platform.

I signalled for the winch to start again and the machine in its cradle commenced to lift from the hatch cover. The ship rolled slightly as the derrick head took the load. I held my breath but the ship did not list too heavily. Slowly the load was raised from the hatch covers, the gear still creaking and groaning.

When it was above the height of the rail, I signalled for the lifting to stop. Then for the load to be winched over the side of the ship. The bosun signalled for the winch to port to pull and the one to starboard to let out. In this way the load was slowly swung out towards the quay and the waiting lorry. The dockers made sure the load stayed steady in a fore and aft position. As the load cleared the rail the ship listed towards the quay and I had to signal for the load to be raised slightly. All was going well but I was still nervous, watching the load like a hawk.

What we were doing was not something that I had anticipated. Oh like a great many things we had studied what to do in theory. I had also used single derricks in this way many times. On tankers we had used them that way to load stores or equipment. Once we had used derricks to load barrels of lubricating oil to take to Buenos Aries. Never had I used the heavy lift derrick for a load of this weight. The container on the swift had been much lighter and a regular shape. This was irregular and I was worried that we might damage some of the pipes and other attachments. In addition I was angry that the dockers had not fulfilled what to me was their obligation to unload the cargo.

The load swung slowly out from the ship and over the quay. I waited until it was above the lorry before signalling for them to stop. The lorry driver manoeuvred the trailer until I was satisfied it was right under the load. This next bit was tricky as the weight of the load was taken by the trailer, the ship stated to come upright. The head of the derrick was no longer over the load and there was a danger that the load would be pulled off the lorry. The bosun had to lower the head of the derrick so that this was kept directly over the trailer. With a sigh I watched the load land on the trailer and all the weight come off the runner. The ship rolled slightly and then settled in the upright position. The dockers took over now. They uncoupled the hook and made the load secure on the trailer. The bosun started to bring the derrick back on board.

I left the load now to the dockers. The foreman was waiting at the foot of the gangway but I ignored his hand and brushed passed. He said something but I did not stop or reply. I know it was petty but I was feeling angry and resentful. In normal circumstances I would have invited the docker's foreman to my cabin for a beer. It was not in my nature really and the next day I invited him for a beer during the afternoon.

" Thank you Bosun," I said. Turning to the third mate who had been watching I ordered. " Get the hatches open and the discharge commenced. Bosun come and see me later and I will have a case of beer for the sailors to share this evening as a way of saying thank you."

What surprised us all on board the Star was that the lorry and trailer with the load was parked near the end of the shed and did not move. We discharged the cargo and then loaded without any sign of movement. Just before we sailed the agent bringing the papers on board for the captain to sign told me that the load was still here for a reason. First the dock gate was too narrow for the load to pass through. Well it was not the dock gate but the turning circle once the lorry had passed through the gate into the road. What they were going to do was demolish the gate and part of the wall so that the trailer could be turned into the road. It appeared that the go ahead for this was tangled in local beauracracy. What made me laugh was that now the authorities suddenly realised that when the trailer had exited the docks, it was too high to pass under the tram wires along the street. They were going to need a gang of riggers to accompany the trailer, taking down the wires and then replacing them as the machine was driven through the streets. As I was told by the captain you might be curious but this is none of your business. You make sure the cargo is loaded properly and the ship leaves on time. What happens to the cargo after it has left the ship is not your responsibility.

We did leave on time and sailed back to Hull. There we loaded a cargo for Turku. Before we sailed there were rumours of trouble in the docks in Finland but we did not have any concrete information. The company ordered us to sail in any case. Once again it was a wonderful trip. Even the North Sea was flat calm and sparkling in the sun. In the Baltic the sea was like glass with hardly a ripple. Approaching ships could be spotted miles away and watched easily until they passed. When approaching land it was easy to see the landmarks used for navigation from a distance. These were used to check the Decca Navigation system. Everybody on board was relaxed.

The ship arrived in Turku late one evening. As soon as we were secured the agent walked on board. He quickly disappeared into the captain's cabin. I had just arrived back in my cabin with the third mate when the phone rang. It was Captain Ross. He asked me to come to his cabin. I poured the third mate a beer and asked him to get a gin ready for the second mate when he arrived after making sure the ship was secure for the night.

Captain Ross looked up from a deep conversation with the agent when I arrived. " Ah Eddie. Mr Kanonin informs me that we might have trouble in the morning."

I raised my eyebrows.

Captain Ross continued. " It appears the dockers union have called a strike at all Finnish ports. The dockers here in Turku are having meeting in the morning. If they join the strike, there will be no cargo work in this port."

" Is a strike likely?" I asked the agent bluntly.

Mr Kanonin shrugged. " From my contacts in the port office it seems very likely. We will not know until the morning."

" Shall I get the ship ready for the discharge in the morning before we find out?"

Captain Ross spoke. " I think we should be ready as though there was no threat of a strike. How long is it likely to last if it does go ahead?"

Again the agent shrugged. " It could be a few days or it could be weeks. It depends on the negotiations. Sorry captain I cannot be more specific."

"Thank you Eddie. I'll be down to your cabin for a safe arrival drink once the agent has finished with me. The steward has all the mail and will have this sorted by now."

The next day I arranged for the crew to get the ship ready for the discharge. The hatch covers were rolled back, the derricks pulled against the mast out of the way and the cargo exposed. The third mate and I stood by the rail waiting for the dockers but none came. The shore cranes were parked at the end of the quay still and quiet. The transit shed doors were shut tightly and there was nobody in sight. We waited but nothing moved on the shore.

A car appeared and drew up by the gangway. The agent stepped out and came aboard.

" Well mister mate, it looks as though the Turku dockers have voted to join the strike. I am off to brief the captain."

I shook my head and ordered the third mate to organise the shutting of the hatches. When that is done I asked him to find the bosun and tell him to meet me in my cabin. Without cargo being handled we would have to plan how to keep the crew occupied. This would be difficult because we had no idea how long the strike would last.

Before I could see the bosun, Captain Ross asked me to see him in his cabin. He informed me that the agent had told him the strike was now official and was Finland wide. That meant that there was no possibility that we could take the ship to another port in Finland to discharge the cargo. The company is looking at the option of taking the ship to Sweden. As things stand, we will have to wait for somebody else to decide what we can do.

As it happened we stayed tied up to the quay in Turku for the next six weeks. The company tried to get the Star to Sweden but the Swedish dockers vowed not to handle any ship leaving Finland or with cargoes bound for Finland. Then the sea pilots came out in sympathy. We were stuck.

All we could do was pray that the strike would not last too long. I sat with the bosun and planned a series of maintenance tasks. We planned them in such a way that it was a rolling system and could be finished off at any time. Then there was not much for me to do other than check the progress every day.

What happened was that the captain, the chief engineer and the second mate all played bridge. They introduced me to the game and we played most days.

One morning a large bearded man appeared at my cabin door.

" I am the mate of the Borland, the Danish ship down the quay. I have come to invite you to play my ship at football in a couple of days. There is a pitch just outside the docks. Our agent can provide a referee. What do you think?"

I smiled and waved to a chair. " It is not Carlsberg but would you like a beer or a coffee?"

He grinned back looking more like one of those old Vikings in films I had seen. " Even for a Dane it is a bit early for a beer. Coffee would be fine."

I picked up the phone and ordered coffee. Then I asked the bosun to come and see me.

When he arrived, I asked him if there was anybody on board who could organise a football team.

" Joe McDewer, the chief machinist, was a player with Kilmarnoch in his youth. He is always on about playing football. I will ask him if he is willing to organise the team."

" Good," the mate of the Borland smiled. " I will let you know what time the kick off should be. We usually play for beer. The team that loses provides the beer that evening. How will that go down with your crew?"

The bosun shrugged. " We will play for beer. I'll go and see if I can find Joe and get him started."

That afternoon Joe suddenly appeared at my door holding his greasy hat in his hand. " Mr Mate. I have been round the ship and found out all those willing to play football for the ship day after tomorrow. I hope you do not mind but I have called a meeting of all those in the mess after dinner this evening. Will you come to the meeting? The bosun tells me that you were part of the Vanguard's team which won the Kotka cup one summer. Will you play for us? The third mate has signed up."

I laughed. " Joe, I will be pleased to play. Football is my passion. I'll see you all this evening. Oh by the way, we will have to establish what we will wear. There are no company football shirts on board. I will ask the captain if he knows where we could borrow some shirts.'

" Thank you Mr Mate. See you this evening."

I told the captain of the planned football match and to my surprise he was enthusiastic. He immediately went to the cargo office and phoned the agent. Later that afternoon a van drew up at the gangway and a man carried some cartons and put them on the deck. The sailor on duty organised for these to be taken to the cargo office and then came to tell me. When I opened the first carton I found some football shirts. Red with a white sash. The second carton had blue shorts. I ordered the sailor to take them to the mess ready for the meeting.

That evening almost all the crew were jammed into the crew mess. Joe was about to start the meeting when the captain walked in. He waved everybody to relax and took a seat at the back.

Joe was for the first time straight and confident. " I have a list of those who have volunteered to play. From the list of fourteen I have picked a team. It is a bit speculative but I have consulted everybody I could and found out as much as possible about the individuals I have chosen. Actually it amazes me as to how many have played football at reasonable level."

He then read out the team. I was surprised to find he included me and the third mate in addition to the third engineer. He asked if we could all be on the quay tomorrow morning for a kick about and a discussion of positions.

Captain Ross then spoke. " I think this is a great idea. All you have to do is win for the honour of the ship, the company and Britain. These cartons contain football shirts of various sizes. Now I believe that the loser supplies the beer for a party the evening of the match. In the unlikely event of us losing, I will supply the beer for the party. I will be there to cheer you on. Good luck."

I could see from the reaction of the crew that Captain Ross had just won the admiration of all the men.

We won the football match. Much to the amusement of the Danes Joe produced a can of beer to revive anybody who fell down with an injury. Then there was the biggest drinking session on the Danish ship I had ever taken part in.

The dockers came back to work after almost six weeks on strike. The ship was in pristine condition having had that much attention. On the docks however the export cargo was piled up. We heard that lorries were waiting to deliver more as soon as the go ahead was given. The company informed us that the ship was to load as much cargo as was safe. This meant on deck as well as in the holds.

I laid out the cargo book to calculate the stability of the ship. This was a measure of whether the ship would always return to the upright when rolling in a seaway. Usually because the ship was never down to her marks and the cargo was spread through the holds, the calculation was completed when the cargo had been loaded. I worked out that if the ship were to load as much cargo as possible, I would have to undertake the calculation many times as the cargo was loading.

While the discharge was progressing, I walked to the cargo office in an attempt to find out in which order the cargo was to be loaded. The shore cranes rattled and creaked as the cargo was taken ashore. The dockers appeared to be working as fast as they could to clear the backlog of import cargo. Forklift trucks and tractors with their trailers loaded high with boxes rushed passed. All was now activity after the weeks of no movement.

Inside the cargo office all was confusion. Pieces of paper were piled on any surface. Clerks were shouting at each other and down the phones. The clerk in charge of the Star's loading showed me the schedule of loading. He gave me a copy that gave estimated weights of the various consignments. I thanked him and left him to the chaos of the office.

Once back on the ship, I phoned the second engineer. He gave me the weights and positions of the fuel tanks. These would have to be included in the calculation. Everybody seemed to be tense as though worried about the propriety of loading this much cargo.

In the end the discharge was accomplished. The import cargo was cleared away and everything made ready for the loading to start the following morning.

I spent most of the morning in the cargo office attempting to influence the order in which the cargo arrived at the ship. This was important. I had to make sure that the heavy items came first so that they were loaded low down in the ship. This would provide stability when the ship sailed. We came to an agreement and I went back to the ship to monitor the loading.

It was a tense time. The dockers worked over time. The cargo kept coming and being loaded on board. I had the second and third mates making sure that I was fed the information about the weights of each consignment. These I fed into my calculation, making sure that the ship would be stable on the way home. The holds were full and we shut the hatch covers. Then the dockers spread dunnage on the hatch covers and the deck cargo started to be placed on this dunnage. I furiously did my calculations and when I was satisfied that the cargo was safe, I called a halt. The cargo superintendent came on board and pleaded with me to take just one more consignment but I refused.

With the cargo loaded, we waited for all the paperwork was delivered. Nervously because the stability issue was so tight with all the cargo on deck, I checked the calculation again. The result was that there was adequate stability to sail the ship safely back to Hull. With the bosun I checked the tarpaulins covering the deck cargo to make sure that they were watertight. Then we tested the lashings and found that they were tight and secure. The ship was all ready to sail

Once the pilot was on board, the Star sailed from Turku. All the time I had been sailing on the Star I had never seen her so low in the water. The pilot made a joke about this referring to bloody dockers ruining the Finnish economy. I had not thought about the strike in that way. To me it was a case of the company not getting any revenue and the effect this would have on our operations. That thought was to come back to haunt me later that year but at the time with the cargo packed into the ship and the freight rates being paid to the company for its carriage was not something that worried me. It obviously worried the Finns or the pilot would not have spoken. There was to be a period of belt tightening until the exports started to flow again.

It was a glorious day with hardly any wind even though it was getting towards autumn and the advent of snow and bad weather. The ship sailed serenely between the islands still mostly green though there were signs of shrubs starting to turn brown.

The ship turned sharply to port along the channel, heeling to starboard in the usual way. When the pilot ordered the course to steer and the ship stopped turning, it did not return to the upright. It remained like a drunken sailor leaning sideways.

There was a stunned silence on the bridge. All eyes were staring in my direction. I frantically went over my calculations in my head. There was nothing wrong with the stability of the ship according to my sums.

" Well?" Captain Ross asked bluntly, his expression hard and accusing.

" My calculations gave us adequate stability for the voyage home, Captain. I have no idea why this has happened."

" Do something, chief officer before we get to any rough water!" There was panic in the pilot's voice.

I lifted the phone.

The second engineer answered. " Engine room."

" Pump some ballast into number three centre tank, Nigel. We seem to have a problem."

" Will do Eddie. What happened up there? My bloody tea is all over the engine room deck."

" We seem to have a lack of stability. I'll tell you about it this evening."

The ship stayed heeled to starboard and all on the bridge held their breath. The ballast in the tank did its job and the Star came upright again. We sailed for about a mile and then turned to starboard. The ship heeled to port but when the ship was back on course came back and stayed upright again.

" What you did seems to have worked," Captain Ross shook his head and frowned. " Call me when we approach the pilot station. I'll be in my cabin."

Over dinner that evening I joined the Captain and the Chief Engineer at their table after the third mate took over on the bridge.

Captain Ross looked hard at me. " Have you redone the calculations?"

I bristled but stayed expressionless. " Yes. Using all the weights I was given and the position of the cargo, we had adequate stability. The ship should have come back to the upright."

" With the ballast in place, we are over loaded, you know."

" I am aware of that. We will use a little oil on the way back and some water so I will figure out how to make sure we are showing our load line when we arrive in Hull."

The chief engineer coughed. " I might be able to help. Just before we leave, we put some fuel into the high tank in the engine room. I could put most of this back in the bilge tanks before we arrive."

Suddenly there was silence round the table, the Captain and me looking in horror at the chief engineer. Captain Ross broke the silence.

" Did you not think to tell Eddie?" His voice was flat as though he was trying hard to keep is anger in check.

" We always transfer fuel in that way. I have never been asked for the figures before.'" The Chief engineer did not appear to understand what he had caused.

I could not contain my anger. I struggled to remain seated and not reach across the table to grab him. The experience of the ship heeling over and then not coming back upright was too close, had happened to recently. On very few occasions had I felt like hitting another person?

I was beside myself, my body trembling with anger. I usually did not swear. " What the fucking hell was you thinking of? Bloody hell. I told the second engineer why I need accurate figures for the fuel weights and positions. The ship almost capsized because of you."

Captain Ross interrupted. " That is enough, Eddie. It will not do us any good throwing accusations at each other. Melvin did not think. What we need to do is think about how to make sure the ship is not over loaded when we arrive in Hull."

I was so angry I was passed the time when I was able to control my emotions. Throwing down my napkin, I pushed back my chair and stormed out of the dining room. I did not look or say anything to the chief engineer. I relieved the third mate on the bridge. Keeping watch, concentrating on a voiding other ships and navigating the Star calmed my temper. By the time the third mate returned to the bridge at eight o'clock I had my temper under control.

Eric told me. " Captain Ross would like to see you in his cabin when you have done your rounds of the ship."

Half an hour later, I knocked on the Captain's door. On being asked to enter, I found the chief engineer sitting with a gin and tonic by his elbow where it rested on the table.

Captain Ross smiled. " Pour yourself a gin and tonic and sit down. Melvin is here to talk things through."

Once I was sitting on the settee with a gin and tonic on the table, Melvin spoke. " Look Eddie I am sorry for what happened. I have to admit I did not think. We have done that with the fuel every trip so it was not something different. I did not realise how much a few tons of oil being pumped to the service tank would effect the stability of the Star."

I smiled in reply for the first time since dinner. " I have calmed down now, Melvin. I suppose I was affected by the way the pilot and Captain Ross looked at me when the ship heeled over. It was as though they were accusing me of miscalculating the stability. Can you tell me how much fuel we will use on the way back to Hull? Also the water. Then we can sit down and work out how to pump out the ballast, move fuel and water to make sure the ship is showing her loading marks when we arrive in Hull.

Captain Ross looked relieved ad poured us both another gin and tonic.

We arrived in Hull safely and the plimsoll line was showing as we passed through the locks late that evening. I was surprised to see the agent waiting on the quay for the Star to dock. Usually he would be on board early in the morning because nothing would happen during the night.

I soon found out why after being summoned to the Captain's cabin once the ship was secure.

Mister Brown the agent was blunt. " I have ordered a car for you early tomorrow morning so that you can catch the train to London. Your tickets are in this envelope. The chief officer, Terry Connors has broken his leg this afternoon. There is nobody else available so they need you. Captain Brookes will be waiting to sign you on and the Vanguard will sail tomorrow afternoon."

Captain Ross shrugged. " I will be sad to see you go, Eddie. The deck department has been well run while you were here."

After signing off, I said goodbye and went back to my cabin to pack.

Chapter 13

The Vanguard looked much the same when the taxi turned the corner of the shed to drop me at the bottom of the gangway. I did notice that the cranes were stowed and the hatches closed as though the ship was ready to sail. There was no sign of any dockers though it looked as though there were people still working in the office. Charlie Lucas, the third mate who I had met several times, was standing at the top of the gangway watching me get out of the car.

With a broad grin, he rushed down the gangway to help me with my bags. " Hello Eddie. I see you made it on time. The clerks are completing the paper work. Captain Foster says we sail at two to catch the tide, so you were cutting it bit fine. He is waiting for you in his cabin."

I had never met Captain Foster. He proved to be a man of medium height though over weight. The way that he sat in his chair emphasised the way his stomach overflowed his trousers. His face had the look of somebody who drank too much. I noticed that his hands shook slightly when he signed the articles to witness my signature. He did however have a reputation as a competent captain.

After I had signed all the paperwork, he did inform me that we had a special cargo as he put this trip. The Vanguard was built with four passenger cabins but these were hardly ever used. On previous trips, we had carried the odd businessman who was combining a business trip with a mini holiday. This trip we were to carry four of the office secretaries. It appeared that all the office women had been given the chance to sail on the Vanguard. The company held a ballot and these girls had been successful. Captain Foster was a little sceptical on how it would work out.

" They will have the run of the ship as far as it goes," he concluded in his harsh Glasgow accent. " That is the places where the officers go. They are forbidden to go down to the sailors' decks. I did tell them that they could go onto the bridge at any time as long as they did not interfere with the running of the ship. As with any other passengers carried before on the ship, I will hold Captain's drinks before dinner in the evening. I am sorry but that will not involve you because you will be on watch. Now go down and get ready to sail."

" Yes sir!" I retorted with a mock bow. Captain Foster's face clouded but he did not react outwardly.

After we had cleared the locks and were off down the river, I had an hour to spare until my watch. I spent this in the cargo office pouring over the cargo plan and manifest to familiarise myself the cargo aboard the Vanguard. It was the usual type of cargo.

We were passed Greenwich and the change of pilots when I came on watch at four o'clock. Bobby Spencer the second mate, another man I had never met, reported that all was in order. He was of medium height with black hair, a swarthy complexion and round open face.

" See you at dinner." He grinned. " I am off to get a shower and prepare to meet our passengers in the captains cabin. Pity you will miss all the fun."

I called Captain Foster just before we approached the pilot station. When he came on the bridge I did note that he looked a trifle vague and his speech little slurred. I felt bad but decided to keep my eye on how he was dealing with his duties while I had the chance. After the pilot left it was time for dinner and the third mate came to the bridge to relieve me.

The four secretaries were in the dining room when I arrived. I noticed that they were spread two to a table. That is two with the senior officers, two with the junior. I never did work out whether it was Captain Foster's orders or whether the steward had taken the initiative.

Captain Foster took me over to the junior officers table. The second mate, third and forth engineer, and electrician were there. The second engineer was never relieved for dinner because the time taken to clean up was too long. He would have a meal plated up and left in the kitchen for when he came off watch.

" I don't think you have met the chief officer. Mr Gubbins this is Jane and Margaret. They work in the head office."

They both rose and shook my hand.

" Hello," Jane smiled. She was slim with long blonde hair. Her eyes gave the impression that she was laughing at the world. I was to find out that she was never silent. She always had some thing to say no matter on what subject. Her dresses were very short and hugged her figure.

Margaret nodded to me hardly able to look me in the eye. She was small, well about five feet two. Her hair, as were her eyes, was brown, curly and short. She was quiet and hardly ever said anything unless spoken to directly.

I took my seat on the captain's table. Captain Foster introduced the two girls.

" This is Mr Gubbins the chief officer. Susan and Ruth."

They both waved and said hello.

Ruth was a tall girl or more truthfully a woman looking as though she was as old as me. She wore a tailored suit with a white blouse. Her brown hair reached the collar of her jacket. Ruth was the secretary to the personnel manager.

Susan sat next to me. She looked at me with large blue eyes from a very serious face. She was verging on the chubby but not fat. She dressed in a floral dress that I noticed came halfway up her thighs when she sat.

I quickly eat my meal and stood to leave before the coffee came. Susan raised an eyebrow.

I smiled. " I have to get back on the bridge and take over from the third mate so that he can have his meal. I do the four to eight watch, morning and evening. I'll se you later."

At the end of my watch, I walked round the ship as usual checking that all was in order. Over the time I had been a chief officer I had found this inspection period quite calming after being on the bridge. Those members of the crew who were still up gave me a few words of greeting. After the tour, I always reported to the captain in his cabin. Depending on the captain, I would sometimes have a drink.

Captain Foster was not in his cabin. I thought about going to find the second engineer who I had hardly met but heard voices coming from the saloon. The captain, the chief engineer and the four passengers were there playing cards. Well two girls and the officers were playing cards while Susan and Margaret were sitting reading.

Captain Foster smiled and waved to a table in the corner laden with bottles. " Pour yourself a gin and tonic."

After making sure the drink was just right, I reported on my rounds of the ship to Captain Foster." Everything is in order sir."

Captain Foster nodded and returned to his game. I sat next to Susan. She smiled shyly and put down her book. We sat for a while talking of the sea and her life in London. After a time, I said goodnight and went back to my cabin.

I was surprised the next morning after I had had my morning consolation with the bosun at about six thirty, Susan walked into the wheelhouse.

" I hope you do not mind me coming to the bridge but I was awake. Captain Foster told us we could come to see the officer on watch whenever we wanted. I will not get in the way."

I smiled back. " You are welcome. Would you like a mug of coffee?"

After I had made the coffee, we stood close on the bridge wing looking out into a rather grey day. There was an autumn chill in the air. The sea was gently creased with just a touch of white caps. The ship pitched slowly and there were a few creaks and groans in the structure.

Pulling her coat closer, Susan spoke suddenly. " Have you met Mister Karlson?"

I looked at her wondering where this conversation was leading. " No. Why?"

Susan looked directly at me her expression sombre sending chills up my spine. " I am in Captain Harris' department. I think you know him from this ship. Anyway, he brought this man into the department one day. I did not like him from the start. He had that lean and hungry look which many men have. His eyes are hard, showing no emotion. He was introduced as an efficiency expert, whatever that is. All I know is that he then proceeded to ask questions about all we did. I am worried about what will happen in the company. I have this feeling that the reason we have been given the chance to come on this voyage is to soften the blow when they get rid of some of the office workers."

I did not know what to say. " I expect you are worrying too much. The company have to become as efficient as possible. We will have to wait and see what happens."

I put my arm round her shoulder and squeezed. She laid her head on my shoulder. I could feel the trembling of her body and was suddenly very nervous. Whether there was anything in her suspicions, I had no idea. If she was this scared about what was happening, I told myself, I will have to pay attention to what is happening outside the close confines of the ship. We stood like that for a while and then I had to move because a ship was bearing down on our starboard side.

" Go and get ready for breakfast. I have to avoid this ship. I will see you later."

Turning the Vanguard to starboard, I passed round the stern of the other ship and then put the Vanguard back on course. I lent on the rail of the bridge wing deep in thought. Even though there had been a nagging itch at the back of my mind, this was the first occasion when the changes taking place in the shipping industry had been made specific. I had been aware through reading newspapers and magazines that shipping was changing. There was the introduction of containerisation. The dockers in London had mentioned this to me in the context of container berths being built. The dockers were adamant that they would not work this new technology. Then I remembered that the fear among the dockers was that these new ways of loading and discharging ships would lead to a loss of jobs.

Everything in the new methods of handling cargo was designed to speed up the process so that ships could carry more cargo over a given time period. Then there were ideas about enabling cargo to be loaded or unloaded straight from lorries without the need for transit sheds. On the Vanguard and other company ships there was already a trend to load cargo on pallets that remained in the hold. This meant that there was no need to manhandle the cargo at any stage. There had already been meetings with the dockers and stevedoring companies about the need to reduce the numbers in each gang.

The third mate came to relieve me and thoughts of changes in operations fled as I handed the ship over to him. Warning him that we would be approaching the Elbe River soon and to make sure he called the captain in time.

A few evenings later having transited the Kiel Canal and sailed northeast through the Baltic Sea, I came off watch, did my rounds and joined the second engineer for a drink. Early because I had had interrupted sleep the night before, I went back to my cabin.

I made myself a coffee, undressed and sat at my desk filling in the overtime sheets and the logs for that day. It was peaceful. The sound of the sea against the hull and a gentle rolling. I put the ledgers away and laid my uniform out ready for the morning.

There was a knock on my door. I pulled on my trousers and when I opened the door, Susan was standing outside. " Come in. Sorry about my lack of clothes but I was ready for bed."

She smiled and followed me into my cabin. " You did not come to see the captain tonight. I was wondering if everything was all right. I could not get to the bridge to see you after dinner. The girls wanted to sit on the boat deck and watch the evening settle."

I waved her into a seat but she sat on my bunk, dangling her legs over the edge. Once more her skirt that was short to start with rode up her thighs. I went to the kitchen and fetched her a coca cola from the fridge. When I got back she was lying full length on my bunk, her shoulders held up by the pillows. For the first time after handing her the coca cola, I lent over and kissed her. Her arms came round my shoulders and she kissed me back.

We made love that night to the sound of the generator and the swish of the sea. Susan clung to me as though she wanted this to happen forever. Early in the morning she kissed me and left to go back to the passenger cabins.

When we arrived in Helsinki, the girls were collected from the ship for a few days exploring Finland. Funnily that night I missed Susan in my bunk.

The ships agent delivered a message from the cargo department of the company. It told me that they had secured the shipping of a very special paper cargo and if we managed to get this back to the UK without damage, the company would get a long term contract. You will have to make sure that this cargo is loaded safely, checked for any damage and looked after on the voyage back, the message concluded.

I worked out that the best way of making sure the paper was safe was to load all the other cargo leaving just enough room in the centre of the hold. This would mean building up the other cargo in a wall so that there was a deep well into which to lower the special cargo. In fact this is how we loaded any special boxes sent from the embassy for repatriation back to the U K.

Susan and the other girls came back to join the ship in Kotka. Bobby Spencer suggested that the officers who were off duty take the girls off to a restaurant for a farewell meal the night before we sailed. For once I declined and offered to look after the ship that night. Susan was bitterly disappointed but I pointed out to her that it was important that I planned the final loading of the cargo before going to bed. When they all came back to the ship late that night, they piled into my cabin and dragged me from my bed. Then full of bonhomie and merriment, they proceeded to conduct an impromptu party. It was very late when Susan joined me in my bed and she then promptly fell asleep before we could make love. I had to wake her when I was dressed ready to supervise the loading of the cargo that morning. For some reason I had breakfast with just the captain and the second engineer. Bobby Spencer and Charlie Lucas looked the worst for wear when they joined me later. All I could do was grin at having to look after the loading on my own. I thought back to the times when I had been in a similar state and the officers who had covered for me.

The cargo of newsprint rolls were loaded the next day leaving a deep square pit in the centre of the hold. Though at the time I did not really comprehend the significance, the rolls were loaded leaving an individual lifting strap in place. This would enable the discharge gang to connect the strap to the crane hook and lift the cargo free without any need to place slings around the rolls before lifting from the hold. Placing slings around the cargo entailed a great deal of physical effort on the part of the dockers and was one reason why there was a need for large gangs. With this method, the gang sizes could be reduced without compromising safety because there was no manhandling of the cargo. All that was required was for the dockers to attach the crane hook to the sling and make sure the paper rolls did not hit the structure during discharge. It was another indication of the new ways of speeding up loading and discharge without the need for more dockers. As Dillon sang, times they were a changing.

The newsprint rolls were piled high around the pit forming a ten feet high wall. Into the hole we were to load the rolls of special cargo. I stood at the head of the gangway looking along the quay. There was no sign of the cargo. The dockers trooped down the gangway and disappeared into the shed for their coffee break. We waited and still the cargo did not appear. During the afternoon the stevedore manager came walking along the quay and waved to me as he climbed the gangway.

" Mister mate I am afraid I have sent the dockers home," he said as he reached the deck. " We have been told that the high glossy paper is not ready so will not be loaded today. You can complete the paper work and sail."

I stared at him and then grabbed his arm, pulling him over to the hold. Even though he was much bigger than me he followed meekly.

Pointing down the hold, I banged the combing to emphasise my words. " Do you see that? What the hell do you think will happen to that cargo when we sail. The first heavy sea and that will come tumbling down. You have to get the dockers to move the cargo before they do home."

The stevedore manager shrugged. " It is too late. They will not return. You will have to do something about that."

" Bugger you!" I said in a tight voice. " Leave my ship now."

His eyes flew wide but he turned on his heels and left the ship.

To the third mate who was standing by my side, I ordered," Get me the bosun quick. Then go and tell the captain that I will let him know when we are ready to sail."

While waiting for the bosun to join me, I could only stare into the hold. Still angry with the dockers, my mind was racing. Every conceivable way to make the cargo safe passed through my head but all involved a great deal of work and, more to the point, special equipment.

The bosun confirmed my worst fears when he joined me and looked down the hatch. " What the bloody hells are they thinking of? They should have made that lot safe before leaving the ship."

I looked at the bosun. " Is there any way we can get the sailors to do anything about that?"

The bosun shrugged. " You know the sailors mister mate. They will do anything you ask. They have all heard about the way you risked yourself to get that container back on board the Swift. They do not have the equipment or the expertise to solve that. I would not let them take the risk. I am sorry chief."

I shook my head. " Even I would not ask them to move the cargo. Have we anything we can use to shore that lot up?"

It was the bosun's turn to shake his head. " Not really."

His grizzled face weather beaten from too many storms was lost in thought. " We have some large cargo nets we could use. They might not do much in a storm but they will give some support in normal weather."

I smiled at him. " Thank you, Dick. Get the men turned to and do the best you can. Then pray for fine weather on the trip back. I had better go and tell Captain Foster."

Whether it was mine and the bosun's prayers or just plain good luck, the weather on the way back to London was relatively calm. Even so Susan noticed that I was up tight and nervous. Even when making love, if the ship took a sudden lurch, I would sit up in bed intently listening for the sound of moving cargo. She would pull me back down and try to calm my nerves. It was with great relief tinged with sadness that I watched as we picked up the pilot and sailed into the protected water of the Thames. The sadness came from the fact that I would have to say goodbye to Susan. In true seaman's fashion I was treating the whole episode as a pleasant interlude but would once she had left the ship sail away to other pleasures. All the girls were there for a last lunch as we sailed along the river.

We docked in Purfleet the newsprint berth. With trepidation I ordered the hatches to be opened. The bosun joined me as the hatch covers rumbled back looking as nervous as I was but trying not to show it. When the hatches were back, it was revealed the cargo in exactly the position we had loaded it in Kotka. With a collective sigh of relief, we both grinned at each other. Not one roll had shifted and there was no damage. Even though it was afternoon, the dockers clambered aboard and soon the cargo was being discharged. The rolls were loaded straight into lorries and carried directly to the printing works.

The taxi arrived and the girls were ready to leave. Susan came to say goodbye, giving me a kiss. I promised to see her if it was possible once the ship came to London again.

Once all the cargo was discharged at Purfleet, the Vanguard was navigated up river to Surrey Docks to load an export cargo. There we were informed that we would be carrying two passengers this voyage, Captain Harris now Marine Superintendent and Lars Karlson the efficiency expert.

After we sailed out into the North Sea, Captain Harris invited me to come to his cabin for a coffee one morning. When I arrived, Captain Foster and Lars Karlson were already there.

" Sit down Eddie," Captain Harris waved to a chair. " Pour yourself a coffee."

When I had my coffee and was sitting, Captain Harris spoke. " Eddie this is Lars Karlson. He is going to Finland to talk to people about making the system more efficient. I am accompanying him to put into a practical shipping context what ever is decided."

He looked at Captain Foster. " Mister Karlson would like to take the opportunity while on board to quiz the officers about their feelings as far as making the operation more efficient."

Captain Foster grunted. " Asking the turkeys if they like Christmas."

Lars Karlson stayed calm. " I will explain why the more efficient operation is needed. As you must be aware, the nature of cargo handling is changing. There are new ways of what could be termed cargo packaging."

I interrupted. " You are not saying that the company is going for containers? That system is only being implemented on a few routes and not short haul."

Lars looked sharply at me. " You appear to know a great deal of what is happening."

I smiled. " I read the papers and magazines. Lloyds list has a section on new technologies. I have read that to make cargo operation more efficient all areas of the transport chain had to been integrated. The ships, port terminals, trucks and trains had to been adapted to handle the cargo without the need for changing the packaging."

Both Captains Foster and Harris were staring at me. Lars Karlson was frowning.

Lars Karlson stated. " We in the company have already started to implement some of the methods needed to speed up the process. Like pallets loaded straight into the ship, rolls of newsprint with strops in place and greater use of fork lift trucks in the hold

Captain Foster got to his feet. " I have to check the progress of the ship and then lunch."

I did likewise.

That evening after dinner Captain Harris joined me on the bridge. There was at first a great deal of traffic so he stood on the bridge wing watching and not saying anything.

When the traffic had diminished, I grinned. " Do you miss all this?"

He sighed. " Yes at times. When I am in a boring meeting, I wish I were back at sea. Most of the time I am pleased to get home to my wife most evenings. To change the subject. You impressed mister Karlson back there this morning. He has talked to a great many seamen but you are the first who appeared to have some understanding of what is happening in the shipping industry."

I shrugged. " All I do is read the magazines and papers. You ought to know that we have plenty of time while on watch to think about these things. As for flags of convenience ships, I was sailing out of the Persian Gulf years ago when the first one hundred thousand ton tanker sailed in, the Universe Apollo if I remember right. She is registered in Liberia even though she is owned by a Greek. Even Shell registered some tankers under the Liberian flag. It is much cheaper I suppose. What will all this efficiency drive mean for the Baltic Steamer fleet?"

Captain Harris hesitated. " The obvious result will be less ships needed to carry the same amount of cargo. We are nowhere near that yet."

I laughed. " No. I imagine the main stumbling block will be to get the dockers to agree to work longer hours. They are bound by rules and what they call custom and practice."

Captain Harris smiled. " There is always the possibility of moving the Finland operation from Surrey Docks to a port where the dockers are flexible. Anyway, I must get going and the traffic is increasing. Keil Canal later tonight."

As we sailed from Keil into the Baltic Sea, I was in my cabin drinking coffee with the second engineer. The phone rang.

It was Charlie Lucas the third mate sounding almost hysterical. " Eddie. Captain Foster was just leaving the bridge after we cleared the pilot when he collapsed. He is sitting leaning up against the door frame and all I can get out of him is groaning."

My mind was racing but I tried to sound calm. " I'll be right with you. Call the chief steward and tell him to get the stretcher on the bridge."

I dropped everything and raced up to the bridge. Captain Foster looked bad. His flesh was the colour of putty and there were beads of sweat on his brow. Charlie Lucas was bending over him.

" You take care of the ship," I ordered as the chief steward came into the wheelhouse accompanied by the bosun and two sailors.

The chief steward, the member of the crew with a first aid certificate though all the deck officers had had some training when taking their masters certificates, took charge. He had the bosun and the sailors get the captain onto the stretcher and then carried back to his cabin. Once certain that all had been done, I went in search of Captain Harris.

He looked up from the book he was reading when I came into his cabin. " Good morning, Eddie. What can I do for you?"

I hesitated for a second and then said. " Captain Foster has been taken ill and is in bed in his cabin. The chief steward is looking after him. I do not know if it life threatening. I thought you should know."

He heaved himself to his feet and followed me out of the cabin. When we reached the captain's cabin door, I waved him inside. " I will go up to the bridge and make sure the third mate is ok. He had quite a shock."

Later that day with the captain in bed, I sat with Captain Harris in my cabin.

" Will you be taking over now?" I asked bluntly.

He smiled and shook is head. " Though young Eddie the idea attracts me there is no way in which I could take over. I am on the ship as a passenger and only signed on as a supernumery. That is done to get round the passenger ship regulations. As such I cannot legally take over as master of the ship. I am afraid that in a legal sense you will now be in charge until Captain Foster recovers or another captain joins."

I shook my head. " I thought that was the case. If I need advice will you be available for me to ask?"

Captain Harris held up is hand. " I cannot think when you would need my advice but I will be here if you need me."

I nodded. " Thank you."

At midnight I went to the bridge to talk to both the second and third mates. I pointed out that I was going to keep my watches but might need some help to cover for the captain.

All went well and Captain Foster appeared to recover a little. We radioed the agent in Helsinki to arrange for a doctor to meet the ship. Captain Harris true to his word did not interfere and stayed in the background. Lars Karlson continued to talk to the officers and to work on a schedule that would satisfy the criteria for more efficient operations.

The problem arose when we were a day out of Helsinki. I was keeping my watch early one morning. The bosun had come to see me to discuss the day's schedule of work, the steward had delivered my coffee and toast and dawn had broken on a grey overcast day. Jesse Lawrence, the radio officer came into the wheelhouse with a piece of paper in his hand.

" Eddie, you had better read this." He handed me the paper. " It came in a few minutes ago."

I took the paper and red. " Captain Foster. The Finnish pilots have gone on strike over pay and conditions. There will be no pilots available for the approaches and docking in Helsinki. The government have passed an ordinance giving all those ships that use Finnish ports regularly exception from the pilotage rules as long as the strike lasts. Please confirm that you will be willing to pilot the Vanguard into Helsinki. You are to berth at number six berth when you arrive."

I shook my head. " I suppose I will have to pilot the ship into the port. Send a reply in Captain Foster's name that we will bring the ship into Helsinki."

Jesse grinned. " I bet you did not expect this when the captain was taken ill. I'll send the message straight away."

When the third mate came to my relief at eight o'clock, I ask him to look out the sailing directions for the approaches to Helsinki. " Put these alongside the charts of the approaches and the port."

I had a good idea of what was entailed when sailing into Helsinki. By looking at the sailing directions and the charts I was going to make sure I was familiar with the approaches. The sailing directions are a book of instructions about what to look for when entering or leaving a port. There are pictures of coastline and details of the lights and leading marks.

After breakfast I went back to the bridge and familiarised myself of the approaches to Helsinki. After an hour I had convinced myself that I could navigate the ship through the islands off the port of Helsinki.

When we approached Helsinki the next morning there was cold drizzle blocking out the horizon. The wind was blowing this out of the northeast making it cold, the first sign of winter. My heart started beating too fast and my palms were damp. I had expected to be able to see the land when I came back to the bridge after breakfast. The third mate plotted the position of the ship and adjusted the course to make sure the ship was on track. I tried to keep a calm face and went out onto the bridge wing with the binoculars.

I was staring ahead when the drizzle eased. The islands off Helsinki came into view. I was able to make out the first leading marks, one above the other.

" Put the steering onto manual and get the sailor on the bridge," I ordered the third mate.

He spoke into the tanoi. Very quickly one of the sailors appeared in the wheelhouse and took over the steering when Charlie Lucas engaged the manual control. He pointed out the course.

Charlie stood beside me on the starboard bridge wing looking anxiously through his binoculars for the leading lights as we passed an island in renewed drizzle. He spotted them and indicated to me where they were. I waited as the bottom leading mark, which was the nearest, slowly came in line with the higher one, which was further away. Just before they were in line I ordered the wheel to be turned to starboard and watched as the bow turned. To my surprise, I had judged things right and when the marks were dead ahead of the ship. One was exactly above the other. I gave the order to steer a course that would keep them one above the other ahead of the ship.

Quickly I walked to the other side of the ship, my raincoat damp and heavy. I wiped the raindrops off the peak of my cap, clamped the binoculars to my eyes and stared ahead trying to make out the breakwater entrance to the harbour. The drizzle eased and the entrance with the leading marks was visible. Once more I waited patiently until turning the ship onto the leading marks and making for the harbour entrance.

With a flourish and a wave to the harbour master watching on the breakwater, I turned into the harbour and slowed the engine looked along the main quay trying to make out berth six. When I spotted it, I was astonished at how little room there seemed to dock the ship. The third mate had left to take up is position on the poop for mooring and Bobby Spencer and his gang were on the focasle. I slowed the ship some more and headed for the berth.

Edging the bow towards the quay, I ordered Bobby to put a spring wire ashore. This was a wire that was attached to the shore and went towards the stern of the ship. By holding this and letting it out a little at the time, we had control of the ships forward movement.

The second mate shouted out the distances from the ship ahead. I waited as the ship slowed more until the third mate informed me that we were clear of the hip astern. I ordered the spring to be held, turned the ship to starboard and stopped the engine. Gently the ship came to rest against the fenders hanging from the quay. All ropes were then sent ashore and tightened. The ship was safely berthed. I rang the engine room to tell them we were finished with the main engines and dismissed the wheelman.

He grinned as he passed. " That was well done mister mate."

I grinned back. " Thank you Moody."

After making sure everything was in order on the bridge I went down to my cabin. Captain Harris and Lars Karlson were standing on the boat deck.

Captain Harris smiled. " I knew you would make a good captain, Eddie. Well done."

They left the ship to have negotiations with the stevedoring companies, the unions and the port authorities. Captain Foster was taken to hospital for a check up leaving me in charge of the ship. It was difficult to juggle the demands of the captain's role in looking after many visitors to the ship and the chief officer's duties looking after the cargo work. I have to admit that both Bobby and Charlie rallied round and we managed to cope.

That weekend in Kotka after navigating the ship around the coast, I invited Bobby and Charlie for a drink. Charlie declined because he was off to Helsinki but Bobby did not plan to go ashore. We sat in my cabin talking quietly.

I had heard that Bobby was off to university after Christmas. I was curious. It was the first time I had ever had an inclining that there was an opportunity to go to university without A levels.

After a while, I asked him bluntly. " What made you decide to go to university?"

Bobby frowned. " A number of things actually. I was aware that the company I was with were talking of getting rid of ships and putting some under the Liberian flag. Alarm bells rang in my head so to speak. I started to pay much more attention to news reports, the Lloyds List and other shipping magazines. I was looking for another shipping company when I came across an article reporting the setting up of a degree course in shipping studies. Curious, I sent for more information. When it came, I found out that I needed a Master's certificate to get on the course. I was disappointed."

I frowned. " But I understood you were going in the new year."

He smiled. " When I read the rest of the information I found they were running a preliminary course designed to get those with a mates certificate up to standard. I applied and was accepted."

I was interested suddenly though at the time I could not have reasoned why. " Have you the information or the address?"

He smiled in turn. " I have the address of the admissions tutor. I would think about it if I was you."

I frowned in turn. " Why?"

He shrugged. " The same thing is happening here as happened to me. This Karlson will work out what is efficient and then start reducing the fleet. That will mean fewer officers needed to man the ships. There is always the chance that he will take this opportunity to look for cheaper methods of manning the ships. This might mean flagging the ships other than under the British flag."

" There is no way the Baltic Steamers will flag under anything other than the red ensign."

He laughed. " Coming from you that is amusing."

" What do you mean?"

Again he shrugged. " You are one of the most informed seamen I have ever met."

" All I do is read the magazines and newspapers."

" Oh no, Eddie. You actually think about the consequences of what you read. That to me shows a budding academic. I'll get you that address."

The conversation drifted away from his studies and onto other topics. The subject of my writing for information about university studies was pushed back into the background. I had too much to think about. Dealing with the agents, port authorities and supervising the loading filled all my time.

The next day, Captain Harris and Lars Karlson arrived back on board. They invited me for a drink at lunchtime.

" How were your meetings?" I asked over a gin and tonic.

Lars Karlson answered. " There were positive signs that we could get a better system of unloading and loading cargo. It looks s though we will be able to cut the round trip from London or Hull from three weeks to two."

Captain Harris spoke in a reassuring tone. " It will take time to organise. The consequences for our personnel have not even been thought of yet. But Lars has convinced me that as a company we will have to change."

I frowned. " If what I think is right, it will mean less time in port. Lets take a schedule based on what the Vanguard does now. It is four days at sea both ways. That is eight days given good weather. If we get bad weather now there is a chance to catch up the schedule. Coming back to the eight days. That would leave six days for discharge and loading. So speculating. Leave London on Thursday night. Arrive Helsinki Monday night. Discharge Tuesday. Sail to Kotka Tuesday night. Load Wednesday and Thursday. Sail Thursday night. Arrive Surrey Docks Monday night. Discharge Tuesday and Wednesday. Load Wednesday and Thursday. Sail Thursday night. How does that sound?"

Lars was looking at me with a surprised expression. " That sounds what I had in mind."

Before Captain Harris could speak, I said. " It might be logical in an office in London. The trouble with all theories is they do not take into account the people involved. People have feelings and aspirations. They do not like change."

Lars Karlson grunted. " That is all very well but when there are changes needed it is better to make the changes sooner than latter. That way something will remain in the end. If nothing is done, all might be lost. That is the trouble with ordinary people. They fear change but can end up losing what they most value. Shipping is changing. We have to act now."

I was about to retort when Captain Harris spoke. " Enough of this gloom. How is Captain Foster?"

I shrugged. " He has been sent back on board. The doctors say he will have to take things easy on the voyage home. Then he will have to have an appointment with his doctor."

Captain Harris stood. " I will go and see him."

I left at the same time deep in thought. Before meeting Lars Karlson, I had been aware for some time of the changing technologies and organisation of shipping that was taking place. It had been reported and written about in the shipping press. Like most people confronted by something they were unfamiliar with, I had buried my head in the sand and thought it would not affect me. The reports were about intermodal transport on longer routes. There were articles about roll on roll off on shorter routes. There were also articles on barge carrying ships. On the other hand I had joked about the voyages to Finland being a real pleasure and that the crews were paid to do something they enjoyed.

The connections started to click in my mind. I thought about my conversation with Bobby Spencer. Would I like to go to university? Suddenly a vision of my old school headmaster came into my mind. I was back standing in front of his desk in that oak panelled office. Mister Challacombe was sitting staring at me over his half moon glasses, his bald head shining in the light streaming in at the window. When he spoke his double chins wobbled. His chubby hands rested on his desk. He was telling me that pupils from the top stream in his school went to university not into the merchant navy. Then I thought he must have been laughing as he looks down on me from heaven.

I knew then that I had to at least explore the idea of going to university. I would get the address from Bobby and write for an application form. Then I would see where it would all lead. Doubts flooded into my mind. Doubts about whether I was intellectual enough to study at university level. All I had studied was for my certificates of competency. They were hard but very practical. They did not stretch the mind or answer any broad questions. Deep in my subconscious there were doubts about my willingness to give up the sea life. Since coming to sea at sixteen I had really enjoyed my time. Indeed from the very first step onto a ship I had felt at home, I had felt that I was in my natural world. Would I be able to give this all up for the life of a student? Something in my inner being told me I should give it a chance. I reassured myself by adding that if it was not for me, I could always go back to sea.

I had no time to dwell on these thoughts. The stevedores demanded my attention. The agent demanded my attention. The chief engineer demanded my attention. For the rest of the time in Kotka, I was tied up with ships business. Then we sailed and I had to navigate the ship out of Kotka. On the way back to London I composed a letter to the university requesting an application form.

Captain Foster was taken ashore in an ambulance when the Vanguard docked in Surrey Docks. Next day I was relieved to see Dick Mortimer getting out of a taxi.

I was at the top of the gangway when he climbed on board. " Hello Eddie. I have come to relieve Captain Foster. What a bugger. I have only had half my leave. My wife was not too pleased I can tell you. Captain Harris tells me you looked after the ship."

I smiled and ordered a passing sailor to collect the captain's bags to carry them to the captain's cabin. " When Captain Foster took ill I had to take over. I think I managed quite well."

Dick laughed. " From what Captain Harris told me, you handled the situation well. I hear he pilots went on strike and you took the Vanguard into port. On another subject. What did you make of Lars Karlson? I met him in the office. He struck me as a cold fish. He is only interested in efficiency not the consequences to the company personnel."

We arrived at his cabin. " I am afraid he has a point though. I do not like his attitude to people but shipping is changing both financially and technically. What he is trying to do is make sure the company can survive into the future. Enough of this for now. I have to get back to the discharge now that I have a captain to take over his duties."

Dick laughed and waved me away.

For the next three trips there was hardly a cloud on the horizon. Everything seemed to go right and smoothly. The only blot on the landscape was the now conscious worry about the future. All the officers now discussed the subject of efficiency and what that would mean for them and their futures. They now accepted that things were going to change. Every time a group met for a beer or a gin and tonic the main topic of conversation was the future. This was unlike sailors. They thought of the future in terms of their next port or their next leave. They were always certain that after their leave there would be a job waiting for them. For many of the sailors on the Vanguard, this ship had been their life since it had been built. By convention they had signed an extra sailor so that each could have a trip off every seven voyages. Now that arrangement looked as though it could be in danger of finishing. This would especially be true if the company started to operate from different ports. At times I could feel the tension in the air.

The company relieved me for leave a few weeks before Christmas. I took the opportunity to inform the university that I would be available for an interview. The university were very quick to arrange to see me. The interview was strange. All the way there I was very apprehensive about whether I would have enough technical knowledge to satisfy their requirements. The interview however was a discussion of my opinions and thoughts about the future of the British Fleet. As I had been reading a great deal on this subject, I thought I handled the discussion well. After a lunch provided by the university the tutor told me that an offer of a place on the course would be forth coming in the post. On the way back home, I kept coming back to the idea that if I accepted the offer my life at sea was also coming to an end. I wondered whether this would be acceptable both emotionally and socially. When the offer came, I sat looking at the letter and form for a long time but in the end accepted. My mother tried to understand but to her way of thinking, I had a very good career and why did I want to give it all up. Though I attempted to explain about the changing nature of shipping, it passed her by and all she could think of was me giving up a well paid job for the uncertainty of an uncharted future. She did accept that it was my decision and, as with most things, she would support me even if she did not agree with me.

After a pleasant Christmas, I received a demand from the company to report to head office the next day.

Chapter 14

The journey to London to see Captain Harris was fraught with apprehension. Having spent one of my previous voyages discussing with Lars Karlson the changing nature of shipping and the need to slim down the fleet, I wondered what would await me. The mind plays tricks at times like these and all negative thoughts appear to be uppermost in the thinking. On the one hand the apprehension causes one to wish the journey would take longer so one will not have the problem so soon. While on the other hand one wishes the journey over quickly so that one's fate would at least be known.

My worst fear was that I was going to be made redundant. The very word redundant caused a tightening of my stomach muscle, making my palms become damp and my breathing to shorten. Even now I wonder at my reaction. I told myself over and over again that only a few weeks before, I had agreed to go to university in September. No matter what happened, I would be leaving the company anyway, I assured myself. The reply came instantly as though it had been waiting in the dim reaches of my mind ready to jump out and confront me. Leaving under my instigation of would have been on my terms. Like a blind man negotiating an unfamiliar room, I staggered from one negative emotion to another.

As though on a roller coaster, I would slip into the complete opposite scenario. I speculated that as shipping was changing, the company was about to build a container ship and they wanted me to standby while it was being built. This idea filled me with excitement, like a child feels when sent to the sweet shop. I did understand deep down that this was all speculation and I would not know until I met Captain Harris in his office. That acknowledgement did not stop my mind running wild like some montana clematis climbing over a shed.

When I arrived at the head office building, the receptionist smiled in recognition and waved me in the direction of the lift. I did not have to ask because I knew the way from the times I had been in the building. Captain Harris' office was on the second floor and I took the lift. He was waiting for me when I opened the door to his office. Before ushering me into his inner office, he asked his secretary to brew some coffee. The office was a large room, oak panelled with the walls lined with bookcases. The desk was just as large, leather topped with a red phone. By the window overlooking the street were a couple of armchairs and a coffee table. Captain Harris waved me into one of these comfy chairs. He picked up a file from the desk and sat in the armchair across the table from me. The secretary came in with the coffee. I recognised Ruth from the time she sailed with me that voyage on the Vanguard.

" Good morning Eddie," she smiled. " How are you?"

" Hello Ruth. I thought you were secretary to the personnel manager."

She laughed. " Captain Harris asked me to become his secretary and it was agreed. Oh by the way. Susan is in the general office. I know she would love to see you. It is at the bottom of the stairs along a corridor at the back."

When she left, Captain Harris raised his eyebrows but declined to comment.

" We have to see Sir Richard Birch when he asks for us," Captain Harris was referring to the managing director of the company. " Ruth will call when he is ready. Now tell me about this Susan. There has been a rumour ever since the selected office staff came on that trip on the Vanguard. It is hinted that one of the girls went further than the others with one of the officers. I take it that that was you and Susan."

He was grinning like I had never seen him do before.

I grinned back. " That is none of your business. All I will say is that she came on the bridge at times and we talked about the efficiency drive in the company."

Captain Harris lifted the phone. " Ruth. We will be going out to lunch at the Blue Angel. Will you ask Susan if she would like to accompany us?"

Shortly after the door opened and Ruth came in. " Sir Richard Birch will see you now."

Sir Richard Birch was sitting behind a vast desk in a very large office when we arrived on the top floor of the office block. The picture window looked out over one of those walled gardens that are so much part of the London infrastructure. The carpet on the floor would not have been out of place in some millionaire's apartment on Park Lane. He looked up from some papers he was reading to study us from over his half moon spectacles. He was a big man with stubby fingers, bushy eyebrows and thick neck. His hair was swept back and thick.

" Captain Harris and Eddie Gubbins, good to see you both. Take a seat," he said waving casually to two leather chairs on the opposite side of his desk. As I sat, I noticed the paintings on the wall and wondered whether they were originals

He smiled but his eyes were hard. " It is traditional in the company for the managing director to greet anybody on their promotion to the position of Captain."

He paused to let what he was saying sink in, obviously amused at my reaction. I was stunned. Of all the things I had imagined as the train travelled from Southampton to London, being promoted to Captain was not one of them. I did not know what to say. I felt as though my mouth was hanging open but I made a supreme effort to keep it closed. Captain Harris was smiling.

Sir Richard pushed an envelope across the desk. " In here is the gold laurel leaf for your cap and the four gold bands," he stood and extended his hand. " Congratulations Captain Gubbins. You come highly recommended from Captain Harris."

I shook his hand and said thank you. We then left the office and returned to Captain Harris' office. I was still in a daze. My mind was not working properly. Then it cleared when I thought of that day when my grandfather had announced to all the family that Edmund was going to be the first captain in the family.

It had been if you remember at one of the family get togethers at my grandparent's home when I was about six years old. Granddad put his large hand on my shoulder and announced. " Edmund is going to sea when he grows up. He will be the first Captain of a foreign going ship in the family."

The sound of his voice had dropped into the sudden silence as everybody in the room nodded sagely. It was so long ago but his voice seemed to echo in my mind that day. I had to admit that he had been right.

All through lunch I was the same with that voice echoing in my mind. When we collected Susan from the foyer, she congratulated me. In the pub, she sat as close as was deemed proper with one of the senior staff sitting with her. She asked me about my family and what I had been doing for my holiday. I answered in short sentences my mood still buoyed up by my promotion.

On the way back to the office, she held my hand. Captain Harris and Ruth showed their amusement by studiously avoiding looking in our direction. When we arrived back at the foyer, I asked Susan what she had planned for the next weekend. She looked at me, her eyes big and round behind her glasses.

" I am flat sitting for a friend. Would you like to join me?"

We arranged the time and place. She kissed me on the cheek and went off down the corridor a smile brightening her face. It was a very pleasant weekend though my mother was curious. She was very huffy when all I would tell her was that I was going to spend the weekend with a friend. It was deliberate on my part to keep a part of what I was doing a secret. It may not be relevant now but then I had reached that age when mothers started to think about their sons getting married. There was always the nostalgia when she met another of her friends with grandchildren. I did not want to have to listen to her extolling the virtues of marriage. If I had told her about spending the weekend with Susan she would have added two to two and made about ten. As it turned out it was a very rewarding weekend.

After joining Captain Harris after leaving Susan that lunchtime, he gave me the instructions. I was to report back to the office in two weeks. The Arrow was to discharge at Hays Wharf opposite the Tower of London. I would be taken to the ship and take over from Captain Moncur.

I did something then which was out of character. Once I had a new cap with the laurel leaves, I visited the grave of my grandfather. It was cold and snow flurries were being blown on the wind but I felt a warm glow inside. In reality I had never understood this need to visit the graves of loved ones. Memories are stored in the mind to be brought forth whenever reminded of loved ones through some place, event or anecdote. The sound of something triggers off a thought and in many cases a picture of some past event. The sight of a view or a car or some other thing brings memories flooding back. To my mind there is no need for physical evidence like a gravestone to trigger off these memories.

Still for once I stood at the foot of his grave with my hat in my hand and spoke to him. " Granddad. I have done what you told me to do. In a weeks time I will join the Arrow as the Captain. Thank you for your confidence in me. I hope I have made you happy."

Turning away from the grave I seemed to hear a voice telling me that I had done well.

I joined the Arrow as Captain at Hayes Wharf where HMS Belfast is now displayed. In those days it was a cold store berth and the Arrow had a refrigerated hold. It carried bacon from Poland to London. Captain Moncur was pleased to see me and had everything ready for a speedy transfer of the ship. I signed all the papers, took charge of the safe keys and watched as the brass plate with Captain Gubbins replaced that of Captain Moncur on the cabin door. After seeing him down the gangway and into a waiting taxi, I climbed back on board realising for the first time that I was officially in charge of this ship.

I had to undertake all the tedious tasks that the master had to finish before the ship could sail. Like seeing agents, office staff and some cases the police. The role of captain is not as glamorous as it appears to the outsider. The few hours before sailing besides the paper work, the master has to deal with all those people. Once they were all ashore, I was free to take over the navigating of the ship. This is how I remember that first time I went on the bridge of a ship as the Master.

After being called to the bridge, I adjusted my black tie in the mirror making sure that the knot was just right. The white shirt was pristine clean and my trousers newly pressed. Taking my jacket from the hanger, I mentally shone the four gold bands forming the diamond on the sleeve. Once in place, I fastened the gold buttons. Certain that this looked fine, I picked up my cap from the desk and adjusted it on my head. The new gold laurel leafs gleamed in the light streaming through the window of my cabin. The mirror showed that I looked the part of a ship's Captain.

When I reached the bridge, the pilot was waiting. He congratulated me on my promotion when I joined him. He was the river pilot who navigated the company's ships from Gravesend to either Surrey Docks or the London Pool.

" Congratulations on your promotion. Are we ready?" the pilot asked.

" All ready," I replied feeling strange at giving the orders. " We can sail."

Over the radio, the pilot requested Tower Bridge to be raised. I stood on the bridge wing watching the red lights flash and the traffic coming to a standstill. The two halves of the bridge slowly separated and rose into the air.

" Right Captain, we can go," the pilot remarked with a smile.

" Let go aft," I gave my first order as a Captain of a ship and watched the ropes slowly come on board.

The pilot grinned. " Slow ahead," he ordered the third mate.

I stood and watched as my command slowly turned to take the stern away from the quay.

" Stop. Half astern."

The ship steadily left the berth until there was enough room to turn successfully into the river. I lent against the varnished rail making sure that the four gold rings on my arm were plainly visible to anybody who happened to be watching.

The rail flanking the road leading to Tower Bridge was crowded with people watching as we sailed closer to the bridge. I made myself conspicuous to the watching people, standing straight and proud on the bridge wing.

The ship sailed under the open wings of the bridge, the tracery of the ironwork above my head. Then we were out into the river with the entrance to Surrey Docks to the south and Saint Katherine Dock to the north. The ship picks up speed.

I instructed the third mate look after the pilot and went into the radio room to tell the radio officer to inform the company that we were out of the Pool of London and heading for Gravesend and the sea pilot.

The ship sailed serenely down the river passed the Royal Hospital at Greenwich and on to Gravesend. The steward brought coffee and cakes.

As we approached Gravesend, a launch set out from the pilot station jetty. The river pilot turned to me and said, " Thank you Captain. I will see you when you return. The ship is all yours."

As he left the bridge, I realised for the first time that I was in complete charge of the ship. The wheelman grinned at me.

" Slow ahead," I ordered the third mate. He moved the telegraph and I heard the bell ring. The engine noise softened as the ship slowed. The pilot boat manoeuvred alongside and I slowed the ship some more. The sea pilot climbed the ladder and the river pilot left.

He waved to me as the pilot boat left the ship and headed back to the shore.

" Half ahead," I ordered and the noise of the engine increased after the third mate had moved the engine telegraph.

The sea pilot arrived on the bridge. " Good morning Captain. I'll take over now. Congratulations on your promotion."

" Good morning. I will be in my cabin if needed. The third mate will look after you. Call me when we are passing Southend pier."

Reluctantly I left the bridge and went down to my cabin. For a while I engaged in the various administration tasks that any Master had to undertake when the ship left port.

The call came as the ship passed Southend. Looking out of the window I noted that the sun had gone and the mist had descended making all around appear grey and dull.

When I came back to the bridge, the second mate had taken over from the third mate. The ship was heading out to sea through the sand banks at the mouth of the Thames. The red bulk of the pilot boat could now be seen about ten miles ahead. The pilot ordered the course set for the ship to rendezvous with the pilot boat

The pilot manoeuvred the ship so that the wind was on the side away from the approaching cutter. and slowed the ship.

" An uneventful passage down the river, Captain," he remarked. " Hope you have a pleasant voyage. She is all yours now."

He shook my hand and accompanied by the second mate left the bridge. I stood on the bridge wing watching as the pilot climbed down the ladder into the waiting cutter. When the cutter swung away from the ship and the sailor was pulling in the rope ladder, I turned and pushed the engine telegraph to full ahead.

" Steer 075," I ordered the wheelman and watched as the bow turned and then steadied. The second mate joined me on the bridge and worked out the position of the ship.

Looking round the ship from the bridge I found everything in order.

" Its all yours, second mate," I said and walked from the bridge.

When I reached my cabin, placed my cap on the top of the chest of drawers and my jacket on a hanger, it hit me. For the first time since setting out on a career at sea, I had nothing to do with the actual running of the ship. The ship would be navigated by the other officers and they would resent any interference from me. Even though I was responsible for the ship and the conduct of the voyage, many of these responsibilities had been delegated as was the nature of seamanship, to the rest of the crew. In many ways the captain is a distant figure who is in charge but not needed most of the time at sea. A figure in the background who could be called if there were problems but kept away when all was running smoothly.

I poured myself a gin and tonic and got stuck into the paper work promising myself that I would not keep looking out of the window. It was very hard to stop myself walking back onto the bridge to check on progress. In truth I would not be wanted anywhere near the bridge until we approached the pilot station off the River Elbe. When I got the call from the chief officer that we were approaching the Elbe River it came as a relief. I now had something to do other than sit and try not to worry. I came alive once more as the ship approached the pilot station. I gave the orders for the wheelman to take his station. Then I manoeuvred the ship so that the pilot could climb aboard.

I was lucky. All the trips went relatively smoothly in the sense of there being very few problems. We did not return to London but sailed first for Leith in Scotland and then to Hull. The North Sea was bad with sharp waves and driving rain. When the wind dropped there was fog but I managed to get through these physical problems safely.

I was surprised when the radio officer informed me that Lars Karlson and Captain Harris would be joining us in Hull for a couple of nights. I surmised that it was an on going part of their efficiency drive. I informed the chief steward to have the spare cabins made available for them.

Captain Harris and Lars Karlson arrived soon after we docked. After settling into the spare cabins, they joined me for a drink.

Lars Karlson looked pleased. " We have agreement in principle for a quicker turnaround in London by basing the London Finland service at Harwich. I am here to finalise the arrangements in Hull. The Swift has been sold. The Arrow is next. I will leave you while I go to the port offices."

When he had left, Captain Harris sat drinking his coffee and looking out of the window at the cranes starting to discharge the cargo. He appeared rather distracted. I wonder what he had come to tell me.

With a sigh, he s began. " The company is no longer the close family it used to be. I cannot criticise Lars Karlson for that. It is the changing nature of the shipping world. Now everything is efficiency with no regard for social policy. I am afraid the fleet is getting smaller. As Lars said before he left, the Swift has been sold and will arrive in London to be handed over to her new owners tat the end of the week. I will have to be back in London for that. The Arrow is up for sale and will be gone by Easter. That leaves me with a problem. The company will have too may captains for the size of the fleet. That means some will have to go. Eddie this is nothing personal. On the five years you have been employed you have been a loyal officer. However you are the junior captain. I am afraid there is no gentle way I can say this. You will have to go back to chief officer until there is another captain's position on offer."

In a way I had anticipated this moment. Not outwardly but in the back of my mind. I had not confronted the thought explicitly but it had niggled away below the surface, ever since I had been appointed. Unconsciously it must have one of the motives for my agreeing to go to university to study for a degree. In that way the announcement did not affect my equilibrium too much. I had hoped no taken for granted that I would remain a captain on the Arrow until I left to go to university in the autumn. Indeed I had at times been working out how much leave I would have due so that I could leave and have a holiday before starting my studies.

I tried not to let too much of this show. " I can in a way understand your position, Captain Harris. In the light of what has been said over the last year this was coming. There is one thing I must say. I have worked hard to become a captain. I am reluctant to give up the position. How about this? I will agree to being demoted as long as I retain my salary. In addition I will need it in writing that I will be the next promotion to captain once a vacancy arises

Captain Harris looked sad. " You know I cannot agree to those conditions. I came here especially so that I could tell you myself. Unfortunately I am not the one who makes the decisions. The managing director and the board lay down the company policy a far as reducing the personnel are concerned. It was decided that we should retain our senior staff as far as possible. What will you do?"

I smiled. " Captain Harris. You were the first master I sailed with in Baltic Steamers. You taught me a great deal about navigating in ice. You showed me how a captain should conduct himself. I have to be honest with you. I have agreed to take up an offer to go to university to study for a degree in the autumn. I was hoping to stay with the company until that time. When I had a chance I was going to come to the office and tell you."

Always before seemingly calm and collected, Captain Harris looked thunderstruck. " Well well. I cannot say I am all that surprised. Of all the officers I have had to deal with you are the most analytical. I ask again. If you hand in your notice what will you do?"

" I will find a job closer to home."

" That is rather silly. I cannot see you getting a job as a captain elsewhere."

I smiled. " It is a matter of principle now. Look I have made my mind up to go to university and will find another job. I will hand in my notice after you inform me the time has come for me to revert to chief officer. Now if you have finished your coffee, shall we inspect the ship?"

Later that day the trades' union representative for Humberside came on board to make sure all was well. He had heard through the union channels that there might be a clear out of staff and he was checking whether it applied to the union member son the Arrow. In effect that meant most of the officers because being a member of the union gave a certain amount of protection. Put it this way. Though most officers never overtly talked about such things, some felt it would never happen to them, in the event of an accident for which they were accused of negligence or unprofessional conduct the union would pay for them to be legally advised and represented.

This sort of insurance was very important. For instance, In the case of a captain or master to give him the legal title, if anything happened in the navigation of the ship, he would be held responsible. This is the case even if the captain was not on the bridge at the time. Always in such circumstances there is n inquiry held by the government. A master could lose his certificate if the judgement went against him. This would mean that he could no longer work on a ship. He would lose the occupation he had been trained for and examined. In a few cases he could be sent to jail. Therefore the representation by a lawyer at the enquiry was vital.

I knew Edwin Thomas from my visits to Hull before and invited him to my cabin for a drink after he had met the other officers. Captain Harris had gone ashore to meet Lars Karlson.

When he was sitting in my cabin with a beer in his hand, he said almost cheerfully. " Troubled times for the British Fleet, Eddie. I hear from some of the men that there maybe redundancies in the Baltic Steamer Company. The Union in London had wind of this a few months ago when the company sold the Swift. It is now on its last voyage before being handed over to its new owners."

I shrugged. " I have read the papers. Funny you should say that about redundancies. The marine superintendent has just informed me that the company will have to put me back to chief officer because of the reduction in ships."

" What did you say?"

" I told him that I would not accept that unless they paid me masters salary. He made me understand that I would have to accept chief officer's salary."

" Did you agree without seeing me? I would get the union negotiator in London to talk to the company on your behalf."

" Actually it is not too much of a problem. I have agreed to leave the sea and go to university in the autumn."

He interrupted. " That degree they have set up into Nautical Studies designed for men with Masters Certificates?'

" That's the one. Anyway, I have informed them that I will not accept a chief officer's salary. I have no idea whether they will tell me to leave. They might even relieve me this trip. To me it is a moral stance not really about the money. If they tell me to leave I will have to find another job until September."

" I think you are rather silly to make such a stand. The union would negotiate on your behalf. If you are intent on leaving, you could leave things to me. I have contacts all over the place so might be able to help."

" Ok I will leave things to you. Have another beer."

When we returned to Hull two weeks later docking in the early morning as the sun was rising, I had a message from Edwin Thomas that he would be on board to see me when he had time. There was no word from the company concerning my demotion so it appeared I would be captain of the Arrow for another voyage.

When Edwin Thomas boarded the Arrow, he came directly to my cabin. I poured him a coffee.

" I have news for you," he said smiling. " How long have you left with Baltic Steamers?"

I shrugged. " It looks as though I have at least one more voyage. There has never been a contract as such. Just an understanding that after each leave the company would have me back."

" I was in London for a meeting last week. There I met Dick Talbot the rep in Southampton. He told me that British Rail in Weymouth were looking for a couple of relief personnel for the summer. They want them to start after Easter. I said I had somebody looking for a local job before going to university. When I mentioned your name, he said he knew your father and had met you a few times."

" Yes. Dad introduced us before I started at sea. He wanted me to join the union but I told him I would not until the union got cadets a pay rise. A year later the union negotiated a twenty five percent pay rise for the cadets an I joined the union."

" Well, he said he would enquire about the job. The upshot is that you have the position of relief chief officer with the Weymouth section of British Rail. The job is available for the first Tuesday after Easter. They will be writing to let you know the details."

" I will arrange for my notice and then for a reference if required. I should be able to have some time off before joining British Rail."

The next opportunity I had I telephoned Captain Harris. I was honest with him and explained what I had planned. I asked bluntly if I could stay in command of the Arrow for another three trips that would take me to within a month of joining British Rail. Surprisingly considering that I was leaving, he told me that my request would fit in with his plans. The Arrow was to be sold before Easter to a Greek company.

It did not work out as planned. When it became time for me to leave, Captain Harris asked me to stay for another trip because there was not a free captain ready to relieve me. Later during my academic studies I realised this was the fear complex kicking in. What I came to understand is that there is a trend in these situations in all of industry. At times when there is uncertainty in a company, where there is a danger that the company will shrink, those very employable workers will look for a position with another company. They will do this in the hope of getting out of the danger of losing their job. Thos who are not so employable elsewhere or who are nervous of change stay put. This is what was happening in Baltic Steamers. As soon as there was a hint that the company was going to get rid of ships and personnel, many officers did not sign on again but found berths in other companies. It was easier to do than would have been the case with Shell where the officers and many of the sailors were on two year contracts.

I agreed but made sure I would leave in time by handing in my notice in writing. At the end of the trip I was called to the port office in Hull.

It was Captain Harris sounding very nervous. " Eddie I know you have a position with British Rail but we are still trying to find a relief for you. Can you do another trip?'

I tried to stay calm but inside I was boiling. " That means I will leave the week before Easter and only get a few days before I have to join British Rail. Legally I can walk off the ship this week because I have given the required notice both verbally and in writing."

I could almost hear him swallow. " I know all of that but we are short of masters. The best chief officers have left the company and all the ones left including, as you know the one on the Arrow have not the experience to take over. Will you do as I ask?"

I shook my head to myself. " I will agree to your request. I suppose I could demand a bonus but that is not in my nature. Have you sent off my reference?"

Captain Harris laughed. " I sent it off straight away after I received it. Funny you should ask. I received a phone call from their marine manager a few days later. It was somebody I sailed with as a cadet and have met frequently since. I told him what I thought of you. For some reason you will not have to go for an interview because he will take my word about your competence. I will phone to inform him what is happening here. I expect he will be in touch with instructions. Thank you Eddie. Best of luck with your degree."

Even then with the promise of Captain Harris, it did not prove easy. The Arrow docked in Hull on the Monday before Good Friday. I was due to join British Rail in Weymouth the following Tuesday. I signed off the crew members who were going on leave and dealt with all the paperwork. I packed my cases with all the things I would not need and waited for my relief to board the Arrow. I found that the relief captain had orders to load for Poland and then after discharge bring the empty ship back to London to be handed over to the new owner. All day Tuesday I waited but no sign of the next master. The company assured me that somebody was appointed. All day Wednesday and still no captain. On Thursday, I phoned the company and informed them that I would be leaving the ship that lunchtime even if another captain was not forth coming. At ten minutes to twelve a taxi came round the shed and pulled up at the bottom of the gangway. Bill Douglas climbed out and paid off the driver.

I made sure my bags were ready and sat waiting for him to get to my cabin. At the knock on the door, I shouted for him to enter.

The look on his face told me better than words that he was not happy. " Bugger you young Eddie. Why the hell did you have to leave now? I have only had a few days of my leave. My wife is steaming.'

I laughed bitterly. " Bill I have had my notice into the company for the last two months. Come on. Put your bags down and come and have lunch. After lunch I will hand over to you."

Following my hand over of the Arrow to Bill, I called for a taxi. The bosun arranged for my bags to be carried from my cabin. I followed down to the quay. Once the taxi turned away from the ship. I looked back to thoughts that this was the end of my time with Baltic Steamers.

After only three days at home, I drove my car through Dorset to Weymouh. The beach was sandy and the sea sparkled in the sunshine as I drove along the front to the port. When I turned through the entrance to the berths, there were no ships tied up to the quay. Finding a parking place, I carried my bags to the offices. The receptionist appeared to expect me and indicated where I could leave my luggage. Then she led me up the stairs and into a small sparsely furnished office. Looking out of the window I saw that the office overlooked the quay. The man behind the desk was small and slim with grey thinning hair. He looked at me through large framed horn rimmed glasses.

" Mister Gubbins?"

" Yes."

He stood and extended his hand. " Brian Masters, the marine superintendent of the Weymouth station.

Charlie Harris recommended you so there was no need for an interview. Would you like a coffee?"

At my nod he spoke into the phone. " As I informed you in the letter, you are to be the relief chief officer. We have relief second mates and captains. What it involves is relieving chief officers on each of our ships so that they can have their time off. There are five ships in the fleet. The two ferries, Sarnia and Ceaserea. Then two relatively modern small cargo ships, the Elk and the Moose. Lastly there is the Winchester that has eight passenger cabins mostly used by British Rail personnel. You will be informed each trip f when you have to swap ships. Any questions?"

I was still puzzled at not having an interview that I did not have any response. " Not at the moment. I expect something will occur to me later."

He looked at me. " How did you get here?"

" I came by car."

" I will arrange for a car park pass for you to put in your car. Now report back here at about seven o'clock. Go and get a meal. There is a good restaurant along the front."

After a meal I reported back as instructed at seven. I was a trifle bemused that it was assumed that I was the right person for the post. In essence I had never gained any employment without an interview. This post had been offered to me on the recommendation of Captain Harris. Actually looking back, I had started my working life in a position found for me by my uncle.

I went straight to the office of Brian Masters to find him looking out the window. There was a great deal of noise and activity outside. I noticed that dockers had suddenly appeared on the berth. Then there was the familiar sound of a ships engine and the poop of a ferry appeared in the window.

" Your ship," Brian Masters pointed out of the window. " Once it has docked, I will take you on board and introduce you to the captain. You can then find the chief officer and take over. I will arrange for your bags to be brought on board once I know where you are to be accommodated."

It became a strange existence for me. As Brian Masters had instructed me, I was to be the relief chief officer. What this entailed was for me to join a ship while the chief officer had his days off. When he returned, I would leave that ship and join another. Sometimes I would get a few days at home myself but very often I would leave one ship and wait either in the office or in town until another docked that day. I would then relieve the chief officer on that ship. It was as you can see a nomadic existence. The length of time I had to wait depended on the ship I was joining. With the two ferries, they docked at about seven thirty morning and night. They sailed at midnight and midday. Therefore I would leave one of the ferries when it sailed and wait until the other docked if required. With the three small cargo ships, they were scheduled to sail before the ferries because they carried the cars. This surprised me but the ferries were not roll on roll off. Their holds were used to carry flowers and tomatoes that were off loaded onto the boat train and despatched to London for retailing the next day.

One thing about BR shipping was that they had laid down procedures for most eventualities. For instance they had a system of what could be called positive reporting that I had adhered to through out my sea life. That is that no action is taken unless a positive report is received concerning a previous action. It was the second mate's duty before the ferry sailed to go through the ship and test all the watertight doors. He had to report to the bridge that all the doors were shut before the ferry could sail. This was carried out despite there being an indicator board on the bridge that showed the position of all watertight doors. Some shipping companies had a system of assuming that something had been done unless. Hence the tragedy of the Herald of Free Enterprise which happened years after I left the sea. There a ferry leaving Zeeburger left the bow doors open so that water flooded the car deck. This caused the ship to capsize. When I heard what had happened I could not understand why this regime had been implemented in the first place. Many seamen wondered whether it was pressure of time and the need to sail on time.

As part of their procedures was the policy of making sure that the Chief Officers could take over from the Master at any time. Again this was in direct contrast to the Baltic Steamers where a master jealously guarded the demarcation of the position from other members of the crew. As I have described, I had experienced this first hand when Captain Johnson had become ill aboard the Vanguard. To this end I was issued with a logbook into which was entered each time I took one of the ships into and out of port under the supervision of the Captain. All the captains had exemption from the need to carry a pilot either in Weymouth or the Channel Islands. The appropriate authority had examined them. They could however under the regulations supervise one of the chief officers to take the ship in and out of port.

Soon after joining when the ferry was leaving St. Hellier, the port for Jersey, Captain Delap informed me that I should prepare to take the ferry into and out of St. Peter Port as my first manoeuvre.

That day I stood on the bridge of the ferry and guided it through the breakwaters of St. Peter Port. The docking technique was simple. Enter with a flourish, get a rope on the knuckle of the berth, turn the ship using the rope and stop right opposite the gangway in one motion.

Even to this day I do not know whether it was deliberate or an accident. I had never seen it happen before though it was only my third trip. The sailors on the focastle missed with the rope. There was nothing to stop the ferry instantly and by the time I had reversed the engines, the ship was in amongst the yachts tied up to buoys in the harbour. The yachtsmen were not best pleased. I remember one man and woman coming onto the heaving deck of their yacht waving heir fists at me. What made the sailors laugh was that they were stark naked. It was obvious what they had been up to before being cruelly interrupted by a large ship just missing their boat. The betting on whether they resumed once we were clear occupied the crew for ages afterwards.

With a great deal of difficulty and engine movements, I managed to manoeuvre the ship alongside the quay. Captain Delap ordered me not to remonstrate with the sailors when the ship had docked. He assured me it had happened to him. Actually, he praised me for the way I had got the ship out of that difficulty. He then made me take the ship out of port backwards which I did this with no problems

Later I left the ferries and joined the Winchester that was a small cargo ship. It carried cars, the era of roll on roll off had not penetrated Weymouth yet, and other cargo. On board were six passenger cabins all oak panelled. This was one of the most aesthetically pleasing ships I have ever sailed on.

Two things happened over the times I was sailing on that ship. In Jersey every year there was a horse race meeting where top horses from the mainland took part.

They were carried on the Winchester. The hold was transformed into stalls for the horses and grooms to look after the horses used the cabins. I did not know until we were to carry horses that they need a calmish sea to be carried successfully. They are prone to being seasick. We anxiously studied the weather forecast all that morning as we waited for the horses to arrive that evening. The trainer arrived early and came to the office with me to also study the weather forecast. All appeared well so it was decided to carry the horses. They had to be loaded by crane but this was accomplished successfully. The grooms took turns to be in the holds to keep the horses calm and to make sure they were fed and watered. The rest of the grooms used the cabins to get some rest.

The trip was uneventful and the horses were delivered safely. The crew spent the trip trying to find out the chances of these horses in the races. After much deliberation they settled on one horse and when we arrived in St Hellier, one of them was despatched to place bets. A few trips later we found out that the horse had lost. When we carried the horses back to Weymouth, the crew threatened to kick the horse. Needless to say they did not carry out the threat and the horses were successfully delivered to Weymouth.

On another occasion when I was sent to the Winchester again, my girl friend came for a trip to Jersey. As an employee of the company I was able to get a ticket on the ferry. The Winchester was going to spend the night in Jersey. Our intention was to meet up when the Winchester arrived. When he heard, Captain Turner ordered me to go and collect her from the ferry and put her in a cabin on the Winchester.

It was a glorious trip with the weather warm and the sea calm. My girlfriend spent the voyage from

Weymouth on the bridge keeping watch with me. She was anticipating the approach to the Channel Islands. We saw the Casquets lighthouse in the distance and the Captain joined us as we approached the passage between Alderney and Guernsey.

With a grin he suggested she go and fetch the afternoon tea and cakes. The ship was rolling gently to a southwesterly swell. She had great difficulty in keeping her footing and not spilling the tea as she negotiated the stairs up to the bridge with a large tray. Captain Turner was grinning even more when she finally placed the tray on the chart table.

As we approached St Peter Port the Captain took over the navigation

" Starboard," he ordered the wheelman waving his arm in that direction. " Steady on Woolworths."

At this command, my girl friend collapsed in helpless laughter remembering the Navy Lark we used to listen to on the radio. She never believed that sea going was like that but this convinced her.

Later we sailed from St Peter Port to St Hellier passed what to me is the most beautiful lighthouse in the world.

After discharging the cargo, the Winchester was moved further into the harbour from the ferry berth. In that part of the port the harbour dried out at low tide. When this happens the ship sits on the bottom. All power has to be turned off because there is no cooling water.

We went shore that night after dinner to a nightclub with some of the other officers. It was a drunken happy evening. When we arrived back at the ship, my girlfriend was astonished to be confronted with a row of oil lamps hanging at he top of the gangway. We had to light one of the lamps to find our way below decks to her cabin. Without the sound of machinery, every footfall echoed throughout the ship. None of the crew could move without everybody else on board hearing their footsteps and other noises. It was very eerie and like a ghost ship.

In the morning when the generator started the vibration and the noise coming to punctuate the silence mad my girlfriend sit bolt upright in the bunk. I had to reassure her that all was well. The ship came alive and I left her to supervise the loading of the cargo.

I joined the ferry for my last three voyages the first week in September. I realised this was to be my last voyages before going to university. I took the boat train to make sure that if I had a drink with my friends before leaving, I would not have to drive home.

The first trip back from St Hellier was eventful. A gale was blowing out of the southwest right up the Channel from the Atlantic. The sea was rough and even with the stabilisers, the ferry pitched through the waves. We received an SOS from a yacht that had lost its mast in the storm. It was north of Guernsey close to our course back to Weymouth. It was hard picking out the yacht in the breaking waves but in the end the sailor lookout spotted it rolling violently. The crew were clinging to the handrails but managed to wave when we approached. Captain Turner decided to stand by the yacht until the lifeboat came. We attempted as much as we could to sail alongside in such a way that the ferry provided shelter and mitigated the full force of the waves.

There is one problem with this course of action. At slow speeds the stabilisers that are designed to stop the ferry rolling too much do not function. The ferry rolled violently from side to side as we tried to shield the yacht from the worst effects of the storm. Passengers found it difficult to remain in their seats with no seat belts to hold them in place. It was chaos down below. All we could hear was the sound of breaking glass and plates. We had a call to the bridge saying that some of the passengers were injured. What had happened I found when I arrived was that a few passengers had ended up in a heap in the scuppers by the side of the ship.

I reported this to the captain while organising the first aid trained crewmembers. The Captain ordered me to go back to the bridge and ask over the loudspeaker system " Are there any Doctors on board?"

I had always wanted to do this. It had been one of those funny dreams we sometimes have.

" Are there any doctors on board? If there are could they report to passenger deck C as some passengers are injured," echoed through the ship when I spoke into the tanoi. As it happened there were four and they tended to the wounded until we arrived in Weymouth and ambulances met the ship. It turned out that beside cuts and bruises, four passengers had broken limbs.

It was rather surreal that last voyage. Before we left Weymouth I was called to the passenger gangway. When I arrived I was confronted with a little old lady remonstrating with the sailor on duty.

He looked at me with raised eyebrows. " This lady has a dog sir. She is insisting on taking it with her into the passenger cabin."

The lady looked at my gold rings. " At last. Somebody with some authority. This man insists I put Dougal in the kennels as he calls them. He will not survive the voyage if he is not with me. Tell him to let me take Dougal with me."

I tried to keep my voice calm and authorative but it was a struggle because Dougal was one of those small dogs peeping out from under her coat looking at me with big eyes. " I am afraid he is speaking the truth, madam. The rule is that all dogs must go in the kennels during the sea trip. The information was printed on your ticket.

She looked at me as though I was a bad smell under her nose. Turning to the sailor she said in a resigned voice, " Show me where the kennels are."

I took her arm. " I will show you the way."

The kennels were in reality a number of wire cages on the poop deck. Once Dougal was made comfortable in his cage, the lady insisted on staying with him. I found her a chair from the saloon and she settled down to spend the voyage with her dog.

It was s peculiar feeling as I stood on the focasle and watched the entrance to St Hellier harbour slip by. It would be the last time I sailed through those breakwaters as a ships officer. I had enjoyed my time with British Rail even though it had been a nomadic existence. The same sentiment came over me as the ferry left St Peter Port on Guernsey. It was the second mates watch for the first half of the voyage so I went down to my cabin and packed my bag for the last time.

Captain Delap found me there. " As this s your last voyage I would like you to take the ferry into Weymouth."

Thus I found myself in charge of the ferry as we approached Weymouth harbour. I watched the mound slip by and turned the ship to starboard. Taking my position on the after steering position, I ordered the engines astern. With a flourish the ferry smoothly entered the harbour. I was conscious of the people standing on the end of the quay watching. With a feeling of joy I ordered the ropes ashore and the engine ahead. Smoothly the ferry came to a halt with the door exactly opposite the passenger gangway. I stood and looked around. With a sigh I rang finished with engines on the engine telegraph. Captain Delap grinned and shook my hand. I followed him to his cabin and signed off.

I changed and folded my uniform into the case. My bag was ready. My relief came on board. Shook my hand and that was it. A sailor came and took my bag. As I walked down the ship to the gangway, every crewmember I passed shook my hand or patted my back. They were all wishing me well at university.

I settled into a seat on the boat train. As it left the berth I had one last look at the ferry and then the train turned onto the street through Weymouth and that was it. My time at sea was at an end. Now I had to get ready to face a new world, an unfamiliar world. Where life was going to take me from now on I had no idea but so ended my time at sea.

The Call of the Sea

The sea is calling, always calling
Even when the sailor has long left voyaging behind.
The sea calls, ever calls,
Over the noise of this sometimes dreadful life.
To sail away , to leave this life behind,
But to where?
That is what adds to the thrill.
Let the voyage be long or short,
Let the oceans be calm or fierce,
In the urge to sail away,
Lies man's eternal quest
For something new.
Why oh why does man always strive after the new
When accepting the present would save a lot of heart
ache.
It has long been a mystery to me but,
More than in any other profession,
The sea offers a greater chance to satisfy this need.
The sailor never arrives
Because each new port is a stepping stone to the next
And on to the next
Until the nomadic lifestyle grows too much.
It maybe that the sailor observes other people
Settling into a pattern of life which brings rewards
Such things as family and home,
Anchored to other views of living
Rather than constantly on the move.
So the sailor leaves the sea
And puts down roots.

Or does he?
The sound of a seagull screaming ,
The wind moaning around the roof of his house
The sound of waves lapping on the shore
Will awaken in the hidden recesses of his mind
The longing to feel the excitement once more
As the ship goes silent,
Ready to leave for the sea.

Printed in Great Britain
by Amazon